REBIRTH

BRIDGETTE HOOPER

SOLISSE ◆

AMICITIA ◆

ANGUID ◆

THE KEEP ◆

CLAUDERE

IUXTA ◆

DOLOR ◆

IMPELLOR ◆

KAIROSSEN

LATEBROS MOUNTAINS

NITORUM ◆

THE ISLAND

SENEX ◆

DRAGON BONDS OF THE FEROX

AISLING (ASH-LYNN)	MORANA
KOEN (CO-EN)	NEERA
KAIDA (KAY-DUH)	SOREN
ORYN (ORE-IN)	NYSSA
AMERIE (AM-ER-EE)	CALEN
CIELLE (SEE-ELLE)	AYLIM
ELAILA (E-LAY-LUH)	OSIRIS

FAVILLA

to anyone who has had to fight to get back to the light

Reader,

War is here.

It is neither gentle, nor kind.

Scenes or descriptions may be upsetting to some.

Please read at your discretion.

ONE

AISLING

Time wasn't real anymore.

Rock pressed in against her from every angle. Each breath echoed back at her, too loud against her aching eardrums.

Aisling stopped shivering long ago. The cold was part of her now. A constant frigid dampness clung to her skin like a parasite. Her bones screamed with every movement as if they, too, were frozen. Her body begged for food. For an ounce of humanity.

Time passed. Hours. Days. She wasn't sure. With every heartbeat, she fell further into the infallible darkness until it was all she was. She couldn't see her hands, couldn't see anything but black. She was nothing—just a shadow moving in a blank space, invisible to everyone but herself.

It was worse than the void. Worse than the sticky tendrils of darkness that pulled at her very soul.

She would not scream. There was no point. Her shouts would be music to Cruento ears, and she would never give them that satisfaction. Not even as panic consumed her. As grief and despair and rage coursed through her veins, her every breath.

Favilla slept soundly somewhere in the darkness. Her heavy, even breaths were now a metronome for Aisling, a blanket of white noise to drown out the sound of her own panicked inhales.

The dragon had done nothing at their first encounter but sniff Aisling before lowering her head and falling into a deep slumber. Her hot breaths were the only thing to give Aisling an ounce of warmth in the time that had passed. She curled into them and pretended it was Morana's body beside her.

The bond shivered like it did whenever Aisling thought of her dragon, but she ignored it. The more she tugged on it, the tauter and more painful the delicate golden string around her soul became. Morana needed to heal.

Battle scenes flooded back whenever Aisling attempted to close her eyes.

Morana's screams. Her pearlescent flesh ripping between the beasts' teeth. Rivers of blood trickling down her magnificent scales. Pain and fury and terror in her amethyst eyes.

Aisling's already cold blood froze with the memories.

She replayed the image of Aedan's nearly lifeless body slumped on the ground, blood pooling around him. The pale shade of his normally vibrant skin. The hollow look in his barely alive eyes.

How badly had he been injured? Was he alive now? He had to be, or the Cruento would have brought her out of this hole and paraded her as a conquest.

If she had listened to Koen, if she hadn't gotten off Morana, none of this would have happened.

She pictured Koen's face, furious and gorgeous, as he raged at her for her idiocy. His deep voice would caress her skin with every shout, every word. The scent of ginger and citrus would envelop her while he threw her to the sand again and again in punishment.

Aisling bathed in the image and allowed it to bring her a scrap of comfort as the darkness threatened to take her under.

Favilla shifted but didn't wake. Her food, some rancid form of raw meat, remained untouched somewhere in the room. Aisling hadn't been acknowledged in however long she'd been stuck inside the cave. She froze in fear when the giant metal door opened and Favilla's food was delivered, only to be ignored every time.

There was only one door. After Favilla dismissed her, Aisling went around the giant room countless times with her hands in search of a handle or knob, but found nothing. Only the large door stood as an entrance and exit from the cave of hell she'd been thrown into. There was nothing for her to grasp from the inside and nothing to leverage the door open.

How long had Favilla been down here? Almost a decade? Aisling's stomach churned with the thought. Maybe that's why all she did was sleep. It was an escape for her, just like Aisling escaped to this world in her dreams.

The Ferox was commanded to kill Favilla on sight, but Aisling would not do it. All it took was one glance into the dragon's bright sapphire eyes and she knew she would never be able to harm her. They were experiencing the same pain, the same loneliness, the same terror and despair. Favilla deserved to live as much as Aisling did.

That's why Aisling made the switch, wasn't it? She wanted the opportunity to fight, to experience everything she could. She wanted to feel alive.

Rage bubbled to a boil in her blood. She did not forsake everything to end up helpless in the hands of the enemy.

Aisling would bathe the world in Morana's darkness and destroy everything the Cruento held dear. She would make them bleed, make them beg. She would douse the world in fire and shadow and dance to the song of their screams.

Dozens of locks clinked against the door from the outside. The handle turned. Metal scraped against stone as it creaked open. She cringed against the dull candlelight that peeked in and illuminated the massive doorway.

The light disappeared, leaving her once again drowning in unfaltering darkness.

Footsteps echoed against the stone and stopped just feet from her.

"Hello, Aisling," cooed a slippery male voice.

TWO

KOEN

"Lazy," Oryn panted despite barely blocking the punch. Koen slammed the heel of his hand into Oryn's chin, his rage a rabid animal inside his chest. Oryn countered with a deluge of punches. None made contact.

Koen wanted more. He wanted to hurt. Wanted to lose himself to the fury inside.

He leaned into the fight and forced Oryn to retreat a step. Again and again, he attacked, reveling in the power of his anger. It lived inside his chest like a parasite, infecting every breath, every drop of blood, until it was all he felt, all he became.

Oryn ducked low and swiped a long leg at Koen's ankles, sending him sprawling into the sand. "Enough," Oryn gasped.

Koen stood, not bothering to wipe the sand from his leathers. "I'm not done."

"You are," Oryn commanded. "No one will fight you tonight, Koen. Kaida and I instructed the girls that they are forbidden from sparring with you. And you will not go looking for a fight." He rolled his shoulders back, his long hair still infuriatingly perfect despite the last hour in the Pit. "I've asked medical to make you a sleeping draught."

His stomach hollowed. "No."

"It isn't an option," Oryn responded, a rare tightness in his voice.

"You can't make me—"

"I can. And I will."

"But—"

"You are worth nothing right now, Koen. Look at yourself." Oryn's emerald eyes danced over Koen's disheveled hair and mismatched leathers with distaste. "You are a ghost of yourself fueled strictly by the rage in your heart. You are a liability to us like this."

The word sank into his skin. *Liability.* That's what he had said to Aisling all that time ago. He hadn't meant it, of course. She had only been a liability to him.

The second she showed up on Morana's back, he knew he was destroyed. When he met her warm eyes and saw the power in her, the power she had no idea she held, he knew he would never recover.

"We could hear something," he said weakly, desperately searching for a way out of the draught.

Oryn's eyes softened. "Say we do find her tonight. Are you well enough to help her? Would you be at your best to fight?

Koen blinked. He hadn't slept more than a few fitful hours in seven days. Seven days without a single shred of information about Aisling's whereabouts. The Ferox was running ragged trying to find her. Hours were spent in the sky and on the ground, frantically searching for any piece of information they could get. He and Neera explored every forest, every dense patch of trees and rocks in the entire kingdom during their endless patrols. And when they weren't searching, they were interrogating.

He had lost count of how many Cruento men he had killed in the last week. Emboldened by their capture of a Ferox, they bragged and peacocked all over the kingdom. Falcons directed Koen to their locations. Kaida let him loose.

The Blade of the Ferox lived up to his name.

Word spread. All it took was four days before the falcons stopped and the Cruento slunk back into hiding, their forked tongues hidden behind their teeth.

And Aisling was still gone as if she had disappeared from the world altogether. Like she was a figment of his imagination, a fever dream.

Morana trudged into the Pit, her violet eyes wild and unfocused as she regarded him. A now constant trail of shadow leaked from her mouth. Despite her healing scales, she leapt into the air, expelling heavy shadows with every flap of her wings. Neera followed, the bond between them tight with worry as she flew into the darkness after her friend.

No one—dragon or human—had been able to control Morana since she returned from Impellor. The doctors worked on her wounds quickly with poultices and well-placed stitches, but it wouldn't have mattered if they didn't. Morana was not going to stay grounded. She was ready to raze the world to nothing but ashes and blood. Her shadows were a constant threat. She voiced her rage and sorrow at all hours, a painful song to everyone in the Ferox.

Kaida refused to allow the dragons to practice flying and sparring together. Morana's rage was too contagious. In a single week, the Lair had descended into near chaos. Each dragon felt Morana's pain as acutely as if it were their own. They were on edge and volatile—a dangerous concoction when paired with the ability to breathe fire. Gareth and the rest of the dragon hands resorted to keeping buckets of water available at all times to douse the pockets of flames as best they could, but no one could stop the shadows.

Oryn sighed heavily as a deep rumbling echoed from the Lair. He watched the two dragons enter the sky with a morbid sadness. "I fear if we do not find Aisling, they will take it upon themselves to exact revenge. Morana's pain is too vivid, too excruciating for them to fight." He glanced at Koen. "First Favilla, now Aisling. They do not take lightly to their bonds being taken from them."

"Favilla wasn't bonded, though."

"Nyssa and Favilla were as close as Neera and Morana. When Favilla disappeared, it was like Nyssa's heart shattered. She was..." Oryn shook his head, his voice softening. "It was an awful time."

Koen remembered bits and pieces. He had only been in the Ferox for a few years before Favilla was captured. The aftermath of her being gone was like a shockwave, one he purposefully forgot.

Oryn's eyes darkened, the timbre of his lyrical voice deepening. "The dragons will destroy everything, Koen. Morana and Aisling's bond is the single thread holding our continent together right now. Should something happen..."

Koen bit back his nausea. Oryn's message was clear: if Aisling died and Morana lived, the world would be saturated in eternal shadow as punishment. Morana would eliminate the sun. Neera would cast a sky of flame. Soren would bake the world with his blue fire. The rest of them would demolish whatever was left standing. And Koen would help.

Oryn's hand found his shoulder, pressing a grounding warmth into his skin that he desperately needed. "To take care of her, you must take care of yourself first. She would rip you apart for allowing yourself to act like this." He squeezed once before disappearing through the Pit doors, leaving a cold emptiness in his wake.

Oryn was right, as always. Aisling would have something to say about the way Koen had been acting. His lack of sleep and lust for blood. His indifference to eating or speaking. His inability to allow himself a single second to rest and think. She would cut him down with that brilliant tongue of hers and a smile that sent his pulse racing.

That was the image that plagued him as he cut down each Cruento in the crumbling castle a week ago – her soft smile and warm eyes. It was all he saw as he surrendered to the savage rage inside. For hours he tortured the men for information. Each one of them bled for Aisling, for Kairossen, before he allowed them death. He slaughtered them one by one, basking in the scent of their fear. Morana stumbled into the open room at some point, bloodied and rabid, and watched with glee as each man met their end at his hand. But none of them spoke. None of them gave him any information. In the end, he was in a room full of shredded bodies and puddles of blood, and his heart remained empty.

Koen looked to the empty sky and wondered where Aisling was. Wondered if she could see it, if she could feel its power and peace.

Exhaustion made itself known, now nearly impossible to overlook. His legs were lead. He could barely lift them through the sand. He trudged down the spiral staircase to his room, pointedly ignoring the empty one beside it.

The bond sizzled and twisted, taking his breath with it. It was a feeling every member of the Ferox had grown to know too well in the past week. His hand clenched at his chest. Footsteps raced down the hall a second later as he reached his door.

Amerie raced to his side, her hazel eyes wild, her mouth opening and closing silently like a fish. She clenched his shirt and pulled him up the stairs and into the common room. The rest of the Ferox was inside, all breathing heavily as they weathered the same pain through their bonds.

His heart faltered as he met Kaida's raging silver eyes. She stood in the middle of the room, her hair down and unbrushed as she continued to deal with Aedan's injuries. Her jaw was set in a tight line. Oryn appeared in the doorway a moment later, silent as an owl.

Kaida's voice came out in a broken whisper. "Morana felt the bond."

Koen was grateful for Amerie at his side and her hand planted firmly around his bicep as his knees threatened to buckle.

"Soren is taking her on patrol right now. She's panicking. Frankly, she's a danger to all of us like this." Oryn took a step closer, his brows bunched tightly together. Kaida spared him a sidelong glance before looking at Koen. "Soren will let us know if the bond strengthens in a certain location. It was his idea. I'm not sure if it will work, but it's not a bad idea, and we don't have any other options."

"What can we do?" Cielle asked. Dark circles hung beneath her eyes, mirroring the rest of their family. She had taken the most patrols since Aisling's disappearance. No doubt she was full of silent, oppressive guilt for being unable to save her at Impellor.

Elaila glanced at her sympathetically. She had gone through every memory of her time with the Cruento in painful detail, looking for any hint or clue as to where Aisling would be, but came up with nothing. Her time with them had been blindfolded and in the dark, shuttled and sedated inside caravans of crops and goods. Oryn had soldiers stationed on every major intersection in the kingdom. Nothing passing through went without a thorough check.

Kaida shook her head. "Nothing. Right now, this is our best shot at finding her. We can't have the dragons dispersed. We still have a job to do."

Fuck the job, Koen wanted to scream. Fuck everything that wasn't about finding Aisling.

Amerie gave his arm a single squeeze in silent agreement. Oryn stood in front of Kaida, their eyes meeting and dancing with an intensity that charged the room. "Stop the twin thing," Amerie groaned.

"Just tell us," Elaila whispered, her soft voice a blade to the tension.

Oryn's jaw feathered before he took a step back. "What was said through the bond?"

Kaida lifted her chin, her throat bobbing. "She didn't say anything. It was a feeling. An emotion." She swallowed again, her voice notably weaker. "Aisling was terrified."

THREE

AISLING

"How are you liking your new home?"

Aisling refused to answer. She cataloged his deep voice, noting the way it remained even and steady despite the vitriol bubbling just beneath the surface. The man laughed softly. "Silence is a valuable tool, I'll give you that. It makes sense for the Shadow Bringer of the Ferox to mold to the darkness. You're doing an excellent job." He paused for too long. "We have no plans to kill you, Aisling. I will let you know the truth. You're far too valuable."

His voice was venom against her skin, burning and acidic and horrifying.

"Imagine what we will accomplish with a dragon rider in our ranks? How much damage we can truly inflict?" He let out a low whistle. "The Ferox is going wild looking for you, you know. It's rumored Morana is willing to bathe the entire world in shadow for you."

She bared her teeth at the name of her dragon on his lips.

"She could do that. But it still wouldn't help her find you. We've been here for years now with no one the wiser. Your people are always so close, but never close enough. It must be frustrating to be on the losing end of a war." He sighed dramatically. "I wouldn't know. It's been easy here for us, if I'm being honest. We can rebuild after Impellor in peace. Favilla here," his voice faded as if looking at the dragon, "has been a vital part of our force. She doesn't know it, of course, but she's been Cruento for years now. Loyal and devoted, like all women should be."

Aisling clamped down on the nausea crawling up her throat. The Man paused for a painful minute.

"We lost a lot of men in the battle at Impellor, Aisling. Too many men. We have to rebuild our ranks." A smile tinted his voice. "We have to rebuild an entire population from the ground up. And what better person than a dragon rider of the Ferox to help us."

The air leeched from her lungs as his words, his intentions, seeped into her skin.

The Man's voice reeked of power, of command. "You will breed an entire new generation of Cruento, Aisling. One of power and skill. Your sons will tame and teach our beasts. Maybe with you here, you can convince sweet Favilla to allow her offspring to mate. She's a bit stubborn, this one. Even unconscious, she seems to be able to alter her children's ability to bring life into the world."

A hint of happiness ran down her spine despite the oily heaviness of horror in her blood. Favilla was creating beasts that couldn't breed. If they wanted to have their best weapons, they had to keep her alive.

He let out a heavy sigh at Aisling's silence. "We've been on a delayed schedule since you arrived. We needed you to acclimate, of course. It takes time to get comfortable in the darkness, even for you. But you were too good an opportunity to pass up. You will be worth it in the end." He cleared his throat. "Unfortunately, Favilla hasn't been putting in the work she's required, so you'll see quite a show today."

His shoes clicked against the stone ground as he walked away. "I know you like the darkness, Aisling. But even those who love it find themselves breaking in its power. I look forward to that day, my sweet." The door opened. "Until then, my men will ensure you are taken care of."

He walked out. Three sets of different footsteps walked in. A small candle at the entrance illuminated enough for her to see a blur of movement before a pair of hands found her. She reacted reflexively in a flurry of fists, only to be brought down by another body.

It was a blind beating in total darkness. Aisling couldn't fight back while her arms and legs were held down against the stone. Blood pooled in her mouth and trickled down the side of her cheek. Her abdomen ached, bruises already forming as they continued to punish her for some unknown crime.

The hands disappeared after a few minutes. She lay limp on the ground, her starving body exhausted. Every sharp inhale burned. The back of her head thrummed in pain. Someone laughed, low and grating against her skin. "Every day, gents. Job just got a whole lot better!"

They chuckled.

Chains rattled from outside the door, silencing their happiness. The floor shuddered under her as the chains moved closer, clinking louder and louder with every harrowing second that passed. A meaty hand tangled in Aisling's hair, lifted her onto her knees, and pulled her head back at a painful angle. "Time for the show," a faceless man cooed at her ear, a smile in his voice and his spit against her skin.

Something made of nightmares, amorphous and terrifying in the darkness, came through the door. Black scales glittered in the light of the single candle. It repositioned itself in the room, somehow too small now with the number of bodies inside.

Panic slid through Aisling's veins with the realization.

Favilla didn't stir as it stood behind her.

Didn't make a sound as it defiled her sleeping body.

Aisling raged. The stone floor ground into her knees while she fought against the man's hold and screamed for Favilla to wake. She couldn't help pulling on the bond, couldn't stop herself from yanking on it with everything she had as she watched the horror unfold.

"Hush, pet," the man holding her murmured, squeezing his fingers tighter in her hair. "She's used to it by now, yeah? Maybe you'll get used to it, too." His hot breath lingered against her ear. She cringed involuntarily. "Watch closely. You'll finally learn what your type is made for."

Aisling screamed. She sobbed and cursed and slung threats into the ether against the guttural sounds the monster was making, against the laughter of the men in the room.

Favilla didn't move.

After an eternity, the monster stopped. Aisling's voice was hoarse as it lumbered out with its chains dragging along the stone floor in a lazy stride. The man tightened his grip on her hair. "Let us know when you're ready for your turn, pet. It's not every day we get to play with a dragon rider."

"Boss said she's off limits," another voice called from the door. "She's already been spoken for."

The man holding her hissed and threw her to the stone floor too quickly for her to shield. The ground slammed into her face with a sickening crunch. With a huff of a laugh, one of the faceless men blew out the single candle, leaving her once again bathed in darkness.

It swallowed her whole, leaving nothing behind.

They weren't going to kill her.

This... this prison they put her in was simply a preview of what her life was to become.

Aisling couldn't stop the vomit as it raced up and out her bleeding mouth and splashed against the stone. Tears poured down her bruised and bleeding cheeks. She crawled toward Favilla with trembling arms. Favilla didn't move save for the even, unbothered breaths lifting her chest. Aisling rested at the dragon's side and willed her heart to slow, her breathing to even out. Willed herself to stop shaking.

How had her life come to this? Her new life had become worse than a nightmare. One she couldn't escape from.

Would she ever feel the cool breeze of sunrise against her skin? Would she ever feel the wind dancing through her hair as she and Morana took to the sky?

Would she laugh again? Feel human again?

Emptiness sank into her bones, weaved through her ribs, and made a home in her heart.

Was there a point in trying to fight it? She was drowning in stone with no way out. Favilla had been here for years. If she couldn't find a way out, how could Aisling?

She was nothing. No one.

Maybe the universe was tired of her ignoring the signs it threw at her. This might be the only way she would listen—to be locked away with no chance of escape from a world she naively thought she belonged in.

She was to be used for breeding. To be nothing more than a vessel to bring new life into this world—new life meant only for hatred. And if she had daughters? Aisling shuddered at the thought. She tucked the tiny seed of hope she held onto deep inside her chest to protect it against the rotten soil of her fear.

The weight of her new reality slammed into her, leaving her breathless. She leaned into Favilla's scales, horrifyingly grateful to have another soul at her side as her fate hung precariously over a sea of darkness and despair.

FOUR

KOEN

Koen stayed awake long enough for Soren to relay to Kaida that Morana had felt nothing. Soren would fly with her into the night until she calmed down or exhausted herself enough to return to the Pit.

Koen didn't remember taking the draught or getting back to his room. He didn't remember crawling into bed with Aisling's necklace and letting the pull of darkness drag him into bleak nothingness for hours.

Golden rays of light filtered in through his windows and rested against his skin with a foreign warmth. He groaned inwardly and reluctantly cracked his eyes open, flinching against the brightness.

Kaida's words devoured him.

Aisling was scared. Wherever she was, she was scared enough to scream down the bond for Morana. It was the only thing she had communicated this entire time.

He shut his eyes and breathed heavily through his nose.

Alive. She was still alive.

But the possibilities of what could be happening to her swam in his mind, none of them good. He knew what the Cruento were capable of. He'd seen it firsthand.

He'd seen Elaila when she first came to the Ferox. She slept beside Osiris for months on end. She refused to look any of them in the eyes. Her back was hunched, her shoulders curved in and bowed, her hands constantly trembled at her sides. The bruises on her body faded, but the ones on her soul took over a year to heal. He almost cried in relief the first time she had spoken to him. She finally woke up, finally came alive, and it was such a stark difference from the terrified young woman Osiris had brought in.

Would that happen to Aisling? Would the hurricane of fire and light she was be doused when they got her back?

He ripped his eyes open and filled the bath with ice-cold water. Without a second of hesitation, he stepped in and ignored the sharp pain and breathlessness that threatened to freeze him. He needed to purge the thoughts, the what ifs, from his mind. Needed to purge himself of the fear and gut-wrenching anxiety that grew with every hour, every day she wasn't back.

He dressed quickly and willed himself to keep his mind blank. He needed to refocus, to keep a level mind. Oryn was right. When Aisling was found, he needed to be ready.

"If you're offered the draught again, share some of it with me," Cielle murmured beside him in the hallway. He flinched at her closeness, oblivious of her presence until that second. She lifted her brows. "Just me."

"How long was I out for?" His voice was rough and raspy.

"Two days."

He clenched his jaw. Two days he could have been helping. Two days he could have been doing something useful.

"Relax, Koen. You needed it. You looked like shit." She jerked her chin in the direction of the Lair. "Morana's bond has been empty since. The rest of the dragons had to take shifts to relieve Soren. Oryn ran to Impellor and did Aedan's council meetings. He's back."

A bolt of fear and then silence from Aisling. It was almost worse than hearing nothing at all. "Is Morana back?"

"Yeah. Neera was finally able to herd her back in. She's been posted in front of Morana's room to keep her from escaping."

He reached down the bond and sent a current of love and appreciation to Neera. Seconds later she responded with a flood of emotions he couldn't fully digest. Cielle followed him into the common room. He stopped abruptly at the sight of the man sitting at the table.

Aedan sat beside Kaida. His right arm hung in a sling. His left hand cradled a steaming mug. The tan glow of his skin had paled ever so slightly. He glanced up at Koen through his sandy hair, unbrushed and hanging just past his shoulders. His eyes, still bright but haunted, flashed as his mouth tilted upward in a wry smile. "Koen."

"Aedan. It's good to see you up." The last time he had seen the King he was covered in blood, his normally warm face ashen and hollow. He was rushed from Soren's back into Kaida's room with a chaotic team of medical at the bedside. Koen glanced at Kaida. Her silver eyes were warm and soft as she gazed up at her King.

Cielle placed a mug of tea in front of Koen and sat at his side. She smiled warmly at Aedan. "How do you feel?"

The King shrugged. "I've been better."

"Medical says he's in good health now. A little battered and bruised, but healing well." Kaida pushed her long hair over her shoulder. "He's going to be staying here for the foreseeable future."

"Until the castle is habitable again," Aedan added. "Then I'll be out of your hair."

"What if we like you in our hair?" Amerie asked from the doorway.

Aedan's eyes glimmered. "My dear, don't get any ideas. I only have one working arm."

"And his left arm at that. Totally useless," Kaida smiled. Koen noted it—the almost permanent thaw of her silver eyes and the warmth in Aedan's. His chest caved at the memory of the fire in Aisling's gaze, the honest softness and devilish gleam that made her come alive.

A hand grasped his under the table. Cielle squeezed it once, bringing him back to reality, and released him. "Any news from your people?"

Aedan shook his head, the light in his eyes dimming. "Nothing. Anwir has recovered from his injuries and was just here a few hours ago to update me. He has scouts in every town and city. Impellor is in ruins. The people are rebuilding tirelessly with the help of our soldiers. But no one seems to know anything, and if they do, they aren't risking it."

It took everything in Koen to keep from throwing his mug against the stone wall.

"They saved me, you know," Aedan said quietly, his stare latching onto Koen's from across the table. "Aisling and Morana."

The room went silent. Aedan's eyes flickered. "It was chaos on the ground. My men were fighting, but the rebels kept coming. We couldn't discern friend from foe. My soldiers didn't want to strike down innocents, but it became a blood bath with their hesitation." He shook his head. "I knew I was dying. And I had accepted death, because what cause was better to die for than for the freedom of my people? For the land I love? But Aisling came out of nowhere."

Aedan let out a breath of a laugh. "She was yelling at me, actually. But she kept me tethered to the light. I felt her dragging me and I just... I knew I would be okay. When she dropped me, I heard Morana scream, and I knew something terrible had happened." He blinked against the wet sheen in his eyes. "Then she was gone. And all I remember thinking before I blacked out was how badly I missed her voice."

Koen couldn't breathe.

Aedan cleared the emotion from his throat. "We will find her." His voice grew stronger. "We will find her and bring her back home, back where she belongs. And she will know nothing but my undying gratitude and adoration."

The common room was silent. Even the fire popped without sound.

"Come," Kaida whispered, gently tugging on Aedan's good arm. "It's time for a walk." She subtly shook away the glossiness of her eyes and glanced sidelong at Koen for only a blink before ushering the King from the room.

"Koen?" Cielle whispered, her voice cracking as she broke the heavy silence.

Grief as he'd never known it drowned him. Wave after wave of unyielding sorrow slammed into his exhausted body.

He was breaking and couldn't stop it.

He couldn't be inside anymore. He had to do something, or he wouldn't make it.

Koen stood, sending his chair flying behind him and crashing to the floor. With a yank, he pulled on the bond and ran out the door of the common room, ignoring the shouts of the girls. He blew past Kaida and Aedan, the former yelling something he didn't hear over the roaring in his head.

Neera met him in the Pit a heartbeat later with her gorgeous wings splayed at her sides. He swallowed a broken sob as their eyes met and hurtled onto the saddle, clipping in as his dragon ascended into the clouds and away from the place Aisling had unknowingly destroyed him.

A storm brewed. Dark gray clouds caressed his face. He ached for rain, for something to wash away the burning rage and complete and utter despair in his heart. Neera felt it and took him to the sea where the crashing waves matched the fury in his soul.

Rain fell. Neera kept him under the clouds, ensuring he felt every drop against his skin.

Aisling was good and kind and soft. She had chosen this life—chosen to stay and fight.

Koen begged her to keep fighting, wherever she was.

FIVE

AISLING

Time passed. Slowly, quickly, she wasn't sure, but it passed all the same.

The beatings came regularly. Aisling's body turned into a single unending bruise. One of her fingers had broken at some point. The taste of her own blood was too familiar on her tongue.

The thrashings came more often than her food did. Hunger gnawed. Her stomach echoed in pain against the stone walls around her. The experiences of her first life came in handy. She knew to chew the meager slice of stale bread they gave her slowly. To swallow slowly. To drink water in between bites to keep from getting sick and to feel fuller.

Favilla's food was delivered on a schedule. She would begin to stir, stretch her wings, eat, and sleep for hours on end while the monster had its way with her. She was never awake for more than ten minutes at a time.

Aisling listened and watched as best she could in the pitch-black darkness. Without fail, almost immediately after eating, Favilla's snores would fill the room.

Aisling felt around the floor, found a piece of some unknown food, and shoved it in her mouth. Her stomach roiled against the slimy texture of raw meat, but she had to know if she was right.

Memories of her first life came rushing back of when she would eat whatever she could get her hands on. She dove through dumpsters. Ate food off the ground. Stole. She almost laughed at herself for believing she would be better than that in her new life as she forced herself to swallow the rancid meat.

Bone-deep exhaustion hit her just minutes later. She lowered to the ground and coiled her broken body into itself. Her leathers were torn, her shirt bloodied and ripped, allowing the cold to seep further into her skin. She longed for a blanket, for a hint of comfort, and curled as close as she could to Favilla for a hint of warmth.

The darkness laughed at her.

Aisling whimpered as her eyes closed.

"We was beginning to think you kicked the bucket," a raspy male voice said from the darkness. She inhaled sharply, her sleep-addled brain thrown into a panic at his closeness. He giggled. "Did ya get your beauty rest, pet? Three days should be more than enough."

Aisling's eyes widened. Three days?

Her hands traveled down her body, ensuring her clothes were still on. The man laughed. "Not your time yet, pet. Beastie's the main attraction now. You just missed the show." He slapped Favilla's hide. "Don't worry. There's always tomorrow." His footsteps faded. Metal scraped against stone and skittered toward her. "Oh. We took a bite out of you while you were out. You won't miss it." A dark chuckle hummed from his throat. "Eat up or there won't be enough left on you to make it fun."

The giant iron door slammed shut. Aisling loosed a shuddering breath and sat up, her head dizzy and grasping. Had it really been three days? There was no way to tell.

Her right hand throbbed. She flexed her fingers, pausing at the tacky feel of old blood in her palm. Her left hand explored it and pulled back in shock.

Her pinky finger was gone.

Only blood and empty space remained.

Aisling wanted to cry. She knew she should be sobbing, but her body wasn't cooperating.

Her soul cried. Her bright, new, shiny soul was now littered with tiny fissures, each one deepening with every second she was left in the darkness.

There would be no coming back from this place, Aisling decided. Her soul would never be full again. She would forever remain broken. Forever remain shattered.

They would take pieces of her until she had nothing else to give.

She could not let it happen. Would not let it happen.

Aisling crawled to the trough of water against the back wall. It was cool and crisp against the cracks in her throat as she drank directly from the surface. With a hiss, she dunked her right hand in the water and ignored the grisly fact that she would have to drink whatever fluids her wound put in it later. The cold numbed her pain enough for her to think.

She hunted for the plate they had left her. A single piece of bread and old cheese met her tongue. She chewed slowly and put the pieces of the puzzle together.

Favilla continued snoring just feet away, unaware of what Aisling had discovered.

There was only one way to get a dragon to do what you wanted without being bonded to it. Only one way the Cruento could have transported Favilla without dying. Only one way they could have another creature violate her without being torn to shreds or turned to ash.

Favilla was sedated. For years now, she'd been drugged, barely awake for more than a few minutes at a time.

Aisling's heart thundered. Did Favilla even know how much time had passed? Did she know what was happening to her?

Rage coated every fiber of Aisling's being. How long would they wait before they deemed it necessary to sedate her? At what point would she stop being a novelty?

The fight came back to her blood in a fit of fire and shadow.

She would never let it happen. The only way the Cruento would take her would be when she was dead and her body was of no use.

Aisling crawled along the ground and blindly collected every remaining bit of Favilla's food. She tucked all of it behind the door. She found Favilla in the darkness and slowly, gently, stroked the scaled armor.

"We're going to get you out of here, Favilla," she whispered. She sat in the bleak nothingness and allowed herself enough hope to plot as best she could with the unconscious body of her only potential ally beside her. "We're going to go home."

SIX

AISLING

Hours after Aisling allowed herself to fall asleep to the memory of sunrise with Koen at the cliffs, Favilla stirred.

Aisling sat up. A quiet panic rose in her chest and sent blood rushing to her throbbing hand. She ignored it.

Hot air doused her face. "Morning, Favilla," she whispered, knowing full well that she had no idea what time of day it was. The dragon inched closer. Scales gently touched the top of her head as Favilla inhaled deeply, taking Aisling's greasy, matted hair into her nostrils with each breath. "My name is Aisling. I'm Morana's bond."

Favilla stilled.

Aisling was forever grateful for the bonding between dragons. Favilla couldn't hurt her, not without hurting Morana. The hot air disappeared from above. A moment later a long snout pushed against her stomach. Reflexively, she lifted her hands to the sleek scales and searched for the bright blue eyes in the darkness. "You've been gone for a long time, Favilla. The Ferox never stopped searching for you."

The dragon tremored in her hands at the Ferox's name. Aisling swallowed her emotion. "I don't know how long we have before they come back, but you have to listen to me," she pleaded in a whisper. "The Cruento captured me, too. I don't know where we are or how we got here. I don't think you do, either. I want to get us out of here, but I need you to be awake."

The locks on the door clicked obnoxiously against the metal. Aisling's heart thundered in her chest. "They're drugging your food, Favilla. They're keeping you sedated. I'll tell you everything after they leave," she rushed, "but you have to pretend to be asleep right now. And do not eat the food."

Aisling pushed Favilla's snout down as the door opened. She took a few silent steps backward before sitting on the hard ground. The men hesitated to enter until they were content with Favilla's stillness. They took their time with Aisling, making sure her bruises and cuts would never heal. She took the beating silently. They would never have the satisfaction of hearing her hurt as her body became nothing but a plaything for them.

They left food for Favilla in front of the door. It reeked of raw meat and deception. Favilla sniffed it once, twice. Aisling coughed, glaringly aware that blood was the warmth seeping between her lips, and gingerly rolled to her side. Every movement was agony. "Please, Favilla. You have to trust me," she whispered.

There was no logical reason for Favilla to believe her. After years of torture by humans, why should she? But Aisling clung to the bond, praying it would be the thing to save them both.

Seconds passed. A minute.

Favilla's breath blanketed her face.

Aisling choked on a sob. "Thank you." She cringed as she lifted herself to sit. Favilla's tail swung behind her like a chair back. She almost cried with the thoughtfulness, the blind trust. "I'm going to tell you everything I know. You aren't going to like it, but it's the truth. Is that okay with you?"

Silence.

"Morana and I do this thing when we talk to each other. She blinks once for yes and twice for no. But I can't see you, so..." she pursed her lips. "Can you click your claws? Once for yes. Twice for no."

An immediate click. She wanted to smile at the familiarity of talking to a dragon, but her face wouldn't comply.

Aisling filled Favilla in on as much as she could. She told her about Morana and the island, her plane stepping ability, and all the battles fought. She updated Favilla on everyone in the Ferox, dragons and riders. Her heart shuddered as she recalled their faces knowing she may never see them again. She tucked the memories into the back of her mind where they couldn't hurt her.

"You've been here for almost ten years. We haven't stopped looking for you. This entire time our only goal has been to find you." And kill her, but Aisling didn't mention that. She gulped, her throat suddenly tight. "The Cruento have been using you. They... you..."

Aisling's throat constricted to a painful vise. She sniffled and shook her head as if she could force the words to fall from her mouth. Favilla inched closer until her snout rested atop Aisling's leg.

"They've been using you for breeding while you're sleeping," Aisling whispered. "The creatures you make are what they use in battle against us. We don't have a name for them, we just call them beasts. That's what they are. They are only alive to fight. They're smaller than the Ferox and so stupid, but they fight until they die."

Tears fell freely down her cheeks. She didn't bother wiping them away. "The beasts cause the chaos. In the chaos, the Cruento make moves for their cause. We've brought down most of them, but they keep making more."

She rested her bloodied hands on Favilla's snout, suddenly overwhelmed with exhaustion, both physical and mental. "We have to get you out. If we get you back home, they can't make any more monsters. They can't win if they don't have you. So you have to stop eating the food. You have to be awake." Aisling paused, knowing what she was about to ask of the dragon was simultaneously selfish and horrific. "It means you have to be awake when they hurt you."

Favilla made no sound. Her breathing remained even and calm. Aisling's heart physically ached for the dragon. Favilla had to be so overwhelmed to learn all of this, to know what had been happening to her for so long without her knowledge or consent.

The sound of a claw hitting the ground once echoed against the stone walls.

Yes.

An agreement.

Aisling couldn't stop the sob that left her lips or the shaking of her shoulders. "I'm so sorry," she whispered through the tears, her broken body aching with every heaving breath. "I'm so sorry that you had to find out like this. You never deserved to be treated this way. I'm so sorry that it took so long for us to find you. But I promise I'm going to do everything I can to get you back home. And when we get out, we're going to turn these men into nothing but ash."

Another single click echoed from the stones into her heart. *Yes.*

Favilla let out a barely audible groan in their silent tomb. It vibrated through the room in waves. Aisling heard wings attempting to open, heard the magnificent beast attempt to stand, but her body was too weak to function. Favilla's head lifted from the ground and Aisling knew she was wringing her long neck in frustration and anger, too weak to do anything else.

It broke something in Aisling. The bond involuntarily shuddered at Favilla's pain, and Aisling prayed Morana could interpret that it wasn't hers. That it was pain by association, by shared trauma, not physical pain. She could not risk Morana coming to find her. If they got their hands on her beautiful dragon...

Favilla's head dropped to the floor in defeat. Aisling reached over blindly. "You can have my food, okay? It isn't much at all. I don't even think you could consider it a snack. I know Morana wouldn't, but it's something that isn't drugged. You have to tear up your food with your claws to make it look like you ate it and I'll spread it around to keep it from piling up. We can't let them think we know anything."

The dragon didn't respond. Aisling stroked soft circles on the scales. Time. Favilla would need time to get over this, if she ever could. Aisling sat in silence while the beast felt her hurt, her anger, and woke up to the nightmare that had been her life for almost a decade. They sat together in the darkness for a long time, comforted by the presence of the other as their worlds threatened to collapse.

The locks clicked and turned outside. Favilla lifted her head.

"Favilla!" Aisling hissed, panic pounding through her. "You have to pretend to be asleep from now on. They cannot know you're awake until you're strong enough to fight back."

She put her trembling hands on either side of Favilla's head and forced her strength into the dragon. "I'm here with you for all of it. I'm not leaving. Whatever happens, you aren't alone anymore. Remember that when they step through the door." She hobbled a few feet away and prayed Favilla would be strong enough to handle what was about to happen.

The door cracked open. The light of a single candle swept in further than normal. Aisling watched Favilla's eyes shut, her breathing even and steady as if asleep, and bit back the burning in her eyes. Favilla's body was so thin, so emaciated. Where Morana was muscle and power,

Favilla was skin and bone held together by dulled scales. Even her wings looked sunken and hollow.

Aisling lifted her lip in disgust. How dare they treat any living thing like this? Like Favilla. Like Elaila. Like the countless women and girls they hoarded in their pathetic attempt for power.

She would die before they had her.

One of the men chuckled as the light drifted in front of Aisling. The sound of chains echoed from the hallway outside. The floor shook with every heavy footstep. The door opened wide, and two more men stepped in, both pressing themselves against the rock walls with swords strapped to their backs.

The massive beast walked in again, its black hide covered in a web of thick silver chains. Aisling couldn't make out its shape against the darkness it blended in with. One of the men came to Aisling's side and forced her to her knees against the stone in a routine she knew too well. His fingers twisted in her hair and yanked her forward until she was just feet from Favilla's face.

Aisling reigned in her screams and swallowed her fury. She would not show weakness. She would be the strength Favilla needed to get through this.

The beast lifted and sank its claws deep into Favilla's hide.

Favilla didn't move as she experienced her horror for the first time.

A silent tear escaped Aisling's eye as watched the brutality.

Let the men think her weak and breaking. Let them take bets on how soon she would be pliant under their hands, molded to their whims and needs.

They didn't know Favilla was awake and experiencing it all. Every second, every brutal thrust.

They didn't know Aisling had memorized all of their voices. She had memorized each of their hands while they beat her. They didn't know that she would ensure each one of them suffered as thoroughly as they made Favilla suffer. As they made Elaila suffer.

They didn't know she would be their executioner. She would be the one to snuff out their lives one by one until their evil had been eliminated from her new world.

SEVEN

KOEN

Morana appeared through the storm like a strike of lightning. Her wild eyes found Neera's. She let out a string of wails and chirps that had Neera tensing beneath him.

The bond, finally calm with help from the sky, flooded with panic. It coursed through his veins with an unyielding bitterness. A second later, it lit on fire with a rage so hot Neera had to expel her flames into the sky. Morana answered with a shoot of shadow.

Aisling.

"Was it her?" Koen shouted over the storm. Morana blinked once. He gripped the pommel with white knuckles. Every thought eddied from his head. "Go, Neera. Find her."

Something like relief flashed in Morana's violet eyes. She turned south against the storm. Neera flew at her tail, matching her speed stroke for stroke.

Alive. Aisling was still alive.

He blocked out the reasons for her panic and rage. Refused to let himself think past the wind and rain soaking him so thoroughly he might never be warm again.

Hours passed with nothing to show except Morana's agitation over the Latebros peaks. Exhausted and freezing, Neera finally convinced Morana to return to the Pit. The ride back was solemn, almost painful.

He had allowed a small glimmer of hope to sprout in his chest. The rain drowned it before they landed in the Pit.

Koen walked the dragons back to the Lair and stopped to talk to Gareth briefly. The Dragon Master ensured both beasts would get extra helpings of dinner. Declan rushed in another heap of blankets to Morana's room, his face full of sorrow at the defeat in the dragon's eyes.

Neera sighed heavily and walked past her room to sit in front of Morana's. The bond flickered with a thick sourness he knew immediately as hopelessness. He rested his hand against Neera's scales and sent a wave of warm gratitude down the bond. He'd never been more thankful that their bond hadn't turned to speaking yet. If he said anything, even in his mind, he feared he would break.

Koen left the Lair only to run into Elaila around the corner. "Where have you been?" she hissed, her normally delicate face twisted with concern. "Kaida is beside herself. She's waiting for you in the common room." He tucked his chin to his chest and took a steadying inhale. Elaila's face softened. "Where did you go?"

He wanted to scream that he was searching for Aisling loud enough for her to know she wasn't forgotten. Loud enough for her to know what he felt for her. That he was fighting for her. That he wasn't going to rest until she was back.

But he shook his head, unable to verbalize any of it, and walked to the common room in his sopping wet clothes with Elaila on his heels. Kaida stood in front of the fire, arms crossed over her chest and staring into the flames. The rest of the Ferox sat scattered throughout the room, each inhaling sharply as they noticed him. Aedan's face twisted into a grimace just in time for the leader of the Ferox to turn Koen's way.

Kaida's molten silver eyes bore into his. He knew he would be grounded for this. Knew she was going to rip into him until he had to stitch himself back together. It wouldn't be the first time.

"Where the *fuck* were you?" she whispered, her voice uncharacteristically emotional.

Koen didn't care anymore. There was no point in hiding it. "I couldn't be here anymore. I couldn't..." he shook his head, jaw clenched. "I know I should have told you, but I couldn't even talk, Kaida." His voice cracked. "I was about to break, okay? I had to get to the sky. Had to find somewhere I could breathe before I went insane." He cleared his throat, keeping his eyes on the floor. "Morana showed up. She felt the bond again. I wasn't going to let her go alone. We followed the bond as best we could."

A shuffle sounded at the doorway. Anwir stopped on his heels, his dark eyes wide as he took in the tension in the room and the full force of the Ferox. Scattered healing bruises marked his face and spindly arms. "I'm sorry," he murmured, his weasel-like voice as annoying as ever, "I don't mean to interrupt."

"Just come in," Kaida snapped. Anwir flinched and nodded before standing in the back corner behind Aedan.

"We didn't find anything," Koen continued. "Morana couldn't feel the bond. But..."

Oryn leaned forward in his chair at Koen's pause. "But?"

"But she acted strange over the Latebros. Agitated. Annoyed. I don't think she even realized she was. When we passed over them, she acted normally again." He knew he was grasping at smoke, but he couldn't shake the feeling that Morana was right. That Aisling was close, just out of reach.

The room was silent save for the cracking of the flames. He lifted his head. Kaida's eyes searched his with a fierceness that made him involuntarily cower. "If you ever," she hissed, "leave like that again, I will have you grounded for an entire month. That includes any battles. I will have Neera fight without you. Do you understand?"

He nodded once, unable to keep the grimace off his face at the thought of his dragon fighting without him.

"You think Morana knows where she is?" Oryn prodded gently.

"Yes. Something bothered her there." Koen shrugged. "Neera and I felt and saw nothing out of the ordinary, but Morana was almost too agitated to fly. I don't know how she didn't realize it."

Aedan gestured for Anwir. "I want an entire legion posted at the Latebros. All of the mountain passes we know of on the surface and underground are to be searched thoroughly. Find new passageways. I don't care if you have to dig into the mountain. I want every single nook and cranny visited by at least two sets of eyes. Hourly reports through falcon and given directly to me, sealed. If there is any tampering, all involved will be imprisoned until I can use my right arm again, and that includes you."

Anwir nodded curtly. "For how long?"

"Until I say otherwise."

Anwir moved silently in answer and disappeared through the doors.

"I believe you," Aedan said gravely to Koen. "We trust our instincts. Nothing else is working."

Koen looked at the rest of the Ferox, hating the pity in their eyes. "If Morana isn't able to fight, we'll be weakened. She needs Aisling. I had to... I can't not look for her." He swallowed thickly and dared a glance at Kaida. "I'm sorry for leaving like that. It won't happen again."

He turned on his heel and walked out the door, forcing his wet, frozen body to make it down the stairs and into his room.

Not since the last time he snuck out for some girl in town whose name he couldn't even remember from all those years ago had Kaida looked at him like that.

Shame flooded him. He had never *felt* so much before. Every emotion was going haywire until his mind was a storm determined to wreck him.

The fire in his room was almost dead. He didn't have the energy to care.

The door opened. Kaida stepped in. She walked past him and stoked the fire, bringing it back to life. Wordlessly, she opened his drawers and pulled out a set of dry clothes, placing them on his bed before settling on the couch and staring into the flames. Koen stripped where he stood, letting his soaked clothes fall to the floor with a slap, and dressed. "Honestly, Kaida, I didn't mean—"

She lifted her hand. "I know. It was meant more to scare the others. I know Amerie is dying for a night out, but I can't let her out of my sight. I can't let anyone think it's okay." He sat on the side opposite her. She tucked her legs under herself. "What did Morana feel?"

"Soren didn't tell you?"

"I told him I'd get the answers from you."

"Panic. And rage."

Her throat bobbed. They sat in silence for a long time watching the fire grow. His body thawed slowly. Kaida's voice was just above a whisper when she broke the quiet. "I thought Aedan was going to die."

He snapped his head toward her. She didn't break her gaze from the flames.

"I thought he was going to die. And I panicked because I realized how fucking weak I had been. How cowardly. All that time, I could have told him that I loved him. That I couldn't imagine my life without him. I have been in love with him since I worked for his father all those decades ago. I truly cannot remember a time in my life when I wasn't painfully in love with him." Her voice wobbled. "I was full of regret when medical worked on him. My mattress was full of his blood. There are red stains on the stone floor in my room that will never come out, and I don't want them to. I want that reminder." She turned to Koen, her eyes lined with tears. "It took him nearly dying for me to realize I couldn't live without him. I think you know that feeling."

His relationship with Kaida had always been a mix between a mother and an older sister. She was caring and overbearing. Quick to listen and quicker to provide unsolicited advice or comments. A solid presence he had come to respect and love. She had never been so raw. Never been so open with her emotions.

"Vulnerability is something I've decided to start working on. Vulnerability and honesty. So I'm going to be honest with you, Koen. I don't know if we'll get her back."

His heart stuttered.

"But if we do," she continued, "you have to be honest with yourself. And with her."

He blinked the burn from his eyes and shook his head. "I feel like I'm losing my mind, Kaida. I didn't realize... I never..."

Her hand rested on his arm. "Of all people, I understand. But it's not too late. She's alive. She's fighting, wherever she is. Morana would never have chosen a weak one." She squeezed his shoulder and smiled faintly. "Aisling took us all by surprise. She wormed her way into our hearts like she belonged there long before any of us could understand what happened."

She stood and stretched her tiny body toward the sky. "If it helps, I knew how you felt immediately. So did everyone else. I think you two were the only ones who didn't realize it."

He cringed. She breathed a laugh. He crossed his arms and leaned back against the couch. "So did you tell him?"

She stopped at his door and glanced over her shoulder with a warm smile he'd never seen before. "I did. And the vulnerability? It was worth it."

She disappeared behind the door, leaving Koen with nothing but the thoughts in his head and the eternal ache in his chest.

EIGHT

KOEN

Sleep pulled at his eyes with an unrelenting strength. He let his heavy lids finally fall.

The door burst open.

"Get up," Amerie demanded, her normally effervescent voice low and laced with rage.

Koen sat up. She was dressed in fighting leathers. Daggers hung from her waist and twinkled in the light of the fire. "Why?"

"Kaida just got a falcon."

Everything in him stilled. A rush of adrenaline kickstarted his heart. "Aisling?"

Amerie ripped open his drawers and threw his leathers onto the bed. He obeyed the silent command and dressed. "Someone at the tavern is talking about her. In detail."

There was no way to control the burst of rage down his spine. Neera mirrored it instantly until he felt her fire popping in his soul.

"Oryn is in Impellor again. Elaila and Cielle are patrolling. Kaida needs us to go."

He didn't need convincing. Amerie smirked as Koen strapped his blades across his back and broke into a devilish grin at the numerous daggers he grabbed from his closet on his way out the door. Calen and Neera met them in the Pit, wings splayed in anticipation.

It was a quick flight to the center of Anguid. A few people milled about in the dark streets. Most houses and buildings were plunged in darkness, their inhabitants sleeping and safe. Lively music lilted from the open doors of the tavern on the outskirts of town. Warm torchlight glowed from inside its windows.

Neera growled low in her throat as she lowered to the ground in front of the tavern, landing with impressive stealth despite her size. Calen dropped Amerie off without landing and took to guarding the sky.

Amerie lifted her brow and unsheathed a thin dagger. "Shall we?"

Koen was no longer capable of conversation. Every cell in his body glowed with the promise of blood. With the thrill of hope that he might find Aisling.

Amerie shot him a playful wink and threw open the doors to the tavern, her hips swinging as she flounced inside. The music stopped. Every head turned their way. Jaws fell open. Koen stood behind her, his eyes searching the room through red-tinted vision.

"Oh, don't stop on our account," Amerie cooed, batting her bright hazel eyes in faux innocence. "We heard there was quite a party going on tonight." She rested her hip against a table of men and picked up a full pint, downing it in seconds. The man beside her gaped. She patted the top of his head. "I needed that more than you, trust me. You can take up the debt with the King."

Koen scanned the room. All eyes were locked on Amerie. All but one.

A young man sitting alone in the center of the room stilled. His eyes widened at Koen's glare. Slowly, his already pale face blanched to a sickly gray.

Footsteps echoed from behind the kitchen door. A thin older woman walked into the silence. Her dark gray hair sat atop her head in a sleek knot. She crossed her arms over her chest and leaned against a wall with a brow lifted at Amerie. Her low voice was raspy and oddly comforting. "Took you long enough, darling."

"Sorry, Cammie. He wanted to look pretty."

Cammie glanced at Koen and smirked. "He did a good job." She lifted off the wall and walked toward them. Koen continued to stare unblinking at the now trembling man, letting the vicious acid of hatred curdle in his gut. The rest of the tavern watched in complete, utter silence.

"It was just him," Cammie whispered at Koen's side. She stared out the door before her. "Everyone else is innocent. I've never seen him before and don't care to see him again. The men around him warned me, then I sent for you. They're good men. Do not harm them." She paused. "I don't care what you do in here, just make sure he pays me for that fucking drink."

Cammie left her tavern and entered the cold night air without another word.

Amerie hopped off the table and came to Koen's side, twirling her daggers with practiced ease. "Now, gentlemen, we know you're enjoying your night, and we hate to break up the revelry, but there is someone here who is just dying to talk to us."

Her blades stopped moving. She extended an arm, the playfulness in her bright eyes replaced by untethered rage, and pointed the tip of her dagger at the man in the middle of the room. Every measured step she took toward him echoed in the silent tavern. "Tell me, love, what's your name?"

The man didn't speak. His lips pursed in a tight white line.

Amerie pouted. "Poor thing! You're shy. It's okay. I know it's hard for you to talk to women. Especially pretty ones." His eyes flared with the insult. Amerie laughed. "It's fine. I'll get your name eventually. Or maybe I won't, who knows?"

She sat on the edge of his small table. "What I do know," she started, her bubbly persona drowned by the fearsome predator she was, "is Koen will make you wish you hadn't opened your stupid fucking mouth."

The man's lungs hollowed. Amerie spoke to the rest of the room without lifting her eyes from her prey. "Every single one of you better be out of this building by the time I turn around." The entire room stood. "Not you three," she said, pointing to three men closest to the man's table.

Their faces paled. The rest of the tavern emptied in seconds as each customer shuffled past Koen to the door, their eyes downcast. The click of the lock echoed against the empty silence inside.

One of the three men spoke. "We didn't—"

"I know," Amerie smiled. "But our friend here seems to have his tongue tied, and I normally like to hear what crimes have been committed before I kill someone." She winked at the trembling man at the table. "Normally. Not always."

Koen stalked toward the center of the room. He stopped behind the man's chair, noting his thin neck and weak arms. He had only a single rusted dagger at his waist.

. It was always like this. Rarely had he ever come across a Cruento man who was truly strong in any way. It almost annoyed him, but he was too far gone to feel anything but revolting hatred.

"Now," Amerie turned her attention back to the man in front of her. "What is your name?"

He didn't speak, but his shoulders tensed.

Amerie tutted. Koen grabbed the back of his neck, his hand almost large enough to wrap around it entirely. The man gasped and grabbed the edge of the table. "Debil! My name is Debil!"

Koen didn't let go.

"Debil," Amerie pursed her lips. "Tell us why we were called down here."

"No."

Koen's grip tightened. Debil's spindly fingers pulled at his hand, but he barely felt them.

"He was talking about Aisling," one of the men along the stone wall stated, his nervous face pale and sweaty. "He…"

Her name flipped a switch. Koen's dagger was in his hand before he had time to think. He plunged it into the back of Debil's right shoulder. The man screamed and writhed against the hold on his neck. Koen didn't remove the blade or his hand.

"Go on," Amerie coaxed the man with a sweet smile.

He swallowed audibly. "I don't feel comfortable repeating it, ma'am. It's not right."

Neera mirrored Koen's rage. A snarl ripped from just outside the tavern door. Amerie cackled as Calen landed on the roof, shaking the entire foundation of the tavern. The men jumped. Debil whimpered.

"Cammie is a very dear friend of mine. Very dear," she emphasized. Koen wanted to roll his eyes. Cammie loved Amerie for spending ungodly amounts of Aedan's money at her tavern. They were no more friends than he was with the farmer who raised cattle for Neera. "She vouched for you three, you know. I would hate to have to tell her that her word is no longer worth anything."

Three sets of eyes widened. The man in the middle cleared his throat. "I won't repeat his vile words. What he said is plain torture, ma'am. It's inhumane and disgusting. If what he said is true, I don't think anyone could live through what he described – man, woman, or dragon."

"He should be ashamed of himself for speaking of a woman that way. Let alone a woman of the Ferox," the man on the end seethed, his eyes latching onto Debil with nothing but hatred. "He deserves no less than to be turned to ash by your dragons."

Amerie slid her glance to Debil. "Anything you'd like to say?"

A strained laugh came from his lips. Amerie's brow pinched as she followed his gaze to a satchel crumpled under the table.

"Don't—" Koen started, but she already opened the flap.

Amerie paled, the fire in her eyes extinguished in a hollow breath.

"I was supposed to bring it to you tomorrow," Debil rasped against Koen's hold, "a little gift for the Ferox left at the front door. But this works, too."

Amerie lifted her stare to Koen. Utter devastation lined her face. It terrified him.

He threw Debil's face into the table hard enough for bone to crunch against the wood. Amerie's knuckles blanched, her grip tightening against the leather as Koen reached for the bag. He pulled it from her with a single yank and peered inside.

Glistening white armor peeked up at him—Aisling's armor.

Covered in crimson and brown.

And in the middle of the armor, a stark contrast to the bright white and dried red, lay a delicate finger spotted with dirt and blood.

He knew that finger. Knew how it looked curled into a fist as it hurled toward him. Knew how it curved around a mug of tea. Knew the hand it belonged to. The arm. The body.

Every thought eddied from his head.

He was empty. Hollow.

There was no more rage or wrath. No more fire in his soul.

"Want more? I can get it for you," Debil whispered, an acidic smile in his voice.

Amerie moved faster than Koen had ever seen before.

Her dagger sliced across Debil's face too quickly for the light of the torches to reflect off the blade. He tumbled off his chair and onto the floor with a wretched cry. The blade in his shoulder sank deeper into the flesh as he rolled onto his back, blood crawling through the gaps between his fingers covering his face.

"She is worth more than you would ever have amounted to," Amerie whispered, her lips pulled back from her teeth in a sneer. She stalked toward Debil's writhing body. "No one will miss you. Your name will never be remembered. You will die alone, covered in your own piss and blood. And my dragon will feast on your corpse only to shit you out like the waste that you are."

Calen bellowed. Neera joined. The bond roared to life.

Koen's rage, his heartbreak and devastation, came back with a power so raw, so vicious, his blood sang. He unsheathed his sword and a dagger. The three men along the wall didn't move or dare breathe as they watched the Blade of the Ferox come to life.

Koen took his time.

Blood splattered the walls. Urine stained Debil's pants just as Amerie predicted.

On the floor, a bloody, orderly line of Debil's fingers. An offering to Aisling.

Amerie picked at her nails with her daggers while Koen worked. For every question Debil refused to answer, a piece of flesh fell from his body. A bone broke. A limb stopped working.

"Where is she? Where is Aisling?" Koen asked an hour later, covered in Debil's blood. His voice was unrecognizable even to himself. This man was a killer. This man was desperate and on the verge of insanity.

Debil's wet cough echoed against the stone walls. "You will never find her," he rasped. Warped pride lined his glazed eyes. He lay sprawled in his own fluids unmoving save for his mouth. "Aisling is ours now. We can do whatever we want to her, and no one can stop us. She's lost to you. She will die there, and none of you can help her. Morana will be nothing without her. Your dragons will be weaker. And you will bleed before we kill you." He grinned at Amerie, his teeth coated in bright red. "I'd love to see how powerful you feel when there's a line of us waiting to fill every—"

He stopped making any sound. Blood trickled from the corners of his lips. His glazed eyes emptied with each gasping, wet cough.

Koen's blade glittered in Debil's chest, embedded in the wooden floor beneath him.

"You always have to ruin my fun," Amerie groaned. She pocketed her dagger, rolled her eyes at the gurgling body on the floor, and turned to the three men. "Tell us everything he said."

"Help me drag him to Calen?" Amerie dropped a pile of coins from Debil's bag on the table for Cammie.

Koen didn't look at the dead body in the middle of the tavern—the body that knew where Aisling was and purposefully went to the grave with the secret on his tongue.

So close. He had been so close to finding her and failed.

If the horrors the men told them were true…if Aisling's finger told him anything…

"Koen."

He blinked from his thoughts.

"He was never going to tell us where she was. You were right to end his blabbering. He was a waste of time. And space. Calen will enjoy him as a little treat."

His raw voice barely lifted above a whisper. "Do you think she's—"

Amerie stepped in front of him, fire blazing in her eyes. "Don't you dare."

"What they were saying—"

"Aisling has lived in two worlds at the same time, Koen. She healed Morana with fucking *flowers*. She knocked you on your ass the first time you sparred." Her voice tightened. A rare flash of emotion danced across her face. "If I had to bet on any of us, I would bet on her. There's something to be said about keeping hope in your heart. And she's full of it. Hope for her future, for her life." She shook her head and blinked quickly. "She wants to live. And she's going to. She will accept nothing else."

NINE

AISLING

"You're weak as hell, Favilla," Aisling groaned as she forced the dragon to walk around the cavernous room for the thousandth time. "We both are, really," she conceded. Favilla snorted once over Aisling's head, dousing her in a mist of hot air. It did nothing to warm her. The chill of the room had set in her body, in her bones, with a painful stiffness she couldn't shake. "Let's do your exercises first. Then I'll do mine. Deal?"

One claw clicked against the ground with a sharp snap. Aisling swore it contained a bite of sass. She attempted to smile but fell short. "Wings first." She felt along Favilla's side until the huge wings were directly above her. "Just some stretches to start, in and out."

The dragon listened. Aisling lifted her sore arms and felt the leathery skin extend and contract, felt the bones and muscles wake up from their years of disuse. After a minute of light stretching, Aisling gave her a light pat. "Beautiful. Let's do some work now. Extend them all the way and lift and lower like you're flying. We have to strengthen that back."

Favilla groaned as she followed orders. Aisling sucked in a breath at the sound of her pain echoing against the stone. They had spent hours and hours exercising already, maybe days of it, and each groan of Favilla's discomfort sent shards of ice through Aisling's heart. She traced small circles on Favilla's side, putting every ounce of understanding and comfort in the touch as she could.

"Again."

"Again."

"Again."

Favilla obeyed every order despite the obvious ache in her atrophied muscles. Aisling swallowed her empathy and focused on the goal knowing they wouldn't make it ten feet in the air before Favilla's wings gave out. "Perfect. Good job, beautiful girl. Rest now. It's my turn." Favilla collapsed on the ground with a sigh.

Aisling took a few tentative steps in the darkness using her arms and hands as guides until she found open space. By the tenth jumping jack, she was breathless. Her body burned against the exertion and lack of nutrients. It was dying for a circadian rhythm. For a hint of sunlight. For a breath of fresh air. She pushed anyway, letting the pain fuel her.

Squats. Attempted pushups that ended in fail after fail as her beaten body screamed for rest. Punches and kicks. Planks and crunches as best she could with the searing pain in her sides and her missing finger.

She heard Koen's deep voice in her head. Saw the glimmer of warm honesty in his eyes from their morning run. His laugh. The playfulness in his smirks.

Out of all the faces Aisling knew and loved, his was the only one to bring her comfort in the darkness. The only one that allowed her heart and mind to relax enough to get a few fitful minutes of sleep. She felt safe in his memory. Safe in his phantom presence.

A need to apologize to him consumed her. If she had just listened to him, she wouldn't be here. If she had just stayed on Morana, both she and her dragon would have been fine.

But Aedan deserved to be protected. She might never know if he survived, but she liked to imagine he was with the Ferox, healed and laughing in the common room.

And Favilla deserved to be saved. She deserved to know that she hadn't been forgotten or replaced.

Aisling rested on the ground with her hands above her head as her chest heaved for more air. Drops of sweat lined her brow despite the never-ending chill. Everything hurt. Between her frequent beatings and the exercises she forced on herself and Favilla, her body wasn't able to handle much more. Her dirty leathers hung off her body. The gnawing ache of hunger was now permanent.

But she would endure it because Favilla was finally awake. She was moving and getting stronger. She was alive again, and Aisling would handle whatever came her way to ensure Favilla got another chance of life like she did.

The beast eggs were collected sporadically. Aisling counted at least five eggs each time Favilla expelled them. She cringed every time they fell to the floor and rolled on the stone ground with an empty thud. Favilla was nearly inconsolable when the first one fell. The first egg she felt, the undeniable proof of what had been done to her. Proof of how her body was betraying her. It took everything in Aisling to keep the dragon contained. She refused to let Favilla crush them. Nothing could hint that they were planning something.

The men had no idea. They laughed and jeered at Favilla's resting body as they rolled her eggs out of the room. The door barely closed before Favilla's deep growl reverberated against the stone. The pair of them, two females battered and abused, would sit together in silence for long periods in the never-ending darkness and silently save each other from their despair.

Aisling didn't know what time it was as she stared into the bleak blackness of the stone ceiling above. She had no idea how many days had passed, but she knew she hadn't eaten in far too long. Knew she was exercising too much for what her body was able to handle. But rest was not an option. Sitting and letting herself waste away was not an option. If she was going to die, she was going to die strong and fighting.

Koen would make her spar. He would force her to get up and fight. Oryn would tell her the best time to train was when her body was exhausted. Morana would not accept weakness. Kaida's brow would arch.

So Aisling stood and wiped the sweat from her brow. She launched into a series of punches and kicks that had her breathless in seconds, but she kept going, imagining Koen on the receiving side. Imagining his smile, his encouragement, as he made her into the best version of herself.

She wondered if he knew how much he had helped her. That his words, harsh as they might have been, forced her to fight. Forced her to become who she was supposed to be. She was alive again, her soul alight even drowning in darkness, because of him.

A stroke of gratitude ran down her spine that her last sunrise had been with him.

The locks clinked outside the door. Favilla instantly forced her breathing to even and calm within seconds. Aisling wiped the sweat from her brow, ignoring the shaking of her limbs, and leaned against the back wall as she sat and prepared for the oncoming barrage of pain.

Favilla's food squished against the door as it opened. Slow, measured footsteps echoed against the stone walls.

"Hello, Aisling," the slimy voice she despised cooed. Her jaw clenched as she realized she would rather be beaten by his minions than hear the mystery man speak. "I've missed you. Just checking in to make sure you're well taken care of."

She scoffed, the only sound she would let the Man hear.

His voice inched closer. "It's been almost three weeks now if you need help keeping track. Three long weeks of no one coming to save you." His foot scraped along the ground just feet from her. "You would think they'd want their Shadow Bringer back."

She bit her tongue, saving her waning energy for something worthwhile. He laughed, acidic and abrasive against her skin. "Word is Morana is looking for a new rider. Someone who can actually hold up her end of the bond."

He was bluffing. Morana was constantly tugging on the bond. There was a terrified urgency in each pull that grew stronger with every second that passed. Aisling never answered it. There was no point in working up her dragon more than she knew she already was. She would never forgive herself if something happened to Morana.

"We all know that isn't you, don't we? You can barely hold a sword. You were like a well-wrapped gift left on the doorstep. We never expected you to fall at our feet. You did it all yourself."

His deep, resonating voice inched closer. Too close. She pushed into the rock at her back as the heat from his breath caressed her face.

"No one can save you, my sweet," he whispered. A smile tinted his voice. "Think about it. Favilla has been with us for almost a decade now. Wouldn't they rather put their effort into finding her – a fire-breathing dragon? There is no reason for them to look for you anymore. You've been deemed dead. A little girl who fell too far over her head. A girl with no family, no friends, no skills. Why would they waste their time with you when they could find an actual weapon?"

She clenched her teeth and forced his words to fall off her skin like oil and water.

"You've lasted longer than I anticipated, Aisling. While that's frustrating, it makes me eager to see what our offspring will be like. Will our sons be the ones to finally tame the beasts? Will they rise through the ranks and lead like their father?" He laughed. Aisling's lungs hollowed. "Maybe one of them will become King and rule with an iron fist. How wonderful would that be – one of Aedan's blessed favorites breeding his replacement?"

Fuck him. Fuck the Cruento. She was not an object. She was not to be bred like a prized mare or given to the highest bidder. She would never be his. Rage boiled so hot inside her soul that she wondered if she would crack.

Aisling leaned forward and spit blindly in the blackness before her.

She didn't see it in the darkness. Didn't feel the whoosh of air until it was too late. His knuckles met her eye with a splintering crack. Her head slammed against the rock behind her.

"I was going to let you out, but I think more time down here will do you well, Aisling," he whispered, his infuriatingly calm voice just inches from her face. "Take this time as a gift. Think about how you want to benefit our cause. One way or another, you will be put to use."

The door slammed shut. She lifted a shaky hand to her already swelling face and grimaced when it came back covered in blood.

Her head pounded in pain. Favilla chirped softly over her, blanketing Aisling's face in hot air.

"I'm fine," she reassured the dragon, overwhelmed that a soul who had been through unspeakable trauma was concerned about her. She wiped the blood from her hand onto her crusted shirt, immune to the pain coursing through her. "Let's take a quick nap. We'll start back with the exercises when we wake up."

She didn't need to say that it depended on when the door opened again, when Favilla would be fed next, or when they deemed it time for Aisling to bleed again. She didn't need to say it depended on how bad the injury to her head was.

The Man's words hung heavy in her mind, tattooing themselves on her brain. She would never forget the sound of his voice. Never forget the threats and promises. Every time she allowed the seed of hope to peek out through the darkness, his words would echo, and the hope would shrivel in on itself.

Favilla rested her head at Aisling's feet. Her mind calmed at the dragon's closeness, no longer the firestorm of rage it was just moments before. Bolts of pain shot across her face and down her neck, but she ignored them.

She needed a clear head. Favilla depended on it. Her future depended on it.

TEN

KOEN

A torrent of flame flooded the bond.

Koen was on fire, burning from the inside out with a heat so excruciatingly strong he was positive he was dying.

He sat up with a gasp. The dying embers of the fire illuminated his room with a soft orange glow. Stars littered the night sky behind his window.

Again, the fire down the bond, this time mixed with something dark and misty that sent a raging chill down his spine.

He leapt from bed and threw on a pair of pants, not bothering with a shirt before he raced to the Lair. Doors slammed behind him. The thunder of footsteps followed him to the Pit where he stopped. He threw his arms out to stop the rest of his family.

Morana raged in the sand, her teeth bared, shadows curled around her like the caress of a protective lover. The violet of her eyes was brighter than he'd ever seen, almost glowing against the night sky and the brightness of her scales. The rest of the dragons stood in a circle around her with their wings outstretched to form a wall. She bared her teeth, snapping her maw at them like a cornered animal. None of the other dragons made a sound. Morana's rage was enough to fill the Pit and the ether.

Kaida pushed Koen's arm down gently, her wide eyes locked on Morana. She stepped into the Pit in nothing but a long shirt, her legs bare. Aedan reached for her, but she shrugged him off and walked straight into the circle of claws and fire.

Soren's head lifted above the rest. He let out a plume of blue flame large enough to cover the entire opening of the Pit. The dragons took a step back and allowed Kaida to slip inside. Her steady hands lifted through the shadows.

Morana's eyes narrowed. At Kaida's touch, Morana snarled deep enough for the sand to vibrate. Aedan took a step forward, but Soren did nothing. He let Morana snarl at his bond, respect and understanding in his eyes as he stared at her tiny body swarmed by scales.

Kaida rubbed small circles against Morana's hide. Slow, patient strokes.

After a minute, Morana lowered her head. Her lips covered her teeth. Kaida murmured under her breath. Morana's eyes closed, exhaustion loosening her neck and wings until they sagged. Kaida rested her forehead against Morana's. She whispered something.

Morana whimpered.

Neera's bond tightened to an almost unbearable level of pain. Koen held his breath against it. Elaila and Amerie covered their mouths, their bonds undoubtedly feeling the same pain he did.

Kaida continued to speak softly to Morana, her voice a low hum in the heavy silence. Soren chirped once and turned toward the Lair. The rest of the Ferox dragons followed, but Neera remained steadfast at her friend's side.

"Koen."

His legs reflexively followed Kaida's soft command. He stood beside Neera, resting his trembling hands on her comforting hide as he braced for the worst.

"I need you to take Morana to the island," Kaida said softly against the bright white scales, her lashes damp. "You and Neera. Just for a few days. She needs time to breathe. I think you can understand." She pressed a soft kiss on Morana's cheek and looked at Neera. "Stay with her. We will only be a few minutes." Neera blinked solemnly in answer and curled her body around her friend's crumbling form with devastating gentleness.

Koen numbly followed Kaida past the rest of the Ferox, down the stairs, and into his room. He stood by the fire while Kaida grabbed his bag and filled it with clothes and toiletries. She threw him a change of clothes. "She felt her again."

He swallowed. "What did she feel?"

"You felt it."

He balked, his shirt halfway on his head. "That's not possible."

"It is. If the emotion is strong enough, it can travel not just between the bonded pair, but the entire bond." She clenched her jaw. "All of us felt her."

He stared at Kaida, not fully comprehending what he was hearing. That fire, that pure rage...

"The second blast was Morana's response. It's why it felt...different." Kaida shivered. "The dragons were barely able to keep her contained. Soren thinks Morana needs somewhere she can breathe."

"The whole island is full of memories of Aisling," he rasped. "That's where they met. That's where everything happened."

"I know," she responded. "But it's the only place that would be safe for Morana to unleash her wrath. We can't risk the people. Kairossen is already in shatters. We can't have a rogue dragon on top of everything. Aedan has enough on his plate already."

"This isn't about Aedan," he countered, unable to keep the ire out of his voice.

Kaida turned to him, silver fire back in her eyes. "Make no mistake, Koen. I feel for you. Truly, I do. I want Aisling back as badly as you do. I miss her terribly. But I am the leader of the Ferox. I command the dragons of the sky. We are in a war. Unlike you, I'm able to see more than what's directly in front of me."

"She's not in front of me!" Koen shouted, the tether on his sanity fraying dangerously thin. "She's not here, Kaida. And I can't see or think or breathe anymore. So forgive me," he seethed, "if I can't see the bigger picture because she blinded me to everything else."

Kaida zipped his bag and walked to the door. "Just a few days. No longer than a week. Let Morana clear her head. Neera will be there to keep her contained."

"And if she can't?"

Kaida froze for a moment. "Just keep her safe."

"The Cruento—"

"Haven't made a move in almost three weeks. We destroyed their only chance of beating us. None of them are brave enough to fight without their stupid beasts and we killed them all. It will be weeks more before they do anything. Anwir has everything monitored to within an inch of his life. Aedan has made the consequences clear. Do not worry about the Cruento. We're confident enough that we will stop patrols for a few days to allow everyone to rest."

Red tinted his vision. His voice came out dangerously low. "You're giving up on her."

"I will never give up on her," Kaida hissed, her eyes flaring. "I will look for her until the day I die. But we're exhausted, Koen. Cielle has done every night patrol for weeks and helped rehouse those in Impellor. Amerie and Elaila have scoured maps and searched every city and town they could for days. Elaila relived every traumatic memory she could remember to help Aisling. Oryn is taking on all of Aedan's council duties on top of everything else." Her throat bobbed. "If we do not rest, we are of no use to her."

He shook his head. "I can't stop looking for her. I won't."

"Then don't. Explore the southern coast. Let Morana search for the bond as much as she wants. Just keep her safe." She turned the doorknob. "Take this time for yourself, too. Figure out what you want to say when we get her back. Be brave." She shut the door.

He finished dressing quickly, his mind whirring. He grabbed his bag and jogged to the common room where Elaila poured a cup of tea and stared out the giant windows into the night sky. He threw whatever food he could find in his bag.

"We'll find her, Koen," Elaila faced him. "They aren't as smart as they think they are. If I got out, she will too."

"Don't sell yourself short."

"I'm not. I'm stating the obvious. She survived an entire life before this one. If I had to bet on anyone, it would be her."

He zipped his bag and glanced at her, unable to stop his mouth from opening. "Did you know? Was it obvious?"

He didn't know why he asked. Didn't know why the question was bubbling on his tongue since Kaida mentioned it.

A knowing grin lifted her lips. "Since she landed in the Pit."

"How?"

"You may think you're stoic, but your eyes never are."

He ground his teeth. "Amerie and Cielle?"

She laughed. "Amerie still won't shut up about it."

"What won't I shut up about?" Amerie strolled in and took a bite of a stale muffin.

"Why are you still awake?" Koen grumbled.

"Koen and Aisling," Elaila said.

Amerie smirked. "It's plastered all over your face, lover boy. I don't blame you. She's stunning. And so clever." She took another bite. "She looks at you the same way."

Elaila gasped. "Amerie!"

Cielle walked through the door, the dark purple under her eyes growing deeper by the hour and glanced between them. A surge of guilt ran through him. Maybe Kaida was right. They did need a break. "Want me to hit her?"

Neera tugged on the bond. Koen walked out of the common room, his ears ringing as the girls argued behind him. He strapped into the saddle and zipped his coat, not bothering with the gloves. Neera launched into the air with Morana at her side.

The cold night air greeted him like an old friend. He breathed it in deeply, clearing his lungs before he cleared his head.

They arrived at the island just as the sun rose above the horizon. The stars winked and flickered out against the brightening sky. Golden light blanketed everything below them in a symphony of color and life.

Deep green grasses covered flower-conquered slopes. Blue ribbons of water danced through the rock and dirt. Splotches of gray craggy rock jutted out amongst the softness.

Morana led them further inland to a valley where a bright blue river snaked through the mountains of rocks and grass. He climbed from the saddle and stretched while the dragons drank their fill.

Morana lumbered to an opening in the hill held up by two large vertical boulders. She disappeared into the darkness as if she had been a mirage. Neera followed blindly and disappeared with her friend without so much as a look back at Koen.

He wanted to sleep. Wanted to curl up under Neera's wing like he had as a child and sleep until everything was right again. But he started walking, needing to feel Aisling's presence somehow, over hills, through streams, until the ground beneath his feet turned to sand as dark as Morana's shadows. He sat at the water's edge with his arms around his knees, letting the waves lull him to a quiet mind.

Aisling was somehow everywhere and nowhere, a haunting presence he craved tainting the land around him. Every gust of wind, every rustle of the grass or curl of the waves was her.

This was where her story started all those months ago. She sat along this same black sand beach to escape from her other life, a life he planned on knowing more about, when Morana fell from the sky and changed her fate forever.

Would she still have chosen this life if she knew what was in store for her?

It didn't matter, not now. This reality mattered.

He couldn't find her. Not without burning the entire kingdom to embers.

But he could be there for part of her soul—the living, breathing extension of her heart. He could ensure that part of her was safe and cared for until she returned. And when she returned, he would be nothing but honest with her.

He walked back to the cave after the sun had fully risen and pulled out Aisling's necklace, holding it close as he watched Morana sleep.

ELEVEN

AISLING

A foot slammed into Aisling's side with a sickening crunch.

Blinding pain careened through her.

Men laughed.

Fresh blood sat atop caked layers on her skin. Her bruises had bruises. Her breathing was becoming more laborious with every minute that she disintegrated in the stone. Her heart stuttered often. She could no longer feel the pangs of hunger.

Her body wasn't healing fast enough between beatings. After giving what little food she had to Favilla, hers wasn't ingesting enough to get through them. The exercises she weakly attempted drained her.

"Had enough?" one of the men sneered as he lifted her by her hair and threw her into the ground. Her head bounced off the rock with a wet thud. The urge to vomit overwhelmed her, but she had nothing to give.

She knew the man's voice, the cadence of his slurred words, his heavy hand. It had been so long in the darkness that she knew who was walking toward her by the heaviness of their steps.

He leaned down until the spittle from his lips wet her cheek. "Word is you'll be taken off the market soon. Boss thinks you're just about ready to break. I think you're broken." His hand trailed down her front and squeezed her breast painfully. "I plan on being there when he realizes you aren't worth it. Since we know each other so well and all."

He squeezed her again. "I'll wait 'til then, though. Bruise you up real good so no one else takes a liking to you."

Her next breath was stolen as he kicked her side again. Something snapped and echoed against the rock around her. Aisling drowned under the unending shockwaves of pain. She let out an almost audible whimper—the only sound she'd ever allowed herself to make in their presence.

The door shut after a minute with a click. A heartbeat later, Favilla's hot breath swarmed her. A low rumble vibrated through her neck as she sniffed Aisling's blood and tears.

Aisling's soul was breaking. She swore it wouldn't happen. Swore she would make it through, that she was strong enough now to handle anything. She had traveled worlds. Had endured more than anyone else she knew and still hoped for better.

But the torture never stopped. She was starving. Broken. Dying.

Favilla was nearing her breaking point, too. Aisling could hear her claws scraping into the ground with every visit. Could sense Favilla's tension every time the door opened.

"It's almost time, Favilla," she whispered, her voice raspy and wet. Every breath was agony. "Do you feel strong enough to fly?"

They didn't have to get far. If Favilla's dedication to her exercises was any indication, they could at least make it a few miles. Maybe more if they caught the current. Aisling would pull on the bond as soon as they left this room. Yank on it as hard as she could until Morana appeared. Even if she died in the process, she could finally lead the Ferox to the nest.

Favilla hesitated before she clicked her claw once on the ground.

Yes.

It felt more like a question than an answer, but Aisling didn't have the energy to think about it. She clutched an arm around her broken body. Her head thundered with pain. Sleep beckoned, and she wasn't strong enough to fight the pull. "Make sure I wake up?"

The sound of a single click against the floor was the last thing she heard.

"Aisling."

Something pointy nudged her ribs. She groaned against the pain, flickering her swollen eyes open to nothing but darkness.

"Ah. You're up," the Man said, his familiar voice a bullet to her heart. "Glad to see my men have kept their anger in check." Her side screamed in pain as he nudged her again with the pointy end of his shoe, but she reigned it in.

He tutted. "So close, my sweet. Maybe one more day. What do you think? One more day before you're finally mine. I'll let my men have their fun for a little longer. It's not every day that a member of the Ferox is pliant before us. They deserve to have some fun after all their hard work."

Aisling said nothing, her hatred and rage too much for her weakened body to express.

Time passed. Aisling heard his steady, unhurried breaths as if waiting for her to respond. His voice inched closer. She shivered involuntarily at the venom lacing his words. "Your silence, while endearing, is laced with defiance, my sweet. And I will not tolerate it." A nauseatingly warm finger slid down her arm. "Your type is meant for two things: obedience and breeding. Nothing more. I think you need a reminder of that. A collar would do nicely, yes?"

Her breathing hitched at the cold tip of a blade at her throat. Slowly, just shallow enough to keep her alive, he pierced the delicate skin and dragged it across her neck with a searing burn. Warmth seeped down her collarbone, onto her chest, and past her shoulders.

A smile tinted his voice. "I am going to break you, Aisling. You will show the Ferox they're fighting a losing battle. Show Aedan his reign is a pathetic sham. And you will provide me many strong sons." He traced the line of her jaw with a finger. "It will be an honor to be the one to ruin you."

She barely swallowed her cry before his footsteps melted behind the door.

Her breaths came short and fast and excruciating. Tears fell over the mounds of caked blood and grime on her face. Her body trembled. With anger. With fear. With hopelessness. She couldn't decipher any longer.

With a shaky hand, she lifted her fingers to her neck. Sticky blood met the ripped pads of her fingers. She rubbed it between her thumb and index finger, craving the warmth against her frozen skin.

The sobbing started a heartbeat later. She couldn't hold back anymore. Couldn't stop the wails that came from the deepest part of her soul and echoed back at her, unable to leave the chamber, the prison, she'd been caged inside.

She wouldn't live through another day. She was starving. Her ribs were broken. Her head was one more solid push away from breaking. The men would get tired of waiting and take her as they took Favilla.

They had to leave. Had to get out before the cave turned into their coffin.

She would rather die trying to live than die giving up.

Favilla sat beside her. Aisling leaned against the scaled body, grateful to have someone else to share in her misery. "We can't wait any longer, Favilla," she croaked in a barely-there whisper. "The next time the door opens –"

Favilla let out a low rumble in answer.

Together. They would go together.

TWELVE

KOEN

"Get her up, Neera. She can't sit in there forever," Koen growled. Neera shook her neck in agitation. She grumbled in response before walking back into the cave.

The sun had started to set. After a quick nap with the dragons, Koen scouted for meat but found nothing worthwhile. He had food in his bag, but the dragons needed to eat.

Frustration oozed down the bond. He tucked in his smile, knowing Neera hadn't meant to send it. Sharp, intense sounds rang out from the cave. The snap of teeth against air clipped through the darkness, mingling with the dull vibrations of their annoyance with each other. Finally, Morana's shiny scales appeared from the darkness. She lumbered to the entrance with a glare latched on Koen. Neera came up behind her, wings splayed and neck twisted.

He crossed his arms. "I know you ate when you were here before. Aisling told us about a field of livestock. Take us there, and we'll come back as soon as you're done. I promise."

Morana's violet eyes flared with the memory. The brightness of her stare was long gone. In its place was a blank, bleak nothingness. There was no more anger. No more determination. Just wretched emptiness.

It was the same look Aisling had when Koen called her useless. The same look of quiet defeat.

He cleared his throat, ignoring the bolt of shame the memory brought. "We will get her back, Morana. If it takes my entire life, I'll get her back to you. But she will be pissed if you aren't taken care of, and I don't want to deal with that. So let's help each other out, okay?"

An olive branch for the dragon who came close to killing him too many times to count.

Morana blinked slowly. Her sad gaze left him and turned to the river. Koen knew Morana was giving up with every minute that passed. Her soul was too tired, too broken. Weeks without her bond had turned her into a frayed shell of the terrifying dragon she was.

Did Aisling feel the same way? Wherever she was, was she close to breaking?

Koen braved a step closer and waited for Morana to snap, but it never came. His hand rested against her neck. "You cannot give up. She would never forgive you. You can feel her, right?"

Morana didn't move. Didn't acknowledge she had heard him.

"Aisling is fighting. That's why you chose her. Without her, you would have died on this island. She came back day after day, splitting her soul between two worlds for you, Morana. She chose to leave an entire life, an entire world, behind to be with you. Do not make her regret her choice."

He turned toward Neera, her beautiful eyes glowing with emotion that echoed down the bond. He climbed into the saddle and clipped in. "Take Neera to eat, Morana. She's hungry."

Morana didn't move for a long minute. Then, slowly, she lifted her head to the sky and shut her eyes. A wail came from her soul, loud and haunting against the idyllic backdrop. A chill ran down his spine as the dragon sang her grief to the clouds, her entire body shaking. Neera's bond hollowed into something twisted in agony for her dearest friend, a pain so devastating it took his breath away.

The wailing turned defiant. Lilting sadness morphed into fiery rage. Her maw opened wide. Shadows crept into the air and danced with the swirling wind as she let out a roar strong enough to rattle the heavens.

Morana shook her neck wildly before splaying her wings and launching into the air. Neera returned the roar with a vengeance, rocking every bone in Koen's body before she followed her friend through the skies.

The sea spread in every direction as they left the island behind. The last remaining rays of sunlight glimmered on the surface of the deep blue water in hues of pink and orange. Land appeared. Different shades of brown stood out against the long green grass. The dragons hit the ground without a sound, startling the cows before they had a chance to run. The pair made quick work of the herd, leaving a handful to escape while they ate their fill as quickly as they could.

Dust billowed around three horses racing toward them. Koen stepped out of the saddle and onto the ground, ready to meet them. He left his knives on the island. Being in the company of two dragons was enough to quell any fight.

He raised his arms in placation as the men neared. Two younger men rode on either side of an older man, his hair wiry and white. Their horses whinnied and stomped against the ground when Neera and Morana fixed their gazes on them.

"We aren't here to harm you. My name is Koen. I am a member of the Ferox," he said calmly, dipping his chin toward the dragons. "The dragons are on a mission from King Aedan." Saying he was on a mission was a bald-faced lie, but what the men didn't know wouldn't hurt them.

They didn't seem alarmed. The oldest man jerked his chin to what was left of his livestock. "What of my herd?"

"The crown will pay you handsomely for helping during the dragon's time of need."

The man nodded once, and Koen reigned in his surprise. He expected far more of a fight. The livestock up north was strictly for the Ferox, but down south, especially as far south as Senex, they had more freedom with how they use their animals.

The older man studied Morana for a heavy beat. "Where's the girl?"

Koen worked to keep a straight face. "Girl?"

"Yeah. A while ago this one," he pointed at Morana, "came and ate half our herd. There was a young woman on its back. Long brown hair. Pretty thing. She convinced it not to hurt us."

He could picture it: Aisling sitting bareback and yelling at Morana, wind twisting through her long hair. He could hear Morana's growl of displeasure with her scales covered in blood like she was now. He shook his head, his voice threatening to break. "She's not here."

"Shame," the man sighed. "I thought I'd get to introduce her to my boy here." He threw a finger over his shoulder to the man on his right. The son looked strong, sturdy. His sandy blonde hair was pulled back into a small knot at the back of his head. Koen wanted to punch him.

"She's something fierce. I didn't catch her name, but I knew if I saw her again, I had to introduce them. You don't let a woman like that go without at least giving her your name."

Heat curled in Koen's gut. He swallowed it. "Her name is Aisling. She's Morana's rider." The men's eyes widened. They knew the dragon's name. Knew of her power. Morana stared back without blinking, crimson blood dripping from her maw. "Aisling was captured by the Cruento three weeks ago."

"Bastards," the man cursed. His sons shook their heads in disgust. "We don't see much of their action down here. It's mostly farmland, nothing they want to bother with. But I've heard stories. I've visited the towns they've demolished. Never seen anything like it." He ran his hand through his wild hair. "I've heard what they do to those poor girls."

It took everything in Koen not to scream at the man. He wasn't saying anything Koen didn't already know. But he was talking about Aisling.

Those things he'd heard, the injuries he'd seen, not just with Elaila but with the women all over the kingdom, he wasn't sure who he would become if Aisling suffered the same horrific treatment the Cruento were known for.

"We know nothing," the man said, "but you can be sure we'll send word if we hear so much as a whisper."

Koen swallowed thickly and nodded his thanks. The man turned his horse slowly, keeping an awestruck eye on the two dragons in front of him. "I hope you find her. And when you do, give them hell." His foot dug into the horse's side. The three riders disappeared toward the rest of the herd in a cloud of dust without sparing a single look back at the dragons.

"Get enough?" Koen asked as he climbed up Neera's back. The bond pulsed with a quiet contentment. He held onto it as Morana led them back to the island and curled herself into a tight ball inside the cave. Neera fell asleep shortly after, leaving Koen alone to stare at the stars and wonder if Aisling was able to see them where she was. If she knew he was thinking of her more than he breathed. If she knew to hold onto hope.

THIRTEEN

AISLING

A familiar heavy rumble of chains sounded from outside of the room. Vibrations rolled across the floor through Aisling's aching back. Her muscles tensed.

It was time.

Favilla growled softly and clipped her claw once. *Yes.* Yes, it was time. She dropped to the ground only a few feet from the door and shut her eyes. In the next second, her breathing was slow and even.

Aisling remained sprawled on her back as the door opened slowly. A dim light crept in as they checked Favilla's somnolence. Satisfied with what they saw, the door creaked open to its full width. Two men stood on either side of the doorway while the other dragged chains and forced the shadowed monster into the room.

Aisling had never gotten a good look at it. She didn't turn her head to watch. Didn't move as one of the men from the doorway nudged her with his foot. "We have orders to take you with us, pet. After the show, of course."

She'd run her own head into the rock wall before she let them take her anywhere.

The beast walked toward Favilla.

The man chuckled over the low rumble from the monster's throat and mumbled, "Enough time for me, I think."

The fabric of his pants shifted as he knelt beside her.

He ripped Aisling's shirt down the middle.

She didn't fight it. Not yet. Every ounce of what little strength she had left had to be savored until the last possible second.

"Save me some," another man called out. The man above her laughed.

His hand was on her chest.

She clenched her jaw but didn't move. Didn't make a sound. Not as his hand wandered. Not as his breathing turned heavy.

Chains rattled as the beast settled behind Favilla.

His hand found Aisling's waistline. Found the button on her leathers.

The monster growled as he lifted to mount Favilla.

The button of Aisling's pants popped off and danced across the stone floor.

The man's hand slid to her waistline.

The room glowed orange. A deep raging heat passed just over her supine body.

There wasn't enough time for the men to scream before they were scorched.

The hand left her skin with a curse. Aisling stood, her nearly dead body pulsing with pure adrenaline, and punched his backlit silhouette in the throat as hard as she could. With Favilla's flame as a light, she took everything Koen and the rest of the Ferox had taught her and emptied it on the man. He fell to the ground. She sat on top of him, pinned his biceps with her knees, and let loose.

A strike for the Ferox. A punch for Elaila and all the girls lost to these vile men. A punch for Morana and her wounds. A strike for Koen.

Blood painted her face. She didn't stop.

She slammed her knuckles into his nose, relishing the sharp crack as it shattered. For herself.

The man didn't move. Favilla's flames dimmed. The scent of crisp burnt flesh hit her nose.

Aisling reached down and found a dagger at the man's waist. His arms lay flaccid at his sides. She jabbed the blade in and out of his hands until there was nothing left but ribbons of bone and muscle.

Never again would he be able to touch a woman as he did her. Never again would he be able to touch anyone. Not even himself.

Favilla stood to her full height, a beautiful black dragon against the backdrop of fire and fury. A strip of clothing hung from her mouth as she chewed. A rumble of happiness rolled through the room when she swallowed. Aisling pocketed the bloody dagger and stepped over the burnt remains of the one other man in front of the door. Favilla turned her attention to the shocked, frozen monster behind her.

It was gigantic. Its snout was shorter than a dragon's. Its back legs were elongated. Its feet looked more like clawed flippers than feet. And its eyes... there was sadness in the black pupils. A desperation, almost, for Favilla to kill it. Aisling held her breath and waited for the flames, but Favilla didn't make a single move toward the creature. She huffed once before walking away.

Together Favilla and Aisling walked through the door.

Only three torches lit the stone hallway. They gave off barely enough light to see through the darkness, but it was more light than Aisling had seen in eons. She flinched against it.

The hall was massive. Favilla fit easily as they turned left out of the door, neither of them sure of where they were going, but they knew they didn't have the luxury of hesitating.

It was too quiet. There was no movement, no shouts or screams. Aisling clenched her sore jaw as the hallway ended at a fork. To the left was a narrower tunnel with more flames. To the right, the hall stayed the same size, but there was almost no light.

Her breathing was ragged as she turned right, relying strictly on the pull in her gut to lead them the right way. She didn't know where she was going. She could be leading them to the entire Cruento base. The hub. She could be leading herself to slaughter. Or it could lead nowhere, leaving them pinned against rock.

She didn't care. As long as they were out of that tomb, she didn't care where she ended up.

They followed the steady curve of the hallway toward the right. Favilla's presence warmed Aisling's exhausted back. Aisling held her breath with every step as she waited for the inevitable.

They passed another massive room with the door open wide. Inside was nothing but a single torch and a large trough of water like the room they were in. She cringed. The beast that violated Favilla was as much of a prisoner as they were.

A dull roar hit Aisling's ears. Her blood ran cold. She hesitated for only a moment. Favilla's snout urged her forward.

It got louder.

Aisling pictured a legion of men waiting for them. She pictured the Man who promised her a life of pain waiting in the distance with her blood dripping from his blade and a smile on his face.

The air turned thicker. Still cold, still harsh, but thicker. It sat heavy in her lungs and against her skin with a damp edge. Droplets of water fell on her head. The light disappeared as they passed the last torch. Darkness encased her, but she didn't flinch. It was part of her now.

Water tickled her feet. The ground angled downward at a steep decline. She clutched the stone wall, praying she was still strong enough to make it out. The atrophied muscles in her battered legs screamed with the angle. She kept going.

Favilla let out a low chirp as a tiny dot of brightness appeared through the darkness. Aisling gasped and winced against her broken ribs.

Light.

Not candles or lamps.

Sunlight.

She ignored her screaming body and hustled forward. Ignored the unsteady, faltering beats of her heart and dove into the adrenaline pounding inside of her.

Water drenched her feet, undulating with a steady, lulling rhythm. The scent of brine and crisp wind assaulted her nose. She let out a weak whimper as the tiny seed of hope she kept buried deep inside sprouted.

The sea.

She didn't stop the joy that flooded the bond. She threw it down and prayed Morana was able to feel her.

Favilla used her snout to push Aisling forward, her pace faster than Aisling could manage with her broken body. The light grew bigger, brighter. It beckoned them with its siren song. Its promise of freedom.

"Down here!" a muffled male voice shouted in the distance behind them. A chorus of screams followed. The sound of heavy footsteps echoed down the eternally long tunnel. Their swords clinked together as they ran, the sound bouncing off the stone around them.

Her hope disappeared. The seed shriveled and crumbled in the pits of her chest.

Aisling was going to die.

Maybe she simply wasn't meant to live. She was just a placeholder for someone else. Friendship and love were meant for that soul, not hers. It would make sense. Both of her lives had turned into something ugly. Something wretched.

Koen's face danced in her mind. Her memories had blurred with exhaustion and pain, but she could still picture his warm eyes and the playful smile she had grown to crave.

She would never be able to apologize to him for not listening. She would never feel the electrifying rush of his voice against her skin. Never hear his deep laugh again.

She pictured the rest of the Ferox.

She pictured Morana.

Her soul shattered into splinters for the second time in her short life.

She roared down the bond knowing Morana wouldn't be able to hear her words.

Aisling threw down her thanks, her gratitude for Morana giving her such an amazing life in such a short time. She thanked Morana for being the one to see her when she thought she was nothing. Thanked her for showing Aisling that her soul was not a waste. She shouted her eternal love. Her praise and devotion.

Her body stopped working. Her legs locked. Her breath turned acidic.

Aisling wondered if it would be easier to fall into the now knee-high water and let herself drown before they took her. Go out on her own terms by her own hand.

A set of jaws clamped around her and lifted her sideways from the water. Hot air enveloped her in rapid bursts. Water sloshed below like a churning stomach. A cool mist sank into her skin as her dirty hair hung lank in the air. The dagger fell from her loose leathers and clanged against the stone below.

The light got brighter. She could see the blue behind it. See the frothy waves crashing angrily against a set of three vaguely familiar rock archways standing tall and formidable in a line. She could see the bright sky of sunrise. Hear the morning cawing of birds as they hunted for breakfast. She could feel the sea spray as the waves crashed just outside.

This would be a good way to die, Aisling decided. A peaceful view. The breeze of the same ocean she sat at when she met Morana and took control of her soul's path.

The screams of the men raced ever closer. Their fury tainted the air with a heaviness, a venom, that she'd grown accustomed to.

How ironic, she thought, to finally start living and have your life cut short.

Adrenaline disappeared. Her body gave up. Black swarmed her vision, and Aisling closed her eyes as unconsciousness took over.

She had fought enough.

FOURTEEN

KOEN

He woke with a start.

Morana was screaming.

Not wailing, not growling. Screaming.

Her head twisted from side to side as her neck extended to its full length. Her massive feet stomped on the ground and her tail whacked the walls hard enough for the rock to shake and fall around them.

Neera backed away from her friend toward the entrance of the cave, shielding Koen from the madness with a wing. Their bond was taut with fear. He could taste it sharp and stinging against his tongue. He peered under Neera's wing and watched Morana thrash against some invisible force.

He stopped breathing.

Something happened to Aisling.

No one knew what happened when a bond was shattered. They debated on the effects of the death of either dragon or human, but no one had experienced it.

Morana was experiencing it now.

Neera trembled. Their bond went silent, both she and Koen in complete and total fear as the dragon in front of them shattered.

As Aisling died.

Koen's breaths came too shallow, too fast.

The world spun around him. Sweat pricked his palms.

The crisp breeze of dawn sent his bones shivering.

He didn't know what to do or how to help. He said he would take care of Morana, take care of the little piece of Aisling's soul that he still had, but that part was breaking before his eyes. He could do nothing to help either of them.

She was dying, and Koen would never see her again.

His legs buckled. He sank to his knees. Tears fell down his cheeks. Emptiness devoured him. He didn't fight it.

Neera stood between Koen and Morana, a look of utter devastation and hopelessness on her face as the two most important souls in her life broke.

The sun rose to the screaming of a dragon losing part of its soul. There was no chatter of birds. No rustling of wind. Time itself stood still in mourning.

Morana stopped. Her eyes flashed in the hazy darkness of their cave.

Neera tilted her head to the side.

Morana answered with something like a sob, her eyes wild and wide. A second later she ran through the opening of their little cave, barely missing Koen with her wings as she launched skyward. Aisling's necklace crunched under her feet, and her blood sank into the dirt. The last remaining part of Aisling Koen had, gone.

Neera was at his side a moment later. The bond pulsed with something he couldn't place. She nudged him with her snout, a desperate urgency flaring in her neon yellow eyes. He didn't want to chase Morana. She should be free, sent somewhere far away where she could have time to heal. But Neera was insistent, yanking on the bond with enough force to make him stand. He barely made it onto the saddle before she took to the sky.

Morana was a beacon of light in front of them. The sun glittered off her pearlescent scales as she flapped her wings at a speed he didn't know was possible. They flew over the land they visited last night. It was nothing but a blur of green and brown as Neera plunged forward, following Morana as she made her way up the coastline. Waves thrashed the rock below with an intensity he'd never seen before. It was like the ocean heard Morana's pain and answered with its own.

They passed farming villages. Passed the Latebros. He watched for signs of distress, but Morana didn't seem to feel or see anything as she devoured the air, the land, the sea.

The black peaks of the Latebros mountains disappeared behind them. Morana lowered over a thin stretch of brilliant white beach. She let out a guttural roar that sent Neera's bond sizzling with confusion and concern. A heartbeat later, the bond went blank with shock.

Morana rumbled again and again before throwing herself onto the beach. Sand flew under her feet. Neera landed just behind her and broke into a run toward a pile of black rocks on the water's edge.

Koen's mouth dried.

It wasn't rock.

Black scales. A tail. A wing.

Bright blue eyes opened.

Neera exploded with shock, shaking the bond violently until Koen could hardly breathe.

Favilla.

He knew her long ago when he first joined the Ferox. She was barely the same dragon.

Her hide was ripped to shreds at her haunches in both new and old grooves. Her black scales were dull and lifeless. Every rib showed through her skin. There was no more muscle on her. No power like before.

Neera and Morana stopped before her, both silent as they took in their friend.

Morana sniffed the air and splayed her wings to their full length.

Every muscle in Neera went rigid.

Favilla blinked in recognition and chirped softly, the sound broken and weak. Her wing lifted open to the sky.

Koen launched from the saddle and into the sand with a guttural cry.

Aisling.

Her limp body was in his arms in the next breath. With shaky fingers, he checked the pulse just below her jawline. A faint erratic beat met his touch. Morana hovered above him, her worried whines loud and oppressive.

Koen shouted Aisling's name, but she didn't wake. Didn't stir. He turned to Neera, his panic and shock all-consuming. "Go, Neera. Get them. Get everyone. We need them all *now*." He glanced at Favilla before meeting his dragon's yellow eyes again. "As fast as you can. Tell Soren we need medical for both."

Neera was gone in the next breath. He brushed the crusted hair from Aisling's face and sucked in a breath.

She was so thin. Her cheeks were hollow. Every inch of her beautiful face was covered in blood, new and old. It caked her split lips. Bruises covered her in layers. Her right eye was swollen. The back of her head had a fist-sized knot. Her arms were covered in lacerations. Her pale skin was cold despite the warmth of the sun and the dragon around her.

Every thought eddied out of his head as he pushed her matted, bloodied hair off her neck.

Her throat had been cut. Not deep enough to kill, but deep enough to scar.

Deep enough to terrify her.

He looked lower, bile and fury boiling inside his throat. Her right hand was missing a finger. Her shirt, covered in blood and dirt, hung open down the middle. Every inch of her emaciated stomach was painted purple and green. He worked to keep breathing at the sight of her pants torn at the waist, button gone.

Morana thrummed above him. She lowered and sniffed Aisling, lifting her lip and baring her teeth at the damage inflicted on her bond.

Their gazes met. Inside the bright violet eyes, Koen saw the silent promise. The oath of destruction. The promise of retribution.

Favilla groaned as her body turned on the sand and exposed her stomach to the sun. She stared at the open sky with heartbreaking awe. Koen flinched at the dips of her ribs and deteriorated muscles. Morana lowered her head over her friend's body and chirped soothing words to the dragon they had thought lost forever.

Aisling's chest rose and fell slowly in his arms. He kissed her cold forehead. "You're safe, Aisling," he whispered, hoping his words were reaching wherever she was inside.

FIFTEEN

KOEN

"You need to rest."

"I am resting."

Amerie rolled her eyes beside him. "You look like shit. At least take a bath. This is not something she needs to smell when she wakes up."

Cielle walked in, her eyes immediately narrowing on Aisling's sleeping body. "Anything?" Koen shook his head. "Medical said it should be soon," she offered.

"At least Morana is better," Amerie muttered as she left Koen's side and walked out the door.

Cielle dropped a plate on the coffee table in front of the fire. "I brought you some food."

Koen glanced at it, uninterested. "Thank you."

She forced a mug of tea into his hands. "You have to eat something."

He couldn't remember the last time he ate. After everything that happened, it seemed so inconsequential.

"Amerie was right, you know. You do stink." He shot her a glare. She returned it. "Take five minutes for yourself. I will stay right here. If she moves at all, I'll grab you." She nudged him from the chair until he fell off. A soft laugh left her lips as she sank into the seat and wrapped her hand around Aisling's. He glanced once at Aisling's sleeping body before shutting the door and running the bath.

Two days. She had slept for two days and was now on her way to a third. The tubes and fluids were gone, but she was still asleep.

The scene on the beach replayed in his mind on a constant loop.

Neera returned with the entirety of the Ferox and a team of medics, all of whom looked green as they stepped off the dragons. Nyssa lowered over Favilla's body with a steady stream of comforting chirps that had Oryn's emerald eyes glistening. Soren bellowed his rage into the sky as he took in the two broken bodies in the sand, the sound traveling into the ether with a promise of retribution.

The girls came to his side in a whir of cries and shouts. Koen refused to let go of Aisling until Kaida's hand found his shoulder, gently urging him to comply. He placed Aisling on the sand and forced medical to do their checks around him.

Elaila stood a few feet away, her eyes wide as she saw the extent of Aisling's injuries. Tears fell down her cheeks and she sunk onto her knees, her hands covering her mouth in horror. Cielle was there a heartbeat later cradling her friend against the flashbacks of her own trauma.

Medical gave the all-clear for Aisling to fly back to the Pit where the rest of their team was on standby. Koen didn't hesitate. Aisling was a feather in his arms as he jumped onto Neera's saddle and into the sky. Morana flew beside them, her eyes nothing but purple flames.

He didn't allow medical to put her on a stretcher when they landed. Morana snarled at them and followed Koen as far as she could through the Pit before she could go no further. She sniffed Aisling again, a low rumble in her throat before nodding at him to go. Koen lurched down the stairs into his room and placed Aisling reverently on his bed. Medical followed inside like a swarm of rushing bees. They pushed him to the outskirts of the room as they began working. Kaida appeared a minute later at his side.

They called out Aisling's injuries with robotic, unfeeling precision.

Facial fractures. Missing finger. Multiple concussions. Starvation. Numerous lacerations. Blood loss. Internal bruising. Broken ribs.

Kaida's eyes flared brighter with every injury listed. Koen's soul quivered, his mind and body both numb and violently alive at the same time.

The team cut Aisling's clothes off. His jaw clenched tight enough for his head to scream in pain. Kaida outwardly gasped at the damage. Every hill and valley of Aisling's ribs showed. Her hips protruded at a sharp angle. Her body was layer after layer of bruise as if she had been painted blue and green.

The rest of the Ferox burst through the door and went silent at the sight.

"We will clean her," Kaida said to the medical team, her commanding tone leaving no room for argument. They nodded while hooking Aisling up to numerous tubes and fluids. An hour later, they left a basket of bandages and gave Kaida basic wound-care instructions before they walked out. Kaida came to the bedside and brushed a shaky hand across Aisling's swollen cheek. She didn't turn her head. "Girls."

Amerie and Cielle were already in the bathroom. They brought out buckets of warm water, soap, and towels. Both girls ignored the tears running down their cheeks as they came to the other side of the bed and stared down at their friend.

"Oryn."

A hand was on Koen's shoulder, guiding him from his room. It led him wordlessly up the stairs and into the Pit.

Koen didn't think as he threw himself at Oryn. It didn't matter that this man had raised him, had saved him from himself time and time again. Oryn knew what Koen needed and let him loose.

His fist met skin, met bone, and it wasn't enough. He needed more. He needed blood, needed to destroy.

Neera appeared. Nyssa appeared. Oryn ordered them to leave.

For an hour, Oryn allowed Koen to attack him. By the end, Koen was breathless, his face lined with a mixed sheen of sweat and tears. He collapsed on the sand, every breath a billowing fire in his lungs. Oryn sat beside him and wiped blood from his nose with his sleeve.

"Sorry," Koen rasped.

Oryn shook his head. "Feel it, Koen. Allow yourself to feel it all: the rage, the hurt, the sorrow. Feel it, acknowledge it, but do not let it rule you. She's back. She's alive. Focus on that." He looked at the midday sky. "When she wakes, she will need you. Not your vengeance or fury. She will need *you*."

The bath ran cold. Koen dried himself and dressed without looking at his reflection in the mirror. Oryn's words haunted him.

Who was he? This woman had changed him so irrevocably, so fully, that he didn't remember who he was anymore. He no longer felt invincible or even strong. Would she even need him? Or had her experiences harmed her so badly that she wouldn't acknowledge him when she woke? Would she even be able to stay in the same room as a man?

Cielle smiled warmly as he walked back into his room. "Much better. You look and smell human again." She stood from the chair and planted a soft kiss on Aisling's healing forehead. "I wasn't kidding about eating, Koen. You won't be worth anything to her if you aren't taking care of yourself."

She shut the door behind her. He glanced again at the plate she left and begrudgingly ate half of whatever was on it before moving it out of the way. He sat on the chair and rested his elbows on the edge of his mattress to watch the steady rise and fall of Aisling's chest underneath his blankets. Exhaustion pulled at him. His eyelids fluttered shut.

The door opened. He let out a groan.

"Don't huff at me," Kaida whispered. "Favilla started talking." His eyes opened. Kaida and Oryn stopped at the foot of his bed, both staring at Aisling with a mix of concern and leashed anger.

"And?"

"She told Soren as much as she could before she fell asleep again. It's been difficult for him to understand everything. Favilla's confused and disoriented." Kaida tore her eyes from Aisling. "Favilla said Aisling was locked in the same room as her. The room was described as pitch black. All stone. No windows. No light except for a single candle when they would get visits."

His mouth ran dry. "They've been underground this entire time?"

"The details are murky. Favilla said Aisling figured it out and that's how they were able to leave. We don't know what *it* is. But she remembers what the outside looked like when they escaped."

"We're hoping that Aisling can corroborate," Oryn supplied. "The two of them could lead us to the nest when they're well."

"You want her to go back there?" Koen asked, his voice laced with disbelief.

"The entirety of the Ferox and Aedan's men will be with her. We would never ask her or Favilla to go back alone."

He swallowed thickly. "Did Favilla mention anything about the Cruento?"

"Nothing important. She's overwhelmed right now. It's been almost a decade since she's seen the light or sky. Her body and mind are broken. She needs time to heal before we make her relive it all."

Three weeks underground was torture for a human who was meant to have her soul in the sky. But a dragon? It was worse than torture. It was worse than death.

The three of them sat in silence for a long time. Sunlight peered inside the windows, glowing golden with the setting sun. Oryn glanced at his twin expectantly. Kaida clenched her jaw.

"What?" Koen asked, his voice flat and empty, his psyche too exhausted for secrets.

Kaida swallowed. "Favilla said she owes Aisling her life. And when Aisling wakes up..." Koen waited. Kaida's eyes glistened. "She wants Aisling to know that she's sorry for taking so long. That she's sorry she couldn't stop them from hurting her sooner."

His blood ran cold. Aisling's torn shirt. Her ripped pants. The scar on her neck. It had to be why Elaila couldn't stop crying at the beach. Why she had yet to come see Aisling.

"We don't know what it means," Kaida whispered. "Don't overthink it. Wait for her to tell us before you set the world on fire." She walked out the door.

Oryn slid his all-knowing gaze to Koen's. "Aisling will want to burn the world down, Koen. Be the one holding the match. Let her light it." He followed his twin, gently shutting the door behind him with a click.

Silence enveloped the room. The fire cracked.

Koen felt it in his bones. Felt the realization settle. Felt the lightness, the heaviness, all of it at once. What he'd been wondering for weeks, now cemented in his chest.

He rubbed small circles on the top of Aisling's bandaged hand with his thumb. Her skin was finally warming. He stared at her, letting her presence and steady breathing finally lull him into sleep.

SIXTEEN

AISLING

Aisling's bladder screamed for relief.

How was that possible? She remembered dying.

The light at the end of the tunnel, the beauty of the sea just beyond the opening. She remembered her body giving up, Favilla's jaws around her, and the shouting of the men just behind them. She remembered throwing her love to Morana and letting the darkness take hold.

Morana.

The bond was still there, still glowing around her bones. She stroked it once in an experiment. Instantly, a flood of warmth rushed through her.

She cracked open her swollen eyes, terrified of what she was going to see.

Dark stone.

Stone walls, stone ceiling.

But a faint orange glow to the right. Warmth.

The first bright rays of dawn from floor-to-ceiling windows on her left.

She glanced down. Blankets. A bed.

And holding her right hand, Koen.

Her heart stuttered to life inside her chest.

Even in sleep, she could see the concern on his face—the tightness of his mouth, the slight pinch to his full brows. His hair was disheveled in the way she liked. A shadow of dark hair peppered his jaw.

She watched his chest rise and fall and listened to the fire pop, breathing him in, his scent almost overpowering after so long.

Aisling's body ached. Every part of her hurt. But she felt *alive*.

She ignored the pain and lifted her left arm from the blanket. Her fingers slid through his thick hair, and she smiled as the dark silky strands tickled her skin.

Real. This was real.

Koen stirred, his russet eyes blinking open in confusion. He lifted his head and froze as their gazes met.

"I've wanted to do that for so long," she croaked.

Koen didn't move. Didn't blink.

"I'm not dead, right?" Aisling asked after a few pounding heartbeats, her voice a low rasp. He shook his head. "Favilla?"

"Alive," he breathed. "Healing."

His voice danced along her skin, and it flushed as if it remembered him.

Aisling had survived. Favilla was finally back where she belonged. Somehow, against all odds, the two of them had made it back home.

Part of her couldn't believe it. This was the image that plagued her in the darkness, one of comfort and warmth. Had she just fallen into the reveries of her mind? Had insanity finally claimed her?

She glanced again at the room, at the light and the fire, needing to hear the truth again. "I'm not dreaming? Morana is here? She's healthy?"

He nodded, his throat bobbing. "You're awake. Morana is in the Lair, thrilled you're back."

Aisling stared into his warm eyes, eyes that singlehandedly kept her from breaking in the darkness. "I'm so sorry," she whispered, unable to stop the tear that crept down her face.

He sat up in confusion, his hand never leaving hers. "What?"

"I didn't listen to you. I should have stayed on Morana's back. I should have -"

He kissed her hand, his brows pinched as if in pain. Her eyes widened. "I'm so glad you're back," he whispered. "How do you feel?"

"Broken," she responded instantly. It was the first word that came to mind. She knew her body was broken. Her mind might be, too.

Something dark flashed over his face. "What do you need?"

She cringed. "I really need to use the bathroom. But you don't have to -"

He was standing in the next breath. With a swipe of his strong arms, the blankets were thrown off. She didn't look down at her body, didn't want to see the damage she knew was there. Koen gently reached behind her bruised back and lifted her to sitting before wrapping his other hand around her legs and swiveling them to hang over the edge of the bed. His arm tightened around her waist as he lifted her seamlessly to her feet. "How's that?"

Aisling stood against his chest, blinking quickly against the dizziness while she got her bearings. She glanced up at him after a few swaying seconds. "This is new," she gestured to the splattering of hair on his jawline.

Koen absentmindedly lifted his free hand to his face as if just realizing he hadn't shaved and frowned. "What do you think?"

She rolled her eyes. It made him roguishly, impossibly handsome, she wanted to say, but her bladder was begging for relief. After a steadying breath, she gritted her teeth and attempted a step.

Her leg gave out. Her abdomen clenched in pain. Koen's arm tightened around her, pulling her closer to his chest. "A little sore," she admitted breathlessly.

He pointed to a basket beside the bed. "Medical left pain medication for you if you want it."

She shook her head. Even in another world, she did not want to end up like her mother. She could handle this pain like she handled everything else. "Just the toilet, please."

Koen pulled her flush against his side. They walked slowly into the bathroom, and he opened the door for the toilet. She braced her hands on the wall and looked at him over her shoulder. "I won't be able to go if you're here."

His brows lifted. "I'm not leaving you alone. You just woke up. You can barely walk."

"I'm perfectly capable of sitting on a toilet."

"Are you?"

She glared at him. "Want me to prove it?"

"And if I did?"

Aisling rolled her eyes. "Can you run a bath for me?"

"You can't take a bath yet."

"Why not?"

He blinked, searching for an answer. "Because."

Aisling grinned, the movement foreign. "Turn on the water, Koen. And sing or something." She shut the door on him and held her breath as she lowered to the toilet. Koen was right, but she would never admit it. She shut her eyes. The sound of running water echoed from outside. She relaxed. Her body sang in relief as her bladder emptied and decreased some of the pain in her back and stomach. She opened the door when she was done, unsurprised to find Koen right outside. "Didn't trust me?"

"Not in the slightest," he smirked. Warmth flurried down her spine. She swallowed against the overwhelming rush of relief his presence brought. Wafts of steam curled from a thick blanket of bubbles in the tub behind him. "Bath?"

"Please," she answered, the promise of hot water too good an opportunity to pass up. Her skin was no longer coated in blood and dirt, but she needed to scrub. She needed to wash the cave from her skin herself.

"Are you able to stand here for a minute? I'll grab one of the girls."

A bolt of panic ran through her. "No."

"Okay," he nodded, reaching for her. "Let's get you back to bed, then. They can bring you in the bath when—"

"No—don't go," she pleaded, her eyes latching onto his. "Please."

She knew she sounded desperate. Knew her need to have him close defied logic and sensibility, but she needed him there in a way she couldn't articulate.

His throat bobbed. He dipped his chin in answer. "Okay."

Relief swamped her panic, drowning it before it overwhelmed her. She exhaled slowly before glancing down and cringing at the plain white shift covering her. "This is so ugly."

"It's from medical. Amerie also hates it. She tried to dress you multiple times. Kaida almost killed her."

"They've been here?"

"Constantly. Almost too much depending on who you ask."

"And if I ask you?"

A flicker of delight flashed in his dark eyes. "Far too much."

She swallowed the emotion in her throat. "Close your eyes."

Koen obeyed. He held his hands out for her as she maneuvered out of the plain dress. It fell to the floor in a heap. She unwrapped the dressings from her arms and hands, pleasantly surprised with how clean the wound to her missing pinky looked. Her eyes lifted to the mirror without her permission.

Broken was the perfect word.

No part of her was untouched or undamaged. She remembered every blow, every drop of blood, every threat made against her. Her body was nothing but a map of Cruento torment and brutality.

The lack of food was evident. She looked like she did in her other life before she made the switch, all bones and skin. Her face was a mix of cuts and bruises. The swelling over her right eye wasn't as bad as it felt.

She let go of Koen's hand and traced the slice along the bottom of her neck.

It would be there forever. Thin as it was, it was still going to scar. It would be a permanent reminder of every second of pain and anguish in the dark where she was reduced to prey. Where she was marked as an object, a prize. Where she was made to wear a collar to prove her lack of worth.

"Aisling?" Koen whispered. She cleared her throat and tore her eyes from her reflection. Her hands found his again.

"I'm getting in now. If you hear me fall or drown you can look, but not until then." She stifled a groan while her body gingerly maneuvered into the tub. A moan slipped loose as she inched down and the warm water crested over her shoulders. The scented bubbles tickled her nose as she breathed them in. Her eyes widened at the familiar scent of ginger and citrus. She glanced at the bathroom, noticing the subtle differences she'd missed just seconds ago. "This isn't my room." Koen stilled. "Look at me."

The gold in his eyes flickered to life as he stared down at her. He knelt beside the tub so they were eye to eye. "It's my room."

"Why?"

"I wasn't thinking. When we brought you back, this was the first place I thought of."

She paused. "Who found me?"

"Me. Well, Morana, technically. But Neera and I were with her."

Of course it was Morana. Her beautiful, magnificent beast. She stroked the bond again, smiling as her dragon answered with warmth. "When can I see her?"

"Maybe another day or two. Medical will want to give you another look first."

"Can you carry me to her now?"

His jaw clenched. "No, Aisling. Not yet. Kaida would actually kill me." He paused. "Morana might, too."

"How long was I there?"

"Twenty-two days."

The Man in the cave hadn't been lying, then. "How close were we?"

His brows pinched. "To what?"

"To home. Here."

"You weren't close at all." His jaw feathered. "You were on a thin stretch of beach along the Latebros coast."

Aisling ignored the rush of fear in her veins at the thought of the black mountains. At the oppressive, dark stone she had come to know too well. "Favilla?"

"You were between her wings."

Aisling shut her eyes and shook her head. Those stupid exercises worked. She reached for his citrusy soap and lifted her brow. "Can I use this?" He dipped his chin in answer. The soap jumped out of her hand where her pinky should have been and landed on the floor. "That's going to take some getting used to," she mumbled.

Koen handed her the soap, his face tight. "Does it hurt?"

"No." She had more to worry about in the darkness than a missing finger. And now, knowing she was alive and home, she couldn't care less for the finger she left behind. Aisling lathered herself as best she could, noting each imperfection marring the beautiful new body she loved. She let out a gasp of pain as she reached for her back. Koen took the soap from her hand and gently sat her up. A breath of a moan left her lips as he cleaned with just enough pressure to keep her from hurting.

"I haven't had a bath in a while," she said with a hint of a laugh while she held onto the lip of the tub. "I forgot how nice it is."

Koen's hand stopped moving. A tense silence hovered in the air.

"It was just a joke."

"It isn't a joke, Aisling," he gritted back with a fury in his eyes she'd never seen before. "None of this has been a joke."

A single flame burst alive in her soul. "I was there, Koen. I know none of it was a joke. I was trying to make light of the situation."

"Why?"

Because she had been terrified. Because she had accepted her death. Accepted never seeing him again, never seeing Morana again.

Because she finally felt safe enough to laugh.

"So I don't cry," she responded dryly. The fire in his eyes died on impact.

"I'm sorry," he breathed, "I didn't—"

"It's fine." She sighed. "Can you run to my room and get my shampoo? My hair feels disgusting."

He opened a drawer under his sink and pulled out two bottles. "These? One of them is conditioner."

Something inside of her shuddered. She swallowed. "Perfect."

"Amerie wanted to wash your hair. Medical said not until you woke up."

Aisling lifted her hand to her crusted, matted hair. "Amerie had the right idea."

He knelt behind the tub. "Lean your head back."

"I can do it."

"I know you can. Lean your head back."

She blinked in confusion but listened. He filled a cup with water and ran it over her hair.

Aisling braced for the panic. Braced to be swamped with memories of the pain and torture of human touch, but nothing came. Her eyes shut as his fingertips massaged her scalp. Caked blood and dirt disappeared, leaving a lightness she hadn't felt for weeks in their wake.

She didn't know when the tears started, but they fell down her cheeks and into the bath as the morning sun crept through the windows and warmth seeped into her skin.

His hands were the first gentle touch she'd had in a lifetime. The first time her hair wasn't being yanked or pulled in weeks. The first time she wasn't beaten in what felt like years.

She was safe. She was safe at home. With Koen. With Morana. With the Ferox. She was alive. She had made it out and back into the light.

The fissures in her soul shivered with hope.

"Am I hurting you?" he asked, his voice tight.

"No," she whispered. "Not at all."

"You're crying."

"Yes."

A storm of questions swirled through his eyes. "One more rinse. The water is getting too cold."

"Do I have to wear that dress again?"

He snorted and ran the water over her hair a final time. "No. Stay right here." He disappeared. Drawers opened and shut just outside the door. He appeared again a minute later with a pile of bunched clothes and placed them on the vanity. "It's easier for medical to treat you if your clothes are looser." He extended his arm. "Come on. Let's get you warm."

Slowly, with his eyes closed, Koen helped Aisling from the bath and held out a fluffy towel. She dried off as best she could and carefully dressed in the simple white tee he provided. It hung to her mid-thigh, showing off an array of purple and blue splotches on her legs. "It's pretty long," she murmured and glanced at the pants. "I can't put those on."

"Do you need help?"

"Can I just wear this? It's easier."

Koen opened his eyes and glanced at the hemline. His face tensed for only a moment. "That works." He wrapped his arm around her waist and guided her from the bathroom.

She stilled in the middle of his room. "I don't want to take your bed from you."

"You aren't."

She glanced up at him. "I am, though. I can go back to my—"

Koen hooked his arm under her knees and swept her off the ground before placing her on his bed. He pulled the blankets over her, and her argument died on her tongue as warmth and comfort devoured her. "Thank you," she whispered, resting her head against his pillow. "I feel relatively alive again."

Somehow, she was exhausted. Her eyes fluttered shut as the smell of him enveloped her. The smell of home. Of safety and life.

Koen's knuckles brushed along her temple and down her jaw. She hummed at the touch.

"Aisling," he whispered, his voice strained. She opened her eyes. His brows were pinched. His jaw was clenched tight. But inside his gaze was a warmth, an honesty, that she'd seen only once before. Something inside her soul fluttered awake.

The door clicked open. Aisling flinched at the sound. Koen's touch disappeared from her skin. She missed it immediately.

Amerie walked in and stopped with a gasp. She stuck her head out the door and shouted loud enough for everyone in Anguid to hear. She barreled forward, pushed Koen to the side, and swallowed Aisling in a hug.

"Amerie!" Koen snarled. His hands wrapped around her shoulders. "She's hurt!"

Amerie's grip disappeared. She grimaced. "Shit, sorry. I forgot. I'm just so happy to see you, you have no idea." She sat on the bed by Aisling's feet. "I knew you'd come back to us, babe."

Cielle and Elaila burst through the door. Elaila's eyes filled with tears as she ran her fingers down Aisling's cheek. "Brave, brave girl," she murmured.

Cielle crawled into bed and rested her head on Aisling's left shoulder. Her eyes darted to the back wall where Koen was leaning. "Never had so many girls in this bed before, have you?" He scoffed but didn't dim the gentle smile on his face. She reached for Aisling's wet hair. "You need a comb and a new pillow."

"On it!" Amerie shouted, disappearing through the door as Kaida and Oryn walked in.

"She's back," Oryn said softly, taking Aisling's hand in his with a gentle squeeze. She fought the sudden urge to cry at his calming voice.

Kaida stepped beside Elaila. Her silver eyes flashed as she took in the wet hair and Koen's shirt, but she said nothing. She smiled, genuine and breathtaking, "We missed you, Aisling."

"Hair rescue coming through," Amerie muttered as she climbed onto the mattress. Cielle snatched the comb and gently worked it through Aisling's hair while Amerie fluffed the new pillow at her back.

Aisling's throat constricted at the sight of her family around her. A sight she accepted never seeing again. She smiled as they talked at once in different conversations. She had missed it—missed the feeling of safety and love and belonging more than she ever realized.

She peered over Oryn's shoulder for the one who made her feel safest of all, but Koen had disappeared.

SEVENTEEN

KOEN

"She's perfect," Koen leaned against Morana's door. "Hurt. Sore. But perfect." The rest of the dragons purred in response; a general exhalation of tension relieved as Morana's euphoria ran through them all. "I think it will be at least another day or two before she can make it here. She's hurting more than she lets on."

Neera's bond fluttered through him. He smiled at his dragon over his shoulder, a lightness in every breath he took. Morana leaned forward and nuzzled him with her snout in thanks. He lifted his hands to her scales. She never let him touch her before. Not until Aisling. "Rest, Morana. You need it, too."

He walked to Gareth's door, leaving Morana in her massive pile of blankets and Neera resting just next door. "Favilla?"

Cielle's father pointed down the dark hall. "In Soren's old room. He took the empty spot beside it on the end."

Favilla slept with her wings fully outstretched and stomach rolled to the ceiling. Soren's massive head appeared out of nowhere. He peered over Koen's shoulder. They watched Favilla's stomach rise and fall steadily, every bone in her body protruding at painful angles.

He couldn't imagine the atrocities Favilla went through. Aisling had only been there for three weeks. Her injuries were horrific. Favilla had been there for almost a decade.

"She'll be fine," he whispered to himself. Soren's eyes slid to his. "In time." He gave Soren a quick pat on the head and said goodbye to Gareth before leaving the Pit. The fresh air greeted him as always with a song and a jolt of peace he craved. It danced in his lungs and cleared his head as he walked into the Keep.

He took the stairs to the lower level, immediately falling back into memories from long ago as the sounds and smells of the kitchen seeped through the air. It was his favorite place when he first came to the Ferox as a growing boy. Kaida was tired of being woken up at all hours by him asking for food, so she took him to Leonard and begged him to take Koen under his wing. After lessons with the twins, he would spend a few hours every day in the kitchen learning how to feed himself.

Leonard's deep tenor echoed through the hall in song. Koen couldn't keep the smile off his face as he walked into the warm kitchen where bodies buzzed chaotically against the clanging of pots and pans. He came up to Leonard at the large stove and clapped him on the shoulder.

Leonard turned, his white hair frizzy at the edges from the steam in the air and his wire-rimmed glasses halfway off his nose. He let out a booming laugh and brought Koen in for a hug. "Koen! Finally, he appears. Took him long enough."

"I know," Koen grimaced. "I've been busy."

Leonard wiped his hands on the rag over his shoulder. "Yes, yes. Busy saving the world, I know. You're late. The last bit of cake is gone."

Koen groaned. "Next time can you save me a slice?"

"So it can stay here uneaten and go bad? I think not." He scoffed. "He thinks I save cake for him. Everyone wants my cake. I have no favorites." The chef leaned his hip against the stove. "What can I make for you?"

"Nothing, actually. I was wondering if I could..." he gestured at the stove.

Leonard's eyes widened. "He comes to me and asks for cake and a space to cook! The nerve." He threw up his arms. "Be my guest. But you know the rule." He pointed menacingly.

Koen pushed Leonard's index finger from his face. "When I'm done you won't even know I had been here." It earned him a string of unintelligible mumbling. He washed his hands and gathered his ingredients before settling in front of an empty stove. The kitchen knife was as light as his daggers as it sliced through vegetables with ease. Leonard peeked into the pot after a few minutes. "It's called soup," Koen whispered.

The chef leveled an unamused glare at him. "For who? You sick?"

"No. For a friend."

Leonard's eyebrow lifted. "A friend, eh? Tell me, how many friends do you have? Don't count me. I'm not your friend."

"Kaida and Oryn."

"Those are your parents."

"They aren't."

"They are. Go on."

Koen scoffed. "Okay. Elaila, Amerie, Cielle."

"Coworkers."

"They can be both."

"So far, I am counting zero friends."

Koen rolled his eyes and placed the wooden spoon on top of the pot. "Aisling."

Leonard paused. "Aisling. She's back?"

"Three days ago."

Leonard blinked. "And you're making her soup because?"

"She's hungry." Truthfully, he didn't know why he was making her food. He didn't even know if she was hungry or able to eat, but he couldn't do nothing. Not now that she was awake. Not when she looked at him with those soft eyes like he had saved her.

"Ah." Leonard sniffed at the pot. He disappeared for a minute and came back with a small mesh bag of herbs. "Throw this in." Koen tossed it in the pot blindly. There wasn't any room to argue. Leonard's instincts were always right. "How is she doing?"

He didn't know how to answer that. Her body was broken. But her mind was still sharp. He wanted to cry at her playfulness and sharp tongue, both somehow still alive after everything she'd been through. But when he washed her hair and saw her tears...

"She'll be okay," he murmured. Leonard didn't press. "She brought back Favilla."

Leonard's spoon clattered to the floor. "Favilla is back?"

"You knew her?"

"Of course I knew her, you stupid boy. I have been here since the beginning."

"Oh. Well, yeah. She's back. She's healing, too."

Leonard's face darkened. "What did they do to those girls?"

"We don't know the details yet. Favilla will fill us in when she's ready."

"And Aisling?"

Koen stirred the soup and listed every one of Aisling's injuries. He knew them by heart. He could picture each one with painful precision. Leonard let out a low whistle. "Tough girl."

"Yeah. Yeah, she is."

"Beautiful, too." Koen clamped his mouth shut. "And you're making her soup."

"No, I just made the whole story up."

Leonard smacked him with another spoon from his pocket. "Don't sass me in my own home, boy."

Koen laughed and rubbed the growing welt on his arm. "Yes. I'm making her soup."

"Good instincts. Soup is the best place to start. It's very comforting. Like a hug in a bowl." He pulled out a glass container and placed it on the counter. "Put it in here."

He disappeared while Koen emptied the pot and came back with a canvas bag. Leonard sealed the container and put it in the bag before handing it to Koen. "You make sure she eats. Anytime she needs the kitchen, you come, day or night. And when she's ready to bake again, I will be ready to learn from her."

Koen's throat tightened. "Thanks, Leonard. I'm sorry for not—"

Leonard pushed him out of the kitchen. "Tired of your yapping, boy. I know how bad you are at cleaning. Don't come back until you bring that girl with you." He walked back into the kitchen and threw his arm up. "And bring back that container!"

Koen peeked inside the bag as he left the Keep. A slice of chocolate cake sat on top of the bowl.

Koen peeked into the common room.

"She's resting," Oryn said. He sipped his tea and brushed a long blonde hair from his shoulder. "We left half an hour ago. She said she didn't need anyone to babysit her. I think it was her polite way of telling us to fuck off."

Koen laughed like he always did when Oryn cursed. "I'll just drop this off then. Where do you need me? I know I'm behind on patrols."

Oryn's brows pinched. "The Cruento aren't doing anything. They lost their two most valuable treasures at the same time. Take this opportunity to rest. We all are."

"But –"

"Get in there," Oryn demanded. "She said she didn't need us in there. Not you." He walked away with the cup of tea and disappeared down the hallway in the next breath.

Koen opened his door slowly. Aisling was lying down, her face turned to the sun-drenched windows. His stomach flipped at the sight of her in his room, on his bed, in his clothes. She turned as the door creaked and met his eyes with a warm smile that sent a nauseating wave of happiness down his spine.

"I missed the sun," she whispered.

Everything in him stuttered. He didn't know what to say, so he raised the bag. "I brought you some food."

She lifted to sitting. He caught the flinch she tried to hide. "Oh, thank you. But I don't know if I can eat anything yet. I still feel weird."

"Weird how?" He pulled out the soup and placed it next to her.

"Nauseous," she murmured, her gaze fixed on the bowl. She took a deep inhale and shut her eyes. "But that does smell really good."

He handed her a spoon and held his breath as she brought it to her healing lips. She chewed slowly, the groove between her eyebrows softening. "That's delicious. Want some?"

His chest relaxed as she took another bite. "No. It's just for you."

"When did you get it? Medical tried giving me this awful drink. I couldn't tolerate it. Amerie tried feeding me something from the common room and I started gagging."

He groaned inwardly. Amerie. "I just got it from the kitchens. I knew the common room wouldn't have this."

She paused with the spoon in front of her lips. "You went all the way to the Keep to get me food?"

"Saying 'all the way' is kind of a stretch. It's right there."

She watched him for a minute before taking another small bite. "You left without saying anything."

He shrugged. "I needed to get you food." A weak excuse. He needed to get out before he started crying. Seeing her alive and surrounded by everyone he loved did something to his heart. Making her food was a comforting reflex.

"You don't have to do anything. You've done enough."

"You haven't eaten in days."

She cringed. "Longer," she whispered. "I haven't eaten in I don't know how long."

The rage was back. Every inch of him lit on fire. He blinked through it. "You weren't fed?"

"I was. Every once in a while a bit of bread came in. Sometimes a few pieces of cheese."

He cocked his head, the beast inside him begging to be let out. "That's not being fed."

She swallowed more soup. "Favilla was being drugged. That's how they kept her docile. She'd been sedated for years. When I figured it out, I convinced her to eat my food instead so she could wake up."

He didn't want to know the answer, but his mouth moved before his brain could stop it. "How did you figure it out?"

"I ate her food. They said I slept for three days. That's when they took my finger. I didn't even feel it."

The pure selflessness of this woman...

The pure foolishness. The irresponsibility.

His voice came out quieter than he expected. "You starved yourself so Favilla could eat?"

She pursed her lips in answer and rested the spoon against the soup container. Koen walked to the window and ran his hand through his hair, unable to sit or breathe.

"I don't regret it."

He turned toward her. "Why not?" he nearly yelled. "Why would you do that, Aisling? You could have died from that alone. You—"

"I couldn't watch Favilla being raped anymore!" she shouted. The bowl teetered on her lap. She yelped as the hot liquid splashed over the edge of the container and seeped into the covers. Koen was there a second later to take the blanket. When he came back with a new one, tears raced down her battered cheeks. Darkness lurked behind her eyes.

"They were drugging her with every meal. Enough to make her sleep all day and all night. That's how they got her to breed." Her breaths heavied. Koen watched helplessly as she lost herself to her memories and flinched in pain.

"There was this monster that came in every day. They made me watch it happen over and over. She was unconscious every time. I couldn't do it anymore. I thought if she woke up, we might have a better chance of getting out, so I offered her my food even though it wasn't much. And that's why I'm here and not in the situation he promised." She wiped the back of her wrapped hand on her nose and rolled her shoulders back. "So, no. I don't regret it. I couldn't leave her there. I would do it all over again if it meant saving her, too. I think starving myself was a small price to pay for our freedom."

It was as if she had thrown him in cold water and lit him aflame at the same time. He didn't know what to say.

Aisling stared up at him with eyes full of exhaustion and honesty. The fire he loved so much was still there but banked, like the memories of what she went through doused the flames inside. He hated it more than he could remember hating anything else in his life. He hated it more than he hated his father. His mother. The Cruento.

It was a herculean effort not to reach for her. To keep her at arm's length when all he wanted to do was let her know she was safe. He pulled a chair to her bedside, leaned on the mattress with his elbows, and jerked his chin to the soup. "Eat, Aisling."

EIGHTEEN

AISLING

"The Cruento?"

Kaida shrugged. "Silent."

"Did you find anything?"

"Nothing. Nyssa and Soren saw and felt nothing when we flew over the Latebros. From what you've told us and what little Favilla has said, we know a general area to check, but we won't do anything until we can get you two in the sky."

"I can go—"

"You absolutely cannot," Kaida scolded. "Medical will have my head."

"Soren could just burn them."

Kaida's eyes widened in surprise. Her lips tilted up in a smile. "He could. But Aedan would frown at that. He enjoys their odd sense of humor very much."

Aisling blanched. "Aedan. I forgot, how—"

Kaida waved her off. "He's fine. The sling should come off his arm any day now. Not a minute too soon, either. He's been needier than usual."

Aisling leaned against the back of the couch, the same one Koen slept on while she slept in his bed, and released a deep exhale. The two days she'd been awake were a blur of medical visits and Ferox attention. She was constantly under assessment. The girls helped bathe and dress her in the mornings while Koen took Neera and Morana on a long ride. She felt an emptiness when he was gone that she hadn't felt before, like part of her was missing. And when he was with Morana, the feeling expanded until it was almost painful.

"Aedan wants to thank you."

Aisling grimaced. "Oh, that's not necessary. I didn't do anything. He still got hurt."

"You did everything, Aisling," Kaida replied softly. "You saved the King. You kept the man I love alive. There is no way he or I could ever repay you for what you did."

Aisling lifted her brows. "Love? I thought you two were just…"

"Old friends who casually enjoyed each other's bodies on a frequent basis?" Kaida laughed. "We've been more than that for a very long time, but I didn't want to admit it. The second he was able to hold a conversation I told him."

"Did he reciprocate?"

The corner of Kaida's lip lifted. "And then some."

Aisling smiled back without pain, the swelling on her face finally gone. The bruises scattered on her body remained with their dull ache, but she could handle those. She was thrilled something good came from all the chaos of the last few weeks. "So…are you going to live with him?"

"I have no idea," Kaida admitted, taking a sip of tea. "The castle has to be completely rebuilt. Anwir says it should be at least another full year before it's even inhabitable again. So right now, Aedan will stay with us. It's the safest place he can be."

"It's the safest place anyone can be," Aisling murmured. She thought back to the battle. "Anwir was okay? I only caught a glimpse of him before everything happened."

"A concussion and a few cuts. They found him barely conscious under a pile of bodies just feet from Aedan." Kaida looked at the fire. "Koen told me what you told him. About Favilla."

Aisling tensed. "I couldn't kill her, Kaida. I couldn't leave her there either."

"No one is upset with you for what you did."

"Koen is."

Kaida rolled her eyes. "Koen..." She pursed her lips in thought for a minute. "Koen came to me at a pivotal time in his life. I tried to help him as best I could with what he was dealing with mentally. I've never had a child. He's the closest thing I have to one. I didn't know what I was doing, but I think he turned out okay." She swallowed thickly. "So I know him better than he knows himself. And I can tell you that these last three weeks have been the worst of his entire life. He has never been so angry, so inept."

A huff of a laugh left her lips. "Aedan was almost dead. You had been captured without a single hint of your whereabouts. Morana was uncontrollable. And Koen was self-imploding. I was terrified." She took a deep inhale. "Koen is not angry with you. He never has been. He's angry with himself for a thousand different reasons he probably doesn't even understand."

Aisling stilled. "But when I came here—"

"He was an ass. A real piece of work, yes. He regrets it like you wouldn't believe. If I gave him a whip, he would flay himself raw for it."

Aisling grimaced. "I don't want that."

"Nor I." She rolled her tiny shoulders back. "No one is upset with you, Aisling. Do not apologize for surviving. You did exactly what you should have done. I am constantly impressed by you. And I am so very proud of you."

Aisling's heart nearly exploded. Never in either of her lives had those words been said to her. For just a moment, her aches and pains went away. For just a moment, she was floating.

Kaida smiled and walked to the door, taking her tea with her. "Do not rush your healing. Take every minute you need and then some. You've dealt the Cruento a death blow. You've earned every right to relax."

She walked out, shutting the door behind her. Aisling flinched at the sound, so similar to the door in the cave, and shook the memories from her head before turning her attention to the fire. The sun had begun its descent, throwing a rich golden hue across the stone walls that weren't hers. Koen's room was basic and undecorated despite how long he had lived there. Nothing differentiated his room from hers. Maybe that's why she felt so comfortable in it.

It was a lie, of course. She knew why she felt so comfortable there, why she could relax and sleep for a little bit at a time without panicking. She placed her tea on the table, the sharp ache in her side lessening with every passing day, and rested her head against the back of the couch.

She wasn't going to think about everything Kaida had said. Wasn't going to read into Koen's attention and care. Wasn't going to acknowledge what she'd realized in the cave. She was just going to be.

She closed her eyes and let the cracking of the fire lull her to sleep.

A hand slid behind her back. Another slithered under her knees.

Blackness devoured her.

No. No. Not again. She had left the cave. She had made it out.

The grip tightened.

I am going to break you, Aisling.

Adrenaline coursed through her at the sound of the Man's voice. The aching muscles in her arms didn't scream as she lashed out in a flurry of kicks and punches. She felt no searing pain in her sides. No pain at all as she fought back against the touch.

She yanked on her bond, the single glowing thing in the darkness around her.

"Aisling!"

It wasn't the acidic voice of the man who tortured her. It was softer, kinder.

The hands weren't of the men who beat her. Her eyes peeled open.

A pair of russet brown eyes bore into hers. Flecks of gold glowed in the dim light of the dying fire.

Stone hovered above her. And below. And on every side.

The darkness laughed at her.

Her breaths came too fast, too shallow. Her side screamed in pain as the adrenaline faded. "Out," Aisling breathed, her throat nearly closed with panic. "Get me out."

She was in Koen's grasp a heartbeat later. Her arms reflexively went around his neck. She buried her face against him, the one solid thing keeping her grounded against the fear pulsing through her.

He burst up the stairs and into the Pit. Fresh air slammed into her. Crisp gusts of wind greeted her like an old friend. They sank into her lungs and pushed out the panic with every shaky exhale.

She loosened her grip around Koen's neck after a few full breaths and tilted her head up to the night sky. Stars twinkled against the darkness. The moon glowed and bathed her in its brightness. Her body relaxed. "I missed it," she whispered.

"So did she."

Aisling whipped her head to the opening of the Lair. Favilla limped into the sand.

Aisling had never seen Favilla in the light. What she had seen was only from the weak flame of a small candle.

Her black scales were dull and covered in layers of thick scars. She was all bone. Even her wings were somehow atrophied. But her sapphire eyes reminded Aisling of Soren's flame. There was a fight inside, a hint of the dragon she had been a decade ago.

Favilla looked lovingly at Aisling before lifting her head to the sky. She collapsed on the sand in the next step with her stomach toward the moon and a heavy, content sigh from her mouth.

A flare of shadow danced down the bond. Morana appeared from the darkened Lair door, her amethyst eyes locked on Aisling's.

Aisling couldn't stop the whimper that escaped her mouth at the sight of her beautiful dragon and felt her power again. The last time she saw her...

Morana flooded the bond with a litany of emotions, all warm and comforting. Koen gently lowered Aisling to the ground, his hands holding her waist as Morana nuzzled at her stomach. A deep purr left her dragon at the touch. Aisling lifted her hands to the scales, letting her tears fall freely as she finally reunited with the other half of her soul.

"I missed you so much," she croaked after the knot in her throat loosened. She leaned into Morana and rested her head against the shiny plates. "I felt you every day. Every minute I was awake, I felt you looking for me. I felt your love and pain and frustration." Aisling took a steadying breath. "It killed me not to answer you. To feel your sorrow so strongly and know that it was because of me. All I wanted was to be with you, but I couldn't risk you. You know that, right?"

Morana blinked once. *Yes.*

"I'm so sorry," Aisling whispered, her voice weak. "I'm so sorry I got off your back. I'm so sorry you got hurt."

Morana pulled back slightly with a subtle shake of her head. She blinked twice. *No.*

"Yes. It was my fault. But I'll make it up to you." Aisling stroked Morana's cheek. "I never want to be parted from you again."

The bond warmed. *Yes.*

They stood together for a long time, foreheads pressed together and bond pulsing, until Aisling's weakened legs began to shake. Morana leaned in closer as Aisling's broken body folded in half. Koen gently lifted her from the scales and lowered her to the ground. He sat and put her back against his chest, his strong legs on either side of hers. Morana curled at Aisling's feet and rested her head beside them with a content sigh.

Aisling glanced over Morana's body. "Her wounds?"

"Healed," Koen responded, his voice a low vibration on her back.

"How bad were they?"

He paused. "It was bloody. The hardest part was getting her to sit still. She was... defiant after you were taken."

Aisling rested her hand on Morana's head. "Sounds familiar." The dragon huffed in response.

Sand shuddered under them. Neera curled behind Koen, allowing him lean against her, and dropped her gigantic head at Aisling's other side, her bright yellow eyes soft. Aisling stroked her beautiful green scales. "Thank you for keeping her safe," she whispered. "And for bringing me home."

Koen stiffened at her back. Aisling wondered what was happening with their bond, but she didn't have time to ask. The rest of the Ferox dragons came into the Pit in a single file line. Each nuzzled her with their snouts before resting in the sand in a pile of wings and teeth. Even Soren tucked in close—close enough to Neera that Morana huffed a laugh.

Her throat was unbearably tight as she took in the sight. She leaned back onto Koen's chest and rested her head in the crook of his neck, the movement natural and easy. "Better?" he asked.

"Much."

"Should we bring the bed out here?"

She laughed. "Maybe."

He didn't ask her what happened in his room. Didn't press her for details or an explanation. He was just there.

It was all she needed. She attempted to turn to him, but the lancing pain in her side took her breath away. She collapsed back onto his chest. "Thank you for getting me out."

"You got yourself out," he said, his stubbled cheek brushing against her temple.

"No. It was you."

"Agree to disagree."

She smirked. "I've been thinking."

"About?"

"I should move back to my room. I've been hogging your bed. You can't keep sleeping on the couch."

He tensed behind her. "You aren't hogging anything."

"I am. You need your space back."

He was quiet. "Is that what you want?"

No. She wanted to stay in his bed and breathe in the scent of him. She wanted to know he was right there when panic began seeping through her veins, when she felt the world closing in on her. She wanted to know it was real – that she had made it out and he wasn't a figment of her imagination. "You need your space back, Koen."

His voice was rough in her ear. "You don't know what I need, Aisling."

Her jaw loosened, eyes bulging.

"Oh, a sleepover?" Amerie called from the door. Aisling started.

Koen groaned. "Go away, Amerie. Haven't we seen enough of you today?"

Amerie pouted. A rolled blanket hung from her hands. "It's never enough, babe." She stopped in front of Calen. His one eye opened, assessing her before closing again. "Anyway, beastie invited me." She curled into Calen's side. "Looks like I wasn't the only one."

Cielle stumbled in, clearly still half asleep. Aylim opened a wing and huffed a laugh as her bond fell asleep at her side. Elaila came in next. Her eyes soaked in every detail of the scene before she gave a small smile and leaned against Osiris's neck. Oryn and Kaida came in together.

"Aedan?" Koen asked.

"Sleeping."

"You didn't want to invite the King to a family sleepover?" Amerie asked.

Kaida smirked as she rested against Soren's massive cheek. "He's worn out. I thought I'd let him rest."

Oryn made a gagging sound. "Can we not?"

Kaida winked at Amerie before turning to Aisling. "His room starting to smell?"

"Just needed a change of scenery," Aisling responded with a tight smile. Elaila's brow lifted for only a second. Her eyes flickered with understanding.

Aisling didn't have the energy or courage to tell them the truth. She didn't know if she would ever be able to describe the fissures the time in the cave had left in her soul. The gaping crevices haunted her, teasing her with the missing bits of herself every time the darkness laughed at her. Every time a door opened. Every time she woke up in a blind panic or heard footsteps clicking against stone.

Koen's fingers stroked lightly against the back of her arm in response.

"We've never done this before," Amerie said, glancing around. "We should do it more."

"I'll bet a whole week of patrols that you won't make it through the night," Koen responded. "You'll be back in bed long before morning."

"Okay, and?" She rolled her eyes. "I hate getting sand in my hair. It takes forever to get out."

"It does," Elaila agreed. "It's a valid reason." Amerie blew her a kiss.

"I haven't found that to be true," Oryn yawned. Nyssa's head rested on his lap.

"Of course you haven't, you beautiful man!" Amerie crossed her arms over her chest. "You're not normal. The rest of us actually have to work to look halfway decent."

Aisling laughed as they bickered, letting the soundtrack of her family and the warm, solid body at her back wrap her in the peace she feared she would never feel again. Sleep came for her like an old friend, the darkness from before banished into the sky above.

NINETEEN

AISLING

"This brace is a little tight," Aisling muttered.

Medical gave her the all-clear that morning to begin simple movement as long as she wore the thick white brace around her ribs for everything except sleeping. She thanked them profusely for everything, but they only nodded awkwardly in answer before walking out.

"It'll keep you from feeling like you're being stabbed," Cielle replied as she finalized Aisling's hair into an intricate braided updo.

"How do you know how to braid so well? You only have a tiny bit of hair."

The cave had unlocked a new comfort in having her head touched. Aisling craved gentle hands in her hair and along her scalp to erase the memories of her beatings. None of the girls came close to Koen washing her hair, but they didn't need to know that.

"Do you think I never had long hair?"

"Did you?"

"Yes. Then I bonded, and I suck at braiding my own hair. It was constantly full of knots, and I couldn't take it anymore. I chopped it off in the common room with a dagger after patrols one morning. Kaida trimmed it until we decided we liked this look. Amerie nearly died."

Aisling laughed. "Does this brace mean I can ride again?"

"That's not up to me," Cielle shrugged. "I think it depends on who you ask."

"What do you mean?"

"I'd let you on Morana right now. So would Amerie. Elaila would be hesitant, but she'd want you to be happy, so eventually she'd let you. But she would feel wildly guilty the whole time. Oryn might, but only with certain safety measures in place. Kaida would say no. And we know what Koen would say."

Aisling puffed a sigh. She'd moved back to her room three days before and regretted it every second since. Night after night she awoke in a panic, surrounded by nothing but stone and darkness, and hobbled her broken body up the stairs to the Pit to sleep beneath the stars with Morana and Favilla on either side of her.

Amerie threw open the door. "Love the hair." She brushed a quick kiss on Aisling's cheek and patted Cielle's head. "Good work, babe. Too bad you desecrated yours."

Elaila walked in and rolled her eyes as Amerie jumped onto Aisling's bed. She glanced at Aisling's brace. "Heard you got the all-clear to start moving."

Aisling cocked her head. "How did you hear that already? It just happened!"

"We bumped into medical on our way over."

"They came into the common room to tell Kaida," Amerie said. "Oryn mentioned getting you back in the saddle."

Aisling nearly fell out of her seat. "You're joking."

"It's true. Koen's eyes almost popped out of his head," Elaila grinned.

"Shocking," Amerie quipped. She turned an inquisitive glance to Aisling. "What's happening there?"

"It's none of your business, you idiot!" Cielle threw the brush at Amerie's head.

"Come on!" Amerie laughed. The brush narrowly missed her head and crashed to the floor. "In all the years we've known him, Koen hasn't shown a single shred of interest in another living being besides Neera, and even that is hit or miss. Excuse me for wondering."

"Do not answer her," Cielle told Aisling. She grabbed Amerie's wrist and wrestled her off the bed. "We're going to the Pit and I'm going to knock some common sense into her. Yell if you need us."

The door shut behind them. Aisling did her best not to cringe at the sound. Elaila's bright blue eyes didn't miss it. She hesitated and awkwardly repositioned herself on the edge of Aisling's bed. "When you're ready to talk about it, I want you to know I'm here."

Aisling stilled. "I wasn't raped," she whispered, needing to admit it out loud to someone. No one had asked, and she understood why, but she still needed to get it off her chest. Elaila's eyes widened in shock. "Almost. I almost was, but Favilla stopped it before it happened."

She couldn't stop overwhelming guilt from drowning her as Elaila, a woman who was violated time and time again, stared at her in astonishment. What made Aisling so special that she hadn't been brutalized like that? Why had Elaila been the only one to suffer so horribly?

"Kaida told us about Favilla," Elaila said after a beat, her soft voice calm and steady. Aisling swallowed, refusing to allow the memories of the cave any more space in her mind. Elaila reached forward and wrapped her hand around Aisling's. "Just because it didn't happen to you doesn't mean it wasn't traumatic. Any time spent with them is hard, Aisling. Don't ever compare your experience with someone else's. Just because you weren't hurt like me doesn't mean you weren't hurt. It doesn't mean you weren't scarred."

Aisling's free hand absentmindedly lifted to her neck. The slice was raised to the touch, and it took everything in her to keep from reaching for it all day.

Elaila's eyes narrowed. "It's a badge of strength, Aisling. It means you lived."

"They were going to—before Favilla exploded..."

Elaila nodded. "Being threatened with it can make it feel like it's already happened. Especially when you're powerless against it."

Aisling clenched her jaw as the flashbacks bombarded her without permission.

She could feel their hands on her. Could hear her shirt ripping. Could taste her fear and blood on her tongue.

Elaila studied her. "I know why you're sleeping under the stars. I did it, too. For a long, long time. Something is healing about the sky. It changes constantly. It doesn't hold grudges. It can't hold a memory." A glossy film covered her eyes, making the blue inside nearly electric. "Every single day I have to remind myself to be like that. To let go of the memories. To continue moving on, continue evolving, and not get stuck in the same cycle of hate and anger, just like the sky. And it helps."

She wiped a lone tear off her cheek and breathed a laugh. "It's really hard. You shouldn't rush healing. Give yourself time and let it happen gradually. Allow yourself to feel, but always bring yourself back to the present. Pull on the bond. Let Morana anchor you." She tightened her grip on Aisling's hand. "Give us some of your load. We're here for you. You are never alone. I know we've said it before, but you need to hear it again and again until you believe it."

Tears slid down Aisling's cheeks.

Elaila grimaced. "I know it's none of my business, but if you feel safe with Koen, lean on him. He..." she searched Aisling's face, her mouth opening and shutting in thought before she shook her head. "If he makes you feel safe, don't hide from him. Let him hear you. Let him see you. Please don't keep it all inside, or you'll never heal. Trust me." She wiped a tear from Aisling's cheek, ignoring her own.

"Are you healed?"

The corner of Elaila's lips tipped up. "Healing doesn't have a finish line, Aisling. I have healed, yes, but I don't think I'll ever be done, if that makes sense." She rubbed her thumb across the back of Aisling's hand. "You will never be the same woman you were. You will be better than her. Stronger. Brighter. Nearly invincible. But do not mourn your old self. She went through this for a reason. The universe does not make mistakes, and that includes you coming to this world."

A knock sounded at the door. Elaila and Aisling both jumped. Koen's head popped in. His brows furrowed at the sight of their tears. "Sorry. I can come back."

"No," Elaila stood. "I was just leaving." She bent down and pressed a gentle kiss to the top of Aisling's head. Her footsteps were light as she walked out the door, leaving it open as if she could hear Aisling's unspoken request. Koen walked in, his dark hair wind-tossed and eyes bright.

Aisling's skin heated as he assessed her. She cleared her tight throat. "You shaved."

He rubbed a hand along his smooth jaw. "Is that a problem?" She shook her head, swallowing the urge to reach up and touch his face. He grinned. "Ready to train?"

Her mouth fell open. "Really?"

"No. You're not healed enough." He pushed a plate of food in front of her. "The more you eat, the faster you'll get back out there."

Aisling sighed. All she wanted was that soup he had brought before. The food from the common room was fine, but it wasn't the same.

"Everything okay?" he asked softly. She nodded and shoved the food in her mouth, still digesting everything Elaila had said. He watched her before taking a step back and sitting on the arm of the couch. "Oryn wanted to know if you were ready to fly again."

She stopped chewing. "What did you tell him?"

"To ask you."

"Really?"

He smirked. "You need the sky, Aisling."

She stared at him for too long in silence.

Elaila was right. He knew exactly what she needed without her having to say a word. She couldn't keep everything to herself forever without feeling like she was going to explode.

"Do you want to know what happened in the cave?"

His cut jaw tensed. "Do you want to tell me?"

Aisling saw the anger burning in his eyes every time she held her side. Watched him try to keep his control during her bursts of panic. She'd noticed his gaze on her bruises when he thought she wasn't looking. Heard his teeth clench when she flinched in pain. And when she touched the scar on her neck he turned molten, his barely restrained wrath palpable.

Talking about what happened took the power from the memories and gave it back to her, and she needed to feel that power again. Needed to feel in control again.

She stood from her chair, the brace annoyingly helpful. "Yes."

A chorus of bells rang out and shook the foundation of stone beneath them. Her knees buckled with the vibrations. Koen's hands slid to her waist before he lifted her and placed her on the couch. "It can't be, can it?" she whispered breathlessly.

The Cruento couldn't be attacking. The eggs couldn't be ready yet. The man said they needed to rebuild.

The same confusion whirred in Koen's eyes. "There's only one way to know. Stay here." He hesitated before running out her door. She stared in shock just for a moment before forcing herself to stand. Using the sturdiness of the brace for balance, she walked through the hallway, up the stairs, and into the Pit with her legs on fire.

Every dragon and rider mobilized inside. Armor clinked as they donned it with impressive speed. Saddles tightened. Swords and daggers flashed in the light of the sun above. Kaida tucked her sword at her back. "Attack at Iuxta."

"Beasts?" Amerie asked, her normal playfulness hidden behind brutal focus.

"Unknown. We're obviously to treat it as such until we find out otherwise."

Morana's eyes latched onto Aisling's from across the Pit. Sorrow rushed down the bond. Kaida followed Morana's gaze and pursed her lips as she took in Aisling in the doorway. The rest of the riders turned. An awkward silence filled the air. Aisling steeled her spine and stepped into the sand. "I want to help."

"You will help us by healing. It isn't your time yet." Kaida glanced at the other riders before settling in her saddle. Soren was in the air seconds later. Cielle, Amerie, and Elaila shot her remorseful glances before their dragons followed.

Oryn glanced at Koen before turning his emerald eyes onto Aisling. "Heal, Aisling."

Nyssa took him skyward in a beam of gold.

Morana stared at Aisling. Aisling stared at Morana. "Go," she finally murmured, her voice broken. "Go, but do not land. You're to stay in the air the entire time." Morana blinked once in answer. She was a flash of light in the sky moments later. Remorse trickled down the bond.

Tears filled Aisling's eyes. White-hot fury sank into her bones.

She had survived. She fought. She could still help.

Koen appeared in front of her blurred eyes. His sharp face was pained as he wiped the tears from her cheeks with the pad of his thumb. "Let me ride with you," she pleaded.

"No."

"I want to go, Koen. I need to go. I can't... I can't be locked up again."

His jaw feathered. "You aren't being locked up. You're healing. There's a difference."

"I'm sick of healing," Aisling hissed, pushing past him toward Neera. She refused to allow the Cruento to keep her down like this. They'd done enough to her. They wouldn't take her ability to fight, too.

Koen's hand gripped her wrist and forced her to turn. She slammed into his broad chest. Tears sliced down her face as she beat her fists into him again and again. He held her close and allowed her to hit him until she grew tired and collapsed.

"I won't get off her back," she whispered through her tears. "I won't get off. I swear. Just let me come with you."

He cupped her face and forced her to meet his stare. "When I come back, we will start training, and you can tell me everything. We can sleep here under the stars like you do every night. But I need you here right now, Aisling." His voice cracked. "I need you safe."

"What about what I need?"

His eyes darted between hers, an honest promise inside. "Write me a list. I'll spend the rest of my life checking it off." He leaned forward and pressed a devastatingly soft kiss to her forehead. She shut her eyes against the torrent of emotion blazing through her.

Neera took him to the sky, to battle, a moment later.

Aisling stared numbly at the empty Pit. Her family, gone.

What if one of them was captured? What if Morana was hurt again? If Koen got hurt?

She clenched her teeth and walked into the Lair, past Gareth's room, past the empty rooms of the other dragons. Favilla yawned on her back and smacked her tongue lazily. "Get up, Favilla," Aisling commanded. "We're done with this resting nonsense. It's time to train."

TWENTY

KOEN

"Bombs?" Aedan leaned back and whispered incredulously. His sling was gone, but he guarded his torso with every movement. "They've never used those, not even in the beginning."

"They never had to," Koen said. "But eyes are watching, and bombs are far too easy to plant without anyone noticing."

"They decimated Iuxta." Oryn's hair was tied into a low ponytail, the only sign he was remotely rattled. "We only found seven survivors."

Aedan's face paled. Anwir stood behind him, his normally inquisitive face ashen, eyes wide.

"They're changing the goal of their attacks," Oryn continued. "Iuxta is where the majority of the livestock comes from to feed the dragons. By killing the supply, they're trying to starve our best weapons against them."

"All of the food…"

Oryn nodded at the King. "Every single farm was demolished. The entire town, gone."

"Food for us. For the dragons." Koen supplied.

Aedan pinched the bridge of his nose with his thumb and forefinger. "Even if they starve the dragons, which I won't allow, we have an entire army."

"So do they."

"Yes, but—"

Oryn leaned forward. "Yes, we have an army. A fantastic one at that. But the Cruento also has one. We do not know their numbers or skill level. We do not know where they will attack, nor do we know what weapons they have. If these bombs are any indication of what they've been working on, we need to be very, very smart about our next steps."

Aedan clenched his jaw. "Tell me about the bombs."

"They contained Funestum," Koen said. The light went out in Aedan's eyes. "We smelled it before we got there. Had to wait until the wind carried it away."

"How?" the King asked breathlessly. "We have it under guard and lock."

"The castle was demolished. You were under attack. It's not a far stretch to believe a guard ran to help and left the store unattended during the siege." Oryn said softly.

"Do you think—"

"The Cruento infiltrated the castle at some point," Koen replied. He had wondered about it for a while now, but Aedan and Anwir checked backgrounds so thoroughly that it seemed impossible. "Maybe infiltrated the Keep, too."

Oryn nodded in agreement. Aedan tapped his finger absentmindedly on the table. "No one goes without a thorough check. From those with the most seniority to the newest refugees, we need to make sure we haven't allowed a snake into the garden." Anwir took the implied command and left the room.

Koen knew as soon as he smelled the sickly sweet gas that the castle stores had been raided. Neera and the rest of the dragons pulled back instinctively against the smell. Kaida and Oryn's faces paled as they took in the scene below the smoke.

There was a reason Funestum was kept in a secure vault. A reason people were executed immediately and without trial for making it. The devastation was the worst thing Koen had ever seen. Bodies lay swollen with blood dripping from every orifice as the smoke lifted to the clouds. The gas wormed its way into every surface, tainting whatever it touched with acid so strong it burned your vital organs before you had a chance to realize what was happening. Those who inhaled it never lived more than two minutes.

"Did they take anyone?"

"We couldn't tell." Oryn took a steadying breath. "I think this was just a show. Retribution for losing Aisling and Favilla. They didn't want to take women. They wanted to prove that they aren't going anywhere."

Koen tempered the rage inside. Aisling had never been theirs. Never would be again.

"Anwir will look into it. I'll leave tonight to investigate myself," Aedan said.

Oryn's brows lifted. "Are you sure that's wise? Medical—"

"I am the King," Aedan's voice was pure ice, all sense of friendliness gone. "I have the luxury of doing whatever needs to get done." He rolled his shoulders back with a steadying breath. "Kaida? The girls?"

"Kaida has the dragon medical team assessing for inhalation injuries. Every dragon hand will be on watch in the Lair for the next day to monitor for symptoms. The girls are getting the few survivors settled in the Keep."

"I'll see them immediately," Aedan said to himself. "And Aisling? Did she make the journey?"

"No. Morana flew alone."

The King pursed his lips. "Is Aisling up for visitors yet? Or does she still need time?"

Oryn looked to Koen. Koen shrugged. "I think she would love to see you."

"Wonderful," Aedan said, his tense body deflating. "I fear I've waited far too long to express my appreciation. I intended to give her space to heal before I hug her so hard she might crack in half, but now I think it may be coming off as rude and ungrateful." He sighed. "She might know something about these bombs. She spent time with the Cruento. She may have overheard something."

Oryn and Koen both nodded. They knew Aisling knew nothing about it, but if it made Aedan feel better, they wouldn't say anything.

Kaida burst through the door. Her hair hung loose from its braid. A wild look danced in her eyes. She ignored her twin and King and looked at Koen. "She's gone."

The air left the room. Everything in his body froze.

"Explain," Oryn demanded, his eyes hardening.

"Aisling is gone. Morana is looking for her now. Gareth saw her leave with Favilla, but no one has seen them since. Favilla isn't answering Soren and the rest of the dragons are finishing their medical—"

Koen yanked on the bond as he sprinted from the Keep. Neera dropped into the meadow and splayed her wings. He leapt on without breaking his stride. She flew north over the ravine toward the far cliffs in the distance. Morana's shimmering scales glittered ahead. Black wings flapped too close to the cliff edge further in the distance. Koen let out a string of curses as they neared.

Favilla fought the current, her weak body swerving against the power of the wind. Morana growled from above at Aisling sitting saddleless on Favilla's bony back. Koen echoed the sentiment.

"Do you want to explain this?" he yelled over the wind. Morana and Neera floated on either side of Favilla.

Aisling murmured sweet words of encouragement to the weakened dragon. "Not really."

He gritted his teeth. "Aisling."

"Koen."

"You need to come down. You'll hurt yourself. Favilla isn't ready yet. You're going to exhaust her."

The delicate line of her jaw tensed. "You never told me to stay on the ground."

He ran through their last conversation and muttered a curse when he realized she was right. "I said you needed to heal."

"The sky is healing."

His impatience tore down the bond. Neera let out a warning rumble that Morana parroted. Favilla didn't hesitate to lower to the ground. She nearly collapsed as she tucked her wings to her sides and hit land, jostling Aisling enough to make her grimace.

Morana glared at Aisling. Aisling glared back. Koen fought the urge to laugh at the sight of the small, injured woman staring down the dragon of shadow and death. Morana chirped once. Aisling's jaw tightened.

He hopped off Neera and stepped to Favilla's side, arm outstretched. "Come on. We can walk back to ease you into training."

"No."

He fluttered his eyes shut, willing his dwindling patience to stay with him. "Why?"

She didn't answer.

"Aisling." He opened his eyes and his heart hollowed. Aisling's head was in her hands, her shaking shoulders bowed as much as they could be with her brace.

She was in his arms and cradled against his chest a moment later. Neera and Morana walked an exhausted Favilla back to the Pit without prompting, the latter turning a concerned eye on Aisling. Koen sat in front of a large boulder with the sea before them and placed Aisling in his lap.

She sobbed into his chest. The waves below crashed solemnly against the cliffs as if the ocean could feel her pain. He stroked long lines down her arms while she finally let out her hurt.

Time passed with the arc of the sun.

Her tears eventually slowed. She sank into him and wiped her face with her sleeve. "Sorry," she whispered, her voice small and hesitant. "That was embarrassing."

"It's only embarrassing if you let it be. Look at Amerie. She's never embarrassed."

She let out a ghost of a laugh. "You hate her."

"I don't. I love her, but I'm also violently annoyed by her." He brushed unruly hairs from Aisling's forehead. "Do you want to talk about it?"

Every day since she returned he'd been dying to know what happened to her. Dying to know and also terrified of what he would hear.

Aisling sat up and winced slightly as she repositioned herself on his lap to look at him. The steel of resolve traveled down her spine. Her throat bobbed. He couldn't help dipping his eyes to the slender column of her throat, to the scar that marred the perfect skin.

"I do. But are you sure—"

"Just tell me, Aisling. Please."

She took a steadying breath. Her eyes went distant, her voice monotone and low. "The cave had no windows. No light. It was freezing. There was enough room that Favilla and I weren't crammed together. There was a trough in the back full of water. I was beaten before and after Favilla's visits, sometimes in between. They made me watch her get raped. Made me listen to them rolling her eggs out the door as they laughed.

"After the first week, a man came in. He was different than the rest of them. He was more... more commanding. The men listened to him. They called him the Boss. He told me he wasn't going to kill me. That it would be a waste." Tears welled in her eyes. She blinked them away. "He explicitly said he wanted to break me. That he would use me to prove a point to everyone."

Koen's chest clenched as Aisling fought against the tears to relive all of it for him.

"He told me he would keep me for himself. That when I broke, I would be his. I would bear him sons. He wanted them to become the next generation of Cruento rulers. He thought because I was a dragon rider, my children would be able to tame their beasts."

Everything in him stilled.

Her breaths came quickly, the brace moving in time with her shoulders. "I didn't break, though. He got frustrated and said I had one more day before he took me. I guess he was tired of waiting. He gave his men one more day to break me. That's when Favilla and I decided we had to move. They came to use her. One of the men, not the guy in charge, decided he wanted first dibs on me."

Tears fell down her cheeks. "I was exhausted. I knew I was going to die. But I wanted to go out fighting, so I held onto as much energy as I could. He started touching me." Her lip curled in disgust. "That's why my clothes were ripped. He... his hand..." She shook her head, slamming her eyes shut. "That's when Favilla erupted. And when I fought back. I beat him, then took his dagger and turned his hands to ribbons. Favilla and I left the room together and walked through the hallways until we found the light. But the men figured out we were gone and chased after us. And I was so tired."

Her voice cracked. "I was too tired. I knew I was going to die. So I threw everything I had into the bond. I apologized to Morana. I told her how much I loved her and how grateful I was for the little time we had together. Then my body gave up. I wondered if it would be better to just let myself drown. That way, I could go out by my own will, but Favilla grabbed me. That's all I remember until I woke up in your room."

Koen went breathless at the raging fire in her honey-brown eyes. Aisling's fingers traced the line across her throat. "I never spoke once in the cave. He took it as an insult and branded me. It's a collar for obedience and loyalty."

She blinked quickly and turned her eyes to the splattering of gray clouds above. "I don't want to let what happened rule me, but it's almost impossible. I can't sleep in my own bed. I can't breathe without the sky above me. I flinch when I hear footsteps or when a door clicks. I have never felt weaker in either of my lives. I feel like... I feel like they won. They broke me like they wanted, they just aren't here to see it."

His chest caved. There would be nothing he could ever say to make her feel better, but he had to try.

Koen wrapped his thumb and index finger around her chin and turned her to face him. "You are the strongest person I know, Aisling. What you've been through is horrific. But still, you're here. You're trying to ride a dragon even though you have broken ribs. You're trying to live. Do you know how strong you have to be to face death, to accept it, and still want to live after the fact?"

He couldn't keep the awe from his voice. To go through all of that, to live two lives drenched in pain and suffering and still have hope was incomprehensible to him.

"You are no one's property," he rasped. "Not even Morana's." He traced the scar on her neck. "This is not a branding unless you let it be one. What happened to you will not define you because you won't let it. You prove to the Cruento that they didn't get the last laugh."

He wrapped his fingers around the nape of her neck and stroked the scar with his thumb. Their eyes met. He swallowed his fear, his hesitation. "When you are ready to burn the world down, I'll be there with the match."

Silent tears cascaded down her cheeks. "Thank you," she whispered, her throat bobbing. "I know that was a lot to dump on you, but..."

He waited. "But what?" A hint of a blush crept up her cheeks. His voice caught. "But what, Aisling?"

She rolled her eyes and lifted her face to the sky. "I feel safe with you. I know I can throw all of this at you, and you won't shrink away from it. From me. I'm really thankful for you, Koen."

Her words slammed into him. After everything he had done to her, every awful thing he had said before, she still felt safe around him. Safe enough to divulge the atrocities she hadn't shared with anyone else. "Is that why you've been sleeping in the Pit? Because I'm not there anymore?"

She glanced sidelong at him. "How did you know I've been sleeping there?"

"Just answer the question."

Aisling shrugged. "I'm not sure. I just know when I woke up for the first time and you were there, I was so relieved. I know we didn't start off on the right foot, but—"

He felt it—the vulnerability, the honesty, bubbling from his throat. And for the first time in his life, he didn't want to stop it.

"We started on the wrong foot because I was an ass. And I lied to you." Her eyes widened. "I didn't trust myself around you, Aisling. So I pushed you away." He leaned against the rock at his back. "The second you landed in the Pit for the first time I knew I was fucked. It terrified me. No one has ever had power over me like that. I thought if I pushed you away, you wouldn't want to come back. That you'd realize all of this wasn't worth it. But you fought back. You kept showing up. You saved my life. I got to know you better, but it was never enough. I couldn't get enough of you.

"And we became friends. Instead of running, you chose to stay. You chose my home to be yours. You offered me a clean slate even though I would never deserve it. And I thought, I hoped, that you'd realize I wasn't a piece of shit." He forced himself to meet her eyes. "Then you got captured. For three weeks, I lost my mind. Really and truly, I thought I was going insane. I was full of regret for every awful thing I said to you. I was terrified that you'd be gone forever, and you would only ever know me as that awful brute, and I would never get the chance to apologize. I was so weak for pushing you away all that time. Clean slate or not, you deserve an apology."

He took her hand in his and pressed a kiss to her healing skin. "I'm sorry, Aisling. For every awful word I said. For how I treated you and how I made you feel. I'm so sorry that I ever made you feel less than the incredible woman you are."

He wouldn't come back from this. He knew it, and still, he dove headfirst.

"I care about you. Deeply. I brought you to my room to heal because that's where I want you. I want to be close to you. It's all I've wanted since you showed up on Morana's back wild and free and fighting. I cannot focus on anything anymore because of you. And to hear you say that you feel safe with me..." He took a shaky inhale. "I swore to myself that if you came back, I would be more honest. More vulnerable. I swore I would be the real me, not the awful version you knew. You're the only person I want to be vulnerable with. I want you to know that I will work every single day to be the person worthy of your safekeeping."

Koen tucked his chin to his chest and let out a heavy exhale.

Kaida and Oryn were full of shit.

Vulnerability was brutal. He'd never felt so laid bare in all his life. This woman had the ability to rip him to shreds and leave him for carrion. And he'd let her, so long as she touched him.

Silence ensued. He drowned in it.

He'd gone too far. She was healing, trying to work through the complexities of the last month of her life. Not just the Cruento torture, but her plane stepping, her leaving behind an entire life for this one. And instead of giving her space and time, he'd bombarded her with something as stupid as his feelings.

Aisling's hand traveled up his neck with a delicate softness and forced his chin to lift. His breathing went ragged at the sight of her eyes aflame, the honey inside molten and glowing. She traced his temple, his jawline, with trembling fingers. His skin buzzed at the contact, begging for more. She looked at him in wonder as her thumb brushed his lower lip.

He didn't move. Didn't dare speak.

She leaned forward slightly, her mouth barely parted, just close enough for them to share a breath.

"Hey!" Amerie shouted from Calen's back. Both of them jerked back in shock. Aisling grunted and clutched at her side. Koen steadied her as Morana landed beside them, her violet eyes narrowed at their closeness. "We need you both back now."

"Why?" he yelled back, his blood boiling in every different way.

"Someone is here to see Aisling."

Ice splashed in his veins. Aisling's face paled. She met his eyes. "I don't... there's no one else I know here," she whispered.

Koen turned to Amerie. "This can't be done later? When she's healed?"

"No. Oryn and Kaida have him tied up and ready. Kaida seems pissy. Don't make her wait." Calen took Amerie away without allowing a response.

Koen clenched his jaw and turned to Aisling, now trembling in his lap. The beautiful blush on her cheeks had gone bone white. Her eyes were wide and unseeing. He brushed his thumb along her shoulder, willing her out of her head. "We'll go in together. If this person makes you uncomfortable in any way, squeeze my hand. I'll walk out with you."

She said nothing. He helped her stand and climb onto Morana's back.

Her first flight on Morana since her capture, and she was shaking with terror.

He was going to kill this man, whoever he was. He hoped it was the nameless man from the cave. The one who tried to stake a claim to her and her unborn children. He would relish in bleeding him dry.

They walked to the common room in silence. Morana had given her a small nuzzle for comfort, but Aisling was too numb to even notice. He shot the dragon an apologetic look before following Aisling down the hall. Just before the common room doors, she slid her cold hand into his. His eyes fluttered at the simple touch.

Cielle, Elaila, and Amerie stood in different corners of the room, their eyes twinkling at the sight of her hand in his. Oryn appeared in the doorway. He clasped his hands behind his back, the perfect picture of calmness, but Koen could see the concern swimming inside the bright emerald green eyes. "There is a man here for you, Aisling. He wouldn't tell us his name. But he swears on his life he knows you, and you know him. He's begging to see you."

She said nothing, but Koen saw her delicate jaw tense. Felt her tremor strengthen. Despite her terror, she gave a curt nod. Oryn disappeared behind the door.

Aisling turned to Koen with a heartbreaking fear in her eyes he knew he never wanted to see again. The girls echoed it, each pulling out a blade in preparation and stepping closer to form a barrier around Aisling. She kept her eyes trained on him as footsteps sounded in the hall, her hand flinching in his with every step.

Kaida came in first. Her mouth was set in a tight line, her bright hair billowing over her shoulders, a stark contrast to her deep brown leathers. Her hand remained on the hilt of the sword at her side. Oryn brought the man in.

He was younger than Koen pictured. Tall and lanky. His dark skin seemed to glow in the weak light coming in through the windows. His hair hung in a shag to his shoulders. When his bright hazel eyes landed on Aisling, they widened.

Koen hated him. He clenched his jaw and turned to Aisling. She stared into his eyes for another heartbeat before taking a deep breath and turning toward the unnamed man.

Koen waited for her hand to squeeze. Waited for any sign of her discomfort, his hand itching for an excuse to rip out his dagger.

But she pulled her hand from his and covered her mouth with a sharp inhale.

Aisling took a single step forward and collapsed to the floor with her eyes rolled back.

TWENTY-ONE

AISLING

Aisling couldn't see anything, but she could hear the commotion. One of the girls let out a yelp. Feet scuffled on the floor. Metal scraped against stone.

A high, shrill ring echoed in the back of her head.

"Get him out of here," Koen growled. He checked her pulse before leaning closer and whispering in her ear, "He's gone. You're okay. You're safe." Her blood warmed with his words. "Someone calm Morana down," he muttered. "Neera is freaking out."

Footsteps raced out of the room.

The ringing subsided. Aisling's eyes fluttered open after a minute. Koen knelt over her. His thumb stroked her cheek in soft reassuring swipes. Elaila hovered over him with a bright blue rage in her eyes. Aisling swallowed against the sudden dryness in her throat. "This is real, right? I'm here in this world?"

Koen's brow furrowed. "Yes. This is real. You're here with us."

Her mind whirred. There was no explanation for what she had seen.

"Do you know him?" Elaila asked with a cup of water for Aisling in one hand and her blade in the other.

Aisling couldn't respond. Words failed her. She tried to sit up but grimaced at the sharp pain in her side. Koen lifted her to standing and wrapped a hand around her waist for stability. She gulped the water. "I need to see him," she finally breathed.

"Absolutely not," Elaila responded fiercely.

Aisling looked up at Koen. "Please. I need to—I have to see him." His eyes darted between hers, the strong line of his jaw feathering. Whatever he saw in her stare was enough to convince him. He gently urged her forward. Elaila stood slack-jawed in the common room as they left.

Her bones felt like jelly. Her legs barely held her up. She was oddly grateful for the stupid brace that kept her breathing from getting too deep. Koen led her around the corner from the common room and through a heavy door hidden in the stone walls. "We never use these," he admitted.

Aisling shuddered at the damp, dark stairwell before her. A single torch hung on the wall.

Everything inside of her screamed against the darkness.

"You're home," Koen murmured in her ear.

A small part of her thawed. She set her jaw and moved forward against her mind's screams. Slowly, they descended the uneven stairs together, his hand a steadying presence against the dampened stone around them. He led her down a narrow hallway when they reached the bottom. The air grew colder. Plinks of water hit the stone.

Aisling worked to keep her breathing steady.

This was not the cave. She was not with the Cruento. She was home with the Ferox. Morana was just upstairs. Koen was with her. Favilla was out.

Bleak, empty cells covered in layers of moss and other fuzzy green things appeared on both sides of the hall. She didn't look inside, didn't dare look anywhere but right in front of her. They turned a corner. Oryn stood in front of a door, his eyes widening at the sight of her. "Aisling?"

"I need to see him."

Oryn shot a troubled look at Koen. Silence hung heavy between the three of them.

"He won't hurt me." She rested her hand on Koen's at her waist and glanced up at him, begging him to listen. "Trust me."

Koen's fingers flexed at her side. He nodded at Oryn, who unsheathed his long sword before unlocking the stone door behind him.

Every click and creak sent shards of fear down her spine. Memories threatened to come to the forefront of her mind. She banished them.

It was dark inside save for a single candle. A familiar sense of dread slithered in her veins. She swallowed against the constriction in her throat and stepped forward. Koen moved with her. Aisling stopped him with a glance. "He won't hurt me."

Koen blinked in understanding. His hand reluctantly fell from her waist.

Aisling walked alone into another stone tomb, swallowing her fear and confusion.

He stood in the corner, his hands bound lightly in front of him. His simple linen clothes were covered in dirt. His eyes were brighter than she remembered. His hair longer and shaggier.

It was still *him*, though.

"Troy?"

He took a single step forward from the shadows before his knees crashed to the stone floor. His heart-wrenching sob hit her ears a second later. She found herself on her knees before him and pulled his hands from his face.

Aisling couldn't cry. What she was seeing was impossible. "How?" she breathed, assessing every inch of the friend she had left behind.

Troy's hazel eyes devoured her, narrowing at the brace on her torso and turning molten with the scar on her neck. "Ash," he whispered, "what happened?"

Her heart stuttered at her old nickname. "How are you here?"

He wiped the tears from his cheeks and steadied himself. "I don't know. You left. I started dreaming."

"Permanently?"

He nodded and took her hand in both of his. "I couldn't... I couldn't be there without you. I heard about you in my dreams. Whispers about you and Morana. I knew I couldn't leave."

Her eyes fluttered shut. This was impossible. There was no way...

"Whose drink did I spit in?" she asked, needing confirmation it was really him.

His brows pinched. "What?"

"Whose drink did I spit in when I quit?"

"Red Lips."

"What does Morana's name mean?"

"Death."

"What does mine mean?"

His throat bobbed. "Dream."

"What did I take to stop dreaming?"

He paused, pinching his face in thought. "Valerian root."

Aisling's heart nearly exploded. Her friend was here. Her friend from her other life had somehow followed her through worlds. Had cared enough about her to chase her in his dreams.

A true soulmate.

She lifted her palm to cup his cheek. "Did you fire Vivienne?"

Troy's eyes widened before he tilted his head back and laughed, bright and out of place against the heavy stone around them. She felt it against her skin, a tiny flicker of her life before, and couldn't help but smile. "The day after you left."

She threw her arms around him, ignoring the pains and aches of her body. He buried his face in her hair. She breathed him in, the friend she thought she had lost.

Aisling didn't know how long they held each other, but it wasn't nearly long enough.

Troy angled himself deeper into her hair, his mouth right beside her ear. "Who's the blonde?"

She laughed as they pulled out of the hug and ran her knuckles down his stubble-covered cheeks in awestruck disbelief. Her attempts to stand were feeble. Koen's footsteps sounded behind her, but Troy gently lifted her, his eyes hardening as he took in the fading bruises. "What happened to you?" He glanced over her shoulder at Koen and Oryn. "Did they..."

"No," she shook her head. "I have a lot to tell you, though. A lot," she emphasized with a whisper. She looped her arm in his, unable to stop a smile from taking over her face, and turned to the door where the two men stood in quiet, tense confusion. She pointed to Oryn, grateful he had sheathed his sword. "Troy, this is Oryn."

Troy didn't blush as Oryn's gaze lingered.

"And this," she jerked her chin to a steel-faced Koen, "is Koen." His dark eyes assessed Troy with a different sharpness than Oryn. Every inch of him was on edge as if assessing a predator. She rolled her eyes. "Troy is from my other life."

Both men went preternaturally still. Deafening silence encompassed them.

"He doesn't belong down here," she said with as much authority as she could.

Oryn cleared his throat with a subtle shake of his head as he turned his gaze from Troy to Aisling. "That's not for you to decide, Aisling."

She balked. "He—"

"Too much has happened."

"He's not from here!" she shouted against the stone, her smile wiped from existence. "He has no idea what's going on."

"That may be so," Oryn replied with infuriating gentleness, "but he said he's been here for a few weeks now. Anything can happen in that amount of time."

A tendril of flame licked up her spine and shot through her soul. She angled her chin up, allowing the candlelight to illuminate the scar on her neck. "I know exactly what can happen in that amount of time, Oryn."

Koen's jaw clenched. Oryn remained unbothered. "Then you of all people can understand why we're taking precautions. I'm sure he's fine, Aisling, but that's not up to us to decide. He will meet with Aedan tomorrow. The King refuses to take any chances."

"This—he isn't a chance!" she yelled, a flurry of panic running through her. "He isn't a threat to me or anyone else here. He can barely lift a full bag of trash!"

"Hey!" Troy whispered, glaring down at her. He looked back at Oryn. "That's not true."

"I'm trying to help you, you moron," she bit out. "Can't Aedan take my word for it? Bring me to him and I'll explain everything!"

Oryn shook his head. "He's not here. He's coming back tomorrow morning. It's just one night."

"I'll be fine," Troy mumbled, squeezing her hand on his bicep.

She ripped out of his grasp. There was no way she would leave someone she loved in damp darkness to sink in stone. She would not let him sit in this cold, revolting space for another minute. He did not deserve it.

No one ever deserved to be treated like that.

Her breathing quickened.

She rested her hands on top of her head, wincing at the sharp pain in her side.

The darkness laughed at her in a confident taunt. The walls pressed in until her lungs refused to open.

A phantom door opened. Chains rattled along the floor. Footsteps inched closer.

She tasted her blood on her lips. Felt her bones rattling from an invisible impact.

She pulled at the shimmering bond inside, breathless for an anchor as the room began to tilt. As her heart became a rattled beast inside a cage too small.

Her hands ripped at her brace.

She needed to breathe.

She was drowning in the darkness. Drowning in her own lungs.

Koen's scent wrapped around her as he lifted her into his arms. She reflexively buried her face in his neck and begged her lungs to inhale.

He said something too muddled for her foggy mind to understand before he was running. They blasted up the stairs and through a door. Morana was under them a heartbeat later.

The wind met her with its comforting embrace. It forced itself into her lungs, pushing out the panic with every shallow exhale. In a single powerful gust, her fear and dread blew away in the wind. She gasped as her traitorous body finally gave in and sank into Koen's touch, exhaustion heavy in her limbs.

"Troy?"

Koen angled his mouth to her ear. "He won't be there tonight. He'll spend the night in the Keep under lock and guard. There will be windows and light."

She could have cried in relief. Morana stroked the bond with whatever comfort she could. Aisling tightened her grip around Koen's neck. "Thank you."

He said nothing as they rode the wind with the sun and sky as their only companions.

TWENTY-TWO

AISLING

"You can't be serious," Cielle murmured from across the table. "He's from your other life?" Aisling nodded. Cielle leaned back in her chair and crossed her arms over her chest. "How did he–"

"He is cute!" Amerie sang as she dropped her plate beside Aisling's. "Don't tell me you two had a thing. I can't tolerate you taking all the cute ones."

Aisling laughed. "No. It was never like that. Trust me." She tried to keep the smile off her face. "And he isn't into me like that. He wouldn't be into any of us like that." She gestured to the three of them at the table.

Cielle's eyes widened in understanding. Amerie's head dropped and hung heavy between her shoulders. "You're telling me that another beautiful man has come into my life and wants nothing of what I have to offer?"

"That's exactly what I'm telling you."

Amerie went quiet. "We need to start keeping wine here."

Aisling squeezed her hand and looked at Cielle. "Tell me about the attack." So much had happened since then. She listened in horror as Cielle and Amerie described the sickly sweet scent of Funestum and the damage it caused. Aisling knew the bombs were a direct taunt at her. She had taken the Cruento's only ability to make beasts, and now they retaliated by brutal shows of power, killing entire towns of innocent people.

"There were only seven survivors," Cielle finished with a grim shade to her face. "They're in the Keep now."

Aisling pushed her plate away, her sudden nausea overwhelming. Elaila appeared from behind and pulled the plate back in front of her. "You won't heal if you don't eat."

Did she need to heal anymore? If the Cruento were attacking with gas bombs, no one could fight them. They made themselves untouchable and unpredictable on top of being invisible.

"Just focus on now," Elaila instructed from Cielle's side. "Think about eating and getting a good night's sleep before Aedan comes back tomorrow."

"Where did he go?"

"He got the report from the attack and insisted he make the trip to see the damage."

"Most likely why Kaida's pissed," Amerie frowned.

Aisling picked up her fork and forced herself to chew and swallow. "What will Aedan ask Troy?"

The girls shrugged. "We've never seen an interview. It isn't physical though from what Kaida and Oryn have described," Cielle reassured her. "They won't hurt him. And if he's from another world like you say he is, he truly won't know anything."

"I have a feeling it will be very quick," Amerie said. "Aedan has too much on his plate to worry about much else."

"How is he?" Aisling asked.

"Great. Much better than he was." Cielle grimaced. "It was a rough few days when he got back here."

Aisling vividly remembered the color of his blood pooling on the castle grounds. She shook her head subtly, but enough for Elaila to lift a dark brow in concern. "Kaida said she finally—"

"Yes! Finally!" Amerie nearly shouted. "Just wait until you see how cute they are now. They're so in love it's disgusting."

"It is really cute," Elaila admitted with a smile. "It's nice to see her finally happy."

"At least one of us is," Amerie moaned.

Aisling awoke the next morning to the first rays of dawn in the sky above and Morana's scales at her back. Favilla snored loudly at her feet with her stomach again turned to the sky as if she was tanning.

Morana lifted her head and glanced at Aisling. The bond warmed. "Morning," Aisling cooed. She stretched, barely cringing at the pain in her side, and glanced down in confusion at the blanket covering her. "I didn't bring this with me last night, did I?"

Morana blinked twice. *No.*

She bit back a smile. Morana let out a puff of hot air and rolled her eyes as she rested her head on the ground. Gingerly, Aisling lifted herself to standing. It was getting easier. She could almost twist now. She bent slightly and kissed Morana's head before blowing a kiss at a sleeping Favilla and trekking back down to her room.

She bathed in the first light of morning and marveled at her healing body. The bruises were fading quickly. A hint of weight had been put back on. She no longer needed the wound wraps around her hands and arms. Her broken finger was a little wonky, but it added character. She was just happy she could still use it after losing her pinky.

Aisling carefully exited the bath and wrapped herself in her white robe. She sat on a stool and brushed out her long hair. Her eyes drifted down to her neck where the scar stared at her.

Not a branding, not a collar, Elaila and Koen had said. She belonged to no one. This was a necklace of her strength, her power. Nothing more, nothing less.

She swallowed as Koen's words from the day before came flooding back. He had shocked her with his apology and declaration. Had rendered her speechless at the rawness in his voice, the brutal honesty in his eyes.

Aisling knew they had fallen off the edge. Knew that line they teetered on had disappeared the moment she offered him the clean slate all those weeks ago.

And she was ready for it. She was free-falling into him and savoring every second of the drop. If Amerie hadn't shown up at the cliffs, she would have confessed everything without hesitation. He deserved to know how she felt, too.

She was tired of pretending they weren't together. Sick of the palpable tension between them. Tired of not knowing what he tasted like, what he felt like.

With a groan of impatience and frustration, Aisling opened her drawers and pulled out her leathers. She would wear them today. The linen pants, while comfortable, weren't her. She was a rider of the Ferox. She would be dressed as one.

She put the pants on first and nearly fell before sliding them up her legs. Her boots went on next, their plush warmth enough to coax a smile from her face. The tee, normally tight against her skin, billowed slightly over her tender stomach. She ditched the ugly brace for a leather corset and pulled the strings as tight as they could go.

"Come in," she answered to the knock on her door. Oryn's head popped in, his hair shining brilliantly against the sun. She smiled despite their spat the day before. "Good morning."

"Good morning," he said. "Ready?"

"I think so."

"Wonderful. Koen asked me to escort you to the Keep."

"I don't need an escort," she grabbed one of her lighter jackets.

Oryn shrugged. "Maybe not. But I will never pass up an opportunity to talk with you."

She smiled up at him, his calming presence almost intoxicating. "You're a charmer, Oryn. I'm sorry for yelling at you yesterday."

"You had every right to be upset, Aisling. I did not take it personally." He took her hand and wrapped it around his deceptively large bicep.

They walked from the Pit into the meadow separating them from the Keep. "I'm nervous," she admitted after a minute of pleasant silence, keeping her eyes locked on the uneven ground before her.

"For what?"

"For Troy."

"Ah. Why?"

"He came here for me. What if he answers a question wrong? I don't know how to save him." Oryn nodded silently. "And then what? He made the change for nothing? How is that fair?"

The questions kept her up most of the night. The guards wouldn't allow her to see Troy inside the Keep after dinner when she snuck out, and she was nearly inconsolable for hours afterward. Morana and Favilla's presence in the Pit kept her from spiraling. Sleep eventually found her, but it wasn't restful.

"You cannot save everyone, Aisling."

"I know, but—"

"He made the choice to switch of his own volition. He chose to find you. It is not fair to take on the future of his soul while also dealing with yours."

She sighed in defeat. "How do you always know what to say?"

Oryn laughed, a warm, glittering sound. "I don't. Ask Kaida."

"Will I be as wise as you one day?"

He looked down at her with nothing but adoration. "Even more so, dear girl." He opened the door to the Keep and guided her to the throne room. Cielle stared into the massive fireplace. Amerie paced along the back wall, her normally bright eyes dark and serious. Elaila sat at the large table with her hands politely clasped in her lap. All three of them were dressed in full leathers with daggers and swords gleaming at their sides.

"Those aren't necessary," Aisling said through a tight throat.

"Aedan's orders," Oryn replied gently. "With any interview, this is the process."

The girls grimaced at her in apology. She brushed it off. "Where is Koen?"

"With Troy."

She cringed. If Koen touched one hair on Troy's head...

Kaida walked in, her long hair in a slew of delicate braids over her shoulder. "He's coming."

The Ferox stood behind their chairs, hands clasped behind their backs. Aisling held her breath as Aedan walked through the door.

He looked perfect. His hair was longer. He was the tiniest bit thinner, but he looked strong. His skin was no longer leeched of color. There was no hobble to his gait or sign of pain. The brightness in his eyes was overwhelming.

He was healed. He was safe. Aisling bit back the tears as he sat in his chair, face solemn, eyes looking at nothing but the empty space at the end of the table. Kaida sat first. The rest of them followed. Anwir walked in next, bowing his head of dark hair with his eyes planted on the ground before he took his place behind Aedan.

Footsteps sounded from outside. Aisling's heart hammered in her chest as Koen appeared first, his hardened gaze finding her immediately. His throat bobbed before he moved his attention to Aedan. Troy walked in at Koen's side—his eyes wide as he took in the scene before him. His dirty clothes were gone, replaced by a simple linen set. Koen placed him at the end of the table and stood inches behind him. His hand rested on the hilt of his sword.

Aisling forced herself to remain stoic.

"Your name," Aedan demanded after a minute of painful silence.

Troy swallowed. "Troy."

"How old are you?"

"Twenty-two."

"Where are you from, Troy?"

"I-I'm not from this world," he whispered, the fear in his voice sending shards of ice down Aisling's spine. "I'm not from anywhere."

"How did you come here?"

"I dreamed."

Aedan paused. "Tell me why your dream brought you here."

"I'm here for Aisling." The hazy tension in the room solidified. Troy noted it. "Aisling left my world and I... I can't live without her. She's the love of my life." His eyes glimmered with unshed tears. "I had to follow her."

Aisling's eyes fluttered before she shut them tightly, willing her tears not to fall. Aedan said nothing. Troy filled the silence and spoke quickly, a shrill panic in every word directed at her.

"I told you I would follow you anywhere, Ash. That I'd be there to reflect your brightness." His voice cracked. So did her heart. "I wasn't lying. I couldn't live without you. Remember when we were at the park? When we said if we left the world together it wouldn't be a bad thing? If we never came back to our shitty lives it would be fine as long as we had each other?"

She was crying, unable to stop her shoulders from shaking. Troy stuck his hand in his pocket. Koen was there before she could blink, his blade glimmering in the light beside Troy's throat. Aisling gasped hard enough for her side to spasm. Koen's jaw feathered at the sound of her pain, but the blade remained out.

"I have your note," Troy whispered. He looked at the King, ignoring the knife at his neck. "Aisling wrote me a note in her other life before she left permanently and came here. I kept it. Somehow, I was able to bring it with me."

Aisling looked at Aedan in quiet desperation, unashamed of the tears falling down her face. The King didn't look at her, but he held out his hand in unspoken demand. Slowly, with a side glance at Koen, Troy reached into his pocket and pulled out the folded letter. Koen handed it to Elaila who passed it to Aedan.

Aisling held her breath as Aedan opened the note and began reading. No one moved. Even the fire went quiet. Finally, Aedan folded the letter and placed it on the table before him. Anwir whispered in his ear, his dark eyes glancing apologetically at Aisling before returning his attention to the King. Aedan shook his head and stared at Troy. The King's bright eyes marked every inch of him, every shaky breath.

He slid his gaze to Aisling after a minute of tense silence. "You didn't mention me." Something glimmered in the King's gaze, his hardened exterior melting with every second that passed. "Tell me, Aisling. Why won't Troy be able to talk to Koen?"

She stared in disbelief at the King, his handsome face now glittering with a smirk. Her heart relaxed. The rest of the Ferox looked at her in confusion.

Aisling smiled, full and bright despite her wet cheeks, and turned to Koen. "Troy is incapable of speaking to hot men."

Surprise lined Koen's eyes before they darkened, his lips curling into a smile that sent her heart racing. Troy's mouth fell open. A deep blush tinted his cheeks.

"Oh, shit," Amerie whispered with a laugh.

The tension dissolved. Aedan's answering smile could blind. "Troy, you must forgive me. Our world is in chaos, and we cannot afford to misjudge anyone. You are not a prisoner by any means." He nodded at Koen. The straps around Troy's wrists disappeared. "You are welcome in our world."

Troy didn't move. Aisling stood from her chair with surprising grace and threw her arms around him. She held her friend while he trembled and pulled back after a few unsteady breaths to wipe a tear from his cheek.

"Any friend of Aisling's is a friend of mine," Aedan said brightly. "You are part of the Keep now, of course, and there are privileges you will receive, but everyone here has a job. We do not allow idle bodies in our ranks."

Troy glanced at Aisling in silent panic. She regarded him, pausing only for a second before coming to a decision. "Medical. Troy would like to train with the medical team." She shrugged and whispered, "I always thought you would be good at it, remember?"

Troy shook his head in disbelief, a hint of awe in his bright hazel stare.

Aisling cupped his cheek and stroked the smooth skin with the pad of her thumb, still in shock at his presence. She took a heavy inhale and turned her attention back to the table. The Ferox smiled back at her. She looked at Aedan. "Thank you."

Kaida's eyes softened. Aedan's fluttered. He leaned forward, angling his head. "You're thanking me? You, Aisling, are thanking me?"

She glanced at Kaida, but the beautiful silver eyes gave nothing away. Aisling nodded in confused silence at the King.

Aedan shook his head and ran his hands through his sandy hair. When he lifted his eyes, she swallowed a gasp at the emotion welling inside. "You saved my life, Aisling," he whispered. "You kept me from dying. Your voice anchored me here when the darkness wanted to take me." He slowly stood and walked around the table. Koen pinched Troy's shirt and gently urged him back as Aedan stood before Aisling.

"You gave me the gift of life. You kept Kairossen from crumbling beneath my feet." He took her hands in his. "You sacrificed your life for mine and almost lost it in return."

Aisling stared at him wide-eyed.

"Because of you," Aedan continued softly, "the Cruento have lost their ability to take the skies and the innocent. Because of you, the Ferox is whole again. Because of you," he whispered, "my life is full of love and hope."

A tear escaped down her cheek. She heard sniffling somewhere in the room but didn't dare take her eyes off her King's.

"I will never be able to properly thank you for what you've given me, Aisling. What you've given Kairossen and all those who fight with us. I'm afraid we owe you a debt that will live forever." He placed a soft kiss on her hand. "But I would like to try, anyway." Gently, he lowered her hands to her side. He blinked rapidly against the growing glossiness in his eyes and turned to the table. "I've decided. There will be a ball in Aisling's honor."

Aisling's jaw dropped. Amerie squealed her happiness. "No," Aisling whispered, grabbing Aedan's hand. "No, please. That's too much. It's so unnecessary."

"Nonsense." He wrapped his arm around her shoulder and brought her to his side. He lifted his brow at the table. "Does she not deserve it?"

"She does," Kaida replied with a soft smile. The rest of the Ferox agreed.

Aedan glanced back at Troy. "Troy. You must fill me in on your world. Aisling gave me a glimpse before. If you'll allow it, I'd like to pick your mind as well." Troy stared dumbfounded but nodded once. "Wonderful," Aedan muttered to himself. "Wonderful."

Anwir cleared his throat from the corner. His soft voice lilted in the air. "Sir?"

"Oh yes, right. Thank you, Anwir." Aedan sighed and walked back to his seat. "This Cruento business. We should discuss it." He whispered to Anwir. His advisor's brows knitted before he disappeared through the door with a curt bow a second later.

Koen shut the door gently enough to keep Aisling from flinching. She pulled Troy to sit beside her and refused to let his hand leave hers. Koen sat across from her, his gaze darting between her and Troy. She lifted a brow in challenge. He bit his cheek and turned his attention to Aedan.

"Someone under my employ is working with the enemy. Anwir and I are investigating, but it's slow work. Every member of the Keep and Pit will be interrogated, save the people in this room. The supply of Funestum was raided during the attack at Impellor. Only a select few know about it, but there's no telling who they may have told. Out of fifty containers, we only have seven left." He tightened his jaw, looking more like a King than a friend. "The attack at Iuxta only used eight bombs. That leaves well over thirty still in their possession."

A general shudder of unease ran through the table. Aedan made sure to look at every single member of the Ferox. "Under no circumstances are you to fly into the gas. If you or the dragons scent it, do not go in. By the time you arrive, the damage will be done. Come back here, and my soldiers will go in when the air clears. Am I understood?"

They nodded solemnly.

"How do we fight this?" Cielle asked, voicing the same concern Aisling had. "We can't fight bombs."

Kaida slipped her hand into Aedan's. "They didn't get rid of all their beasts. Aisling and Favilla told us they still have some of Favilla's eggs. We will fight with what we can, when we can, and adapt as needed like always."

"Keep training. Keep yourselves battle-ready. We don't know what their next move will be, but we need to be prepared." Aedan sat back with his hand still wrapped around Kaida's. "And practice your dancing. I refuse to employ bad dancers."

TWENTY-THREE

AISLING

"Can I see the note?" Amerie asked Troy with a devious smile an hour later.

"Absolutely not," Aisling said from his side.

"What did you say about me?"

"I said you're nosy," Aisling smiled. "And that you're stunning, et cetera."

Amerie sat back against the couch and smirked. "Can you make lattes, too?"

Troy scoffed. "A latte? Out of everything you can do, that's what you've been making them?"

"Is there something better than a latte?" Amerie prodded.

Cielle rolled her eyes from the couch beside Amerie in the common room. "How were you both plane steppers?"

Aisling shrugged. "I have no idea."

"I didn't start dreaming until she... left," Troy said, hesitating on the word. Aisling rested her head against his shoulder in comfort.

"I wonder..." Cielle shook her head. "Do you think the gift transferred to him once you officially left your other body?"

A gift. That's exactly what it had been, and Aisling never recognized it.

She considered it. "I don't know how it works. Kaida said the one book she found with any information about it was destroyed a long time ago. She thought I came here because my soul needed it. That's how I could walk worlds. And Morana needed me, too. Maybe it was the same for him? Maybe Troy's soul needed—"

"Yours," Troy whispered.

Aisling nodded once, her voice soft. "And I needed yours."

The common room went silent for a heartbeat. Aisling blinked against the emotion on Troy's face. Koen's brow seemed permanently furrowed as he watched them from across the room.

"Did your other body just die, then?" Amerie asked.

"Amerie!" Elaila yelped.

"Yes," Troy answered baldly, his body tensing. Aisling had wondered the same thing but accepted she would never know the answer.

She glanced up at her friend while the girls scolded Amerie. "Would you like to go on a walk?" He nodded once with a flash of gratitude. She braced herself on the arm of the couch and stood. Koen was beside her in the next breath to offer a hand for balance. She took it strictly for the comfort of his touch, her body stronger with every hour that passed and every meal she ate.

"Are you going to be okay to walk that much?" he whispered in her ear as he led her from the common room.

"I thought you said I could start training?"

He cringed. "I did say that, didn't I?"

And much more, she wanted to mention, but she needed to talk to Troy before she tackled all of that. "Can we start today?"

He glanced out the window at the early afternoon sun. "Go on a walk first. See how it feels, and we can go from there."

"Can I at least fly?"

"That's not up to me," he answered, his thumb rubbing small circles on the top of her hand. "But I'll tell Declan to have Morana's saddle ready."

Her chest warmed, accidentally flooding the bond. A puff of shadow answered with Morana's laugh. Troy came up beside her, his eyes darting between her and Koen. "Ready?"

Koen let go of her hand. She nodded and ignored the ache of his missing touch. "Don't let her go too far," Koen told him, his eyes no longer warm and inviting. "If she shows any signs of—"

"Okay," Aisling said, pressing her hand against Koen's chest and pushing him a step back. "He's going to be studying with medical, Koen. I think he can handle a tired girl."

"You sound insane!" Cielle yelled at him from the common room. Aisling bit back a smirk as she looped her arm in Troy's, but she winked at Koen over her shoulder before leading her friend out the door and into the open air. She smiled as it enveloped her in the scent of sea and freedom. A scent she would never take for granted again. They walked slowly in the direction of the cliffs, careful to avoid any problematic rocks.

"So—" she started.

"I'm so sorry," Troy whispered, his voice breaking. "I should have been there for you. I should have realized how much you were going through. I was so selfish."

Aisling stopped. "Troy..."

"No," he pulled out of her grip and took a few steps ahead. "Do not forgive me, Ash. I treated you horribly. You were right in your note. I should have given you the same grace these people did. I was so selfish and hot headed and just... I was not there for you at all." He turned to her, his hazel eyes wild with grief. "I was the one to call the police. I pounded on your door as soon as we closed that day, but you didn't answer. I knew something wasn't right. The cops came, and that was it. They handed me the letter and took you. No one even tried to figure out how you died no matter how much I begged."

He was crying. She stood still and watched her friend relive the trauma of her choice. "I don't know what happened to your body," he whispered. "I don't know where they took you. No one knew who I was even talking about when I called the morgues to ask about burying you the next day. It was like you hadn't even been alive. And I was livid because you deserved more than that."

A flood of tears cascaded down Troy's cheeks. "I was so angry. I fired Vivienne the next day as soon as she walked in. Ryan flipped out and sent me home early. That was the first night I dreamed. I wasn't on the island. I was in a forest somewhere. And I felt it, just like you described. It was peaceful, and I knew you were here."

He wiped his nose with his sleeve and rested his hands on his hips, his pained gaze locked on the sea. "When I woke up, I knew what I had to do. I didn't go into work. I cleaned my apartment and set up piles like you did. I left everything to Eva and fell asleep that night knowing I would never wake up." He pulled out her note. "You anchored me. This stupid letter kept me here. I walked for weeks trying to find you."

He glanced at the Pit and the Keep behind it. "You were right. I was wrong for how I treated you. You deserve a better friend than me, and now that I see who you were talking about, I know you have."

Aisling blinked rapidly through her own tears. "What?"

"I won't stay here, Ash," he said incredulously. "I just wanted to make sure you were here, alive somewhere. I wanted to make sure you were happy. Now I know you are. I can leave with relief knowing you're in far better hands than you ever had been with me."

"You're going to train with medical," she said slowly. "You aren't leaving."

"I am."

"No. You aren't," she said forcefully. "You're not going to run from this life, Troy. I watched you run from the first one. You aren't meant to be hidden."

"I can't look at you without hating myself," he said, refusing to meet her eyes. "I can't look at you without remembering how badly I treated you at the end."

"I don't care—"

"I do!" he shouted. She tensed in surprise. "I care, Aisling!" He stepped toward her, the wind rustling through his dark hair, now hanging just above his shoulders. "I can't ruin this life for you, too."

"You saved me," Aisling hissed. She straightened her spine and dug her heels into the ground. "In the other life, I only stuck around for you. Don't try to change the narrative because you feel guilty." She took a step closer, her familiar anger with him both comforting and infuriating. "I fucked up, too. I handled the whole thing horribly. But you still chose me. And I choose you. You will stay in my life because you are my soulmate, Troy. I wasn't lying in the letter. I love you. I adore you," she rasped.

"You deserve more," he whispered.

"I know."

He flinched like she had hit him.

She smiled broadly as the ground shook under their feet. As her dragon answered her anger and lowered from the clouds. Morana landed behind Troy, amethyst eyes narrowed on his back.

Troy's face paled. He turned around slowly before falling on the ground and sliding backward toward Aisling as he met Morana's eyes, his mouth open in a silent scream.

"I have more," Aisling said calmly, staring down at his frightened face. "I have everything I could ever want or need. And still, I want you here." She cocked her head. "You are not leaving me, Troy. Morana will not allow it."

Morana purred in answer. Her wings splayed to their full length, reflecting the sun's brilliance on her iridescent leather skin. Aisling tickled the bond in thanks.

Troy couldn't leave her, not now that she had him back. Her heart could not live through the heartbreak and guilt again. "I can't live without you," she whispered through a tight throat. "Our souls need each other. I need you here, Troy."

The resolve in his face crumbled. He glanced up at Morana. "Is she going to eat me?"

Koen watched Aisling guide Troy through the fields. Her steps were guarded but strong, her back straight and proud as she again turned to gaze up at Troy.

How many times had she looked at him like that now? At least a hundred, if not more. And the way Troy looked at her...

She had only mentioned Troy once before her capture, and even that was just his name before they were interrupted by the bells of battle.

If she was in love with someone from her other life, would she have made the switch?

Koen shook his head. She would have said something.

Troy glanced down at her again. Even from the distance and through the sea-salt covered window, Koen saw nothing but utter devotion in his eyes.

They would make a beautiful couple, he had to admit. Troy was handsome, albeit a bit too lean and gangly. With his dark skin and bright eyes, he would be a catch for any woman.

A roll of hot fury slithered down Koen's spine. The acidic taste of jealousy coated his tongue.

"Relax," Elaila murmured, appearing beside him at the window. "I can see every thought of yours through your shoulders. You're going to get a cramp."

Koen didn't take his eyes off Aisling, but he lifted a brow. "I don't know what you're talking about."

"Right." She crossed her arms over her chest and smiled. "They're cute, aren't they?"

His jaw feathered. "Very."

"They'd make a very handsome couple. Imagine how gorgeous their children would be?" She tutted. "Do you think they'd have her eyes or his?"

Koen shut his eyes and took a steadying breath. "Is there something you needed? Or are you just here –"

"I'm loving this, actually," Elaila giggled, bright enough to force Koen's attention on her. Her twinkling laugh was usually only reserved for the girls and the nonsense they frequently got into. Her pale cheeks flushed with delight. Koen couldn't stop the smile from lifting his lips.

"You're the worst, you know that?"

"We both know you save that title for Amerie."

He huffed a laugh and turned his attention back to the window. Aisling was growing smaller against the beauty around her, but he couldn't look away.

"You don't need to worry about him."

"What do you mean?"

"He isn't a threat to you. At least, not in the way you're thinking."

"You don't know what I'm thinking."

She rolled her eyes. "Anyone living in Kairossen knows what you're thinking, Koen."

Troy stepped away from Aisling. His wiry arms moved in time with the words coming from his mouth. Koen and Elaila watched silently as he spoke to Aisling, his pain and sadness strong enough that it almost wafted in the air.

Koen held his breath when Troy raised his voice and Aisling startled. His muscles tensed to run, but Elaila shook her head from beside him. "They have to do this. Let them have it out."

Troy yelled. Aisling countered, her spine straightened and chin lifted as she fought back. She took a single step forward.

Elaila smiled broadly at the sight of Morana lowering from the clouds behind Troy. The dragon moved in a way Koen was far too familiar with. Every ounce of her weight landed behind Troy with a purposeful slam. His thin frame started with the shock.

Elaila giggled as Troy fell to the ground and crawled backwards toward Aisling.

They both stared in awe at Aisling standing over her friend. She was bruised and nearly broken, but grace and strength pulsated from her body in undulating waves.

Elaila turned to Koen, the playfulness from before replaced by concern. "She trusts you, Koen."

His jaw tightened. He nodded once. Aisling trusted him far more than he would ever deserve.

"And you trust her."

"Yes."

Elaila stared up at him, her large blue eyes seeing everything he wasn't saying. After a minute of silence, she nodded to herself. "I think it's an interesting thing when a soul finds a home in someone else. Even more interesting when two souls find a home in each other." She cocked her head and smiled at the sight of Troy and Aisling in front of Morana. "He is her soulmate, yes. But he is not her home."

Koen's throat clenched painfully.

Elaila rested her narrow hand on his forearm and smiled. "You deserve her, Koen. Remember that when you try to convince yourself otherwise."

Aisling explained the Keep and the Pit. She told Troy about each member of the Ferox in extreme detail and described each dragon as best she could.

Troy and Morana got along well after the initial rocky minutes. The dragon hummed down the bond as Troy wordlessly, reverently, stroked her scales. Morana flew back to the Pit once Aisling's anger down the bond had dissipated, and she knew Aisling was safe. Troy stared after her in wonder.

"How did you fight the void?"

His brows pinched. "What void?"

"The void between worlds. The big, black, terrifying—"

"I didn't have to fight anything. I just..." he frowned and shrugged. "I just knew what I wanted. I knew I needed you. I never saw a void."

"That's really annoying," she muttered. "You're telling me if I had just made a decision earlier, I wouldn't have had to fight to get here?"

He arched a brow. "If you think I have any answers for this crazy thing we did, you think too much of me. I followed my heart, Ash. That's all." Troy leaned back on his hands. "Now. Tell me what happened to you. Spare no detail."

Aisling told him of the chaos of the last few weeks and the trauma she'd gone through. He didn't ask questions except to see if she was okay. She told him she didn't know how to answer that just yet. He traced the scar across her neck. "Pretty badass."

She huffed a laugh and stared into the late afternoon sky. "That's what they keep saying."

"You should believe them."

"I'm also missing a finger." She wiggled the remaining fingers of her right hand.

"So you're not a ten anymore. Just another nine like the rest of us." He smirked. "You were right. Koen is hot."

She laughed hard enough for her ribs to complain. "I know. What do you think about Oryn?"

It was Troy's turn to laugh. "I will never be able to speak to that man, Ash."

"Try anyway. He's wonderful."

"You're making it worse."

A strong gust passed over them, sinking a chill in her bones. Troy noted it and stood. "Come on. Koen will kill me. And I mean that literally."

Together, they walked back to the Pit. Back to her home. To his new home.

Aisling swallowed against the emotion in her throat. Just weeks ago, she was convinced she would be dead in the darkness, swallowed by her despair. But here she was, surrounded by nothing but love and support and walking beside her friend from another world.

They walked into the common room where everyone but Koen had gathered. Elaila smiled in greeting. "How was your walk?"

"Do you feel okay?" Cielle asked.

"Let her walk in the door," Oryn chided, his green eyes sliding to Troy's. "Was she okay?"

"I'm right here," Aisling drawled.

"She was great," Troy answered. "Tired. A little cold. But perfect."

Aisling balked. There was no blush on his cheeks as he spoke directly to Oryn.

"Of course she's perfect," Amerie said. "Morana would have killed everyone otherwise."

"She's joking," Aisling whispered.

"No, I'm not," Amerie winked at Troy. Aisling poured him tea before collapsing on a couch beside Kaida. She felt silver eyes on her and turned.

"Tired?" Kaida asked softly.

"A little," she admitted, refusing to admit she was exhausted.

Her blood chilled as the peal of bells sounded. As the very foundation of the Pit shook with each ring. She stood with the rest of the Ferox and brushed past a terrified Troy. "Don't leave this place. Stay here until I come back, or I'll send Morana to find you."

He didn't get a chance to answer before she was through the door.

TWENTY-FOUR

AISLING

"You aren't ready," Kaida seethed with Aisling's armor in her hands.

"I'm not staying behind, Kaida. You'll have to tie me to my bed to keep me here."

"Don't give me any ideas." Kaida cursed as she tightened each piece of shiny new armor on Aisling's thin body. She placed a necklace around Aisling's neck, the same vial and light as before. "Don't lose this one. I don't have enough of it to make you a spare."

"What are you doing?" Koen asked breathlessly as he rushed to Aisling's side, throwing his armor on faster than she would ever be able to.

"I'm coming with."

He looked at Kaida. She shrugged and walked off. His jaw clenched. "Aisling. You need—"

"If you say I need to rest," she hissed, "I'll never speak to you again." She took two daggers from a tight-lipped Declan and hooked them into her leathers. "I won't get off Morana," she promised. Morana rumbled her agreement from Aisling's side.

Koen looked between the two of them as he finished clasping his armor. Aisling shamelessly let her eyes wander over his strong body now covered in hundreds of viridian green scales and savored every blink. A hint of a smirk played on his lips when she met his gaze again. "Do not get off Morana. For anything. I don't care who is about to die. Get back here." He looked at Morana. "If she even thinks about unclipping, fly back home."

Morana blinked once. *Yes.*

Aisling glared at her dragon. Koen lifted her onto Morana's back. She lowered into the saddle and clipped in. Her hands shook with anticipation. Koen stared up at her for only a second before and climbed onto Neera's back. Every dragon but Favilla walked into the Pit, their wings and jaws snapping with feverish energy.

"Morana and Aisling know their limits," Kaida called over the din of dragons. "And we know Aedan's rules. There was no note with the falcon, just a location. Claudere."

"That's so close," Cielle called out.

"Quick flight, then," Kaida responded. Soren took to the sky. Then Nyssa. Then Osiris and Aylim. Then Calen.

Morana went next, but not before she chirped at a shocked Troy in the doorway. Aisling winked at her friend as she went airborne and met the sky with a smile on her face. She pressed herself into the saddle as best she could.

The ache in her side was a dull memory as adrenaline slid through her veins. She rejoiced in the wind and sky at her fingertips, against her skin. She had missed this terribly. Morana echoed the sentiment and sent a rush of effervescent happiness down the bond despite the reason for the flight. Neera came up beside them, her dark green scales a stark contrast to Morana's glistening ones. The dragons pushed ahead with pumping wings, each ready and roiling for a fight.

They stopped midair minutes later as if they hit an invisible barrier.

A green tinge tinted the air ahead. The sickening sweet smell hit her in waves.

Aisling couldn't breathe. Couldn't comprehend what she was seeing.

Soren turned with a deep, resonating roar of rage. The rest of the dragons followed him, turning from the horrors with low rumbles in their throats. Morana and Aisling held back for only a few seconds and stared at the devastation below.

Nothing moved save for the flicker of several small fires. Children lay motionless on the ground with their toys broken around them, their tiny bellies overly distended and clothes shredded. Men and women hung collapsed over debris. Animals lay scattered about haphazardly as if they had tried to leave and fell before they could. Blood painted the ground. Stone crumbled.

A whole town, gone.

It will be an honor to be the one to ruin you.

Aisling's soul hollowed. Every fissure deepened until she was sure her slowly healing soul would shatter again.

The Man had ruined her like he promised he would. The Cruento had ruined her. And she had ruined these people.

A torrent of emotion flooded the bond. Aisling ignored it, unable to feel anything in the empty space where her soul used to be.

Morana turned and met the rest of the Ferox in three full swipes of her wings. No one spoke when they landed. They removed armor in silence. The dragons sulked to their rooms.

Aisling pulled Oryn aside. "Can you—"

"I'll get him settled."

She attempted a smile but couldn't make her face obey. He disappeared with the girls into the hallway. Koen stood a few feet in front of the doorway waiting for her. The light of the flames danced against the sharp planes of his face. She steeled her shoulders. "I want to train."

"Aisling—"

"I need to train, Koen," she begged, her voice as broken as her heart. "Please. Help me."

The rage inside was too much. The sorrow. The guilt. The panic.

The powerlessness.

She couldn't handle it anymore.

Koen didn't hesitate. His eyes morphed from cautious to predacious in a blink. He stepped forward until they were only a foot apart. "Hit me."

"What?"

"Hit me."

"I don't want to hit you."

"Remember the cave?" He angled his head. "Remember his words?"

Her blood steamed as everything came rushing back.

The knife against her neck. The wandering hands on her body. The sound of Favilla's scales tearing. Their laughter at her pain against the unforgiving dark stone.

"Remember your skin? Your bruises?" he asked. "Remember the knot at the back of your head and the pain in your side? The pain that isn't gone yet." He prowled around her. "Remember how you couldn't even wash your back? How you—"

Rage flowed through her. Rage she had hidden to heal. Rage she refused to acknowledge, to give power to.

It bubbled up from the deepest crevices of her ruined soul and swam through every blood cell, every breath, until it was all she felt. All she was.

Aisling struck his chest with her fist. Koen didn't flinch. "What's it like sleeping outside every night because you can't sleep in your own room? What does it feel like to flinch every time a door opens? What was it like to hear someone talk about your unborn children as if they owned them?"

Aisling struck again. And again.

Her knuckles ached against his solid frame. She didn't stop.

Not as tears fell from her eyes. Not as her lungs burned or her body begged for her to give it a break. She hit Koen until her mind went blank. Until the cacophony of emotions in her head went silent. Until the beast inside of her calmed and her body finally gave up.

She collapsed into him in a breathless mess of tears and sweat. He said nothing as he picked her up. A door opened and closed. The sound of water echoed against the walls. He lowered her to the floor. She grasped his biceps while her legs shook under her.

"They're hurting those people because of me. Because I took Favilla." Her voice came out in a painful rasp, but she had to get this out, had to put her pain into words. "I came to this world to help. I switched lives to help them. But I killed them instead." Aisling lifted her eyes to his. "I thought... I thought this life would be different, but it's not. I'm still useless here. I'm still worthless. I am a waste—"

Koen pulled her against his chest. His strong arms wrapped around her in a vise grip. She fought it for only a breath before she sank into the touch, molding her body to his.

Aisling allowed herself to have this comfort, this selfish safety, while the rest of her world was receiving a punishment designed for her.

Water overfilled the tub. Koen didn't move. His grip tightened.

Aisling held him until her mind relaxed. Until her body echoed the steady ebb and flow of his breaths.

"You are worth more than two worlds combined," he whispered against her hair.

Her heart cracked so thoroughly she wondered if he could hear it. She'd heard that before—the same words her mother used to sell her for drugs, their meaning irrevocably altered forever.

He lifted her chin with a finger. Aisling melted into his dark eyes, the flecks of gold inside nearly glowing. "You are more than you will ever understand, Aisling. You are..." he paused, his breathing staccato. He lowered his forehead to hers and lifted his hands to either cheek. She angled her face toward his and closed her eyes with a breathy sigh. Her skin buzzed as their noses touched, as his warm breath caressed her face.

His lips brushed against hers, just a whisper of a touch.

Her knees buckled.

Koen caught her and let out a breathless laugh, shattering the silence they'd become entombed in. "I'll clean up so you don't fall."

She blinked furiously as he sat her on a stool and did just that. He turned the water off and stuck his fingers inside the tub to check the temperature. Towels came from nowhere, soaking up the mess in a matter of minutes. He stood with his arms full of wet towels and glanced at her, his throat bobbing when their eyes met. "I'll step out." He shut the door behind him with heartbreaking gentleness.

Aisling wanted to call him back in. Wanted to tell him it was okay if he saw her naked. That she'd already laid herself bare before him. She'd laid herself at his feet, and he did the same, time and time again.

She got into the tub and grimaced as the water sloshed over the edge. She bathed quickly, refusing to give her mind a single second to think. A dry towel hung on the wall, and she wrapped herself in it, glancing around the bathroom for a new set of clothes, but found none. "Koen?" The door cracked open. Koen's eyes planted on the floor. Aisling smirked. "I don't have any clothes."

He glanced at her legs. "Hold on." He disappeared and came back, dutifully avoiding looking at her as he handed her his clothes. She smiled and dressed in his long shirt and linen pants, savoring the scent of him on her skin. With the towel, she dried her hair as best she could and walked into his room.

The fire roared and soaked the air with a comforting warmth. Koen sat on the couch. He watched her sit against the opposite side. "Better?"

She nodded. "Much."

"Do you want to talk about it?"

"No," she breathed. "Not at all." She was so tired of talking about herself and what she'd been through. "You talk to me. Tell me things."

"Like what?"

"Anything. Tell me your favorite color."

"Green."

"Favorite food?"

"Everything."

"Favorite—"

"What's your favorite color?"

She smiled. "Purple."

"Morana's eyes."

She nodded. "Neera's scales?"

"It's cliché, but yes."

Aisling angled her head. "Tell me about your life before you came here."

He tensed. "Why?"

"You know all about my other life."

"I didn't know about Troy."

"Do you not like him?"

"No. No, it's not..." he sighed defeatedly and leaned back, sprawling his long legs in front of the fire. A reluctant grin lifted his lips. "Tell me about him."

"You aren't changing the subject," she said. "You go first. Then I'll go."

"Fine." He looked into the fire, pursing his lips in thought for a few seconds before beginning. "My parents had me when they were both very young. Neither wanted a child. My father enjoyed alcohol more than water. My mother loved pissing him off. He would beat her until she couldn't talk anymore, and whatever he had left was what I got.

"I learned to stay outside. If I wasn't in the house, I couldn't get hurt. But my father caught on and kept me locked inside for long periods at a time. When I started growing, things started changing. I wasn't small anymore. I was stronger. And he was getting weaker and weaker with how much he was drinking. I think he realized it when I started pushing back. That's when he started using anything he could find in the house. I couldn't block well against a chair."

Aisling watched his eyes harden with the memories.

"He wouldn't let me go to school. I had no friends. I couldn't go outside. I could only use the bathroom twice a day. And my mother was just... she was waiting for him to kill her. I think she wanted it, honestly. She had given up. She never helped me, even when my father started using knives."

Aisling's heart stuttered. "Did he stab you?"

"No. Just a few small scars on my arms. They're not noticeable anymore after all of the Cruento stuff. He was too far gone to do any real damage." He ran a hand through his hair and sighed. "One night he drank too much, which was a feat in itself, and he left my door open when he passed out in the doorway. I thought about slitting his throat with his own knife, but I couldn't do it. So I ran. I ended up running toward the cliffs, and I decided to run until I fell off. Then he could never hurt me again." His face softened. "But Neera was there. I almost fell from shock. She hovered right over the edge like she was daring me to jump. I took one look at her eyes and felt it."

Aisling knew what he meant. The same pull that she had felt with Morana at the beach all those months ago. The need to be near the dragon as much as possible.

"She herded me away from the edge and forced me to walk," he laughed hoarsely. "I don't remember how long we walked. But we came here, and you know the rest."

Aisling hesitated. "Where were you from?"

"Dolor."

"I don't know where that one is," she admitted.

"Just south of here a little bit. Not too far."

"And you never talked to your parents again?"

"Never."

"Have you ever seen them in battle?"

"Never looked."

She looked at the fire and imagined Koen as a child, locked away and beaten by his own father. It was like what she went through in a way, but Koen knew his captor. She wasn't sure if that made it better or worse. "I'm sorry," she whispered.

He shrugged. "No one is born knowing how to fight, Aisling. And at some point in everyone's life, they feel useless or worthless. It's what you do to combat those feelings that matters."

She lifted a brow. "That was very wise. You sound like Oryn."

He smiled. "An honor."

"What were they like?"

"Kaida and Oryn? Great. The exact opposite of what I knew. They were so involved, so present. And they kicked my ass. I don't know where I would be without them." He shook his head subtly. "Okay. I said my bit. Your turn."

"What did you want to know?"

He smirked. "What's your relationship with Troy like?"

"Troy is my best friend. My platonic soul mate." She shifted in her seat. "He was thrown out of his house by his parents five years ago. He had to make his way in the world just like I did. We found each other at the café, and it was an instant connection. Kind of like the bond with Morana, but we can talk to each other. He's the one that kept me alive, I think. We leaned on each other when things got too hard or overwhelming."

"What he was saying today before he gave Aedan the letter..."

"It's all true," she admitted softly. The fire danced. She let it mesmerize her if only to keep her from feeling too strongly.

"You love him."

"Yes," she said baldly, turning to Koen. "I love him entirely too much. He was the only reason I didn't make the switch earlier."

"What changed, then?"

"He didn't understand why I was letting myself go and got angry." Her head rested against the back of the couch. "I neglected everything, Koen. I didn't eat. I barely spoke. I couldn't concentrate on a single thing without thinking of all this. I never told him the truth, either. I just let myself wither away to nothing. It was hard for him to watch." She rolled her head toward him. "There was a lot of miscommunication on my part. I handled it horribly. That's why I was so shocked when he showed up. I hadn't explained any of it except in that note."

Koen's eyes narrowed for a heartbeat. "And you two never..."

"Oh, gross," she laughed. "No. He is not into me like that at all. Or any woman, actually. But he's incapable of talking to attractive men, so if he can't speak to you, don't take it personally."

He rested his head against the back of the couch. "Do you think he would agree with you?"

"About what?"

"That I should smile more."

Aisling groaned. "I regret ever saying that."

"I don't regret hearing it," he murmured, his face soft against the light of the fire. She watched it dance along his smooth skin and throw shadows against the sharp planes of his jaw. They fell into a comfortable silence. Aisling's body relaxed against the couch, an overwhelming sense of peace coursing through her bones. Her eyes drifted shut, and she didn't stop them.

TWENTY-FIVE

KOEN

Aisling fell asleep quickly. Koen watched the calm rise and fall of her chest. Her porcelain skin glowed against the firelight. Her face was fully relaxed. The slender column of her neck curved in invitation. Her lips were slightly parted.

He was choking on his desire, his need to be close to her.

Devastation clung to her on the ride back from Claudere. Morana told Neera about it in almost silent rumbles, and Neera flooded the bond with Aisling's fury and sorrow until it became too much for him to tolerate. He waited at the door of the Pit knowing she would want to do something about it. Knowing she wouldn't want to let it fester.

She didn't know what she wanted. There was too much she was feeling. It was written on her face and plastered in her eyes, a lost look full of pain. She hesitated to hit him, hesitated to move, and Koen hated it. The Aisling before her capture would have reveled in a request to hit him. She wouldn't have waited for an invitation.

So he goaded her. He urged the fire and fight back in her eyes. He hated every word that came out of her mouth afterward. There was nothing he could think to say that would convey how wrong she was about herself. He brought her close, praying that his touch would express everything his voice couldn't. Aisling molded to him, and he physically couldn't let go. He didn't care about anything but the woman in front of him baring the most broken parts of herself to him with a trust he would never deserve.

He almost lost it when she looked up at him with those soft eyes. Words felt too thick in his mouth. His tongue wouldn't cooperate with his head. His control nearly shattered at the soft breath from her lips as he tangled his hands in her hair. He wanted more. He needed more. She was unraveling him with every look, every touch, and he loved it.

She hadn't acknowledged his blabbering at the cliffs, but he was okay with it. When she was ready, she would. Either way, he was curiously proud of himself for being honest.

Reluctantly, after far too long of her being asleep on the couch, he scooped her into his arms. All he wanted was for her to be back in his bed. He didn't even need to sleep with her. He was fine on the couch. He just wanted her there.

He opened the door to her room. Troy's head popped up from the couch, his eyes heavy with sleep. Koen banked the urge to rage at the sight of another man in her room, replaying Aisling's words from earlier in his head.

"What happened to her?" Troy stood. He was in sleep clothes, no doubt given to him by someone else. He was far too tall to wear Aisling's.

"She trained a little bit," Koen whispered as he brought Aisling to her bed. "Then took a bath."

"With you?"

He gritted his teeth and gently placed Aisling in her bed, covering her with blankets before turning to Troy. He lowered his voice to a near growl. "And if she did?"

Troy did not balk or flinch like most did when Koen tried to assert dominance. His size and voice normally were enough to send most cowering, but Troy held firm, his bright eyes narrowing. Koen reigned in his surprise.

Troy glanced over Koen's shoulder to check on Aisling before moving in front of the fire. Koen followed. "She told me about you," Troy started. "When she first got here."

He couldn't stop his throat from bobbing.

Troy saw it. He crossed his arms over his chest. "She came to work devastated a day or two later. She crumbled to the floor in tears. I held her until the storm passed. When she stopped crying, she told me she felt useless. And she wondered if it would be better if she ended her life."

Koen held his breath, guilt drowning his lungs.

"Do you know how terrifying it is to watch the one person you love think that they would be better off dead?" Troy hissed. "I didn't know that this was real then. I thought she was just beating herself up with her own imagination. But now—"

"It was me," Koen admitted.

"Why?"

Koen paused. "Why what?"

"Why did you call her useless? Why would you say any of that?"

He didn't have an answer that would absolve him of any of his sins.

"Do you want to see what she wrote about you?" Troy reached into his pocket and handed him the letter. Koen glanced at Aisling over his shoulder before opening it. He kept rereading one line:

"I thought he hated me. But now?"

Their conversation at the cliffs all those weeks ago came back. She admitted she knew what it felt like to want to end her life, but Koen never expected to be the reason for it.

A sickening wave of nausea rolled through him.

The clean slate would never purify him. The honesty and care he showed would never exonerate him for how he had made her feel. To have his acidic words on her mind in both lives was just another form of torture, and she had been through enough.

He had only said them because he was terrified of falling for her, which happened regardless.

He was so selfish. So selfish, and so idiotic.

Troy took the letter back. "I see the way she looks at you, and I see how you look at her. I don't know what happened between that time and now, but I will not tolerate her being treated like that. Ever. By anyone." He glanced at Aisling's sleeping body. "She deserves the world. Whatever world she wishes. Nothing less."

Koen liked him. A lot.

And he hated himself.

Koen cornered Oryn in the stairwell early the next morning. "Send me to Impellor."

"For what?"

"Anything."

Oryn turned, his bright green eyes seeing everything Koen wasn't saying. "No."

"Please, Oryn," he begged. He couldn't be here. He couldn't face her after last night. He had barely slept. Guilt crawled through him with an oily heaviness he couldn't shake. The thought of being around the woman he nearly destroyed was going to kill him.

"No," Oryn repeated. "Whatever happened, deal with it." He walked up the steps and disappeared. Koen whispered a string of curses.

"Language," Cielle scolded. She took a look at his haggard face and sighed. "What happened?"

He shook his head. "I was an idiot."

"Well, yeah. That's nothing new, though."

"I fucked up, Cielle." He turned to her, his pain evident in every pore.

She paused, the crease between her brows deepening. "Should we go on a walk?"

He was out the door a heartbeat later with her at his heels. They took the long path around the Keep and down the cliffside to the beach. The roar of the waves and chirps of birds greeted them. "What happened?" she asked as she sat on top of a large boulder.

"I love her," Koen whispered, the words falling off his tongue. Words he'd never said before. Words he had been too scared to acknowledge. "And I can't."

She blinked. "Why not?"

"Because I almost ruined her." He ran a trembling hand through his hair. "When she first came here, I was awful. I said some horrible things to her, Cielle. Before Impellor, she offered me a clean slate. She didn't want anything holding her back in this life and said she could forget all of it. And I felt better, like I really could start fresh. But Troy..." he looked at the sea. "He told me how much my words destroyed her in that life, too. She wanted to kill herself."

Cielle said nothing. He paced along the beach in quick steps in a desperate attempt to calm the storm inside his chest. "I can't... I'm not good for her. I'll never be able to forgive myself. And she shouldn't forgive me, either. She deserves so much more than–"

"Stop," Cielle said. He paused. Cielle looked at the sky, her eyes squinted against the brightening sun. "You're being selfish, Koen."

He balked. "I'm being selfish? For trying to help her?"

"No. You're selfish for being scared."

"I'm not scared."

"You are. You're terrified because you're so close to finally being happy. And you would rather ruin it than accept the helplessness that comes with love."

"That's not true."

"Really? Because I know how she looks at you, Koen. I see the relief in her eyes when you walk into a room. And you want to tear that away from her because you can't forgive yourself for being an ass a few months ago." She crossed her arms over her chest. "She's finally started healing. Truly healing, not just physically. Do you remember how long it took Elaila to do that?"

Months. It took Elaila months before she could even look him in the eyes, let alone speak to him.

"Imagine what would have happened if you pulled the rug from under Elaila during that time. Imagine how long it would have taken for her to feel better." Her voice tightened. "You cannot do that to Aisling. She has been through too much. I won't let you."

His chin fell to his chest. He was so tired, so overwhelmed. "I don't know how to make it better, Cielle. How do I fix it?"

"You can't. It's already done."

He glared at her. "Then why—"

"You can only move forward. You have to grow. You have to see that you made a mistake and learn from it. Recognize it, and don't do it again. That's the only way." She pushed a short windswept hair from her eyes. "No one knows what they're doing, Koen. We're all learning. You need to remember that you aren't the same guy you were back then. That you've grown exponentially since. Aisling forgave you a long time ago. Don't throw away the clean slate she gave you because of some self-loathing guilt."

He sat on the sand and leaned against her rock. "This is hard," he whispered.

"Anything worth it isn't easy."

He huffed an empty laugh. "You sound like Oryn."

She nudged his shoulder with her shoe. "So you love her, huh?"

"Don't make it weird."

"I don't think it's weird. I think it's wonderful. Have you told her?"

"No. I told her I had feelings for her. Then Troy appeared, and everything happened."

"Ah, yeah. He was a shock."

They sat in silence with the waves as their only companions. He had always been drawn to Cielle. She wasn't boisterous like Amerie but was more outgoing than Elaila. She was the closest thing to a real sister he would ever find.

"She's probably waiting for you," Cielle said after a while. "She wants to train."

He cursed and stood. "Wait. How—"

"Just relax. You're fine. She doesn't know you had this freakout, and I will never tell her." She nudged him toward the cliffs. "Go help her."

He paused and kissed the top of her head in a rare show of gratitude before darting up the pathway and around the Keep. Aisling sat in the common room in her brown leathers, her hair twisted into two braids. Troy sat infuriatingly close beside her. She looked up when Koen walked in, and his heart stuttered at the bald relief in her eyes, just like Cielle had mentioned. "Ready?"

"Yes." She smiled and stood in one fluid motion. Her brace was off again. The corset around her was tight enough that she didn't need it. She planted a kiss on Troy's freshly shaven cheek, eliciting a shiver of jealousy down Koen's spine. "Oryn will take you to medical after you eat. You're going to do an amazing job. I trust you with my body already."

Troy rolled his eyes. "Yes, mom."

"It's Mother to you," she called over her shoulder. She came to Koen's side. "So what's the plan? Are we running?"

"Do you feel like you can run?"

"I think I'm excited enough to try," she admitted. "But I don't think I can go far."

"Well, we know you can still hit."

A deep groove grew between her eyebrows. "Did I hurt you?"

"You got some good ones in." She bit her lip. He cleared his throat and tore his gaze from her mouth. "You should stretch-"

"Why did you take me to my room?"

Koen paused. "You would have been uncomfortable on the couch."

"You slept on it for days," she countered as they entered the Pit.

He dug inside his head for a decent excuse but came up empty. "I know." Aisling stared at him, a thousand questions swirling in those warm eyes. Questions he was dying to hear but would never force from her no matter how badly he wanted to answer them. "Let's try a run."

TWENTY-SIX

AISLING

"I'm not used to taking a bath," Troy admitted when he stepped out of the bathroom, his eyes tired from studying all day with medical. A white towel hung on his narrow hips as he opened his drawer and dressed. Maura had outfitted him with enough clothes to warrant taking an entire drawer in her room in a single day.

"It's nice, though, isn't it?" Aisling asked over her shoulder without taking her eyes off the book Cielle brought her. Her training had lasted almost the entire day. Sand and sweat covered her skin with a familiar grit. Koen hadn't taken it easy on her, and she loved every painful minute of it. Her bath afterward had been a beautiful reward.

"Much nicer than my old place," he murmured as he sat beside her on the couch.

She scoffed. "Anything was better than our old places."

"Your place should have been condemned."

"Maybe you finding my dead body inside will get the ball rolling."

He glared at her. "Not something to joke about."

"I'm not joking." She closed the book. "Did you eat?"

He nodded. "Medical eats in shifts. I might have eaten before you."

"Are you hungry? Did you eat too early?"

"Stop worrying about me," he said softly. "I'm wonderful. I don't think I've ever felt so..." he pinched his nose. "I don't know the word."

"Happy?"

"That, yes. But it's something else, too. Something filling."

She smiled. "I know exactly how you feel."

He leaned against the back of the couch, his long hair damp. "Are we positive we aren't dead?"

"No." He whipped his head to her. She shrugged. "I'm not convinced. I'm too happy. Despite everything, I'm happy. Maybe we are dead. Maybe this is just an ornate purgatory. But I'm going to devour it anyway."

"When did you get so wise?"

She laughed. "Wise? Or am I rambling like an insane woman?"

"Is there a difference?"

"Either way, enjoy it. There's no point in being miserable here. We've already done that."

He stared at the fire for a long minute. "So, Koen."

She grimaced. "What about him?"

Troy smiled, his eyes taking on the same devilish twinkle as Amerie's. "Don't be coy, Miss-Jumping-Into-His-Arms. Miss-Taking-A-Bath-In-His-Room, Miss –"

"I get it," Aisling hissed. His brows lifted expectantly. She rolled her eyes. "What do you want me to say?"

"I want to know what's going on there."

So did she. He had shaken her very soul with his confession, and not once had he brought it up since. Not once had he pressured her for an answer. An answer that had been bubbling on her tongue for weeks. A bubble she was unable to pop. "I don't know," she murmured, staring into the flames. "I—he..."

Troy's hand wrapped around hers. "Talk when you're ready, babe. I'm just having some fun."

She scowled. "So, Oryn."

He dropped her hand. "You're pettier here."

"Pettier or prettier?"

"Both."

Her stomach rumbled. Troy's eyebrows lifted. "I think I'm going to get something to eat." She had forgotten how much she needed to eat when she trained. Her body was begging for something warm and filling.

"Want company?"

She shook her head. "No. Get some sleep. You're studying a lot. Your brain needs rest."

"So you became a mother when you switched, huh?"

Aisling rolled her eyes over her shoulder before shutting the door on him, but her smile didn't fade. There was an innate comfort with Troy and their bickering that she missed more than she realized. She made her way up the stairs and peeked into the deserted common room. The trays were empty, as were the cabinets. She pursed her lips and debated her options before walking out of the Pit and into the meadow.

Night had fallen over Anguid, casting everything in a deep blue haze. One of the dragons spun in lazy circles deep in the clouds, its shape silhouetted by the bright moon. The wind wrapped around her in a familiar embrace. She twirled her hand through each gust, reveling in the feel between her fingers. A feeling she thought she would never experience again just a short time ago.

Her jaw clenched like it did every time her mind drifted to the cave. The flashbacks should be gone. There was no need for them. No need for her to freeze with panic every time she opened her eyes in the darkness. No need for her to flinch every time a door opened or something scraped along the stone floors. There was no need for her to keep checking the empty space where her finger should be.

The Man's voice was on a constant loop in the back of her mind. His venom-laced words were never far away from her every thought. He was a leech on her life, one she couldn't get rid of.

She entered the Keep and took the stairs to the lower level. There was no yelling coming from the kitchen. No banging of pots and pans or steam wafting from the doorway. She peeked in and grinned at the sight of Leonard talking to himself over the stove. "Leonard?"

He started. A bright smile lifted his lips when he met her eyes. "Aisling," he whispered, his voice quiet and calming. "My dear." He came to the door and clutched her head between his massive hands. "You are back."

"I am."

"And I have never been happier." He pressed a kiss to the top of her head and led her inside by the hand. "Sit. You have excellent timing. I've just gotten back from my interrogation. What can I make you?"

"Interrogation?"

He nodded. "Yes, love. They must ensure no one from that dreaded group has made their way into our sanctuary. I am not above suspicion, and I am glad of it. No one should be."

"No one in their right mind would suspect you."

"True. But maybe that's exactly why they should question me." He smiled at her. "I am deemed clean, so you know. You have nothing to worry about in my presence except a full stomach."

Aisling shook her head. "I know you aren't them, Leonard. Out of everyone, except maybe Elaila, I would know."

He brushed a thick hand over her hair. "Let me feed you. Tell me what you desire."

"I don't know," she admitted. She leaned her elbows on the countertops. "But I'm starving."

"Starving, eh?" He lowered his chin and looked over his glasses at her. "Unacceptable. I will feed you."

"Thank you."

"Leonard?" came a small voice from the doorway. Aisling followed the sound. She nearly fell off her stool.

A young girl stared back at her, cocking her head as if trying to place her.

"Zain!" Leonard chided, placing his hands on his hips. "What are you doing out of bed so late, young lady?"

The girl's eyes danced with delight. "I'm hungry."

Leonard tutted. "Of course you are, darling. Of course." He waved her in and rested his massive hand on her thin shoulder. He pointed to Aisling. "Zain, this is Aisling. She's Morana's rider."

Zain's eyes widened in recognition.

"And Aisling," Leonard smiled, "this is Zain. She is my new shadow."

"I want to be a chef," the girl smiled.

Aisling bit back her tears. This girl standing before her looked so much different than the girl she saw under Neera's wings after her first battle. Gone was the hardened look of a child who fought for her freedom and had to grow up too young. In its place was a childlike wonder, a glow of happiness.

"It's wonderful to meet you," Aisling said through a tight throat.

"Don't move," Leonard squeezed Zain's shoulder. He disappeared into the pantry.

Zain lifted a brow. "I remember you."

"And I remember you."

"They said you escaped."

"I did."

The girl didn't hesitate. "And now you're going to destroy them."

A knot grew in Aisling's throat. She tried desperately to swallow against it, but all she could do was nod.

Leonard fluttered to Zain's side and handed her a small parcel. "Eat it on your way back to your room. Do not eat it in bed. Crumbs belong on floors and in bellies, not blankets."

Zain smiled up at him and tucked the parcel under her arm. She gave a sheepish glance to Aisling before vanishing through the door.

"Poor child," Leonard mumbled as he stared after her. "Her whole family was killed by the Cruento one night. She was orphaned in the blink of an eye. Luckily, Aedan houses the orphans here. Koen got word and brought her to me right before the battle at Impellor." He shook his head and placed a basket of ingredients on the counter before her. "Her little smile makes every day better. For weeks she wouldn't. Now, she can't stop. I think it's the food."

Aisling pocketed the image of Koen helping an orphan. She shook her head. "It's you. Not the food."

"Nonsense." He took a deep breath as if to steady himself and glanced at her. "Now, tell me, dear, how are you feeling?"

"That's a loaded question."

"Then unload it."

She angled her head and smiled despite herself. "I feel..."

How did she feel? She was alive. She had made it out. She was a survivor.

But she was broken. Her body, her mind, all of her, was still broken. The tiny chasms in her soul were barely filling despite her best attempts. Every time she felt like herself again, something knocked her back down. Every time she thought she was better, she was smacked with reality.

Leonard stood across from her, his jaw set. "Healing takes time, Aisling."

"I'm tired of it," she whispered back. "I feel like I'm wasting time."

"Time for what?" He lifted his brow. "What could be more important than healing yourself?"

"Killing them," she answered baldly.

Leonard didn't balk. He nodded and turned back to the stove, stirring something in the giant pot slowly. "I have been alive a very long time, Aisling. Far too long I feel some days, and I've learned we cannot rush time, nor cannot force it. We have to accept what it's giving us and trust in the timing of the divine. Whatever is meant for us will never pass us." He rolled his shoulders back. "The time you are given now is vital to strengthen you for whatever is to come. Your revenge will come, but you cannot force it before you are ready."

"I don't know how to accept that."

He shrugged. "You don't have a choice, do you? None of us do. We have to make do with what we are given. Some of us trust time and grow and bloom. Some of us focus too much on our fears for the future or hang in the past and shrink." He turned to her, a low flame in his stare. "You do not shrink, Aisling. You do not bloom. You explode."

She blinked the burning pressure from her eyes. "I don't think I'm meant for—"

"What do you know of what you're meant for?" He placed a bowl of noodles and vegetables in broth before her. "None of us know what we are meant for. We find out when time deems us worthy. And right now, it is not your time." He jerked his chin to the bowl. "Eat."

She stared at him for a long moment before bringing the spoon to her mouth. The soup warmed her soul, sinking into her bones like a hug. She sighed contentedly.

Time. She just needed time.

"Give yourself grace, my dear," Leonard said softly. "In time, you'll find you are exactly where and who you are supposed to be."

Aisling said nothing as his wisdom seeped into her heart. She ate the soup like a woman starved and lifted the bowl to drink the rest of the broth. Her stomach purred in response. "That was wonderful, Leonard. Thank you."

He dipped his chin. "More?"

"No. I don't want to overdo it. But…" she glanced at the empty kitchen.

"You do not even have to ask, my dear," Leonard said with a smile. "Bake. Please."

An hour later, she and Leonard were covered in flour. The kitchen was a mess of ingredients and tools. The ovens were full of their creations. Genuine laughter bounced against the stone walls. She had missed the sticky dough between her fingers and the work and science it took to create something delicious and soul-warming.

"What are you making, Leonard? It smells so good," Koen called as he walked through the kitchen doors. He stilled at the sight of Aisling kneading dough beside the chef. She brushed an errant hair from her face with her forearm and spread another streak of flour across her cheek. He broke into a painfully beautiful smile.

"What am I making?" Leonard asked. "I am learning, boy. I am simply another vessel for Aisling's magic." He glowered over his glasses at Koen. "What are you doing here?"

"I was hungry."

Leonard glanced at Aisling over his shoulder and whispered con-spiratorially, "This boy? He is always hungry. He –"

"I can hear you," Koen drawled, dipping a spoon into the pot of soup. His brows lifted in appreciation as he swallowed. Aisling traced the line of his strong throat with a hunger no food would sate and subtly cleared her throat.

"You will have to work for that," Leonard said, stepping to Koen's side and slapping his hand. "I am tired and can barely knead. Help Aisling, then you can eat this." Leonard looked at Aisling. "It has been a privilege, my dear. Come back anytime. And do not," he emphasized, "allow this boy to eat the soup until he has helped you."

He glared at Koen as he walked out the kitchen doors. Koen rolled his eyes before meeting hers. "What's going on here?"

"Just making bread."

He glanced at the counter where her hands had disappeared in a ball of dough. "It looks...messy." He came to her side, his heat and scent overwhelming. "How can I help?"

"You don't have to. I won't tell Leonard. All I have to do is knead this for a few more minutes."

"You sure?"

"Positive. Go eat." Koen's face flickered with gratitude before he poured a bowl of soup and sat across the island from her. She forced her attention to the dough beneath her. "I was hungry, too. I think from training."

"Training and healing," he said between bites. "You'll only get hungrier from here."

She groaned. "Leonard will get sick of me."

"Impossible."

Aisling bit her cheek to keep from smiling. She kneaded the dough with the heel of her hands in a steady rhythm. "I baked for the café every morning," she told him after a few seconds of silence. "I got in an hour before Troy, hours before sunrise, and did this."

"Did you like it?"

"I loved it. It's a peaceful way to start the day."

"Better than running?"

She laughed. "Much better. Troy would steal whatever I made, and we would eat it after work at the park. Usually, that was all I ate the whole day, so I had to do it well."

Koen studied her, his eyes darting between her hands and her face. "What was your favorite thing to make?"

"The orange and ginger morning buns."

"You made those before."

She nodded. "Yeah, the twisted ones."

"They were so good. Why those?"

Because they brought her comfort. Because she liked losing herself in the twisting and molding of bread. Because the smell reminded her of him. "I have my reasons."

His brows lifted. He glanced at the dough between her hands. "Will you teach me?"

Something in her melted. She nodded and gestured for him to come to her side. "Come on. Cover your hands in flour."

Koen's hands were covered in the white powder a second later. She pulled her hand from the dough and peeled the sticky mess from her fingers before slapping it back onto the ball. She took his thick wrists and placed his palms on top of the dough. "Now press with the heel of your hands."

"At the same time?"

She shrugged. "You can. I like doing alternating hands. It keeps it moving and allows the gluten to develop."

Slowly, he pressed his large hands into the ball of dough, his face pinching at the texture and stickiness. "This doesn't feel right."

"It is," she laughed. "Just keep kneading. It needs time before it's ready."

Leonard's words came hurling back at her. She blinked quickly and swallowed. Koen glanced down at her after a full minute of the most pathetic kneading she had ever seen. "This is gross, Aisling."

"Excuse you," she said, pushing him away with her hip. She lowered her hands back into the dough and pressed in alternating waves. "Go wash your hands, then." She stopped when the dough turned silky and placed it in a loaf tin before moving it to the warming drawer. Koen watched from across the counter in silence. "Now we wait," she murmured to herself as she washed the sticky remnants from her hands.

"For what?"

"It to grow."

Koen's brows furrowed in confusion. "It grows?"

She sat beside him. "You know nothing about bread, do you?"

"Nothing," he admitted. "Just that I like to eat it."

"If you want to learn, I can teach you."

Koen's mouth lifted at the corner. "I'd rather watch you make it."

Her heart stuttered. She pursed her lips to keep from smiling. "It can take a long time. Each loaf has to sit for –"

"I have nothing but time, Aisling." His eyes darted between hers. "I don't intend to waste any of it."

She said nothing as she stared at him. The words she wanted to say danced on the tip of her tongue and tickled her throat. Her heart pounded against her ribs—a caged animal begging to be released.

Aisling smiled as a crack in her soul mended.

TWENTY-SEVEN

AISLING

Rain pattered against the common room windows the next afternoon. Dark clouds rolled through the endless sky from the sea and emptied over Anguid in heavy sheets of water.

Amerie hummed over a puzzle. The fire crackled and popped behind her. Cielle read a thick novel from the library in a plush chair she had dragged in front of the large windows. A fresh latte swirled its steamy tendrils from the table beside her.

Troy walked through the door still dressed in his all-white medical linens and headed straight for the buffet trays. He said nothing as he filled his plate and sat down next to Amerie with a smile. Elaila filed inside at some point, notebook in hand, and poured herself a cup of tea before sitting beside Aisling on the large couch.

No one spoke. A marrow-deep comfort sank into Aisling's body.

This is what she had always wanted, always ached for. And by the sparkle in Troy's eyes and smile on his face, she knew he felt the same way.

A bolt of emotion down the bond shattered the peace. Everyone but Troy gasped. He glanced around in concern at the faces of the Ferox, no longer the quiet, contemplative ones of peace he had seen just seconds before.

Kaida stormed inside, hair braided and up, armor on. Blades crossed at her back. She lasered her gaze on Aisling. "Falcon came in. Oryn's roadblocks got something. Soldiers stopped four caravans."

Aisling blinked rapidly. Elaila spoke first. "How many?"

"At least fifteen women. Three girls."

A fire bellowed in Aisling's stomach. Morana stoked it with her shadows.

Kaida's eyes danced between her and Elaila. "Do you two want –"

"Yes," they both answered in unison.

Kaida nodded once. "Thought so. I need one of you," she pointed to Cielle and Amerie, "to stay here with Koen and Neera in case something else happens. Oryn is in Impellor for the night, so he can't help, though I know he wishes he could."

"What about me?"

The entire room turned to face Troy. Kaida angled her brow. "What about you?"

He shrugged, a slight blush on his cheeks. "I don't know why I asked, to be honest. I just felt left out."

Amerie burst into laughter. "Leave him with me. I'll make sure he has a fun night."

Troy glanced at Aisling for help, but she blew him a kiss and raced to the Lair where Declan already had her armor and swords laid out. She dressed with brutal efficiency, only a small tremor in her hands that she convinced herself was excitement, not nerves.

Soren, Osiris, Aylim, and Morana stalked from the Lair. Rain pelted their scales and repelled onto the sand. Cielle handed Aisling two more daggers before walking into the Pit. Aisling followed.

Kaida stroked Osiris's scales. "The men have been apprehended and are being held by Kairossen soldiers. The women are safe, but we are to stay with them until Aedan's female force arrives."

Aisling glanced sidelong at a stoic Elaila.

"Elaila and Aisling take the reins," Kaida said softly. Cielle nodded. "If it becomes too much for either of you, do not hesitate to leave. Is that understood?"

Aisling and Elaila agreed. They mounted their dragons just as Neera dropped from the sky onto the sand with Koen on her back. Rain dripped off his black leathers. He ran his fingers through his sopping wet hair and pushed it off his face. "What's going on?"

"Caravans."

"How many?"

"Four. Women and girls."

He steeled his jaw and unhooked from the saddle. "Let me grab my sword and—"

"No."

He paused. "What?"

"I said no," Kaida repeated. "You are to stay here with Amerie. If something else happens, you will be needed. We have more than enough people for this excursion."

Koen glanced at the four women, his brown eyes lingering on Aisling. Something flickered in his stare, but he drowned it in a blink. "Okay."

"Tell Leonard we will be needing something warm when we come back. Preferably with chocolate, but I would never tell him what to make."

Koen slid down Neera's leg and landed in the sand with more grace than Aisling would ever have. He smirked. "He'll have a whole buffet ready for you."

Kaida's answering smile dazzled. "That's what I'm hoping for."

Soren took her into the sky in the next breath. Aylim and Osiris went next. Morana paused to chirp quickly to Neera. Koen met Aisling's eyes.

She waited for him to give her instructions. To tell her to be safe or to give her last minute pointers on how to use a sword.

But a warm smile lifted his cheeks as he crossed his arms over his chest and dipped his chin. "Good luck, Shadow Bringer."

Morana was airborne before Aisling could respond.

Rain poured from above and pelted her armor with fat drops. It seeped into her hair but bounced off Morana's scales. The flight was quick. Where they were, Aisling had no idea. It didn't really matter, not this time.

Heavy drops turned into a light drizzle as they landed at a large empty intersection. Soldiers stood in lines across the road to stop and check any incoming traffic. Aisling glanced around from atop Morana's saddle. They weren't near any city or town. A vast expanse of land spread out all around her. Bright green grass and multiple small plumes of flowers littered the landscape. Large boulders created miniature hills. Mud covered the road where dirt had been.

Four large caravans sat parked on the side of the road surrounded by soldiers. A young officer bravely came to stand at Soren's side and dipped his chin in respect to a now grounded Kaida before delving into the details.

"The lead caravan had two drivers. The rest only had one each."

"Where are they being held?"

He glanced over his shoulder to a tight circle of soldiers standing just off the road. "In there. They aren't going anywhere."

"And the women?"

The soldier nodded, his young face grim. "They are all alive and resting in our compound. I hate to admit that we only saw them because one of the young girls was smart enough to push her foot through a slat at the bottom of the wagon." He grimaced. "Their getting smarter. Used to be they would just hide their prisoners in the middle of the crops. But now, they're developing hidden compartments only accessible to the outside."

Kaida's mouth tightened. "So if something were to happen to the men..."

The soldier nodded. "The women wouldn't be able to free themselves, yes."

"Death either way," Elaila murmured, her blue eyes narrowing at the circle of soldiers and rebels inside.

"Exactly, ma'am," the soldier replied, his gaze lingering on Elaila longer than appropriate. He blinked quickly and cleared his throat. "Oryn's missive said to call the Ferox before we—"

"You did the right thing," Kaida answered. "Tell your men to stand down. Take a break. We have this covered." She glanced to the shack. "Do not try and talk to the women. A large group of men with swords is the worst thing they can see right now. Stay far enough away to give them a semblance of peace."

The soldier shouted. His men replied at once, abandoning their posts to stand guard a respectable distance from the small shack located just feet away from the road. Soren and the rest of the dragons formed a perimeter. Kaida turned to Elaila and Aisling. "Cielle and I are here to in whatever capacity you need us. Remember that."

Aisling swallowed thickly and stared at the group of five men. Ropes twined around their wrists and legs. Thick scraps of fabric cut into their cheeks. Their clothes were clean but soaked. They sat with their backs to each other in a small circle.

She glanced inside the small shack where the soldiers had gathered outside. Wan sickly faces stared back. There was no emotion in their eyes, even from the youngest.

Is that what she looked like when she returned to the Ferox? Alive but with a dead soul? On death's door with an expired invitation?

These men were not the ones who beat her. She knew they were dead. But these men here, they were of the same family. And their line needed to end.

Elaila brushed her thumb against Aisling's hand, bringing her back to the present, and started a slow, measured walk to the men.

They glared at the women of the Ferox. Hate glittered in their eyes.

Aisling could only remember their voices. Their hands.

Snippets of the cave rushed back. She clenched her jaw against them.

"Evening, gentlemen," Elaila purred, the light in her eyes dangerous and volatile. "Seems you've hit a roadblock."

The man in the back of the group bared his teeth. Spit drizzled from his gagged mouth.

Kaida stalked around them with Cielle as her shadow. Soren made a show of splaying his wings with an annoyed rumble, shaking the ground beneath them. The men's eyes widened.

"I'll cut to the chase. I want to be back home. I want to be wrapped in a blanket with a cup of tea. And I really, really want to get a good night's sleep. I do not want to be here. But I cannot go home until I deal with you. So," Elaila paused, "let's help each other out."

Cielle removed a gag from one of the prisoners. He cursed and flung obscenities into the air. She didn't blink. "Where are you taking the women?"

"To their rightful owners."

Something inside of Aisling, something primal and hidden deep within the confines of her shattered soul, awoke with vicious intensity. A rage she had smothered for weeks billowed and shook her very core.

Morana ripped a snarl into the air.

Aisling smiled.

Something flickered in the man's eyes. Fear, maybe. Or regret.

She didn't care either way.

"A woman is not meant to be owned," she cooed, angling her head and coming to Elaila's side. "A real man knows that."

The words flowed from her chest into the ether.

She would never be owned. Never be property to anyone again.

"But you are not real men. You are weak, pathetic, spineless worms feasting on the rotten beliefs of a man who is too cowardly to show his own face. You want to own women because there is no possible way," she said as she knelt to the ground and caressed one man's cheek with her finger, "that a woman would ever give you the time of day. You feed off the fear of women because a small, terrified part of you knows that is the only way you can get what you so desperately desire."

The man recoiled at her touch.

But the man without a gag spit at her feet.

Aisling stood and unsheathed her sword, her need for retribution nearly overwhelming. But Morana stalked behind her. Something flickered down the bond, warm and promising.

She glanced sidelong at Elaila, and Elaila smiled back at her, an unspoken agreement flowing between them.

A heartbeat later, Morana bathed the men in shadow.

The two women of the Ferox with broken souls let loose.

Aisling didn't flinch as her blade met flesh. A tiny monster inside her heart purred at the violence, at the justified rage in her blood.

When they were finished, five bodies lay crumbled in pools of their own blood. Aisling and Elaila didn't speak as they sheathed their blades and looked to their leader.

Kaida shrugged and picked at her nails. "Dramatic, but I liked the flair. They weren't going to tell us anything anyway. They never do." She wiped the rain from her brow. "Now to the hard part."

Hours later, after a caravan of Kairossen's best female-only medics and soldiers arrived from Impellor, the women of the Ferox flew home.

The bond hummed with delight, and Aisling leaned into it while the little monster inside her soul fell back into a deep, restful slumber.

TWENTY-EIGHT

AISLING

The morning sun reflected off the shimmering sands of the Pit and blinded her. She barely dodged Koen's punch in time and stumbled to recover. Koen didn't hesitate his assault.

Aisling blocked a blow with her forearm and used it to swing their arms up. Her leg lifted reflexively, and she slammed her heel into his now unblocked ribs. He staggered back with his brows arched in surprise. A sheen of sweat lined his face, making him almost glow in the morning light.

She wondered what it tasted like.

He capitalized on her distraction. She was on the ground in the next breath. Every solid, wonderful inch of him pressed into her from above. He held both of her hands above her head with one of his. They panted together, their faces just inches apart. "Yield?" he breathed.

She glanced at his mouth before meeting his eyes. "Never," she whispered, wrapping her legs around his waist in a single swift motion and heaving herself to the side. He fell with her, his breath coming out in a shocked grunt as the sand met his back. She pushed her knees into the thick tissue of his biceps and pinned him. "Yield?"

The gold in his eyes danced as he stared up at her. "Never," he mimicked after a beat. He lifted off his back with surprising speed. Aisling slid down his body and onto his lap with a gasp. Her hands gripped his shirt to keep from falling. Koen wrapped his arms around her back, bringing their faces close enough to share a breath.

Everything in her stilled.

Koen's gaze darted between her lips and eyes.

She wanted to lean forward. Wanted to brush her lips against his. Wanted so badly to lose herself in him. To finally allow herself to give in and have exactly what she wanted.

Her mouth parted slightly. Every beat of her heart was a sledgehammer to her ribs as she leaned forward.

The ground beside them shook. Aisling yelped and fell off Koen's lap. Nyssa's golden wings shimmered in the light. Her intelligent amber eyes regarded them with a knowing twinkle. "Good morning," Oryn cooed as he landed on the sand. "Training looks riveting this morning. I'm interested in what method that was, Koen? It's rare I see it out in public."

Koen ran a hand through his sandy hair and offered Oryn a glare. "It's new."

"Hmm." Oryn's bright emerald stare landed on Aisling. "Are we ready for some more flying, my dear?"

Aisling couldn't stop the blush from creeping up her neck. She cleared her throat. "Yeah. Yeah, absolutely."

"Wonderful," Oryn smiled. "Shake out your hair, grab your jacket, and meet back here in ten minutes." Aisling nodded and glanced shyly at Koen before scurrying into her room. She leaned against her door and pinched her eyes shut in frustration.

It had been two weeks. Two long weeks and she was still too scared to take the next step with Koen.

The door opened. She flew forward. Troy barely glanced at her before throwing himself on the couch with his arm over his eyes.

"Uh, hello?"

He grunted in answer. Aisling rolled her eyes and walked into the bathroom to wash the sand from her face. Her hands twisted as she rebraided her hair, shaking out the spare particles of sand onto the floor and ignoring the flashbacks of Koen's lap. Troy grunted dramatically again from the couch. She peeked out of the bathroom. "Are you unwell?"

"Why is everyone so nice here?" he whined.

"You're going to have to be a bit more specific."

He sat up. "I just met with Aedan. The King."

"I know he's the King." Aisling lifted a brow. "And?"

"He's so nice. Genuinely, wonderfully, impossibly kind. I don't understand."

Aisling smiled. "He's the best. I was terrified to meet him for the first time. Koen told me I was overthinking it. He was right." She would never admit it to him. "What did Aedan ask you?"

"Politics and issues and stuff. Probably the same things he asked you. But when I thought he was finished, he asked about me."

"What did you tell him?"

"Everything."

She widened her eyes in surprise. "About your family?"

He nodded. "It was like talking with a therapist. I couldn't not tell him."

"Are you okay?"

"I'm great," he whispered. "He's just... he's exactly what you want in a leader. And the Ferox, all the people at the Keep, the medical team... everyone is genuinely kind." He shook his head. "If I had come here in a dream before you, I would have left the old world, too."

"I still could have handled it better," Aisling mumbled.

"Oh, you could have handled it *much* better," he agreed. "But thanks to that stupid little note you left me—which by the way, I read about a thousand times the first day you were gone, I had an anchor to you here and could come yell at you in another world."

"Why did you keep it?" She always imagined him throwing it out without even opening it. But here it was, in her room, in a different life, a different world, on the dresser next to the bed they shared.

His brows furrowed. "Why would I ever get rid of part of you, Ash?"

"I just…" she shook her head. "I never thought I'd see it again. My goodbye note. My admission that I let my old self die."

"You're still you, and I'm still me," he said softly, reaching for her hand. He rubbed smooth strokes over her knuckles. "Your goodbye note ended up being the key to my new life. I will never, ever, get rid of it."

Aisling bent down and kissed the top of his head. "You should frame it." She grabbed her jacket and checked her hair.

"Where are you going?"

"Oryn wants to do another flying session." Aisling and Morana had taken to the sky every day, sometimes twice daily, in the last two weeks, but Oryn insisted on extra sessions. She wouldn't complain. "Wanna join?"

"I have no core strength and a fear of heights." He sat back against the couch. "Dinner tonight? My shift ends right around then."

"Are you asking me on a date?"

"Yes."

"Then yes. I expect flowers and a dessert." She stopped at the door. "Did I tell you I baked again for the first time two weeks ago?"

"You've been too busy getting your ass beat every day to speak to me."

"You're too busy getting smarter and falling asleep before I even come to bed."

He glanced around the room expectantly. "Did you bring me anything?"

"You're supposed to say, 'that's great!', or something along those lines."

He leveled her with a stare. "You're right. I apologize. How was it? What did you make?"

"Just some bread. Nothing crazy."

"Feel better?"

She shrugged. "Yeah, actually. I felt normal again. Like I got that little bit of myself back."

"You'll never be normal, darling." He looked around her room again. "So, did you bring me anything?"

Aisling worked to keep from throwing something at him. "No. I didn't. Koen ate an entire loaf as soon as it came out of the oven." It was still steaming as he ripped it apart and devoured it like a man starved.

Troy's eyebrows arched. "Oh, Koen was there?"

She debated punching him but opened the door instead. "You're right. Everyone is nice here. This is what the other world was missing—people who are actually happy."

Oryn wasn't in the Pit or the Lair, nor was Nyssa. Morana lumbered out with Favilla at her side and Aisling climbed into the saddle. Her dragon flew for the ravine, but Oryn was nowhere to be seen. There was no brilliant golden light beaming in the sunlight from Nyssa. Morana climbed higher into the clouds with Favilla like a shadow beneath them.

The dragons were training Favilla in their own way. Muscles grew where bone had jutted out. Her sunken scales glistened. Her stomach was full, eliminating the sight of her protruding ribs. Her flying looked natural again. She was finally morphing back into a powerful dragon of the Ferox.

Morana hummed her happiness down the bond as they sailed in the endless sky. Their time together as dragon and rider had always been sacred, but now their connection was deeper, their bond nearly divine. The wind caressed Aisling's skin and danced in her hair. She basked in the feeling, the air and the sun and the clouds, and leaned into the joy pounding through her veins.

A blur of bright red scales flashed a foot in front of her dragon. Morana bellowed and pulled back enough to jostle Aisling in the saddle.

Calen dove down a heartbeat later, stopping just inches from Morana's open mouth. He chirped in a challenge with a wicked gleam in his eyes that his rider mimicked. "Ready to play?" Amerie shouted against the wind.

Aylim soared into the clouds, matching their deep gray hue. Cielle scowled. "Morana is going to make him pay for that."

She was right. The bond thundered with shadow. Morana's amethyst eyes latched onto Calen with a predacious intensity Aisling knew all too well.

Osiris made his way through the clouds with lackadaisical grace and boredom in his unsettling white eyes as he took in the scene. Elaila mirrored him, her stare darting between Amerie and Cielle with knowing exhaustion. She glanced at Aisling and shrugged in defeat.

"Let's race," Amerie suggested. Cielle lifted her brow, cautiously enthused. Aylim perked up. "Through the ravine."

"No," Elaila shook her head. "That's exactly where Aisling shouldn't be right now, and that is not what Oryn asked us to do."

Amerie smiled at Aisling. "What do you think, Ash? Too much stone? Too dark?"

"Amerie!"

Aisling smiled at the blatant challenge in Amerie's voice. It was too enticing to ignore. "To the sea or from it?"

Elaila's eyes widened. She glanced at Cielle. "Are you going to say anything?"

"Her dragon breathes shadow, E. I don't think she's scared of the dark."

They had no idea.

"Fine," Elaila snipped. "I'll wait at the end with Favilla. That way we can tell Kaida and Oryn and Koen how stupid all three of you are when one of you gets hurt."

"Perfect," Amerie winked, her face feline with delight. Calen dropped from the clouds. Morana and Aylim followed. The three dragons hovered above the roiling sea before the ravine's mouth. "First one through and out the top closest to the wall wins. No biting, no hitting," she looked pointedly at her own dragon.

"Winner gets?" Cielle asked.

"Bragging rights, obviously."

They shook their heads in agreement. The three dragons positioned themselves in a line, their excitement palpable. Aisling felt the bond twitch, felt Morana's muscles tense in anticipation.

Amerie whistled, and they moved as one.

Aylim bolted forward, her tiny body like a dart with the help of the wind. Calen growled his annoyance at her tail. Morana hung back until they disappeared through the mouth. With a rumble, she flew into the shadows.

Aisling leaned forward and pressed her no longer broken body against her dragon's back. Her blood sang. Her eyes drank in the darkness that tickled her skin as it devoured her.

Morana dove low. Aisling watched Calen above, his muscular body gliding through the rocks with a laughing Amerie on his back. Aylim weaved through the thick shards of stone as if they weren't even there.

The rocks pressed in closer. The light dissipated. Morana pushed through.

Aisling waited for the panic, for the memories and flashbacks to consume her like they did every night even with Troy at her side. She waited to hear the Man's voice in her head, his threats and taunts, but nothing happened.

She smiled as the stone walls closed in. As the darkness hung heavy against her chest. Fresh air was in her lungs. Wind whipped her hair. She was alive. She had made it out.

The darkness no longer laughed at her.

She was darkness. She was shadow and light.

She was the Shadow Bringer.

Morana rumbled in agreement, throwing a rush of pride down the bond. She ducked lower.

And as the stone pressed in, as the final wall of the ravine rushed closer, Aisling laughed. Morana pulled straight up with blistering force. Aisling gritted her teeth against the pull of gravity and forced herself to mold into her dragon's back until they were one.

Amerie shrieked in frustration when Morana flew just in front of Calen's snout, cutting off his ascent in a flash of shimmering white scales.

Cielle cursed as Morana rushed past her and covered Aylim with a flap of her giant wings. Morana's wind pushed the other two dragons down in the tight space.

Aisling shouted her delight as she and Morana burst through the ravine's opening. As the sunlight doused her. As the wind and clouds greeted her.

Morana roared her victory to the sky before dousing it in shadow. Aisling bathed in it.

TWENTY-NINE

KOEN

"Interesting new technique," Oryn murmured when Aisling disappeared through the doorway. "I've never seen it in the daylight before."

Koen grimaced and wiped the sand off his clothes as he stood. "I..."

Oryn smirked, but something lurked in the depths of his bright eyes. "I need you to come with me."

"Where?"

"Down south. A farming village right on the coast—Senex. They caught someone."

Senex. Where he met the farmer and his sons all those weeks ago. "Cruento?"

"Sounds like it. Anwir got word just minutes ago and told Kaida. She asked us to go."

Koen pulled on the bond. "What's the plan?"

"Same as always," Oryn said, rolling his shoulders back. "No need for armor. Grab your weapons."

Neera strolled out of the Lair, her bright eyes immediately latching onto Koen's. Their bond twinged with anticipation. He sprinted to the edge of the Pit and grabbed a few of his favorite blades before leaping onto Neera's back. "Wait," he glanced to the doors. "You said you would meet Aisling here."

"No. I told her to meet here. I never said to meet me." Oryn stroked Nyssa's scales. "The girls already know what to do with her. Don't worry. She's in good hands."

He was in the air with Nyssa in the next breath. Neera followed. After a quick but easy flight, they landed in a familiar field of livestock where three men awaited them.

The older man he met long ago extended his hand to Koen and Oryn. "Name's Arvin." He glanced between the dragons. "No white one?"

"Not this time," Koen said with a half-smile. He nodded in greeting to the sons standing behind Arvin like giant pillars.

"Arvin, it's a pleasure," Oryn smiled, genuine and welcoming. "Please, tell us more about what's happening. We received your falcon and came as quickly as we could."

Arvin's eyes darkened. He gestured for them to follow him to the white barn in the distance. "Young man came to us early this morning looking for farm work. It's not unusual. Lots of folk come looking for temporary jobs to make a bit of money before they move on to bigger things. We need the help." His sons nodded in agreement. "But this one... there was something off about him. I agreed he could stay in the barn to help us with the markets in town for the next two days, but that was it. Didn't feel comfortable having him longer than that. This man is...odd."

Koen glanced at the sprawling farm. A stone house with large windows faced the sea. Cows and horses littered the fields, their scents wafting in the air. Neera and Nyssa followed the men a few paces back. The livestock were silent in their presence.

"Not an hour into working, he starts going off on this tangent about the Cruento and how great their cause is." Arvin turned to Oryn, a serious look in his weathered eyes, "We are not Cruento sympathizers in this house, I can assure you. We disagree with everything they stand for. My wife is stronger than all three of us combined. She's terrifying if I'm being honest." His eyes softened for a heartbeat. "Not everyone can be so lucky to have a powerful woman in their life, but we are. We would never stand for her being treated like that." His voice tinted with pride. One of his sons glanced at his brother and rolled his eyes.

Arvin cleared his throat. "Anyway, we tell him that sort of talk isn't welcome on our property, and if it continues, he will be forced away without pay. He goes quiet for a few minutes before bursting into a story made of nightmares. Almost like he would die if he didn't get it out. A compulsion."

"Stupidity is never silent," Oryn murmured.

Arvin glanced at Koen. "A story about Aisling."

Fire coursed through Koen's veins. Neera echoed it, sending a trickle of her own anger down the bond. "What about Aisling?" he gritted through his teeth.

Arvin hesitated, his eyes dancing between Oryn and Koen. One of his sons stepped up. His voice was brawny and deep. "They plan to get Aisling back. He went into graphic detail about the ways they will assault her when the time comes. Horrible, revolting things that I cannot—will not—repeat."

"We know she escaped with Favilla," Arvin offered. "And we would not be able to live with ourselves if we heard of their plans and didn't alert you." He glanced at Koen. "I told you if I heard anything I would tell you. I was not lying, sir."

Koen felt a rush of gratitude and respect for these men. He banked his fury as best he could and dipped his chin in thanks. Oryn glanced at the barn, the friendliness in his eyes dampened. "What name did he give you?"

"Nabal." Arvin stopped just before the barn doors. "My boys tied him up. He isn't going anywhere."

"Did he mention any specifics? Any direct plans?"

The men shook their heads. "Nothing," the other son said. "It sounded more like idle threats, but we couldn't let it go. Not when it was so descriptive."

Oryn rested his hand on Arvin's shoulder. "You did the right thing. We will handle it from here."

Arvin turned away from the barn and looked toward his house. The silhouette of an older woman, shorter and slightly hunched, stood in a window. "Bloodstains do not bother me, gentlemen. In the end, there's no discerning the blood of a human from that of a beast. Please keep that in mind when you deal with my unwelcome guest."

He led his sons toward the house without a look back.

Oryn unsheathed a single dagger. "Can you remain objective?"

Koen clenched his jaw. Could he? After learning they had plans for Aisling after everything they had already done to her? Learning they wanted her back just to hurt her more? They thought of her as a plaything. As an object.

"Yes."

"Wonderful," Oryn purred. He pulled open the barn door. It was dark inside save for a few rays of light shining through wooden slats. Specks of dust danced in the air with their movement. Koen looked appreciatively at the work the sons had done.

Both of the man's arms were tied to wooden rafters above. His ankles were strapped to wooden pillars on either side, making his body into a human X. He was barely suspended off the ground, awkwardly hovering on his toes. His head hung between his shoulders. His hair was shaved off, leaving a dark fuzz on the top of his head. Lean pale muscle peeked out from his torn shirt.

The man looked up. Blood trailed from his nose in a thin river past his mouth. A few scattered bruises decorated his arms and legs. His dark eyes widened in recognition. Neera and Nyssa stood guard outside the door. His face paled at the sight of the scales.

"Nabal, is it?" Oryn asked. His hands clasped behind his back. The calming, comforting voice was gone. In its place was a voice Koen looked forward to— one of barely contained power and rage that only came out in darkened rooms and bloodied fields.

Nabal nodded, his eyes darting between a slowly pacing Oryn and a too-close Koen. "Release me," he rasped. "I've done nothing wrong."

Oryn smiled over his shoulder at their guest. It appeared warm, but Koen saw the ice just beneath the surface. It sent a roll of giddy anticipation down his spine. "Nabal. I hate for us to have to meet like this, but I've heard some troubling information from my dear friends here and had to confirm for myself." He took a step closer and angled his head. "But first, let me introduce myself properly. I am Oryn, second-in-command of the Ferox, close friend of King Aedan, and bond to the dragon Nyssa. She's right outside and willing to meet you if you so prefer." Nabal's eyes darted between Oryn and the open doors where Nyssa's golden hide glittered in the sun.

Oryn came to Koen's side. "And this is Koen. You know him as the Blade of the Ferox. He hunts both the land and air for men like you. His bond is Neera. You may have heard stories of her ability to control her flames into whatever shape she deems necessary. They're all true." He placed a hand on Koen's taut shoulder. "He is also a dear, dear friend of Aisling's."

Koen glared at the man with a darkness, a rage, that he'd kept inside since Aisling returned. Nabal blanched. Oryn sighed. "I am a friend of hers as well, but the bond I have with her is nothing compared to what she and Koen have. He is very, *very* interested to hear what you have to say about someone he holds so dear to his heart, Nabal." He stopped in front of the now trembling man. "So please, enlighten us."

"I don't know anything," Nabal whispered. "That man out there is lying. Whatever he told you is false. I don't know what you're talking about."

"Hmm." Oryn tucked his chin to his chest in thought. His hand swiped forward from behind his back, the dagger inside slicing at the rope holding their prisoner's left arm. Nabal grunted as his weight transferred awkwardly, one arm swinging. "That is disappointing." Oryn lifted his brow at Koen.

Koen didn't want to use his blades. He sank a punch into Nabal's side, unable to stop his smile at the sound of a deep crack reverberating against the barn walls. Nabal shrieked in pain.

"Now," Oryn said cheerfully, "we can do this one of two ways, Nabal. We can do it Elaila's way, or Koen's way. I'll let you decide."

Nabal glared at Koen. Every weak inch of him shook. "Fuck you."

"Elaila's way it is!" Oryn lunged forward. His blade twinkled in the weak dappled sunlight as he held it against Nabal's throat. Koen ripped the prisoner's pants down to his ankles. Nabal squirmed against the restraints but didn't dare hit Oryn with his free arm.

"Fine! Fine!" he screamed. "Koen's way."

Koen smirked. Oryn let out a dramatic sigh. "Wonderful choice." The blade left Nabal's throat. "Koen's way is very simple. You will answer our questions. You have the chance now to be a good person and tell the truth. But you can lie if you want. It truly doesn't matter.

Your fate is sealed after the venom you spread today. The world does not need more unjustifiably angry men, Nabal. Your hatred and weakness will not be missed." Oryn tucked the blade into his leathers. He glanced at Nabal's naked groin. "Unless you'd like to know what Elaila would do?"

Nabal's answers proved vague at best. He was a low-level Cruento, not important enough to know anything remotely interesting except how to spew hate. He knew of Aisling's beatings when she was with them, but other tales were exaggerated or complete lies. He did not answer a single question about the nest no matter how many clever ways Oryn attempted to get information. There was no concrete plan for the Cruento to capture Aisling again, but hearing her name on Cruento lips sent Koen into a frenzy. Knowing they wanted her back rekindled the fiery rage he had tried so hard to calm since her return.

Fire swelled in his blood with each strike and swipe of his blade. It wasn't nearly enough for what Aisling had gone through, but it was a start.

"You decide how," Oryn muttered an hour later as he strolled from the barn and into the light.

Koen nodded. He would destroy every threat to Aisling without hesitation. She trusted him with her safekeeping. He would do everything he could to deserve it.

When he was done, Neera stuck her head into the barn and ensured nothing was left of the Cruento grub but ash. A small puff of relief ran through Koen's spine. One less Cruento to hurt the woman he loved.

They gave Arvin and his family a heartfelt goodbye and flew north toward Anguid at a leisurely pace. Neera's bond warmed as they lifted over the Keep and found the rest of the dragons painting the sky ahead.

Soren hovered just over the sea. Kaida's bright hair was a twinkling light against his dark scales. Cielle and Aylim caressed the clouds. Elaila and Osiris gently followed the current of the wind. Calen and Amerie whooped as they looped around the rest of the dragons in a never-ending taunt. Favilla soared to meet Nyssa. Their soft friendly chirps filled the air and warmed Oryn's hardened eyes.

And from the clouds like a beam of pure light, Morana dove. Aisling's dark hair unfurled from her braid and danced in the air behind her. A brilliant, intoxicating laugh fell from her lips as Morana spiraled down to the sea and pulled up at the last possible second. The bond warmed, from him or Neera, he wasn't sure.

Plumes of shadow demolished the sun, casting the sky in unyielding darkness. Amerie shrieked in annoyance. Kaida and Cielle laughed. Neera purred as if expecting it.

The shadow dissipated. Morana hung in the air beside Neera. And Aisling, cheeks red and eyes bright, smiled at Koen from her saddle.

No one would ever show him anything more beautiful than what was right in front of him. No paint or pen could recreate the perfection that was Aisling exactly where and who she was supposed to be.

Koen smiled back.

THIRTY

AISLING

"Stop stepping on my toes," Troy hissed.

"Then move the right way!"

His eyes flashed. He tightened his grip on her hand and whirled Aisling around the floor of the empty throne room, now the makeshift dance studio Aedan insisted they use to practice before the ball.

"Three weeks of this," Troy muttered, "and we still have nothing to show for it."

"Speak for yourself," Aisling whispered, pushing him faster to the beat of the lilting violin with far too much ease.

She was stronger than she was three weeks ago. She spent the majority of everyday training with Koen and the girls, both with and without swords. She was given no lenience for her missing finger and never asked for it. She ran twice a day to build her stamina. Koen and Morana joined her for both, but Favilla could not be bothered.

Muscle piled back on with help from her late-night trips to Leonard's kitchen. Koen joined her, mostly to watch her bake and eat whatever she created. Troy tagged along at times and delighted Koen with tales of Aisling in her first life. Koen choked on his food when Troy went into graphic, slightly exaggerated detail about Aisling spitting in Red Lips's drink.

At dinner one random night, Aisling told the rest of the Ferox every detail of what happened in the cave. They listened in horror as she described the voice of the Man who haunted her dreams and what he had planned for her. Aedan's face paled to a sickly shade of gray. Kaida held his hand, the silver in her eyes ablaze as she listened in silence. Amerie's eyes pulsed with rage. Elaila was shaking by the end. Cielle and Aylim took her on a long flight with Osiris before she was able to return. And Koen sat beside Aisling, his presence a helpful additive to her growing strength.

The power came back. Aisling controlled the narrative. The memories no longer controlled her, she controlled them. She was healing. Not just physically, but mentally. Every inch of her was honed into a weapon again, this time much stronger than before.

"I'm leading," Amerie seethed at Koen.

"Over my dead body," he whispered back, glancing over his shoulder at the instructor before glaring at Amerie. "Can you just—"

"Does anyone else want to dance with me?" she shouted and yanked her hands from Koen's grasp. "Anyone who isn't an ass?"

"You need to learn to adapt, Amerie," the instructor said with a sigh, his exhaustion evident. The violinist didn't stop. After this long, he was used to the constant bickering of the Ferox.

"I'd rather dance by myself."

Koen laughed. "Don't worry, you—"

"I'll dance with you," Troy offered, stopping so suddenly that Aisling crashed into his chest. "I need some new scenery."

Aisling's jaw dropped.

"Fine," the instructor said. "I don't care. I just need you to look halfway decent in three days."

Cielle and Elaila twirled around the room, pleasantly oblivious to the mayhem. Kaida and Oryn peeked in and watched with gleeful smiles as their minions struggled to do something that didn't involve brute force.

"Why don't they have to practice?" Aisling asked Koen. He took her hand and wrapped his other around her waist, bringing her much closer than he did with Amerie.

"They know how to dance already. It was part of their life before here."

She grunted her annoyance and lifted her arm to his broad shoulder. He squeezed her hand once before launching them into the music. He was a better dancer than Troy. She ceded her control, letting him take her on a tour of the song.

"Are you leading or am I?" Troy snapped at Amerie. Aisling glanced up at Koen. He bit back a laugh.

The bells pealed. The violinist stopped.

The energy in the room dissipated.

For three weeks, the Cruento had relentlessly bombed towns short distances away from Anguid. Hundreds of civilians died every time, all succumbing to the sickly-sweet green gas within minutes. Some of the bombs were simple homemade ones. Some contained shrapnel. Either way, no one lived.

Hundreds of people, innocent people, dead because of Aisling.

Oryn's stations on the roads around Kairossen had yielded multiple Cruento transports. Women were freed from under crops and goods and taken to safety immediately. The men never saw another sunrise. But their bombs remained hidden.

Livestock supply had plummeted. The farms the Ferox relied on were decimated. Gareth and the rest of the dragon handlers were in constant communication with farmers all over Kairossen. Every farm offered their livestock supply in droves, but transport took time.

A single hungry dragon was a risk. Eight of them were terrifying.

In an act of desperation, Aisling offered Morana fish. She was promptly doused in shadow.

The dragons were silent as the riders entered the Lair. No one spoke as they donned their armor and swords. Aisling threw on the necklace of light knowing she wouldn't use it. There was no need for Morana's shadows.

They flew west until the grass thinned and tinted with red dirt. Ahead, only one plume of green gas danced in the air, its haze thinning with each cloud that passed overhead. A deafening silence pounded against Aisling's ears as another city lay demolished beneath them. She didn't see the bodies anymore, didn't allow herself to register their pain and suffering.

Morana bellowed. She was frustrated, as were all the dragons. Favilla flew riderless and silent, taking in everything. She was strong again. Strong and furious. Every call of the bells brought out the fierce dragon she had been before her capture as she saw the devastation and hurt the Cruento inflicted in her absence.

Soren rumbled as he turned, a dimness in his eyes that the rest of the Ferox, human and dragon, mirrored. They flew back to the Pit. Irritation hung heavy in each of the dragon's wings. Soren leapt into the sky once all the riders dismounted. The rest of them followed. An electric buzz ran through the bonds as flames and snarls ripped through the air just out of sight.

"Fuck it," Kaida said, pulling out her sword. "Sparring. No partners. No death blows."

She whirled on Oryn. He barely got his sword out in time. The rest of them followed suit.

The Pit echoed with the clanging of metal on metal. Sand jumped around their moving feet. Everyone's frustration, their anger and helplessness, flooded the air. The Ferox was made to fight the Cruento, and now the Cruento was able to launch attack after attack unscathed and untouched.

They needed this fight.

Aisling threw her blade forward. Amerie conceded a step in shock before doubling down, both of her daggers nothing but blurs of silver light racing toward Aisling. Cielle came from the other side and slammed her sword into one of Amerie's blades hard enough for it to fall to the ground. She shot Aisling a wink and forced Amerie's attention to lock on her.

Aisling turned. Her blade met Kaida's. She paused for only a heartbeat before attacking her leader. Kaida didn't hold back. Aisling threw everything she had at her.

Her body didn't hurt. Her wounds were healed. Her mind was healing.

The broken body was gone. In its place was pure muscle and unyielding will.

Aisling was herself again. Herself and so much more.

Kaida pulled out a smaller dagger and forced herself closer. The blade hovered inches from Aisling's skin with every swipe. Aisling struggled to block both blades but held her ground, gritting her teeth against the terrifying strength Kaida had for such a small person.

Kaida lunged forward with her long blade. Aisling didn't block the blow like instinct begged. She ducked and sent her leg out instead, connecting her foot with Kaida's ankle.

The leader of the Ferox fell.

Silence ensued.

Kaida lay sprawled on the ground, sand in her hair, eyes plastered to the sky. Aisling panted and lowered her sword to her side. The rest of the Ferox stopped, their eyes wide.

Kaida's laughter filled the Pit, soaking into the sand and floating into the ether with its wonderful silvery melody. She turned her head toward Aisling, a brilliant smile on her face. "Welcome back."

Aisling's shoulders slumped with relief. She extended her arm to pull Kaida up. Her silver eyes twinkled as she stared at Aisling with heartbreaking pride. "Are you ready?" she whispered.

Ready to fight back. Ready to destroy the nest. The Cruento.

Aisling smiled in answer.

Kaida gave Aisling's hand a quick squeeze before addressing the rest of the riders. "We're going to light the nest on fire."

No one spoke. Their eyes darted between Kaida and Aisling. Koen cocked his head at her in question, his brows furrowed.

"Favilla is ready. Aisling is ready."

Oryn sheathed his blade. "When?"

"Dawn. Tomorrow."

Oryn looked at Aisling. "Are you willing to describe the layout to us? Every single detail you can remember?"

"Yes." The memories were still fresh. Between her and Favilla, they could make a map of what they saw.

Elaila frowned. "It's too soon."

"It's not," Aisling reassured her. "We need to stop them before they plant more bombs. People keep dying. We can't allow that. I'm going to be fine."

Cielle glanced at Elaila. "She's right, E. And she won't be alone."

"We are all going," Kaida promised her. "And we will have a plan." She jerked her chin to the doorway. "Clean up. Meet in the common room in half an hour."

They hustled out the door and down the stairs. Aisling burst through her door and threw off her clothes on her way to the bath. Troy popped up from the couch with a giant textbook in his lap, his brows furrowed as she stripped before him. "Care to explain?"

"Not really."

"Well, you have to now," he said, following her as she walked into the bathroom and turned on the water. "Why do you look insane?"

Aisling turned to the mirror and flinched. He was right. Her eyes were wide and wild. A feverish blush clung to her cheeks. Sand hung in her hair. And she was naked, her pale skin finally clear of the blue and green marks she had gotten used to.

"We're destroying the nest in the morning," she said as she got into the bath. The soap slipped from her trembling hands and onto the floor. Troy sighed and handed it to her, crossing his arms and leaning against the wall.

"What do you mean?"

"Where I was kept with Favilla."

He balked. "You're going back?"

"It's the only way they'll know which entrance to use."

"You aren't at all concerned," he said as he slid down the wall and onto the ground, "that you might never come back? That you barely made it out of there the first time?"

"No." It was the truth. She would have her dragon with her. Her Ferox. She wasn't facing the Cruento alone again.

A blaze of heat ran through the bond hot enough to make her gasp. Shadow doused it in the next heartbeat. Troy's eyes widened. "Morana," she explained breathlessly. "I think Soren told them."

"They can talk to each other?"

"Yes. Soren and Kaida can talk through the bond with words. You get to that point the longer you're bonded, I guess. Morana and I can only do emotions."

"Can Oryn?"

"I don't know. I never asked him. But he's been bonded just as long with Nyssa, so probably. You can ask him."

"Why would I ask him?"

She grinned. "Why not?"

Troy stuck his hand into the tub and splashed water on her face. He walked out the door. "Dream on, babe."

"Why are you here?" she shouted out the door. "Why aren't you with medical?"

"I'm studying," he called back. "And it was going well until a naked woman ran through the room."

"This is my room, if you didn't remember!" She toweled off and opened her dresser, shooting Troy a glare. He rolled his eyes and returned his gaze to the book in his lap. She dressed in linen pants and a long white shirt and hastily brushed her damp hair. She patted Troy's head as she walked out. "We'll be in the common room for a while. You can come anytime."

"Family dinner, then," he said softly, turning the page of his book. She smiled and left him to his studies. Trays lined the countertops in the common room. Her stomach grumbled in protest for missing lunch. She filled a plate and took a seat at the table.

"I'm so hungry," Cielle groaned. She sat beside Aisling, and they ate as the rest of the Ferox trickled in, each looking and smelling much cleaner than before. Koen took the seat across from her. They ate quickly before Kaida pulled out maps and multiple rolls of paper.

She lifted a brow at Aisling. "Ready?"

Aisling had only told Koen the details of her escape. She steeled her spine in preparation for the onslaught of her past. "Yes."

Kaida nodded. "Tell us everything you remember. Nothing is too small."

"We need to know the path you and Favilla took to escape," Oryn said. "She filled Soren in as best she could. We need to corroborate with you to get a full picture."

"Dragons can be light on the details," Kaida explained, as if it was a normal thing to be discussing.

Aisling nodded, her chest tightening as she voluntarily brought the memories of their escape back up. She closed her eyes and immersed herself again in the darkness she worked so hard to control. "When we left the room, we turned left."

She had just sliced a man's hands to ribbons. Favilla had eaten one of them. Another lay fried on the ground.

"The hall was straight and had almost no torches, but it was too bright for us for a second. We needed to adjust. There wasn't anything else that I saw as we walked. It forked after a little while." She swallowed. If she had taken the left...

"The hall to the left was brighter. There were more torches. We went right. It curved slightly."

"Which direction did it curve?" Oryn murmured, his voice soft as if to keep her calm in her trance.

"To the right. Then it angled downhill. We walked for a long time. It felt like a long time, at least. We hadn't been able to walk for a while," she quieted, remembering the exhaustion of her atrophied body and the panicked beating of her nearly dead heart.

Cielle's hand covered her own, seeping warmth into her suddenly cold skin. Morana purred down the bond.

"We passed a room on our left. It was where they kept the thing that hurt Favilla."

"Did Favilla kill it?"

Aisling opened her eyes, unbothered by every stare in the room latched on her. "No. It was a prisoner as much as we were. It was covered in chains."

"Can you describe it?"

"Not really," she admitted. "They only lit a small candle when it came in. It was black. And gigantic, at least Morana's size. It wasn't a dragon, though. I know that much. But its feet were more like fins. That's the one thing I can say for certain."

Kaida frowned. "What did its mouth look like?"

"I didn't get a great look." Aisling searched her memories. "But its snout was squished. Like someone took the dragon's and forced it to become smaller."

"No wings?" She shook her head. Kaida grimaced and looked at her twin. "A pistrix, then."

"I've been wondering," Oryn murmured in agreement.

The table was silent. "Anyone want to elaborate?" Amerie whispered.

"A pistrix lives in the sea but breathes air." Oryn pursed his lips. "They're incredibly rare and unbelievably vicious. They're the dragons of the water. No wings, but they have the same brutality and intelligence."

"Then why are the beasts so stupid?"

Aisling started, blinking quickly. "He said..." She paused, hating the way the Man's voice in her head sent a chill of fear down her spine. "He said Favilla was preventing the beasts from being able to mate. Somehow in her sedated state, she was able to alter her eggs. Maybe the pistrix was able to do the same and kept its offspring from any intelligent thought."

Oryn frowned at the information but nodded. "You're doing a great job. Whenever you're ready to continue..."

Her throat constricted but she swallowed against it. "We kept walking. We were in the dark again. There were no torches. And the stone changed. It got damp. The air smelled like the sea. Water appeared. It was just puddles at first, but it got deeper as we kept walking." She stared at the table with her brows pinched, forcing the words to come out stronger than she felt.

"I saw a light at the end. It was small, like a pinprick. I thought I was hallucinating, but Favilla saw it, too. She got excited and pushed me faster. I knew we were close to being free." Her eyes fluttered. "That's when we heard their screaming, and I knew I wasn't going to make it. My body had given up. I knew...I had accepted that I was done. So, I threw a final look at the opening so that freedom would be the last thing I saw. There were three rock archways side by side, all black. And we were at sea level. The waves were crashing inside. That's why there were huge puddles up to my knees. My body stopped working at that point. That's all I remember until I woke up here."

No one spoke. She kept her eyes on the table, forcing herself to breathe normally. Forcing herself to anchor outside of the memory, to let it sink back to the depths of her mind where she kept it.

A foot nudged hers. She glanced up. Koen met her stare from across the table, a flurry of emotion whirring inside his eyes. He rested his foot beside hers, the touch more soothing than she anticipated.

Kaida cleared her throat and unraveled a map. "There is only one stretch of beach on this entire Kingdom with rock archways. Something about the waves and erosion or something, Aedan explained it to me once, but I fell asleep mid-lesson. The west coast of Kairossen doesn't have waves nor the type of rock we have on this side." She pointed at the Latebros mountains. "Here. And here," she pointed to a narrow spot along the western coast just north of the mountain range, "is where we found you and Favilla. Seeing how weak she was, I can't imagine she flew very far before you two made landfall."

"I've seen the archways before," Aisling supplied. "When Morana brought me here for the first time, we spent the night in a cave high above the water. The archways were directly across from us. And I swear they were the same ones when we burned that one cave along the cliffside before Impellor," Aisling said.

Kaida nodded. "I know exactly which ones you're talking about." She looked at the rest of the Ferox. "Make tea. Get comfortable."

They started planning.

THIRTY-ONE

AISLING

"Go. To. Bed," Kaida gritted through her teeth.

Amerie groaned. "Five more minutes."

"Go to bed now, and I'll take you out for a drink and dancing next week."

Amerie launched off the couch and disappeared through the door.

"That girl," Kaida muttered. She turned her attention to the rest of the Ferox. "We will arrive at the nest just before dawn. The bonds will wake you."

They nodded in agreement. Aisling looked out the large windows where the moon hung heavy. They'd been planning for hours. Dinner had come and gone. Troy had joined, and Aisling noted the way Oryn constantly snuck glances at him. He left an hour after dinner citing the need to study. They closed the door and continued planning, digging into every possibility, every outcome, with brutal focus.

Arguments flew. Numerous maps and scouting reports lined the table and floor. Oryn tied his hair into a ponytail at one point - a sign of major distress. A collective tension hovered in the air until the plan was ironed out and recited numerous times by each member of the Ferox without mistake.

The riders walked down the stairs toward their rooms. Kaida's door opened first. Aedan's voice sounded from inside, and Kaida's face softened before she shut the door. The rest of them entered their rooms silently, the heaviness of what they were going to do settling in their bones.

Troy was asleep in bed. His light snoring was the soundtrack Aisling fell asleep to every night. She threw on her sleeping clothes and crawled under the blankets, expecting to fall asleep immediately, but sleep didn't come for her.

She lay awake, staring at the ceiling, the fire, the stars.

Time passed. The moon glared at her. She glared back.

She sat up, frustration heavy in her blood.

Quietly, she exited her room and heaved an exhale before knocking on Koen's door as softly as she could. The sound echoed in the empty hall.

He answered almost immediately. She didn't have to say anything. He opened the door all the way. She walked into the room she knew almost better than her own and stood behind the couch. The fire roared, its tendrils licking the stone around them and dousing the room in a soft orange glow. Koen stood beside her.

"What if it doesn't work?" Aisling whispered.

"Then we deal with the consequences."

"I'm not scared to go back," she admitted after a minute. "But I'm scared for the rest of you. If anything happens, I'm the one that led you there. What if what I remembered isn't enough?"

"Yes, you're the one that led us to the Cruento nest. But we know the risks. Every time we fly out we know there's a chance we won't come back. No one will blame you for anything. You've been brave enough to—"

"None of this is bravery," she said sharply, turning her gaze to him. "Save that word for people who deserve it."

"What part of you isn't brave, Aisling?" Koen asked, his voice hardening. "Tell me why you can't allow yourself to have a single compliment. Why you can't see yourself like we see you."

"I wasn't brave. All I wanted to do was live. I almost died in the process."

"But you're alive now, aren't you?"

She glared at him. "This isn't comforting at all."

"Did you want comfort, or did you want the truth?"

"Neither."

His brows furrowed in confusion. "Then why—"

Her palms prickled. She swallowed the nervous energy bubbling in her veins. "I needed to tell you something in case I don't make it through tomorrow."

Koen's eyes flared like she had just hit him. "Why wouldn't you make it?"

None of this was going to plan. "Let's start over."

"Do you want to sit?" He tilted his chin to the couch. She shook her head. She needed to stand. Needed to say her piece and be able to run out the door.

"You've been... everything to me, Koen," she said, forcing herself to look into his eyes. "In the cave, the memory of you was what brought me the most peace. Memories of you were what kept me from sinking, from breaking."

Her body trembled as the truth she'd kept to herself for far too long spilled out. "I can't go into tomorrow without telling you how much you've meant to me this entire time, and I don't just mean since I've been back. I've been drawn to you since the beginning, even when we didn't get along. I hated myself for it," she huffed, "but I couldn't stop it.

"I do think you should smile more. I love your smile. I love the way you care for me. I love how honest you've been. How vulnerable. And I'm sorry I didn't acknowledge what you said at the cliffs. I was trying to find the same courage as you, it just took me a little longer."

Koen didn't move. Aisling wasn't sure he was breathing. She plowed forward.

"I feel myself with you, like I can finally relax and be at peace. Like my soul can take a deep breath." Her lungs hitched as her throat tightened. "And if I don't make it out tomorrow, I want you to know you've made my second chance at life so much better in these few months than my entire other life combined. I want you to know that I think about you constantly. That I crave being near you."

Aisling's heart slammed against her ribs in a frantic rhythm. The words tumbled from her mouth. "If I don't make it out tomorrow, I want you to know I love you. I'm in love with you. And I'm sorry it took me so long to admit it."

Her entire body trembled. She felt like throwing up and laughing at the same time.

She turned to bolt, the only logical response to declaring her love, but Koen's hand clasped around her bicep and kept her in place. Slowly, he turned her to face him. She stared at his rapidly moving chest, refusing to meet his eyes.

"You love me?" he rasped, his voice thick.

"Yes."

He lifted her chin until their eyes met. The gold flecks were shimmering in his stare, molten in the light of the fire. Her breathing hitched at the intensity inside.

He was her friend, her mentor. He was her safe harbor. He forced her to become strong. He made her want to fight. And she was his in whatever way he would have her.

His hands lifted to her cheeks. Slowly, his fingers traced her jawline until he tangled them gently in her hair. "I love you, Aisling," Koen murmured, lowering his forehead to hers. "Since the moment I saw you, I've been yours."

The words set her blood ablaze.

He lowered his mouth, stopping just close enough for their lips to brush. They shared a breath heavy with anticipation.

But Koen didn't move. He left it up to her.

Aisling lifted to her toes and closed the distance between them, melding their lips together in a searing kiss.

THIRTY-TWO

KOEN

Aisling loved him.

Koen had never heard more beautiful words.

Time ceased to exist. Neera, the Ferox, the Cruento, everything disappeared from his mind.

It was just Aisling—the woman he loved, loving him back.

His fingers twisted deeper in her hair. Aisling's hand cupped the back of his neck, gently urging him closer. She molded to him, her body soft and warm against his, and let out a slow, content exhale. Koen's body trembled with relief and restraint as her free hand lifted to his waist and up his back.

Her lips parted and he took the invitation, deepening the kiss. Every nerve in his body shuddered as he tasted her for the first time. She moaned softly against him, her tongue exploring his mouth with cautious curiosity.

The sound broke him. Koen lifted her without breaking the kiss, nearly going to his knees as her legs wrapped around his waist and her hands slid through his hair. He breathed her in, the sensual mix of jasmine and lavender he had fought against for too long.

Aisling's fingertips grazed his scalp. He groaned into her mouth.

He was going to die of happiness.

They became a clashing of teeth and tongues. Of hot breath and frantic touches. He lowered her to the bed, refusing to break the kiss.

He'd waited months for this. Wanted this more than he wanted to breathe, to live.

Aisling lifted to her elbows. He cradled her head and gently nudged her back with his other hand. For once, she didn't fight him. He crawled onto the bed and hovered over her, bracing one arm to hold her face as the other traced her side, mapping every curve and angle of the body he wanted to know better than his own.

Aisling broke the kiss. She panted, her eyes wild and wide as she stared into his. Her lips were swollen, proof he wasn't just dreaming. "Koen," she sighed.

He clenched his jaw at the raw sound of his name on her lips. "Aisling."

"Not yet," she whispered, a beautiful pink blush on her cheeks. Her chest rose and fell quickly, brushing against his. "I-this is..."

He kissed her forehead and rolled to her side. "Overwhelming," he murmured.

"Yes, exactly." She turned to face him. "But in a good way."

He bent his elbow, rested his head on his hand, and stared down at her in disbelief. He had accepted this would never happen. He accepted he would only ever experience this in his head. But she was here. This was real.

"I tricked you, you know?" Aisling froze. He twirled a strand of her hair in between his fingers. "I made Morana bond with you earlier than she planned."

She blinked rapidly. He could see the memories buzzing through her head. "What do you mean?"

"After our first sparring—"

"When you threw me to the ground hard enough to—"

"Yes," he smirked, the memory never far from his mind. He had wanted to lose control then. Wanted her to bathe him in kisses full of nothing but her hatred so long as she touched him. "When you made me ask Morana those questions in front of everyone. Morana told the dragons she was going to wait until you got settled before she officially bonded. Kaida told us, but I couldn't handle it. I wanted you to be tied here, so I asked her if she chose you. It forced the bond."

Aisling's jaw hung open. "So sneaky."

"I couldn't help it."

The light of the flame danced in her eyes. One corner of her mouth tipped up in a smile. "Weak."

"When it comes to you, yes. Always."

"Is that why..." she paused, her brow furrowing. Her voice came out breathless. "Tell me your truth, and I'll tell you mine."

He smiled at his words on her tongue from so long ago, unashamed at how weak he had been for her from the very beginning.

She stared at him for a long minute before launching forward and crashing her lips onto his. He rolled back with the force, letting her control their pace. The kiss was soft. Punishing and reviving. "That was right after I got here," she whispered, breaking from his mouth far too quickly for his liking.

"I know."

She looked down at him and shook her head. "I had no idea."

"I'm grateful for that. Because everyone else knew instantly." She cringed. He folded his arm behind his head, the other stroking soft lines down the length of her spine.

"What do we do now?"

He tilted his head. "What do you mean?"

"I mean," she rolled off him with a sigh. He clenched his hand into a fist to keep from pulling her back. "Do we tell everyone? Will things change?"

He had thought about it, too, when he allowed himself to dream that she felt the same way. When he'd pictured them like this, talking and kissing and basking in each other, the reality of what they had to do blurry and irrelevant in the background.

"Nothing will change," he reassured her. "Everyone already knows. Well, they knew how I felt."

"How?"

He brushed a soft kiss on her lips, unable to help himself. "They've known me for a long time. According to Kaida, it was obvious, but we were the only two unable to see it."

She winced. "That's so embarrassing."

"Is it?" Koen laughed. "It's more embarrassing for me, then. I got an earful from just about everyone when you were gone. Cielle nearly tore me apart."

Aisling angled her head. "Why?"

He cringed inwardly. Shit. *Shit.*

His throat bobbed. She marked it. "I... when I put you in your room the one night a few weeks ago, I talked to Troy. He told me how badly what I said to you when you first came here affected you. And..." he slid a hand down his face. "And I panicked. I knew I had hurt you, but I didn't know it was that deeply."

Aisling rested her head on his pillow, silently urging him to continue.

"Cielle talked me down."

"Talked you down from what?"

Everything screamed at him to shut up, but he swore if she came back, he would be honest. Swore he'd show her who he really was. "I don't deserve you, Aisling. You're kind and strong and-"

"You felt guilty."

He nodded. Aisling rolled her eyes. "I gave you a clean slate, Koen. And I meant it. I didn't hold a grudge. Yes, your words hurt. But because of them, I changed. I became who I was supposed to be. I didn't allow myself to shrink or disappear like I did in my other life. So yeah, you were a real piece of shit for a while, but without that version of you, I wouldn't be the best version of myself now." A weight fell off his chest, his back. His soul breathed in relief. Aisling smirked. "You have to work on your flirting, though. I know you have better material than what I've seen."

The corner of her eyes crinkled as she smiled at him. It was beaming and bright and beautiful. His lungs threatened to collapse at the sight—Aisling in his bed, not injured, but fully healed. Fully healed, and his.

They stared at each other for an eternity, ignoring the reality of what the next morning would bring. He slid her closer until all they could see was each other, all they could smell and taste was the other. Her fingers gently slid over his chest, his abdomen, his arms, in a silent exploration. A fire lit inside of him so excruciatingly hot he felt he might crack in half at her touch.

"I've never..." she whispered, averting her eyes from his. "You're the only person I've ever been in love with."

"An honor," he whispered, unable to verbalize how much it meant to him.

"How does it work?"

"What?"

"Being in love."

He breathed a laugh. "I have no idea. This is my first time, too. I think we're doing it right."

"This is your first time?"

"Yes."

She lifted her brows in surprise. "Hmm."

"Why?"

"I don't know," she shrugged, a hint of embarrassment in her voice. "I just—you're you." She gestured to his face and body. "I assumed you had a lot of—"

"Aisling." Koen ran a finger across her jaw, silencing her. "You have ruined every other human being for me. In every world. Every life. Falling in love with you was the easiest, most natural thing that has ever happened to me. Do not think for one second that you are something I've experienced before." He leaned forward and lightly pressed his lips against hers.

Aisling's hand grasped the back of his head and kept him against her. Her mouth parted, and he sank inside, the fire in his veins roaring.

A breathy moan reverberated from her throat into his. The sound rolled through him, settling in his bones.

His hand curled in her hair. The other twined around her waist until she was pulled flush against him. She melted into his touch, arching her back as he grazed his hand along her curves and gasping as he cupped her perfect backside.

Her body was healed. She was strong again. She was full and bright and perfect.

Koen broke the kiss to lower his head to her neck. He grazed his teeth on top of her bounding pulse and slid his tongue over it, wishing so badly to mark her, to let the world know she was his. She wrapped her leg around his waist. They inhaled sharply at the same time as she pressed into him in a rhythm that would be his undoing.

Every inch of his body was on fire. The shred of control he prided himself on was now a pile of ashes.

He pulled away abruptly. "You're going to be the end of me, Aisling," he murmured, pressing a single kiss to the hollow of her throat. She panted, mirroring the heaviness of his own breaths. Her leg lifted, but he hooked his hand around her thigh and forced it to stay put.

"I'm sorry," she whispered. "I—"

Koen's brows knitted together. "You have done nothing wrong except force me to hang on to the few tatters of self-control I have left."

Uncertainty tainted her beautiful, warm eyes. He couldn't allow it.

Koen lowered his head again and kissed the scar on her neck. He smiled at her sharp inhale. Slowly, reverently, he kissed the length of it, willing his love and adoration to seep into her skin, seep into the damaged tissue. Willing his soul to heal hers like he'd wanted to do since he found her on the beach.

A tear slid down her cheek. Koen brushed it away with the pad of his thumb. Aisling grinned softly and glanced out the star-filled window. "We have to be up soon."

The fire inside died. He nodded, unwilling to think about anything but her in his arms.

"I should go back."

"No! Sleep here. Stay with me. Please." She couldn't leave. Not now. Not when he finally had her.

Her face softened. A smile hinted at her lips. "Troy will miss me."

"Have you been sleeping together?" Koen asked, his voice much higher than normal.

"Yes." He waited for the anger, the jealousy, but it never came. "I can't let him sleep on the couch forever. But he snores so much."

"I can't promise I don't," he admitted.

She laughed. "Me either."

He tucked her hair behind her ear. "You don't snore. Even in a dead sleep, you're quiet as a mouse. I checked your breathing constantly when you got back, you were so still."

Her eyes flickered. She rested her palms against his chest. "Thank you for taking care of me when I got back. For...for just being there." Her throat bobbed. "I was in love with you before I got captured. And I think the memory of you, the tiny sliver of hope of seeing you again that I held onto, is what forced me to stay alive. To fight. I'm still in shock that I'm even here."

He covered her hand with his own. "We're going to destroy them today," he promised, "so everything you went through will just be a memory."

"A nightmare," she whispered.

He watched her fall asleep with the lights of the moon and fire dancing on her skin, and knew he would make the world bleed for her in the morning.

Koen gasped. Neera tugged relentlessly on the bond. It was a constant, nagging thrumming against his bones. Aisling stirred beside him and blinked quickly in confusion as she looked around the room and met his gaze.

"I have to get dressed," she croaked before sitting up and rubbing her eyes. She cringed at the mess he had made of her hair and glared at him. "This is going to take forever to fix."

He tugged lightly on her shirt, forcing her back down. She smiled as her lips lowered onto his. It was a soft kiss, lazy and unrushed. He felt himself melting into it and pushed her back with a shake of his head. "Enough."

"You pulled me down," she snapped.

"I know. I was talking to myself."

She smirked and rolled off the bed. "You sound insane."

"Go get dressed," he muttered, unable to stand just yet.

"Just because we're together doesn't mean you can boss me around," she said, coming to his side of the bed. She leaned down and kissed his forehead. "See you soon."

Koen watched her leave, his room feeling too big and empty as she shut the door. Together, she had said. They were together. He didn't tamp the joy it brought.

He washed his face with cold water, letting the freeze cool his blood and level his head just enough to function.

The plan. The Cruento.

He ran through it while he dressed. There was no room for error. No room for hesitation.

Doors opened and shut from the hallway. He grabbed his coat and left his room, knocking once on Aisling's door. Troy answered, his long hair disheveled and eyes heavy with sleep. He lifted a brow. Koen peeked inside. "Is she ready?"

Troy looked over his shoulder and turned back before whispering, "Her hair was a mess. What did you do to her?"

Koen couldn't help the purely male smile on his face or the satisfaction in his gut.

Troy rolled his eyes. "Stay here."

Koen leaned against the half-open doorway. Aisling's voice trickled out. Troy laughed, something booming and bright compared to the way he looked. A minute later he opened the door, his eyes hard as he brought Aisling in for a crushing hug and whispered in her ear. She kissed him on the cheek and murmured something too low for Koen to hear.

Aisling's long hair was braided into a crown on the top of her head. Her body was painted in black leather. She was so stunning, so sturdy and self-assured. She was somehow brighter, more radiant, than before she was captured—something he never thought was possible. Her honey-brown eyes glowed as she looked Koen up and down, a feline smile lifting her lips. His blood raced and boiled under his skin.

"Ugh," Troy groaned. He pushed Aisling out. "Be safe. I love you. Come back to me."

"Love you," she whispered, wincing as her door shut.

Koen gestured to the stairs. "Ready?" She nodded without hesitation and led him up.

Would he ever stop being awestruck by her? Would her bravery and strength become mundane someday in the future?

Inside the Pit, the riders wore all black leathers per Kaida's instructions. There would be no armor, nothing to give away their positions. If they were to do this correctly, they would blend into the darkness.

Cielle's eyes twinkled as Koen walked in with Aisling. She lifted her brow in question. He couldn't stop from smirking in answer. She bit her cheek to keep from smiling.

Energy buzzed and crackled between the riders as the thunderous steps of the dragons reverberated in the sand.

Soren walked into the Pit. His red eyes, normally unnerving, were terrifying. They glowed with a promise of blood, of retribution. Nyssa followed close behind, her golden wings somehow dimmed to blend into the darkness.

Koen felt Neera before she entered. The bond was electric the way it always was before battle. He'd come to crave the feeling after all these years. Her neon eyes latched on Aisling beside him, the bond tinting with a question. He sent his answer and pursed his lips at her playful chirping. She ignored him and nuzzled Aisling's chest with a heavy warmth down the bond he had never felt before.

Aisling laughed softly and ran her small hands over Neera's scales. "Hello to you, too, sweet girl," she murmured. Koen smiled to himself as the two parts of his heart stood before him, their love for each other evident.

Osiris and Calen walked in, followed by Aylim, each stopping in front of their riders.

Favilla appeared through the darkness. She was a different dragon than she was when he found her on the beach. Her scales were a brilliant black, somehow darker and deeper than Soren's. The muscles in her legs and back flexed as she stalked forward, her bright sapphire eyes landing on Aisling with predatory intensity before standing at her side.

Morana came in last. Every scale glimmered in the low light of the torches above.

Aisling buzzed beside him as the bond coursed through her body. No one made a sound as Morana stood before her rider, amethyst eyes radiant in the darkness, and rested her massive forehead against Aisling's.

Favilla lowered her head to the sand at Aisling's feet. At Morana's feet.

One of the girls gasped. Koen's heart stuttered. Neera's bond went silent.

It was an invitation. An offering. A promise of utter, complete devotion.

Aisling opened her eyes, immediately locking on Morana's. Her dragon blinked once in answer to a silent question.

Aisling knelt to the ground. She traced small circles on Favilla's black scales and murmured too quietly for anyone to hear. After a minute, she stood, brow furrowed as she stared at the still-bowed dragon.

Favilla lifted her head with a graceful arc of her neck. She stared down at Aisling, her blue eyes sharp like chips of ice, and lifted her leg to stomp once on the sand beneath her.

Aisling smiled. She stepped back to Koen's side, a feral gleam in her eyes as Morana and Favilla, dragons of light and darkness, of fire and shadow, moved behind her.

Kaida cleared her throat and stepped forward. "Do we have any questions about how we will proceed?"

"Do we need to go over the plan again?" Oryn added, his bright green eyes nonjudgmental as he scanned the riders. They shook their heads. Kaida's eyes darted to the doors. Her breathing hitched. Koen followed her stare.

Aedan lurked in the doorway. He was not the King everyone knew and adored. He was a man terrified for the woman he loved. A revolting tinge of fear lined his eyes and face. He leaned against the doorframe, arms crossed in front of his chest, lips pressed in a tight line.

Kaida shook her head imperceptibly. Her voice came out soft, reminding Koen of how she sounded when he was young, full of maternal care and patience. She met the eyes of every rider. "I am proud of you for what you had to go through to get here. Each one of us has had our issues, our struggles, and still, we strived for more. We have fought against oppression and hopelessness. We are the beaming light of hope in the sky when the people of our Kingdom thought the darkness would consume them."

Her throat bobbed. "Today we have the opportunity to banish the darkness for good. I wouldn't go into battle like this with anyone else. You are all strong. You are brutal and efficient and brilliant. I am proud to call you my riders. I'm proud to lead you. And I am so violently proud to be fighting beside you." Her voice cracked. "I love each one of you. And I want to see every single one of your sorry asses back here when we're done. Do you understand?"

No one spoke. Amerie swallowed audibly, her hazel eyes glassy. A single tear ran down Elaila's cheek. Koen's eyes burned as he took in the rest of his team, his family, and fought against the rancid thought that they might not all return. A thought he refused to believe was possible until Aisling's capture.

Oryn stepped to his twin's side and took her hand. Her eyes fluttered shut at the touch. "We leave in five minutes," he said gently, the meaning of his words implied. The girls mobilized first. Elaila reached for Aisling. Amerie and Cielle embraced. Soft sobs pierced the thick air. The dragons huddled together with nuzzles and chirps.

"Koen," Oryn called with his hand outstretched. Numbly, Koen walked to the twins. Oryn's warm hand rested on his shoulder. "We are so proud of you," he whispered, lowering his head until they were eye to eye. "You have grown into a man anyone would be proud to know and love. It has been an honor to be present in your life in the way we have."

Koen's throat constricted too painfully for him to swallow.

"If something should happen to both of us," Kaida said, her expression even, "you are to lead the Ferox through whatever comes."

Koen shook his head. No. Nothing could happen to them. It was impossible. They were invincible. A force of nature. Death itself would cower to the twins.

"Yes," Oryn insisted. "Soren knows. The rest of the dragons and Aedan know. They are in agreement."

He clenched his jaw. "I can't."

"You can. And you will," Kaida responded without hesitation, her voice hinting at a command.

He stared at the two of them, the faces he knew better than his own mother and father's. The faces he had wanted to make proud since day one. "I love you both," he whispered, his voice barely above a whisper. "I-you..."

Oryn's grip tightened at the words Koen had never said before. Something in his eyes shuddered. "We love you, too. We always have." He glanced behind Koen and hesitated. "Am I right in assuming..."

"Yes."

Both their faces lit into smiles. "Fucking finally," Kaida murmured. She kissed his cheek. "We won't hog you. Go on."

Koen forced himself toward the girls. He pulled each of them in for a hug, the feeling foreign. How many years had he been around them and never shown an ounce of affection? An ounce of humanity for the women he considered family-the women he trusted implicitly with his own life?

Amerie smirked, a tear running down her face. "I hope you give her better hugs than this."

Cielle kissed him on the cheek. "So happy for you," she whispered. He tightened his grip around her for a beat, unable to voice the gratitude he felt for her friendship.

"Thank you for helping me," Elaila said against his chest. "And thank you for helping her."

He couldn't speak anymore. He kissed the top of her head in answer.

Aedan joined the circle. He took Kaida's hand and glanced at the riders. "In two days, there will be a ball. I expect to see each one of you there. I have plans to share a dance with all of you." He looked pointedly at Koen and Oryn. "Including you two." They breathed a collective laugh, grateful for the ounce of lightness in the room.

Aedan's eyes darkened, a flash of despair inside, before he yanked on Kaida's hand. She stumbled into his arms. He lowered his face to hers, brandishing her with a kiss in front of all the Ferox. Amerie squealed in delight. Oryn groaned and walked toward Nyssa. The rest of the riders followed his lead, giving the King and their leader a moment.

Koen didn't care that everyone was there. He walked up to Aisling, wrapped his arm around her waist, and cradled the back of her head.

It would not be their last. He wouldn't allow it. But he kissed her like it would be.

She returned it with vigor. Her arms wrapped around his neck, pulling him closer until they were flush against each other. She broke it far too quickly, her breath hot against his face as she held his forehead against hers. "I love you."

He kissed her again once, just a small peck. "I love you."

He wanted them to be the last words she heard before they entered hell together.

THIRTY-THREE

AISLING

The bond was nothing but blazing fury in Aisling's chest.

She stoked it, feeding her rage, her bloodlust, to its glow.

Morana shook her neck in agitation and flew in the middle of the formation with Favilla at her side.

Aisling refused Favilla's bond in the Pit. Favilla deserved the same connection Morana and Aisling had. But Aisling offered her as much as she could. Favilla stomped once. *Yes.* Yes, she would accept it. She would accept whatever Aisling had until she found her soul's match.

They flew in the deep blue sky of pre-dawn in complete silence. The wind pushed them forward in anticipation. On their left, the sea slept. Its waves were calm licks against the stone cliffs.

Aisling refused to let her mind wander and spiral with worry. There was no point.

The mountain stone would hold no more power over her.

They would destroy the Cruento nest in its entirety.

The Ferox would make it out as a unit, just like they went in.

Her blood ran cold when the black tips of the Latebros peeked through the low clouds. Even in the soft glow of the moon, they were hard and ominous. A tangible wave of readiness rolled through the dragons.

Nyssa nudged closer to Soren. The twins sat up, their eyes locked on each other for half a minute, each second agonizing as a silent conversation and declaration of love drifted between them. With a brisk chirp, Nyssa turned right. Elaila and Amerie followed Oryn without looking back. They faded into the clouds within seconds.

A wave of grief blew through the bond. Aisling and her dragon tensed against it.

They lowered and sailed along the surface of the water. The three familiar stone arches stood like a beacon against the waves. Aisling's jaw feathered against the memory of the last time she saw them. Favilla's low rumble was a call to battle. The rest of the dragons echoed it too low for the sound to carry.

Just above the waves and at the bottom of the massive cliffside was a large, dark opening. It was easy to see how they overlooked it with every patrol. The waves covered a quarter of it even at low tide. With an angry ocean, it would be impossible to see. Aisling shuddered to think what would have happened if it had been high tide when they escaped.

Soren rumbled his command.

Aylim dove forward, her scales shimmering silver under the light of the moon. Aisling held her breath as she and Cielle disappeared through the opening.

Favilla went next, bravely disappearing into the darkness that had destroyed her for years.

Morana nudged the bond. It was their turn.

Yes, Aisling responded.

Time had finally deemed her ready.

She would make it out soaked in blood that wasn't hers.

Shadow doused the bond as Morana launched forward and into the opening. Cold instantly seeped into Aisling's skin. A cold she had tried to forget.

Aisling dismounted and clenched her jaw. She refused to hold her breath as the familiar stone laughed at her. As the darkness she had grown to know and hate stroked her skin in fondness. As the water licked her feet, tasting her from its memory.

Cielle pushed herself against the rock wall as instructed. Aylim stood a few feet down the entrance, her eyes latched on the looming darkness ahead. Favilla was nearly invisible in the blackness save for her blue eyes. A bolt of terror ran down Aisling's spine as she took in her glimmering dragon. Morana was a beam of light in the darkness. A target.

Sensing her worry, Morana nudged her toward the wall. They inched forward just in time for Neera to slide inside. Her eyes were neon against the dark, the only thing Aisling could see as her deep green scales blended into the black void around them.

Koen was on his feet in the next breath, silently coaxing Neera further. She stood behind Morana. All of the dragons eyed the dark tunnel ahead with brutal focus. Koen came to Aisling's side and pressed against the wall just as a hurtling wall of black entered.

Soren barely fit. His giant body nearly sealed the opening, cutting off the light of the moon. Kaida slid down his massive leg, the flame in her eyes barely contained. Even her hair was swallowed by the darkness. Without a word, she came to Aylim's side and patted her once in command. The riders dropped their coats on the wet stone and unsheathed their weapons. Kaida and Aylim started the long walk forward. Cielle followed her dragon with Favilla at her back.

The darkness ahead beckoned. It sang a story of pain and suffering. Of threats and promises made. It replayed Aisling's dying moments on a constant loop, accented by the dripping water around them.

She breathed against it, forcing her lungs to inhale fully.

Aisling walked beside Morana. Together they would face this. Two halves of a soul made entirely of darkness come to blanket the world not in shadow, but blood.

Koen and Neera came next. Soren stayed at the entrance. If any Cruento made it that far, he would be the last thing they saw.

Aisling paused, stopping the forward progress. A hint of a glimmer danced in the water beneath. She glanced up to see Favilla looking back at her, her blue eyes blinking once at the silent question. Aisling reached into the cold water and pulled out the dagger.

The blood from the man's hands was no longer on it, but she could still see it – the orange of Favilla's flames reflecting off its blade as she plunged it into his flesh. She pocketed it without a word, ignoring the questioning looks of everyone around her, before walking forward.

The tunnel curved gently to the left.

The ground dried under her feet as they ascended. The calm roar of the ocean went silent.

They passed the beast's empty room. Whatever it was, it was gone. Favilla didn't spare a glance inside. Aisling followed her lead.

The fetid smell hit her moments later. Reek and decay. Damp earth. Death. Waste. Hurt. Pain.

She clamped her teeth together, refusing to allow this place to hold any more power over her.

The light of a torch flickered in the distance. Kaida paused. After a heartbeat, she began walking again, her blades glinting in the light. Aisling's feet stuttered of their own accord when they reached the fork.

To her left was her room. Favilla's room. The room of terror. Of horror and despair.

She fought the sudden urge to burn the stone until the entire mountain collapsed and was nothing but smoke and memories. Favilla echoed the sentiment, her blue eyes ablaze as she stared in the same direction as Aisling.

For a second, for a millennium, Aisling considered it. Considered breaking from the plan and reducing the entire world to flame.

Morana stroked the bond. Koen's hand found hers. She calmed, her rage banking as his breath warmed the back of her neck, eliciting a rush of clarity down her spine.

The mountain didn't hurt her. The Cruento did.

Kaida turned toward them, her eyes darting on all three of her riders, then the dragons. With a curt nod, she turned right and guided them down the fork in the road Aisling had yet to travel.

There was far too much light. Torches lined the stone evenly and frequently. The dragons could not hide. Aisling cringed at Morana's beautiful scales glistening in the flames.

Neera stopped just outside the tunnel. Her giant body didn't fit through the opening. Morana looked back at her friend. The bond frayed. Aisling sent down a torrent of warmth in answer despite the fear solidifying in her blood. This hadn't been part of the plan.

Koen stopped and stared at Neera.

Aisling's heart clenched at the pain in his eyes. The tightness of his shoulders. She wrapped her hand around his. His eyelids fluttered. The muscle in his jaw ticked.

Neera stared at Aisling. The dragon's neon yellow eyes begged her to keep Koen safe, to keep part of her soul alive until they could be reunited. Aisling dipped her chin in a silent promise. She gently pulled Koen forward, forcing him away from the other half of his soul.

His hand gripped hers tighter with every step, like walking away from Neera was the hardest thing he had ever done.

Together they walked beside Morana. Together they steeled their spines and gripped their swords as they walked toward the enemy camp.

The hall widened. Dozens of lights flickered ahead. Aylim bristled. Morana went taut.

Voices sounded from the cavernous space up ahead. Faint, but definitive.

With a single look over her shoulder, Kaida nodded at her riders. Cielle lifted her blade and pulling out a smaller dagger from her leathers. Aisling felt Koen's eyes on her, but she would not look.

Her focus was on retribution.

Morana exhaled softly, dousing them in shadow.

THIRTY-FOUR

AISLING

The two men didn't hear the Ferox approach. They fumbled to light the torches, unaware of imminent death just feet from their noses. They didn't see Kaida lift her blades.

Two bodies fell to the floor. Air gurgled from their emptying lungs.

The Ferox stepped over the bodies, inching further forward in silence.

The heaviness of the tunnel lessened. Sweat and dirt tainted the air.

Morana's shadows dissipated. Aisling sucked in a breath.

It was the hive of chaos and evil. Of pain and oppression.

The mountain had been carved so deeply that Aisling wondered if it had bled. If it felt the same pain she had felt, the same pain Elaila and all the women hurt by the Cruento felt.

The gigantic room was shaped like a bulb, bottlenecking where she stood. It reminded Aisling of a jail. Three floors were carved into walls of the rock high above her, lined with dozens of rooms equidistant apart. Dozens of torches lined the walls.

On the main floor were long tables and benches on either side of a smooth walkway embedded in the floor. Tattered books sat scattered about. Random plates covered in old food piled up beside a large black cauldron full of grimy liquid. At the far end was a single doorway where the smooth walkway ended.

A whimper echoed. A male voice from above shouted against it.

Aisling followed the sound. Her blood ran cold.

Under the upper levels, hidden deep in the stone walls of the main floor, small cells had been carved deep into the rock. They lined the walls and ended on both sides of the massive dark doorway at the far end of the hive. Thick iron rods reached from the floor to the ceiling.

Fingers curled around the iron bars.

Hundreds of them.

Women stared at the Ferox from inside.

No emotion flickered on their faces. No shock, no fear, no hope.

Aisling couldn't discern the color of their flesh under the thick layers of dirt and blood crusted on their bodies. Their clothes, ragged and threadbare, would never combat the cold of the stone around them. Every head of hair hung matted and heavy. A few women dropped their hands from the bars to protectively cradle their swollen bellies.

Elaila had been one of them. Sweet, kind, quiet Elaila had been treated like this.

Favilla had been treated like this.

Aisling had been treated like this.

Morana rumbled beside her.

Aisling stepped forward on silent feet. Past Koen. Past Cielle. Past Kaida.

She stood in front of the cells and forced herself to look at all the women inside. Forced herself to see what her future could have been. A future beaten and pregnant and forced to survive unspeakable horror for the rest of her life.

The women didn't back away from her. They stared, blank and unfeeling, their eyes gray, lifeless voids inside faces too gaunt. Too numb.

There was no respect or dignity. They had no beds, no toilet. A single bucket of water sat in the back corner of each cell. Feces and urine and blood layered the ground.

They were animals caged.

Property. Items. Goods.

The rage she kept hidden far inside herself – the rage she forced into the recesses of her soul in order to heal – became a living, thrashing beast inside of her chest. She had no desire to control it anymore.

Aisling shut her eyes and freed the monster inside, letting it run rampant through her veins, through every cell and bone, until it was all she felt.

Let them see what they created.

The bond fizzled. Morana's wings splayed open behind her. The Ferox inhaled sharply.

Aisling walked to the center of the room. She unsheathed her other blade and tilted her face to the hidden sky. "I'm back, boys!"

A beat of silence. Then hesitation and confusion. Footsteps padded to doors, exposing sleep-addled men in various stages of undress.

Their faces paled at the sight of the Ferox inside their sanctuary of hate.

Aisling laughed, reveling in the sound against the stone. She had never laughed in the cave. Never smiled.

But she was back. Not as an item or a good. Not as property to be claimed.

And she was going to laugh as they bled.

The men shouted as Aylim unfurled her wings at the closed door on the far wall. As Morana and Favilla blocked the entrance to the tunnel, their contrasting wings shimmering against the torchlight.

Aisling spared a glance at Kaida in a silent request. These men didn't deserve to die by flame. They deserved every second of pain they had inflicted on these women.

Kaida smiled in response, her face transformed into something of otherworldly, terrifying beauty. The silver in her eyes shimmered in tandem with her blades.

Men poured from their rooms. Their shouts echoed as they sprinted down the hallways and stairs.

The Ferox did not move. The Cruento came to them—lambs running to dragons insisting on their own slaughter.

Aisling lifted her blades and smiled.

Her body, the one they almost destroyed, pulsed with a strength they could never destroy.

Her mind was blissfully blank as her swords cut through their bodies like silk.

She laughed, loving the taste of their blood on her teeth.

Time stood still or hours passed, she wasn't sure. She didn't care as her blade whirled, as her fury, her rage, took over.

It felt good to burn. To destroy. It was cathartic to purge her trauma onto the very men who dealt it. She let the monster inside herself, the one born of this hatred and pain, eat its fill.

The bond shimmered with rage. She melted into it, forging her beast's wrath with her own until she could feel Morana's power in her blood. Her dragon bellowed. Aisling echoed it, screaming her hurt and despair into the mountain. Hurling her fury and vengeance into every ear, every heart inside.

Blood pooled at her feet. She danced in it, twirling and twisting with her blades as bodies fell. As the screams dimmed, and the roar of men dwindled.

"The back room!" a woman's voice shouted through Aisling's crimson-tinted haze. "The back room!"

Aisling paused her fight and found the owner of the voice. A young girl no older than fifteen, her belly too round, pointed a frail finger toward the back door where the embedded walkway ended. "That's where they keep them," she shouted. "That's where they keep the eggs!"

Aisling didn't hesitate. She bolted forward. Men fell in her wake. Her name echoed behind her. She knew the voice, but she didn't stop. Aylim stepped aside, various clothing bits stuck between her teeth as she chewed and allowed Aisling to pass.

The large black door flung open. Aisling stepped inside.

The girl was right.

Dozens of eggs sat in small nests padded with blankets and enveloped in a steady heat from the multiple small fires scattered along the floor.

Favilla's eggs. Her children.

Beyond the nests, large empty cages stood on either side of a dark door in the back.

Aisling stared at the too-large eggs, her breathing shallow and heavy against the silence of hidden life.

The door opened behind her. She whirled on her heel, blade lifted.

Koen stood panting before her. A thick layer of blood covered his beautiful face. His dark eyes traveled over her in a quick assessment before widening at the scene around them.

"Get Favilla," she croaked.

Koen disappeared. Aisling lowered her blade.

Favilla's head slithered inside seconds later. Koen snuck in under her, his face tight, jaw clenched.

Aisling stared into Favilla's eyes. Her bravado fractured as the dragon took in the proof of her abuse. Proof of the life she had unwittingly created. "What do you want to do, Favilla?" she whispered.

Favilla's answer was instant. Her maw opened, blue eyes blazing.

Aisling and Koen inhaled sharply and held their breath. Gone was Favilla's brutal show of flame from inside the cave. This fire, this power, was different.

It wasn't like Soren's flame or Neera's net. It wasn't metallic like Nyssa's or bright and billowing like the rest of the Ferox.

Dozens of controlled threads of orange and red leaked from her mouth. Each one slithered over the floor and wrapped around an egg. The shells sizzled with the touch. Steam wafted in the air.

Favilla roared, the sound mighty and devastating. It latched onto Aisling's heart with agony so enduring, so visceral, tears slid down her cheeks before she understood what was happening.

The flame ropes squeezed tighter and tighter until the eggs cracked and splintered. Liquid oozed out from the tops and onto the floors. Favilla tugged again and again, her pained scream a dagger to Aisling's chest, until the shells fell to the floor in shards and glistening black bodies slumped lifelessly on the ground.

The flames disappeared as quickly as they came. So did Favilla.

Aisling refused to linger. She brushed past a shocked Koen and walked back into the now silent main room. Puddles of crimson covered the black stone ground. Bodies lay scattered in hapless piles. Fallen weapons gleamed in the torchlight.

Cielle nudged fallen Cruento with her feet to check for life. She plunged her blade into a writhing body with a sneer. Her warm eyes were replaced with a fury Aisling had yet to see in any battle. A weak moan rang out from another pile of bodies. Cielle twisted and threw a small dagger.

It sank into flesh. The moaning stopped.

Kaida lifted her hand to Cielle's cheek, the touch matronly and reassuring. Cielle blinked rapidly. Her shoulders loosened. Kaida smiled as warmth returned to Cielle's wide eyes.

Morana stepped on top of the bodies, unbothered by the crunching bones and squelching flesh beneath her feet, and stopped in front of Aisling. The bond was dark and silent, overwhelmingly silent, as they stared at each other.

The monster inside of her was quiet. The red haze in her vision was gone. She was just Aisling again. Just Aisling, and exhausted.

Her hand lifted to Morana's snout, fingers splaying on the blood-stained scales. Morana rumbled. The bond shimmered low before building in strength and light until it obliterated any of the pain inside Aisling's soul.

Pride and tethered fury. Love and adoration. Awe. Relief. Respect.

All came flooding down the bond, taking Aisling's breath with them.

The swords fell from her hands. Her knees collapsed. Morana's snout caught her.

A pair of warm hands lifted and cradled her. She curled into the solid body, anchoring herself in the smell of home, of love and security.

Here, of all places, she was safe.

THIRTY-FIVE

KOEN

Koen had never seen anything like it.

The woman she had been before was gone. The scrappy fighter he knew had died under this mountain. Aisling was a warrior—a dragon.

Her rage could have ended worlds. So strong it coursed not just through Morana, but all the Ferox. It was a delicious burn, a beautiful additive to his own bloodlust.

The Cruento never stood a chance. They fell too easily. He wanted more-wanted them to truly suffer for what they had done to the woman he loved. He had wanted to take his time with each one of them, bleeding them to Aisling's liking before removing their souls from the world.

"You are safe now," Kaida told the women packed too tightly together in the cells. "We will not hurt you. I will open these doors, but you cannot run." She glanced over her shoulder at the dragons. "They will not let you. The King's soldiers are on their way. You will be brought to safety."

The women stared back with blank, unbelieving faces. His gut churned. How long had they been here? What had they been subjected to?

All he could picture was Elaila when she first stumbled into the Ferox. She was broken and battered. Her soul had been shattered until she was a walking ghost of a person. Would each of these women suffer through the same rebuilding as his friend?

Favilla stepped forward. Kaida kissed the dragon's snout and murmured something in a low, soothing voice. Favilla opened her mouth. Her flame ropes slid across the entire hive, over the bodies and blood, and wrapped around the iron bars of every cell. The women stood back and gasped. Softly, gently, the flames eroded the bars until cracks popped up and down the long walls. Favilla shut her mouth, cutting off the flames.

Koen helped Kaida pull the iron bars off of each cell. The women didn't move.

"You're free," Kaida proclaimed, her voice catching.

A minute passed.

Cautiously, a young woman stepped forward. She stared at the ground just beyond the bars for a heartbeat. And stepped out.

The rest followed her lead. Some leapt over the opening. Some hesitated, a look of fear roiling in their eyes as if the fallen men would wake and brutalize them again.

They coaxed each other out with gentle words of encouragement and soft touches. Tears flowed from every eye, including Koen's.

Every single body emptied from the cells on either side. There was no age limit. Women with white hair and crooked backs shook as they stepped into their freedom. Young women steeled their spines and stepped over the line with soul-deep grace and anger. And to Koen's disgust, little girls no older than twelve shivered with wide eyes beside the older women they trusted. All of them clustered together in the back corner of the room, eyes roaming over the destruction in disbelief.

Kaida spoke to them in the same calming manner her twin possessed. Koen watched the women deflate. Watched them realize they were safe. And clenched his jaw against the incessant burning behind his eyes and tightness in his throat.

"Koen," Cielle tugged on his hand, forcing him to face her. "She's... I couldn't stop her."

He looked around the Hive. Bodies everywhere. Heavy silence.

Favilla was gone. Morana was gone.

He walked past Cielle and Aylim and through the torch-lit tunnel. Neera, his strong, beautiful dragon, remained at the fork. Her bond fluttered at the sight of him before turning acidic with worry. She stepped aside enough for him to fit and nuzzled him as he slid through. He kissed her nose and patted her scales, eternally grateful to return to her.

The other hallway was darker. Colder. And the smell...

He saw Morana first. Her gleaming white scales flickered like a beacon in the torch-lit darkness. She rumbled low in concern and lowered her head. He patted her snout, nodding once in shared unease before the dragon allowed him to pass by her.

Down the dark hall, a massive iron door more robust than anything they had at the Keep was wide open. Favilla's tail stuck out. Koen held his breath as he peered in.

Aisling stood beside Favilla. They stared at the cave void of any light, any life. Her spine was rigid, but her breathing was even and deep.

He glanced around as best he could in the darkness. In each direction, it pressed down on him. The air leeched from his lungs with every second that passed. He was too big, the walls too small.

"You get used to it," Aisling murmured, her voice flat and numb.

Koen roiled against the acid crawling up his throat. What she had described didn't do her torture justice. How she had found the ability to hope in this place was beyond him.

"I didn't hear his voice," she said quietly. "I wanted to hear it. The only time I ever wanted to hear his voice, and he wasn't here."

"You don't know that," he swallowed his panic and stepped further into the dungeon, ignoring the chill of fear that slid down his spine. He took her hand in his. It was too cold. "It was chaos in there."

"I know," she said definitively. "His voice is a tattoo in my mind. I would know it anywhere."

He fought against the need to run from the room. "He could have gone through the pass like we planned. Maybe Oryn and the girls have him."

"He wasn't here," she repeated. "He would never subject himself to these conditions. He was better than them." She turned to him. The fire in her eyes had disappeared. "I wanted to kill him."

"We will find him," he promised, grazing his fingertips down her arm. "And when we do, you can destroy him in whatever way you see fit. I'll help if you need, or I can sit and watch you work with a smile on my face."

She blinked slowly as if barely hearing his words. The emptiness in her was overwhelming. He brushed her hair from her cheek, stroked her skin with his thumb, and watched as her eyes fluttered, as her body and mind remembered his touch. Remembered she wasn't alone. Remembered she was free.

Aisling dared a final measured glance at the darkness and walked out the door, her body silhouetted in the weak orange torchlight from outside.

He had never been so in awe of anyone or anything as she held out her hand for him.

Together they walked through the tunnel with the dragons at their backs. Cielle sprinted in their direction with wide eyes. "Kaida is gone."

Koen paused, registering the hint of something down the bond. "What?"

"Soren called down their bond in a panic." She gulped, her eyes glassy. "Something happened to Oryn. Nyssa is screaming."

His blood ran cold. Aisling's face paled. She turned to him. "Go."

"I can't leave –"

"Go," she repeated forcefully. Her hand pushed his chest with enough strength to make him stumble backward. "Go help him. We will be fine."

"Go, Koen," Cielle pleaded. "We have three dragons."

Aisling lifted to her toes and kissed his cheek. "We'll meet you back at the Pit."

He ran. The bond pulsed with growing anxiety. He found Neera at the entrance, her yellow eyes scanning the sea. She extended her leg without looking back and he leapt up, barely able to clip in before she hurtled into the sky.

Neera called to Soren, the large black-winged mass in the distance. She pounded forward over the mountain peaks until she flew at his tail. Kaida didn't look at them. Her eyes planted firmly ahead to the small pass between mountains. The tension and worry in her small body danced in the air and through his lungs.

Koen heard it before he saw it.

Screaming. Shrill and bellowing and acidic.

A blast of fire burst from the narrow crevice below. The silver gleam of weapons twinkled in the first rays of morning. Hundreds of bodies writhed between black stone. Dragons roared.

He unsheathed his swords. Neera and Soren landed on either side of the narrow pass, their bodies shaking the ground, the very core of the mountain. Kaida was in the air before they landed, her bright hair glowing as she lifted her blades and landed in a chaotic mass of men. Koen followed.

This was not like the Hive. The pass was narrow— a logistical nightmare but the only one that seemed plausible enough to connect to the main hive. Aedan's undercover scouts reported seeing footprints along the seemingly unused ground for weeks in their sealed reports, and Kaida insisted it was an entrance. Planning for it had been an exercise in patience and trust for everyone.

The black stone surrounding them reached into the sky. Dozens of men ran through a small opening behind a single boulder, blades raised, screams at their throats. They came in droves. Waves of them pushed forward with the same crazy, hateful expressions as their fallen comrades inside. They attempted to climb up the cliff face, only to fall onto the blades of their companions.

Calen and Osiris stood on small ledges near the pass opening. Their flames blasted relentlessly against the waves. Below them, the girls fought like two goddesses against snakes.

Elaila swung her long blade with graceful strength, striking down any man who neared her. The blue in her eyes mimicked Soren's flame. Men fell at her feet unceremoniously, venomous slurs on their tongues with their last breaths.

Amerie was uncontrollable. Every inch of her was smothered with blood, and she smiled in the wild, unhinged way Koen knew meant death for anyone on the other side of her blades. He found his way between them and seamlessly fought at their sides, swinging his swords and body in a dance he knew too well.

The men fell, but not fast enough. When one went down, three appeared. Warm iron tinted the air. Sweat and dirt permeated the stone. A rush of panic slid down Koen's spine as the hoard of men pressed forward, their unending mutations overwhelming.

A chorus of blood-curdling screeches echoed from inside the pass, cutting through the sounds of battle like a razor.

Koen's mind stilled.

"No," Elaila breathed, her blade plunging into a man's face. She turned to Koen. "They can't be releasing them here, right?"

Calen and Osiris bellowed above the entrance to the pass. Their wings splayed, excitement and hatred flexing their muscles for the oncoming fight.

Koen swallowed thickly. If they released the beasts here...

Neera's flame curled around the pass like a ribbon. Koen and the girls stepped back as it slid in front of them. Amerie let out a choked sob of relief. Neera squeezed her net tighter and herded the Cruento men together. Their eyes bulged as the flames licked them and they realized who had arrived.

Soren inched forward. Shards of rock the same color as his scales plummeted to the ground in his wake. Koen watched in wonder as the giant dragon stood next to Neera, the two of them making a beautiful, terrifying pair. He extended his neck over the herd of Cruento and exhaled.

There wasn't time for them to scream before their bones were ash. Blue flame was all Koen could see, all he could smell. Neera's net dissipated. Osiris and Calen screeched in delight as Soren stuck his snout into the entrance behind the massive boulder and exhaled.

The screeches stopped.

The mountains rumbled with Soren's power. Koen felt the ground shake and the heavens threaten to fall. The bond fluttered with pride as Neera watched Soren incinerate everything inside, a faint twinge of something warm hiding in the current.

"Soren!" Kaida screamed. "SOREN!"

Koen's relief evaporated.

He looked over the hundreds of burnt, bleeding bodies and found Kaida kneeling on the rock, tears streaming down her face. Both of her small hands trembled over her twin's body.

Crimson painted Oryn's golden armor. His face had leeched of all color.

Nyssa stood over him, her gilded wings dimmed as she stared at the body of her bond.

Elaila came to Kaida's side. Then Amerie.

Koen couldn't move. Couldn't breathe.

He stared at Oryn in disbelief.

He was invincible. He was all-knowing, all-seeing. He was a bright beacon of death and indescribable comfort at the same time.

Oryn was the only man who had ever been a father to Koen. The only man who had been Koen's friend. His mentor. He was the only man who knew exactly who and what Koen was and still loved him for it.

Soren lowered his stomach to the ground and angled his back for Kaida.

Koen moved on reflex. He lifted Oryn's limp body from the ground, refusing to register what he was seeing, and climbed onto Soren's gigantic back. He sat Oryn down in front of Kaida, positioning the body to lean against hers.

Soren launched into the sky. Nyssa flew on his right. The girls jumped on their dragons and flew north toward Anguid without so much as a glance back.

Koen didn't move.

Neera blew a net of flame across the opening behind the boulder, trapping anyone still alive inside between dragon flame or Aisling and Cielle.

He stared at the carnage. Bodies littered the ground. Vultures hovered on the craggy rocks. Sharp beaks and sharper eyes widened in delight at the buffet before them.

Koen would not stop them from feasting. If they wanted filth, they could have their fill.

THIRTY-SIX

AISLING

Soldiers arrived. Dozens of them.

They came by ships and smaller boats and followed Favilla through the tunnels and into the main room with a mix of horror and awe in their eyes as they took in the dead, the blood, the women.

Morana stood guard in front of the women, a post she seemed to enjoy. The women warmed to her, a few brave enough to stroke a brilliant white scale. Morana's happy lilting chirps elicited a smile from some of them.

Aylim paced near the entrance, her psyche heavily affected by the stone around them and the recent rumble of the ground beneath their feet.

Cielle instructed the cavalry on the next steps. Female soldiers would be the only ones to touch or speak to the women. The men were not to engage at all, not even for a helping hand. Kaida's orders fell from Cielle's mouth in practiced perfection: Scout every single tunnel, every doorway, every pass, every loose rock until they covered the details of the entire hive. They were to leave no stone unturned, no tunnel or dark space unexplored. Aedan expected a fully detailed map by the end of the day. The leaders nodded with lips tight, faces ashen.

Aisling spoke to the women. "You will be taken by boat to Salus. There, you will receive medical evaluations and care. You will have a place to stay, a bed, and warm food. You will have water and a bathroom and warmth."

"There will be no men there," Cielle emphasized. "We want you to be as comfortable as possible. If there are any issues or needs, direct a falcon to the King without hesitation."

Aisling glanced over the herd of women, her throat tightening. "I was a prisoner here as well." She traced the scar on her neck. "I'm here to tell you that after today, it gets better. You will have nightmares. You will have flashbacks and moments of terror, but give yourself time. Give yourself grace. You have lived despite it all. You are all survivors. Remember that when you think you won't ever be okay again. Remember your strength."

The women said nothing. Some had tears down their cheeks. Some stared blankly.

Cielle took Aisling's hand and guided her out of the room. They turned left and walked down the tunnel in silence. A small armada of Aedan's ships sat anchored in the churning water outside.

The sea greeted her. Light and fresh air welcomed her.

They mounted their dragons. Aisling didn't look back as Morana sailed forward.

It had been her prison. Her tomb and coffin.

It was also her rebirth.

Oryn's blood tainted the clean bed. Aisling grimaced at the pile of bloody armor and clothes thrown on the floor and Kaida's horror-stricken face as the medical team worked on her twin.

Troy cleaned a deep wound on Oryn's bicep. His brows knitted in concentration as he slathered on a poultice and wrapped it with clean cloths. Aisling's heart tightened at the sight of her friend doing what she always thought he was born to do. Needles and jars of clear liquid went into Oryn's arms. Tinctures lay sprawled across the mattress in different colored bottles.

"Two deep stab wounds," the head physician said calmly to Kaida, pointing to Oryn's abdomen. "They are packed with antiseptics and clotting factors. His armor prevented the blades from hitting any vital organs, but his blood loss is critical."

"Will he live?" Aedan asked from behind Kaida, tears lining his eyes.

"As you know, Your Highness, I don't like to—"

"Will. He. Live." Aedan snapped, a vicious tint to his tongue.

"Yes. He will live." The physician said with a dip of her chin. "He needs rest and fluids. We are running them now through his arms, but he will need oral fluids as well to make up for the blood loss until his body can recuperate."

Aedan's shoulders visibly deflated. Kaida's tears didn't stop. She said nothing while she stared at her brother's face, her pain so potent Aisling felt herself start to crumble. The physician murmured to Kaida and pointed to various spots on Oryn's body.

"Out," Aedan instructed the riders, pointing at the door as he walked toward it. They followed wordlessly. He shut Oryn's door behind him and ran his hand through his disheveled sandy hair. "We're all accounted for?"

They nodded.

"Thank fuck," he whispered. Deep pools of purple hung under his eyes. Stress gleamed in his stare as he took in each one of them, checking to make sure they were all there, all healthy. "How many?"

"Hundreds," Koen answered. "And eggs."

"How many?"

"Three dozen. All exterminated."

Aedan nodded and looked at Amerie. She swallowed, her normal effervescence flat. "Hundreds as well. There were no survivors."

"What happened with Oryn?"

She shook her head. "I don't know."

"We were swarmed," Elaila offered, her small voice strong. "They rushed from the opening too quickly and kept coming in waves. The dragons could only blast so many. Some got through the fire. I didn't see what happened to Oryn either."

"Neera herded all the men with her flames," Koen said. "Soren burnt them, then blasted the mountain before they could unleash their beasts."

Aisling started. That's what the deep rumble under her feet was.

Aedan sighed heavily. "I have to tell Anwir. Is there anything else I should know?"

They shook their heads. "Would you like me to update him?" Koen volunteered.

"No," the King answered. "Thank you, though. Kaida needs time with Oryn. And Anwir is furious with me for keeping him out of the loop. I prefer to have him yell at me than you." He wrapped his long hair in a knot at the back of his head. "Thank you for what you did today. Now go clean up. Rest. I will update you on Oryn in a few hours when things have calmed down." He walked up the stairs, steeling his shoulders with every step.

The riders didn't speak as they walked to their rooms. There was an exhaustion between them, mental and emotional, that Aisling wasn't sure they could ever recover from. She turned her doorknob. Koen followed her in.

They didn't speak as she turned on the water. As they undressed and climbed inside the bathtub. She cleaned the blood off him. He washed it from her hair.

They drained the tub and refilled it before sinking in again, letting the heat soak into their beaten muscles. She leaned her back against his chest and closed her eyes against the warm afternoon sunlight peeking in through the windows.

"Are you okay?" Aisling whispered, the first words they'd spoken in an hour.

"No. Are you?"

"No."

His arms tightened around her stomach.

They got out when the water chilled. She wrapped herself in her robe. Koen threw on Troy's. She crawled into bed and rested her head in the crook of his neck. His arm curled beneath her and pulled her close.

She fell asleep almost instantly, the monster inside of her exhausted and sated.

THIRTY-SEVEN

AISLING

Aisling opened her eyes. Golden rays of sunlight doused her room. Her fireplace was still roaring. Koen's arm wrapped around her middle. He pressed against her back, his breathing slow and even against her neck. She closed her eyes.

Darkness flooded her room when she reopened them. The fire had dimmed to embers. She faced Koen, his brows finally relaxed in slumber.

She didn't know what time it was. Didn't know how many hours or days had passed. Her body was sore but functioning, unlike the last time she left that place. But Oryn's...

Quietly, she rolled off the bed and slid through the door. She knocked on Oryn's. Kaida answered, her eyes bloodshot and swollen. Her bloodied armor remained on. Wordlessly, she opened the door and allowed Aisling entry.

The tubes in his arms were gone. Bandages covered his abdomen. Jars of tinctures and poultices sat scattered on his bedside table. But Oryn's face was relaxed. There was no pinch between his eyebrows of pain as he slept. Aisling stroked the back of his hand, relieved to find his skin warm and dry.

"Have you slept?" she whispered. Kaida scoffed and slumped into the chair beside the bed. "Go bathe," Aisling said with as much command as she could muster. Kaida leveled a glare at her. "Don't look at me like that. You stink. You're covered in blood. I'm going to stay right here. If he even farts, I'll grab you."

"You don't tell me what to do."

"No, I don't. But right now, I do. You're exhausted and he's kind of boring. You have no excuse not to take care of yourself. He would tell you the same thing."

Something in Kaida's eyes flashed. The hardened steel softened. Her shoulders turned inward as she stood and wordlessly walked into the bathroom, shutting the door gently behind her.

"Thank you," Oryn whispered, his raspy voice barely audible. Aisling snapped her head to him. He kept his eyes shut, but a faint hint of a smile played on his pale lips. He squeezed her hand when she tried to pull out and get Kaida. "Don't. You were right. She smelled."

Aisling huffed a laugh as bone-crushing relief coursed through her. "How are you? What do you need?"

"Sore," he admitted. "And tired."

"Are you thirsty?"

"Terribly."

She lifted a glass of water to his lips and angled it slowly as he sipped. "Thank you," he whispered, his voice smoother.

"What happened?"

"I don't know. There were so many of them. Like ants. They just kept coming. Nyssa's flames could only do so much." He grimaced. Aisling brushed his hair back from his face. "How did it end?"

"Neera herded them with her flame according to Koen. Soren blasted them all to ash."

He nodded solemnly, his eyes still shut. "Wonderful."

"Are you in pain? I could have Troy get something."

"No, no. I'll be fine by tomorrow," he reassured her.

"You were stabbed, Oryn," she said dryly. "The only thing you'll be doing tomorrow is putting a dent in this mattress."

"I've had worse."

She knew he meant it. Knew his past was littered with bloodshed and injuries and couldn't stop the question from falling from her mouth. "How much worse?"

His eyebrow arched the smallest bit. He was quiet for a breath. "When we were young, Aedan's father sent us to another land for a job, which was unheard of. We did not succeed. To say that we barely survived is an understatement. We were only there a month before we snuck back onto a ship and came here. That's when the dragons found us." A shudder ran down his body. "I've never seen a place like it. The people... the damage inflicted on them..."

A knock sounded at the door. Aisling glanced at the bathroom. "Answer it," Oryn whispered. "But as far as everyone knows, I'm still sleeping."

She planted a quick kiss on his cheek. He smiled and let go of her hand. She opened the door. Aedan's eyes widened as he took in her robe and unbrushed hair. "She's bathing," Aisling offered.

"Has she rested at all?"

"I think you know the answer to that."

He hung his head to his chin. "I do."

"Did Anwir rip your head off? I have a hard time picturing that."

He grimaced. "Even worse. He was silent the whole time." Aisling gestured for him to come inside. They stood at Oryn's bedside. "I broke his trust. Something I have never done before."

"You had your reasons."

"Anwir has been with me for decades, Aisling. Since the beginning. Of all people, I should have told him." He pinched the bridge of his nose. "I know I did the right thing. No one needed to know but us. Word would get out. The snakes would find their way to the nest and warn them. We couldn't risk that." She nodded. He continued, almost whispering to himself. "I did the right thing. I know I did."

She squeezed his hand once. "You did. We rooted them out."

"No bombs?"

"No. We didn't see any."

He frowned. "Neither did the soldiers after you."

"Maybe they ran through their supply."

His jaw feathered. He glanced at Oryn. "How is he?"

She bit her cheek with the lie. "Sleeping."

"You know..." he said absentmindedly after a minute, "he was the one who encouraged me to go after Kaida." She cocked her head in interest. He nodded. "We've been friends for a very long time. I owe him everything. My life would be nothing without her."

The door to the bathroom opened. Kaida's eyes latched onto Oryn before sliding to Aisling's, then Aedan's. Her hair was unbrushed. She wore one of her brother's long shirts, exposing her muscular legs. "Not a peep," Aisling lied.

Kaida nodded her thanks. Aisling dipped her chin to her King before leaving. She walked up the stairs to the common room and took a plate with two muffins back to her room. Koen sat up as she walked in. His dark hair was ruffled, his smile sleepy. His eyes went to the muffins. "Hungry?"

"Not really," she admitted, "but we haven't eaten in a while." She knelt on the bed and put the plate between them. He waited for her to pick first before grabbing his. "I checked on Oryn."

His brows lifted. "And?"

"Well, Kaida still thinks he's sleeping, but when she went to take a bath Oryn told me he was tired and sore."

Koen laughed but relief washed over his face. "You convinced her to bathe?"

"Barely. Aedan's with her now." She chewed the muffin. "Oryn said they were swarmed. There were too many."

He nodded. "The pass was much narrower than inside the mountain. It was easy for anyone to be overpowered by a rush of bodies. The dragons had to perch on the rock walls. Neera and Soren could barely stand side by side."

"Thankfully you were there," she murmured. If he hadn't shown up, if Soren and Neera hadn't been there...

A shudder ran through Koen. He moved the plate from between them and placed it on the side table. She grabbed a cup of day-old water and guzzled half of it before handing it to him. He finished it in a single gulp and stood to refill it. "I can ask Maura for a new robe for Troy," he called from the bathroom. "I'm sure he won't want to wear this again."

"I don't know. I'm sure he would be okay with you wearing his clothes."

Koen stood in the doorway, a wicked gleam in his eyes. The robe barely closed over his strong chest and the top of his abs. Her heart raced at the smile lifting his lips. "You keep insinuating something."

"Oh? What?"

"Nothing," he smirked and walked back to the bed.

She sighed. "Yes, Koen. I think you are hot. It was my first thought when I saw you."

He rested against the pillow at his back, a cocky gleam to his eyes. "So shallow."

"I thought it was all a dream. I think I get a pass." His arm wormed behind her back and gently nudged her toward him. "Imagine my shock when I found out you were real."

"Shock or joy?" he murmured against her lips.

"Can't it be both?"

His kiss was soft, languid. Aisling melted into it, resting one hand on his shoulder and the other on his chest. The beat of his heart thudded into her palm.

She hadn't gotten enough of him the night before. He stoked a heat so vibrant inside that she felt like combusting with every simple touch. She was glad she had never been with anyone else before. Glad no one had shown her attention like this. It would all belong to Koen. Every inch and facet of her heart was his, and she wasn't scared to leave it in his care. He would hold it like a precious gem, cradling and protecting it against any pain or horror.

The reality and intensity of her love flooded her with insatiable need. She kissed him with an urgency she couldn't contain, an urgency she didn't want to control.

He matched it instantly, lifting his hands to cradle the back of her head. She swung her leg over his and straddled his strong thighs. He sat up and pulled her closer, his large hand splayed across her back as their pounding hearts beat inches apart.

Her robe inched up her thighs. His opened fully at the chest, exposing the glorious panes of muscle she'd stared at for too long with quiet need. Her fingers slid inside, reveling in the warmth and softness of his skin. His curled in her hair and tugged ever so slightly, sending a delectable rush of pleasure down her spine. A moan slipped from her lips into his mouth.

The shred of control he talked about the night before seemed to burn to ash.

She gasped as he cupped her backside, squeezing it at the same time he tightened his grip in her hair and exposed the column of her throat. Koen kissed her chin, her jaw. He nipped just under her ear. Aisling squirmed against him.

She couldn't stop moving once she started. Her hips rocked instinctually against him, the only barrier between them the loosening robes.

Koen groaned, the sound electrifying against her skin, and bit her neck. She cried out, bracing her hands on his thick shoulders. His arms wrapped around her waist and tightened before he flipped her onto her back without breaking his lips from her skin. He lowered his body between her thighs, every delicious ounce of him pressed against her, and explored her curves with rapt fascination.

She writhed against him, her need feral and devastating. It was a need she had only read about or heard through giggling whispers between friends at the café. One she never anticipated she would experience.

Koen stared down at her with vicious, undivided attention. Every fleck of gold in his eyes glowed molten. Her robe slid open. He was there a breath later, a heavy rumbling in his throat with every taste, every touch.

She cupped his face and urged him closer. He curled his hand around the thigh she had hooked on his waist, his fingers digging into her skin with needy pressure. Her fingernails raked along his back and scraped along his scalp. His tongue danced with hers, matching stroke for stroke.

She arched up, desperate for more friction. Koen moaned into her mouth.

Aisling would go through the torture of the cave a thousand times to hear the sound again.

He pulled back, breaking their kiss with a wet pop. "Aisling," he rasped, panting against her.

She froze, eyes wide. "What did I do?" she whispered breathlessly.

He shook his head, a breath of a laugh leaving his lips. "Nothing. I just..." He lowered his head to her chest and inhaled deeply. He met her stare, his eyes clearer than they had been seconds ago. "You destroy me. I thought I had more control. I thought I was stronger. But you like this?"

She stared at him from below, marveling at the planes of his body and the silkiness of his hair between her fingers.

"If I take you now," he whispered, "I won't be able to stop. You won't be leaving this bed. This room. I'll hoard you to myself until we can't function and then I'll start again."

She shivered as he planted a kiss between her breasts.

"I have thought about this for months. I have pictured every detail, every possible scenario. Knowing you were right next door, just a wall away, was a special kind of torture. One I never want to know again. I want to be in control the first time. I want you to be comfortable."

"I am comfortable," she insisted, tightening her legs around his waist. He gritted his teeth. "I want-"

"Do not," he hissed, "finish that sentence. I'm begging you."

She couldn't stop a smile from lifting her lips or Amerie's words from tumbling from her mouth. "I don't consider it begging if you aren't on your knees, Koen."

A glorious wave of shock crossed over his face. "I'll remember that." He kissed her slowly before brushing his nose against hers and smiling. "I think you're hot, too."

Aisling laughed. "You wouldn't have in my other life."

He pulled back, a crease developing between his eyebrows. "Why not?"

"I was not like this," she said, gesturing to her face and body. Memories of her old self floated to the surface. She cringed. "You can ask Troy. It was especially bad at the end."

"Do you miss it?"

"That life?" She grimaced. "No. Not at all. The only thing I missed was Troy, and now he's here."

Koen paused. "I was jealous of him."

"I know. It was painfully obvious."

He kissed the top of her nose. "I was so relieved when you showed up the morning after you made the switch. I didn't sleep that entire night. Neera refused to let me in the Lair."

She traced his jawline with her fingers. "I was never going to choose the other life. I would have kept my soul in the void between our worlds before I stayed another day there. Once I met Morana, once I met everyone here, my soul knew where I was supposed to be." She brushed his lower lip with her thumb. "I think I never found anyone in the other life because my soul knew all along it was looking for yours."

Koen's eyes shuddered. He looked down at her with an intimacy that made her heart engorge, her blood sing. He kissed her, punishing and reverent, and she smiled as the fissures in her soul shrank.

THIRTY-EIGHT

KOEN

He could not get enough of her.

Stopping himself had been an act of godliness made harder by the fact that she wanted it just as badly. Wanted him somehow as much as he wanted her.

He forced them out of bed the next morning when the sun warmed their blankets. They didn't make it to the bathroom before she was in his arms again. He pressed her against the wall and pinned her hands above her head with one of his own. She squirmed against him in a delicious way that sent common sense and reasoning flying from his head. Eventually, minutes or hours later, he broke away, breathless and roiling.

He waited until he could walk outside before going to his room. It was empty now. Emptier than it had been before. He never had much and wasn't one for trinkets, but he wanted Aisling's stuff there. Wanted her comb and her toothbrush in his bathroom. Her clothes beside his. Her body next to his.

His bath was painfully cold.

Common sense came back slowly, followed by reasoning and an awareness that they weren't the only two people in the world.

Oryn. He had to check on Oryn. Aisling said he was talking, but he needed to see it for himself.

He needed to discuss their findings with the King and the rest of the riders. They needed to know if there were next steps, and if there was anything they were missing. He didn't know how it could be possible. They had destroyed the nest and slaughtered every man they came across on both ends.

But Aisling hadn't heard the Man's voice. She wouldn't rest until she did, and he wouldn't rest until she was safe.

He also needed to ask Maura for a new robe for Troy. One with extra fluff as an apology.

Aisling told him to meet her in the common room when he was done, explicitly instructing him to stay out of her room or they would never leave. He would have been okay with that.

Laughter came from the open doors. His heart, somehow larger in the last two days, softened at the sound of his family inside. He stepped in and stopped, his mouth falling open.

Oryn sat at the table between his twin and Elaila like he hadn't been stabbed multiple times the day before. "Morning," Oryn said brightly.

Koen blinked before looking at a smiling Kaida. "What is he doing here?"

"He lives here."

"Give him a break," Amerie cooed, "he's violently in love. His mind is muddled."

Koen couldn't wait until their next sparring practice. He glared at her before looking at Oryn. "Are you okay to be up like this?"

"Perfectly fine, per medical." Oryn brushed his hand across his abdomen. "The wounds are healing well already. Troy says there's already granulation tissue, so we're on our way to being back to normal."

"Soon, but not yet," Kaida scolded.

Koen smiled at the twins. "I'm... I'm really glad you're okay, Oryn." It was an understatement. Seeing Oryn lifeless on the ground covered in blood would fill his nightmares for the foreseeable future.

Oryn nodded his chin in acknowledgment, a knowing gleam in his bright eyes. Cielle walked in next, her eyes widening at Oryn. "What are you doing here?" she asked.

"This is old news," Amerie drawled. "He's fine. Stabbed, but healing. Annoyingly perfect in every way. Not a hair out of place."

Cielle ignored her. "Seriously, are you okay?"

Amerie huffed. Oryn laughed. "I am. Thank you for your concern. Amerie was correct in her assessment."

Amerie stuck her tongue out. Cielle rolled her eyes. Koen walked with her to the buffet trays and filled his plate to the brim. The last two days had been a wonderful chaotic mess he wouldn't have traded for anything, but he was starving.

"Ugh, Oryn," Aisling moaned from the doorway, her voice a jumpstart to Koen's heart. "How does your hair always look so perfect? I did not look this good when I came back."

"You were beat to shit," Amerie laughed. "Oryn got off easy."

"He was stabbed! Twice!" Cielle shouted.

"I stand by what I said."

Koen's spine shuddered at the memory of Aisling on the beach, her face swollen and bloodied. Her body destroyed, neck branded.

As if she could sense his discomfort, Aisling rested a hand on his forearm and looked up at him with an openness he would never take for granted. She squeezed once, and he reigned in the urge to kiss her in front of everyone. She grabbed a plate and picked her fill. It was something he had always loved about her. Once she got over the initial shock of always having food, she ate. She wasn't shy about her hunger. She ate to fuel, to feed the body he...

He sat at the table before his mind wandered and had to excuse himself. Aedan walked in with Anwir close behind. The King poured a cup of tea before sitting beside Kaida. Aisling sat beside Koen, her knee brushing against his thigh. He glanced sidelong at her, the heat in his blood stirring with the simple touch. She smiled knowingly and bit into her toast.

"Care for some breakfast?" Cielle asked Anwir from the buffet line. His eyes widened but he shook his head, a blush on his cheeks, and sank into the corner of the room.

Aedan waited until Cielle sat before he cleared his throat. "We have much to discuss. Are we okay speaking business during breakfast or would you prefer me to wait until you're finished?"

"Speak to us, oh, handsome King!" Amerie said, lifting her glass of orange juice.

Aedan smirked. "Bless the person who ends up with you, Amerie. I hope their energy is as bright as yours."

She smirked. "How's your energy, Your Majesty?"

Kaida laughed, bubbly and bright. "Do you want details?"

"No," Oryn and Koen groaned together. She shot them both a glare.

"Business, then," Aedan said, his smile dimming. The air around the table thickened. "First and foremost, every single woman that was captured is safe. They have all been seen by the medical teams and given what they need to recuperate fully. They have a long road ahead, but they want for nothing. I am forever grateful for what you have done for them." He cleared his throat. "My troops scoured the mountain, both inside and through all of the passes around it. There were no more eggs or beasts. No men left alive."

Blood everywhere. Aisling fighting just far enough away from him to make him nervous. Neera's anxiety humming down the bond. Koen blinked against the flashbacks.

"We found no bombs. No equipment for bomb-making nor any chemicals that could be used. The storage room at the castle is under multiple guard protection at all hours of the day and night. No one can get in or out without numerous obstacles." He pursed his lips. "Anwir and I believe that the Cruento no longer have the means to make the bombs. They haven't attacked in days. And with us ravaging their nest, they no longer have the opportunity to use their sky beasts."

Anwir nodded in agreement from the corner of the room.

"We have a map here," Aedan patted his pocket, "from the soldiers detailing the intricacies of the tunnel system. The tunnels led nowhere but to a few other openings at sea level and the single pass that you infiltrated. My men scoured their texts left inside and found nothing of interest. Their journals revealed nothing but disgusting words that aren't worth a single breath."

"There was a door behind the nest," Koen said. "Where did that lead?"

"To the pass." Aedan pulled out the map and unfolded it on the table. The rest of the Ferox leaned forward and studied the paper. "There was another miniature hive-like room about a mile further in the mountain from the main one that you destroyed. That's where all of the rebels who fought at the pass came from, we assume. Everything either led to the pass or the sea. How they got Favilla inside is beyond me, but she's out now and will never go back."

Aisling tensed.

"I am fairly confident," the King breathed after a long minute, "that we have destroyed the Cruento."

No one spoke.

Aedan looked at everyone at the table and frowned. "That's a good thing. What I just told you, it's good."

Koen couldn't believe it. There had to be a catch, something they were missing.

Aisling spoke up. "Their head guy is still out there. The leader."

Every pair of eyes trained on her. "How do you know?" Aedan asked, not a single trace of annoyance in his voice.

"I know his voice," she said. "I know... I remember him. I would know him anywhere. And he wasn't there."

"There were a lot of men there," Cielle offered. "Maybe in the chaos—"

"He wasn't there," Aisling said again, shaking her head. "I feel it. I know it. Until he's dead, we aren't done." Koen took her hand in his. She gazed up at him and swallowed. "I know I sound insane," she murmured.

"You do not sound insane," Amerie said before Koen could respond. "I believe Aisling."

"Me too," Elaila said, not taking her eyes off of Aisling's paled face. "There is something we're missing. It was too easy." She grimaced and looked at Oryn beside her. "Not like that. Obviously, it wasn't easy, but—"

Oryn graced her with a smile and patted her hand. "I know what you mean." He looked at Aedan. "I agree. Until we root out their leadership, we are not done."

"We may never know their leadership structure," Aedan countered. "We barely know anything about them besides what Aisling and Favilla were able to tell us."

"Then we continue to hunt and kill them until we get it done right," Kaida said, glancing at the rest of the table. "Our dragons have not relaxed. Soren does not believe we've seen the end of the Cruento just yet. We're close. But we still don't know how they transported their beasts to each city. We have to—"

"This will take another decade," Aedan snapped. "Another decade of us fighting madmen! More years of fear for my people and sleepless nights where I wonder if I'm sending each of you to your death."

"Then we will fight," Kaida said calmly, her voice back to that of a leader. "We don't stop. The women we freed yesterday are worth the battles. The innocents killed with the bombs are worth it. Let the Cruento keep trying. It's pathetic and weak to hide faceless behind a cause you say you believe in. Let them show their hatred with their chests. Let them expose themselves." Aedan pursed his lips, his frustration and exhaustion evident with every breath. Kaida slid her hand into his. "We are with you until the end, my King. Until the last dragon falls from the sky."

Something flashed in Aedan's eyes at her words. His shoulders dropped from his ears. He inhaled deeply. "Then fight, we will."

Aisling's shuddering exhale of relief was quiet enough for only Koen and Elaila to hear. Elaila glanced at him in concern from across the table. Koen lifted Aisling's cold hand and pressed a kiss to her chilled skin.

"Oh, that's right! Finally!" Aedan laughed. "I've been wondering how long it would take for you two—"

Kaida wrapped her hand around his mouth, her eyes wide in mortification. "Just ignore him, please."

"No, he's right," Amerie laughed.

"What's with you agreeing with everyone this morning?" Cielle asked.

"I'm a very agreeable person." The whole table groaned. She frowned. "Whatever. I'm just happy they're finally together."

"We're right here," Koen hissed. "We can hear all of this."

"Thank you," Aisling squeezed his hand. "I know it was a long time coming."

"A lifetime," Cielle muttered.

"You don't get to be gross, though," Amerie demanded.

"What do you consider gross?" Aisling asked, tilting her head with a faux innocence.

Amerie grinned and angled her head the same way. "I could show you."

"That's my limit," Koen responded, wishing so badly to wipe the grin off Amerie's face. "In case anyone was wondering."

Aedan leaned back in his chair. "We will be on our best behavior, Amerie. Even tomorrow."

Elaila's brow furrowed. "What's tomorrow?"

"What's tomorrow?" Aedan nearly shouted. "The ball! The ball I have been planning amongst this mess of a life we live. The ball to celebrate Aisling being back!"

"Oh, I don't need all of that," Aisling grimaced. "It's too much."

"Nonsense."

"What if we change it to a ball for the Ferox? To celebrate what we've accomplished together?"

Kaida's eyes glittered. "I think that's a wonderful idea, Aisling."

"Fine," Aedan sighed in defeat for the second time that morning. "For all of you. A celebration of my favorite people."

A knock sounded at the door. Maura sheepishly walked in. "So sorry to interrupt, Your Highness, but I was wondering if I could steal the girls for final fittings?"

"My sweet woman, you are more than welcome to take them from me." He gestured to the food laid out. "Would you care to join us?"

The seamstress blushed. "No, thank you. I've already eaten."

"Final fittings?" Aisling asked. "I haven't had one."

"Maura has all of our measurements saved in her head." Kaida nodded a hello to the seamstress. "Let's go."

"The men will be this afternoon," Maura said as she walked out the door, looking pointedly at Koen and Oryn. The girls stood to leave. Aisling kissed Koen's cheek as she walked out. Amerie looped their arms together and winked at him over her shoulder.

"I believe that girl could start a riot and a cult with that mouth of hers," Aedan muttered as Amerie walked out.

Oryn exhaled. "Let's hope she doesn't inspire either."

Aedan looked at Koen. "Truly, I am thrilled for you. Aisling is..." he shrugged a shoulder with a sigh. "Words fail to convey how strong she is. And how kind and good. How do you describe a soul full of hope?"

"Radiant," Oryn murmured.

"Radiant," Aedan repeated. "That she is. It's like looking into the sun." He huffed a laugh. "How ironic that she rides a dragon of shadow."

Koen nodded in agreement.

"How did she handle being back?"

"Better than I would have," Koen responded. "She was..." He thought back to the fight, to Aisling's raw fury. "She was magnificent."

"And you believe her? That the leader is still at large?"

Koen locked eyes with Aedan. "Yes. She knows him, whoever he is." He rested his elbows on the table and examined his hands. "I found her inside the dungeon she was kept in. I felt the horror, and it was too much for me. I only spent five minutes inside and nearly crawled out of my skin." His eyes slid to Oryn's. "What she told us does not do it justice. My soul shrank against it. But she fought. She escaped and then was brave enough to go back in. And she eradicated them." He paused. "She would have been able to handle them all herself, Oryn."

"We felt her," he murmured, his bright eyes narrowing. "I felt her rage, just like when she was captured."

Koen nodded. "You should have seen her. When she meets that man, whoever he is, he's fucked."

THIRTY-NINE

AISLING

It was the most beautiful dress Aisling had ever seen.

"Maura," she breathed, running her hands over the delicate fabric, "this is..."

"Breathtaking," Cielle offered.

Amerie smirked. "Koen is going to lose his mind."

The seamstress put a final pin in the waistline and stepped back to admire her handiwork. "I think I've outdone myself," she admitted quietly, "with all of your dresses."

"You have. You're a magician," Kaida said.

Maura blushed and busied herself in a notebook. She glanced over her shoulder. "Now, no one speaks of the dresses. I want to see the shock in the room when you walk in."

"Our lips are sealed," Elaila swore. She looked at Kaida and Aisling. "This means from the boys, too."

Kaida brushed her hair from her shoulder. "Aedan's look of surprise is adorable. I would never miss an opportunity to cause it."

Amerie helped Aisling out of her dress. The women showered Maura with thanks and praise before leaving. Kaida led them outside. "I think it's a good idea if we spar as a group. Let off some steam."

"What!" Amerie yelped. "I don't know if you know this, but yester-day—"

Kaida held up her hand. "Would you rather take dance lessons again?" No one spoke. "Yesterday was brutal, yes. But this is to keep our muscles from tightening. We agreed that we still have to be ready in case they aren't gone. Light sparring will help with that."

Cielle frowned. "Swords?"

"No. Just us."

"What if we went for a run instead?" Aisling offered.

Elaila made a face. Amerie gagged. "Don't you dare."

Even Kaida shot her a disgusted look. "Absolutely not."

They found the boys still in the common room. Another plate of food was in front of Koen. "All good?" he asked, a soft smile on his face.

"Terrible," Amerie sighed. "We're going to look like wenches."

Aedan's eyes flared. Kaida put her hand on his shoulder. "A joke. We're going to spar. Keep the muscles loose." The boys stood immediately, Oryn without a single wince of pain.

"No way," Cielle glared. "There is no chance you're sparring with us."

"I'm going to critique," he said plainly, though Aisling could see the frustration in his eyes.

Troy walked into the room, his gaze locking on Oryn. He lifted his basket of supplies. "Wound change."

"But I was going to –"

"Wound change," Troy repeated, lifting his brow in challenge.

Aisling snapped her jaw shut to keep it from hanging open. Who was he? There wasn't a trace of the bumbling, mute man she knew before. And his assertiveness...

Oryn pursed his lips before nodding in submission. Kaida's eyes flared. She met Aisling's in mirrored shock.

Troy kissed the top of Aisling's head in greeting. He glanced at Koen over her shoulder and smirked. "It's time you had some privacy, I think. I'm going to start sleeping in the Keep with the rest of medical," he whispered.

"No! Sorry. We just had a rough day yesterday."

"It's fine, babe. I don't want to take up your space."

"You aren't."

"Stay in her room," Koen offered. Cautious excitement gleamed in his eyes. "She can stay in mine."

Aisling's heart fluttered. "But that's your space, Koen. I don't want to—"

"I want you there," he admitted in front of everyone.

Amerie's jaw hung open. Cielle and Elaila beamed.

Aisling stilled. Part of her wanted to run, but for some reason the enormity of what he was asking felt natural and right. It was what she had wanted since she came back from the cave. There was no reason for her to say no.

She was not going to deny herself anything anymore.

She nodded once. Koen broke into a painfully beautiful smile. She glanced up at Troy. "You okay with that?"

Troy looked to Kaida for permission. She shrugged. "It's okay with me. If Favilla takes a rider, or if something happens..." Aisling and Koen both tensed. "Then you will take a room in the Keep."

"Thank you," Troy said, glancing shyly at everyone. "It's been really nice to—"

"Do not get sappy on us," Amerie threw her arm around his shoulder and planted a kiss on his cheek. "Go heal our handsome man." Troy cleared his throat and gestured Oryn from the room with a confident flare. Oryn obeyed instantly.

"What is that?" Elaila whispered, a grin on her face.

"I'm not sure," Aisling admitted.

Kaida sighed. "I don't hate it." She kissed Aedan's hair. "We're going to spar. If you have time, you're welcome to join."

"I would love to, but unfortunately I have to plan for tomorrow. I'll be at the Keep. Anwir left a few minutes ago to check on the ballroom décor and I have to speak with him." He parted ways with them at the common room door.

Aisling glanced sidelong at Koen, her heart pounding at the feral grin still on his face. The dragons sunbathed lazily in the sand of the Pit, giant bellies up. Morana glistened like a fresh pearl.

"Lazy beasts," Kaida muttered. She pushed Soren's gigantic head with her tiny foot. Red eyes opened, his slit of a pupil narrowing on her. "Take them on a flight or something. Get the wings moving. Try Favilla in the ravine. Just stay close in case."

He grunted, but the dragons moved as one at Kaida's command. Each rider smiled as their beast danced in the sky, the bonds fluttering with contented warmth.

"Now," Kaida put her hand on her hip. "Let's see. I want... Cielle and Aisling. Elaila with me. Koen with Amerie."

Koen and Amerie flashed terrifying smiles at the ability to finally unleash their pent-up annoyance at the other. The rest of riders split into their designated pairs.

The sand danced around their feet. The sun warmed their bones. An hour passed in the blink of an eye.

Kaida was right. The sparring was helpful. Any sore spots Aisling had slowly melted. Cielle knocked her down numerous times, but yielded just as many, too. Kaida and Elaila twirled in the sand in a nauseatingly beautiful yet vicious way.

"I said light sparring!" Kaida shouted at Koen and Amerie. Sweat dripped from both of their faces as they tackled each other to the ground. Amerie sank a punch to Koen's gut. Koen twisted her onto her stomach and pinned her arms behind her back with one of his hands and his knee into her spine.

"Yield," he demanded.

"No."

"Damnit, Amerie," Kaida muttered.

Amerie inhaled sharply. On her exhale, she twisted her torso with a snap. Koen lost his grip and tumbled from his stance. She leapt onto her feet in a low squat and lunged at him, sending him sprawling into the sand. In a single second, she straddled him with one knee in his groin and the other hovering above his neck. "Yield," she panted.

Aisling smirked. He shouldn't win all the time. It was bad for his ego.

Koen grimaced as she sank her knee lower onto his groin. "Yield."

Cielle tutted. "Now her confidence will be unbearable."

"I heard that," Amerie called out, sitting on the sand with heavy breaths. Koen sat up and shook the sand from his hair, pelting Amerie's face with the tiny grains.

"I think that was just enough," Kaida said with a self-assuring nod, only a light sheen of sweat on her face. "Do what you will now, but stay close." She walked out the door.

Elaila brushed the sand from her hair. "One of these days I'm actually going to beat her more than once a year."

"Yeah you will," Cielle promised and threw her arm over Elaila's delicate shoulders.

Aisling looked at Koen, his eyes already on her. "Run?"

"Ugh, no," Amerie groaned.

Koen pushed her hard enough for her to fall onto her back. "She wasn't asking you."

They walked outside. Aisling inhaled the crisp air. "Do you ever get used to it? Or is it always like this?"

"It's always like this," he replied, his chest expanding with a full breath.

She tilted her head to the sky where the dragons flittered in and out of the ravine. Chirps echoed from the darkness. A ball of flame puffed through the top. Soren's growl came next. Morana's bond was calm and complacent. It was all Aisling could ask for.

She ran side by side with Koen past the ravine to the cliffs, following the gentle curve of the land further north than she'd been before. The sharp wind whipped her hair. Her heart pounded in her chest with every step. They stopped at the furthest point where the rocks below were nothing but daggers slicing through the thrashing sea. Gulls cawed and dove against the roaring in shrill bursts. Aisling stared into the horizon, her breaths heavy and fast. "What's out there?"

"Don't know," Koen muttered as he collapsed onto the ground. "Whatever it is, it's too far for us to worry about."

"No one knows?" She sat beside him.

"I'm sure someone does. Aedan has maps everywhere. But we've been so preoccupied with Kairossen and the Cruento for decades that nothing else has been important. Plus, from what I've heard, there isn't anything for weeks. No one who leaves has come back in decades. Going out there is a death sentence."

She tore her gaze from the sea to look at him. His thick hair was perfectly ruffled. Small slivers of dark blonde glittered in the weak sunlight. A sheen of sweat covered his face and forced his shirt to cling even tighter to his strong body. She wanted so badly to run her hands down—

"Don't look at me like that," he whispered, his voice thick.

"Like what?"

He hesitated for only a second before cupping the back of her neck and bringing her mouth to his. She welcomed it, having gone far too long without his touch. Kaida wouldn't pair them together to spar for a while, and maybe it was a good thing.

The bond pulsed. Then plucked. She pulled away from him in pain, scowling as Morana and Neera flew overhead. Their laughing chirps echoed with the wind.

"Nosey creatures," Koen muttered as he watched them sail in the wind. He kissed the tip of her nose. "We should go back. I think I'm late for Maura."

"What are you wearing tomorrow?" Aisling asked while they jogged at a leisurely pace toward the Pit.

"I have no idea. I forgot about it until today. What about you?"

"A dress."

He lifted a brow. "I gathered as much."

"I'm sworn to speak no more about it. You'll have to wait until tomorrow."

"Give me a hint."

"No."

"Fine. Then I won't tell you what I'm wearing, either." They entered the Pit and headed downstairs.

"I hope it's a dress, too."

Koen laughed. She opened her door and walked inside. He came up behind her and wrapped an arm around her chest. "This isn't your room," he breathed against her neck. She paused and turned against the back of the couch until they were face to face.

"About that," Aisling started, hyper-aware of how close he was, "I don't want you to feel pressured. I can figure something out with Troy. Your room is your space. I don't want to ruin that."

A line formed between his brows. "Is this about what Kaida said?"

She nodded. If something did happen, if he did decide he didn't want to be with her anymore, she would need her space back.

He brushed a damp hair from her forehead. "Nothing is going to happen, Aisling. After everything we've gone through, it's as much your room as it is mine. You're everywhere in it. I wouldn't want to live any other way."

"But—"

"But what?" He cocked his head. "Are you unsure?"

"No," she admitted. Her hands found his waist. "I... no one has ever..."

Words turned to ash in her mouth. She had never been treated so well before. Never been so needed or loved. She didn't know how to handle it.

He leaned down and pressed his lips against hers. It wasn't needy or urgent. It was soft and exhilarating, the kind of kiss that turned her weightless. Her blood fizzled. Her fingertips prickled.

"We will never sleep apart again," he whispered against her mouth. "I don't want to go a single day, a single night, without your touch. Because I love you. I love you so much that I fear some days I might crack in half." He pulled back just enough for their eyes to meet. "I'm going to love you until you realize you're worth it, Aisling. Until you realize how important you are. How treasured you are. And then, when you've realized it and think you can't be loved anymore, I'll prove you wrong."

She didn't know when she had started crying, but the salty drops tickled her lips and jaw. The pad of his thumb wiped them away one by one. "Will you move into our room?" he whispered.

She nodded. Words weren't possible.

"That," Troy called from the bathroom, "was so painfully romantic I could cry." He stepped through the door with his hands clasped over his chest. Koen didn't move, but he smiled at her friend warmly enough to make her want to cry again.

"You're such a creep," Aisling managed to croak.

"I remember earlier we decided this would be my room?" He lifted his brow. "And with a speech like that, I don't know how you aren't all over him right now."

"You ruined that," she countered, wiping her eyes. A knock sounded at the door. Koen opened it.

Oryn glanced in at the three of them, his eyes lingering on Troy for a second too long. "We have to go to Maura."

Koen glanced down at his sweat-soaked shirt. "I just went on a run."

Oryn rolled his eyes. "She doesn't care. Trust me. I'm going with my entire torso in a bandage."

"A well-done bandage," Troy whispered beside her. Koen glanced at Aisling, torn.

"Troy will help me move my stuff," she volunteered. Troy scowled down at her. She nudged him with her elbow to comply. "Oh, can you grab him a new robe while you're there?" A fire lit in Koen's eyes at the memory. She let the corners of her mouth tilt upward.

"What happened to my robe?" Troy asked through gritted teeth.

"Coming right up," Koen purred, winking once at Troy before walking out with Oryn.

Troy crossed his arms. "Care to explain?"

"Not really," she admitted. She walked into the bathroom and put what little she had in a pile. "What do you want me to keep here for you?"

"My robe."

"Be careful what you ask for," she smirked. "Did anyone show you the supply rooms where all the toiletries are kept?"

He nodded. "Yeah. Just take all your stuff, Ash. I can grab whatever." He leaned against the bathroom wall.

"How's medical treating you?"

He smiled. "Great. They're more talkative than they seem."

"Is it too much studying?"

"I don't think it counts as too much if it's something you enjoy."

"You like it?"

"I do. You made the right call. I never would have done it myself." He tucked his hair behind his ear. "Are you nervous?"

She leaned against the tub. "Yes, but not about Koen." It wasn't a lie. He had squashed every one of her doubts with both his actions and his words. She couldn't ask for more. "I'm nervous about weird things."

"Like?"

"Like," she pinched her face. "Going to the bathroom. And what if I get my period? What if I'm having a bad day and need space?"

He laughed. "Going to the bathroom is normal. So is getting your period. Which, by the way, you should start tracking now." He lifted his brows. "And if you need space come here. Or just tell him. I have a feeling the man would burn the entire world to cinders and rebuild a new one for you if you asked."

She walked from the bathroom into her room and dumped what few clothes she had onto her bed. "No one has ever loved me like this, Troy," she whispered. "I don't know how to handle it."

He rested a hand on her back, his familiar touch innately soothing. "There's nothing to handle, Ash. You just live. Love and be loved. Don't take a single second of it for granted." He paused. "You should never take him for granted, though. You were right in your note. He is..."

"I know," she agreed. "It's almost painful."

"Lucky, lucky girl."

She turned to him. "So, you and Oryn..."

"What about him?"

"You don't think he's handsome?"

"I never said that."

"You don't blush anymore. And you're able to talk to him. And Koen." She counted with her fingers. "And Aedan."

"Maybe I changed, too," he said with a faux lightness. "Old Troy would have become mute. New Troy, very much improved Troy, knows that life is too short to be worried about speaking in front of deliciously attractive people."

"I'm proud of you."

He pulled her into a hug. "I wouldn't be here without you, my love. I owe you everything."

"Then help me move."

FORTY

KOEN

He didn't see the suit Maura put him in. Didn't remember a single detail of it.

Aisling was going to be living with him. A giddiness he'd never felt before warmed his veins.

"He loves it," Oryn said to Maura apologetically.

Koen blinked. "It's great, Maura. Like always."

She brushed him off. "Which lucky lady is it?"

"Aisling," Oryn answered for him.

"Oh! What a handsome couple the two of you make." She smiled and brushed a gray hair from her cheek. "Wait until you see her dress."

"I asked about it already. She wouldn't tell me anything."

"Good girl," Maura whispered. She threw him a wink. "You'll love it."

He undressed, barely glimpsing at Maura's hard work. "Is there a chance you have a new robe available?"

They left Maura's workshop with Troy's new robe. "I have to meet Aedan," Oryn said in the middle of the hall. "Not Ferox business. You're free the rest of the night."

"No patrols?"

"No. Soren is refusing. He says the dragons need time to rest after everything." He glanced down the hallway behind Koen. "I think he's as tired of the Cruento as we are."

"Who is?" Kaida asked, appearing from nowhere to stand beside Koen. He started at the sudden closeness of her.

"Soren."

She sighed. "Yeah. He's a grumpy old prick right now." She glanced at Koen. "Know anything about that?"

His brows furrowed. "Am I supposed to?"

"What's Neera been like recently?"

"Fine. Normal."

Kaida squinted. She looked at her brother. "Ready?"

"Are you?"

"Born ready." She took Koen's hand and squeezed it. "Relax tonight. Tell the girls. But tell Amerie she is not allowed to leave yet." She walked down the hall arm in arm with her twin with a lightness in their steps Koen hadn't seen before.

He walked to the Lair and into Neera's stall. Her bright eyes regarded him as he leaned against her wall. "What's going on?"

She didn't move. One of her scaled brows lifted in question.

"Why is Soren being a prick?" The bond flickered with a quick rush of sour embarrassment. Koen's eyes widened in understanding. "Has he asked for you?"

Neera didn't move. She shut down the bond, leaving a painful ache in its place. The ground reverberated under his feet. Morana's white head came through the door. She looked at him and blinked once. *Yes.*

His jaw dropped. He looked at his dragon in disbelief, unable to keep the smile from his face. "And you said no?"

Morana blinked once again. Neera snarled at her. Koen leaned his head against the wall. He had been so selfish the last few days. He thought the bond, the heat and the sharpness, was because of Aisling and the whirlwind he sank into. Not once had he considered it could have been Neera.

"You should be with him," he said. "I know you want to be. Everyone knows you and Soren are meant to be mates."

Morana huffed in agreement.

Koen worked to keep the smile from his face. "There's no reason for you to not be happy, Neera." His dragon stared unmoving. He splayed his hand on her scales, eliciting a comfortable flood of peace to restart the bond. "Let yourself be happy. It's worth it."

Morana chirped her agreement. He glanced at his dragon and laughed at the pure human look of annoyance in her eyes. He faced Aisling's dragon. "Is she happy?"

Morana's amethyst eyes twinkled before she blinked once. *Yes.*

Koen looked at his dragon, ignoring the rush of everything Morana's confirmation brought. "We know you've loved him forever. Why not just give into it?" He kissed her snout. "But if anything happens, shut down the bond. I do not need to feel or know any of it."

Neera's annoyed rumble brought a smile to his face as he walked out and peeked into the common room where Elaila and Cielle sat on the couches—Elaila with a pen in her hand and Cielle with a book in hers. They looked up when he walked in. "Kaida says to relax tonight. Can you tell Amerie?"

"We thought she was..." Cielle paused, her eyes widening.

Amerie walked in the door with a bright-eyed Declan at her side. The pair didn't register Koen or the girls as they grabbed food and sat together at the table in constant, unbroken conversation.

Elaila's mouth hung open. Cielle stared for a heartbeat before her lips lifted in a smile. She jerked her chin to the door and Elaila followed.

"What is that?" Elaila whispered in a high voice and peeked in the door. "I never –"

"We need to walk away," Cielle whispered back. "It's like cornering a wild animal. We don't know how she will react. Best to let her be free."

They ditched him, whispering excitedly between each other as they headed toward the Keep.

Koen shook his head and walked down the stairs. His heart pounded with every step closer to his room, the reality of what he'd asked Aisling sinking in. He paused for only a second before he opened his door.

Nothing looked different.

"In here," Aisling called from the bathroom. His eyes fluttered for a moment before shutting in gratitude and relief. He threw Troy's robe on the couch. Aisling sat on the edge of the tub and stared at the open vanity cabinet. She looked up as he came in, her brows furrowed. "Am I supposed to use the same shampoo as you now? Or—"

He took her head in his hands and kissed her, pulling back after a minute. "You can use your own shampoo if you'd like. Or none. I don't care."

Aisling smiled up at him. She glanced at his lips before meeting his eyes. "How was your fitting?"

"I don't remember."

She cocked her head. "How? It just happened."

"Distracted."

"Did you pick up a robe for Troy?"

"It's on the couch."

"Thank you. He was not too pleased about it."

"Did he help you?"

She nodded and pushed him back. "Yes. I didn't know what drawers to use, so I threw my clothes in the bottom one." She led him from the bathroom to the large dresser. "All I have is what Maura made me."

He knelt and opened the drawer. Her clothes sat neatly folded inside, barely taking up any space.

Aisling's clothes in his dresser. Her shampoo beside his. Her towel and robe hung next to his. Her scent in the air.

"Is that okay? Or do you want me to use the closet?" She knelt, glancing at him in concern over his prolonged silence. "Is it too much?" she whispered, a tinge of hurt in her voice. "I can move—"

"No," he responded gruffly, blinking away the burning in his eyes. He was so happy. So violently, brilliantly happy that his body didn't know how to process it anymore. "Where are your books?"

She frowned. "I don't have any. That's what the library is for."

That needed to be remedied immediately. "What else do you need in here?"

She shook her head slowly. "Nothing. I'm all moved in." A small smile graced her lips. Tentative. Cautious. Nervous. "What now?"

"I have no idea. I've never done this before."

She laughed and walked back into the bathroom. The water turned on a heartbeat later. He heard her clothes hit the floor. Heard her sink into the warmth with a low moan.

"Do you remember when Leonard gave you the warm loaf of bread?" he asked as he leaned against the bathroom wall. The water hovered just under her shoulders. Her hair was thrown up in a messy knot.

There were no bubbles, no barrier to keep him from seeing every-thing.

Aisling's face pinched before she nodded. "Yeah. The fresh loaf when I first met him."

"That's the first time I heard you moan," he admitted, "and I nearly went to my knees in the common room in front of everyone."

Her jaw dropped. He lifted his shirt and threw it beside hers. The burn of her gaze on his chest, his stomach, sent a flurry of warmth down his spine as he undressed. He stepped into the water and leaned against the opposite side of the tub with her legs between his.

She swallowed thickly. "I'm glad Oryn is okay."

He arched a brow. "Trying to change the subject?"

"Yes. We never really talked about what happened."

She was right. He willed the heat in his blood to lessen and forced his eyes to stay on hers. "Seeing Oryn like that was terrifying. I never want to see anything like it again."

"How bad was the pass?"

"It was chaotic. At least there was room to move inside the moun-tain. We were fighting shoulder to shoulder against rock."

She bit her lip. "We shouldn't have divided up like that."

"We had to. It got them on two fronts. Even if we hadn't, all of us wouldn't have been able to take them like that in the pass. It was too narrow. We would have gone down one by one. If anything, we should have divided up by dragon."

"I didn't want to go inside without you," she whispered, a familiar blankness he dreaded growing in her eyes.

"You were so brave, Aisling." He fought against the tightness in his throat. "To go back inside like that..."

"That dagger I picked up? It belonged to one of the men who hurt me. I used it to flay his hands when we escaped. I couldn't leave it there."

Koen didn't know what to say. Aisling continued.

"I remembered every second of it. Every drop of water from the sea. Every vile word. Every fist. And I thought I would be able to control myself." She swallowed thickly. "But when I saw the women there like that... I think I turned into someone else. I felt like I did, anyway."

"We felt your anger," he murmured. "Through the bonds."

She frowned. "How?"

"It was too strong. Morana had to share it. It happened before when you were captured, too. It's how we knew you were still alive." He clamped down on the memories, the terror that had nearly destroyed him during those three horrific weeks.

"I didn't know that," she whispered, gazing out the windows on her left. The last rays of the sun licked her delicate jawline. "Does it make me a monster to want revenge on them? To have enjoyed slaughtering them?"

"No," he answered immediately. "Not at all. It makes you human."

"My anger came back the second we came to the cliffs, and I let it take over. I gave in to it because I like it."

He stayed silent. She paused for a minute before continuing.

"I'm worried I will always be angry. That even if we find and kill him, I'll still want the world to bleed. And I'm so scared I'll let the anger take over again when I shouldn't." Tears lined her eyes. "His words will always live in my head. I will never forget the laugh in his voice as he talked about my children." She lifted her chin slightly, exposing her scar to the sun. "I will carry this reminder of him for the rest of my life. Even if he dies, he will live forever in my memory. And I hate that."

She paused. A tear fell down her cheek. "I am not an angry person. I'm not cruel or vindictive. But he makes me feel that way. The cave brought out that monster in me. I don't want it to leak into other facets of my life. I want to lock it in the cave and be done with it."

The water was still between them.

Koen followed her gaze out the window. "Part of living is to learn who you are, but I think you already know who you are. You're right – you aren't angry or vindictive. You're clever and kind and strong. But all of us carry rage inside. Not as heavy or oppressive as yours maybe, but enough to make us stop and question who we are. Luckily, you know the rage isn't you. You can recognize it for what it is."

He slid his eyes to her face, still tight and staring outside. "You will always be angry about what happened to you, and you should be. No one will ever tell you it's something to get over. I don't think you should try and get over it, either. Your trauma is not just a hole in the ground to jump over and be fine. It's more like...a chasm in your soul. You can't simply leap over it. You have to take time to mesh over it with whatever helps like riding Morana or baking or reading. And over time, the ache and hurt start to diminish. The anger lessens. The chasm molds back together. There will always be a scar, but it won't be a hole in your soul anymore."

Something flickered in her eyes. She swallowed, her tiny throat bobbing.

"Say the word, and Neera will blast the mountain to bits. You can watch that horrible place crumble into nothing and know that no one else will suffer like you did. Tell me when you want me to hold the match, Aisling, and I'll do it, no questions asked."

Aisling faced him, and he held his breath at the emotion swirling in her eyes. "You'll stay with me?" she whispered. "You'll keep me from myself?"

Everything inside of him shattered. If he could go into her old life and strangle everyone but Troy for abandoning her for so long, he would. "Yes," he rasped.

"I don't want the mountain blown up," she said softly after a minute of silence. "I think there are animals that call it home. Birds and stuff."

He stared at her for a heartbeat before bursting into laughter. "Okay. We won't do that, then." A hesitant smile flirted with her lips. He reached forward and pulled her toward him, her back against his chest, and held her.

There was something violently intimate about their baths together; their nakedness not lustful or demanding, but vulnerable and comforting. He craved the simple touch more than he ever thought possible. They sat in silence and watched the sky change with the sunset before getting out.

Aisling knelt to open her drawer and dressed in a simple pair of brown linen pants and a white sweater. Koen paused before deciding it was unacceptable. He yanked his top drawer onto the bed and pulled hers out to place it on top. She gaped at him. "What are you doing?"

He slid his drawer into the bottom slot. "So you don't have to kneel to dress."

Her mouth opened but no words came out. She shut it and stepped into him, wrapping her arms around his waist and pressing her cheek into his bare chest. "Thank you."

He kissed the top of her head. "Anything you need, just ask."

He felt her pause and waited. She pursed her lips against his chest. "I could use a calendar. I have no idea where to find one. Troy says I need to start tracking my cycle."

"You don't do that already?"

She pulled back. "No. I - in my first life I was usually too thin to have a normal one. And I haven't gotten it here yet."

"The girls would know more about this. But from what I've unwillingly overheard, it's every three months and pretty painful. I have no idea what it would be like for you since you made the switch."

Her jaw fell open. "Three months?"

"I could be wrong. It could be longer. Or less. I really don't know." It was something he actively avoided talking about with the girls, but it didn't stop them from going into heavy detail about it around him, usually at times he couldn't escape.

She bloomed into a smile. "Every three months would be amazing."

"What was it before?"

"Monthly."

He cringed. "That sounds awful. If Amerie had her cycle every month I think even Calen would kill her."

"So, I guess I just wait for it," she murmured. "Then start there."

Koen stepped back and tilted his head. "Why does Troy think you should start tracking it?"

Aisling blushed instantly. "He just because..." She winced. "So I don't get pregnant."

Koen had run from women for far less, but he had thought about this. He'd thought about everything when it came to her. "Have you thought about that?" he asked gently.

She shook her head and refused to look at him. "No. I knew I didn't want them in my first life. I don't know what a real parent is supposed to look like. I'm terrified I would ruin them. I hadn't thought about having kids in this life, but they were brought up in the cave..."

If Aisling didn't get to this nameless, faceless man first, Koen would.

He brushed the side of her pink cheek with his knuckles. "You don't have to make any decisions yet. Whatever you want, Aisling. Anything you give me I'll take."

"You've thought about it?" she whispered.

He lifted her chin until she met his eyes. "Yes."

Her blink was slow, almost shuddered. "You want to be with me that long?"

"That long?" he scoffed. "I am not doing this just for fun, Aisling. You've been it for me since I saw you. Since you refused to give me your name first. I was not lying about any of it." He took her small hands in his. "This is not temporary. This isn't a fling or a distraction or an escape. This is real. I am yours in every way you can imagine.

"If you don't want kids, I'll be happy. If you want kids, I'll be happy. If you want to burn this world to embers and start a new one, I'll be at your side. All you have to do is tell me." He pressed a kiss to her forehead. "For what it's worth, you would make an amazing mother. I know I don't have experience in that regard either, but I know you. And the way you love and protect, the kindness and generosity of your soul... anyone would be lucky to have you as their mother."

Tears slid down her cheeks. He brushed them away. "But if you want to be safe until you make a decision, tell Troy to bring you the special tea they make the girls. It's only once a week. Kaida says it tastes better than any of Amerie's attempts at tea."

"Kaida takes it still?"

"Yeah," he furrowed his brows, "she's with Aedan."

"But she's...older?"

"I don't understand."

She tensed in his hands. "How old is Kaida?"

"In her fifties, I think. I refuse to ask."

"And she still takes birth control?"

"Yes." He couldn't help the confusion on his face. Aisling took a step back, eyes widening with a blank stare. Her hand fell from his and slapped against her thigh. He filled the space instantly, worry thickening his blood. "What's wrong?"

"Tell me how long people live here," she breathed, staring through him.

"Around two hundred, I think. Some earlier, obviously."

Koen caught her just before she hit the floor. The blush on her cheeks turned ashen. Even her eyes seemed paler as they barely hung onto consciousness. He laid her on the bed and brushed her hair from her face. "What's happening, Aisling? What's wrong?"

His panic was a bright, tangible, terrifying thing as he stared down at her limp body. Memories of her broken in his bed, of her barely holding onto consciousness before leaving for her other world all that time ago, came hurtling back.

Aisling blinked. Again. And again. The color seeped back into her eyes, but her skin was still too pale. She finally looked at him. "I didn't know that."

An overwhelming roll of nausea hit his gut at the relief of hearing her weak voice. "Didn't know what?"

"You live so long." She sat up slowly. "My first life we would have been lucky if we hit eighty. I never would have made it that long, but on average..."

He sat beside her and wrapped an arm around her waist. His heart still hadn't recovered from her spell. "This other life sounded like shit."

Her head rested against his shoulder. "It really was."

"We live around two hundred years on average, I think. Aedan's father lived to be just over two hundred."

"That's why Kaida and Oryn still look so good."

He nodded. "Yes. And why Kaida still drinks the tea. Fertile years last a while."

It was quiet while Aisling digested all the new information. He smiled to himself at the easy familiarity of them sitting together in bed, in a bed they would share. Just weeks ago, he wouldn't have thought it possible.

Gently, she pushed off his shoulder and turned to look at him. "That means we would be together for over a hundred and fifty years."

He nodded.

Her eyes danced between his. "It still won't be long enough."

There was nothing to say to that. Nothing he could ever say to express the raw happiness she brought him, so he kissed her until he forgot about the rest of their world.

FORTY-ONE

AISLING

"Lattes, anyone?" Troy called from the doorway.

Amerie leapt from her chair and met him at the door. His eyes widened at the sight of the women of the Ferox seated side by side with multiple stylists around them. Amerie grabbed a mug from his tray and kissed his cheek before settling back in her chair.

Cielle sighed loudly and stood to help Troy inside. "She's an animal. Ignore her."

"Koen said you might need these," Troy said as he handed them out. Aisling's heart squirmed in her chest. Troy handed her a mug. "Can I see your dress?"

"Absolutely not!" Elaila scolded. "No one has early access, not even you."

Aisling took a sip of the latte and groaned. "Yours are so much better than mine."

"I know." He glanced around the giant room on the third floor of the Keep that Aedan insisted the women use to get ready for the ball. According to him, Maura's gowns were too precious to risk going outside, and after seeing them, Aisling had to agree. "How were the massages?"

Aedan had made an entire day for the women of the Ferox. Aisling and Koen took an early morning run to the cliffs at a blistering pace, but there was a weightlessness in her soul that weeks ago she feared she would never feel again. She bathed quickly afterward, banishing Koen from the bathroom with his dark eyes that screamed trouble. She would not be late for her first massage. She ran to the Keep and made it just in time. Leonard came with trays and trays of food for lunch afterward. Before they ate, he went around the room and formally asked each woman to save him a dance.

"Wonderful," Aisling said.

"How jealous are you?" Amerie said over the lip of her cup.

Troy pursed his lips. "Careful, Amerie, or I might pull an Aisling and spit in your coffee."

Aisling choked on her latte. Kaida lifted a brow. "That's a story I would like to hear."

"When I'm not needed elsewhere, I'll be sure to go into every gory detail." Troy kissed the top of Aisling's head. "Save me a dance?"

"Always." Aisling watched him leave and sighed contentedly as she sipped her drink and listened to the revelry around her. Kaida's silvery laugh broke through Amerie's rambunctious story. Cielle's hands covered her eyes as she howled with laughter. Tears fell from Elaila's eyes. She apologized profusely to her makeup artist.

"Anyway," Amerie said after calming down, "it won't happen again because I don't have my cycle for this event."

Aisling tilted her head. "How often do you get it here?"

"Every three months," Cielle said.

Elaila smirked. "Four."

"Have you gotten yours yet?" Kaida asked.

Aisling shook her head. "No. I have no idea what to expect. It used to be monthly before, but now—"

"Monthly?" Amerie gasped in horror.

"Yes. It was terrible." Aisling placed her empty cup on a side table. "I want to start tracking it, but I can't until it comes."

Cielle's eyes flashed knowingly. "I'll get you a calendar. They make special ones for us, so if Koen offered to find you one tell him to back off." She paused. "Have you thought about taking the tea?"

"Koen just told me about it last night."

"Is he making you take it?" Amerie pressed, her voice and eyes begging for a fight.

"No! Not at all. I just didn't know it was a thing."

"You take it once a week," Kaida explained. "It's the most effective protection we have. And it tastes good, so it's not a chore."

"You don't have to take it," Elaila murmured from beside Aisling. "You don't have to do anything you don't want to do."

Aisling smiled at her friend. "I know. I do want to take it, though. We haven't... I've never..."

"Don't be embarrassed," Cielle said. "And don't do anything unless you're ready."

"I'm worried I'll do it wrong," she blushed.

Kaida laughed. "I promise you that is impossible, Aisling."

"You're in love," Elaila said softly. "You feel safe. Do what feels natural, and make sure to focus on yourself, too, not just him."

"You can always say no," Amerie supplied, earning vigorous nods from every woman inside the room. "I haven't even had a chance to say that recently."

"Oh, not even with Declan?" Cielle asked.

Amerie gaped. "How do you know about that?"

Aisling and Kaida leaned forward in shock. "Morana's Declan?"

Amerie glared at Cielle. "Don't make a big deal out of it. He's just..." a hint of a smile played at her mouth. "He's nice. And easy to talk to."

"That's why you didn't notice us in the common room last night," Elaila smirked.

"Care to explain?" Kaida drawled.

"Not at all."

"She's quiet for the first time, ladies!" Cielle laughed. "Mark this date in the history books!"

Minutes later, the stylists put their brushes and combs down with proud smiles. Maura walked in and helped each woman into her gown behind a large dressing screen.

Elaila went first. The bodice fit tight against her tiny waist with thin shoulder straps and a deep v-cut to her mid-sternum. Tiny beads of pale lavender glistened in the light. Sheets of pale blue and lavender organza were layered in soft airy waves to make up the flowing skirt. A light pink tint stained her lips. Her hair hung over her shoulder in an ethereal braid.

Aisling's jaw dropped. The rest of the women covered their mouths and shook their heads. "Stunning," Kaida whispered. Elaila blushed, adding another beautiful shade of pink to her delicate face as she turned in the enormous mirror against the wall and smiled in satisfaction.

Cielle's gown was taken from the moon. Thin straps held up a cowl neck and showed off her muscular arms. It hugged her curves, flaring just slightly at her knees as it fell to the floor. Shimmering metallic beads were sewn in seemingly random spots all over, but they caught the light no matter which way she turned. Her short hair was slicked back with an ornate silver pin. Dark red painted her lips.

Amerie came out and twirled, radiant as ever in a crimson red gown that perfectly fit her personality. A plunging v-cut stopped just above her navel and showed off her toned stomach. A high slit was cut into the flowing skirt, accenting the muscles of her long, dark legs. It was elegant and sultry with her dark eyeliner and bright red lip. Her hair was a mess of curls in a knot at the nape of her neck.

"Declan is going to love it," Cielle smirked. Amerie flipped her off.

Kaida went next. Her bright hair was curled and pinned to the side of her head in sweeping waves over her shoulder. She had minimal makeup— her artist only added a bit of eyeliner and mauve lip. It was the right decision, Aisling agreed, as Kaida came out in her gown.

It was understated and simple. The satin was the blackest black. It hugged her neck in a halter style and bared her shoulders before caressing every tiny inch of her to the floor. She turned, and all the girls gasped. The back was the deepest cut Aisling had ever seen, ending just above the curve of Kaida's butt. Black satin gloves ended midway up her biceps.

"Shit, Kaida," Amerie whispered. "I know we saw it yesterday, but..."

"Aedan won't know what to do with you," Elaila breathed, her eyes wide as Kaida turned again, showing off her muscular back.

"That's the plan," she purred.

Maura gestured for Aisling. "I heard the good news," she whispered behind the barrier. Aisling looked at her in confusion. "About you and Koen. I'm just thrilled for you two. He's quite the catch."

Aisling smiled. "Yes, he is."

Maura zipped her dress and stepped back, nodding to herself with pride. "Perfect. Go ahead." Aisling held her breath and walked out from behind the screen.

She blushed as every eye fell on her. Cielle let out a low whistle. Kaida beamed. Aisling glanced in the mirror and inhaled sharply at the woman she saw.

Her dark hair was curled in a messy bun at the top of her head. Stray strands framed her face. Her lips were a neutral pink. A simple swipe of blended eyeliner haunted her lids. All of the attention was meant for the dress–a dress that would suit Morana.

The bond warmed as if her dragon agreed.

Soft white fabric plunged at her chest, draping ever so slightly between her cleavage. Thin straps covered in iridescent white beads sat on her shoulders. The bodice clung to her, accentuating the curves of her newly healed body. The skirt gripped her hips and hung close to her legs before flaring in the back. Tiny beads were sewn everywhere in an imitation of Morana in the sunlight. She glanced over her shoulder, marveling at the low cut of the gown and the lithe muscles in her back.

Maura came to her side. She held up a thick necklace of diamonds. "I wasn't sure?"

Aisling blinked in realization and shook her head, resting her fingertips on the scar across her neck. "I don't need to hide it, Maura, but thank you for thinking of me."

"Maura," Kaida said, resting a gloved hand on the seamstress's shoulder. "You have done an amazing job. You should be so proud of the work you've done for us. We truly have never looked better."

Maura blushed violently. "Thank you. It's been an honor doing this for you. We have never done anything like this. Truthfully, I think it's long past due."

Kaida squeezed her shoulder and eyed the deep maroon dress the seamstress had on. "You look as beautiful as we do."

A knock sounded at the door. Maura opened it and glanced over her shoulder. "It's the King."

Kaida's smile was purely feline. "Close the door."

Maura balked. "You want me to close the door on the King?"

"Yes."

The door shut. Maura's eyes were wide as she leaned against it. Kaida looked at her riders. "We have a set of leathers set out for each of you in the Lair in case anything happens tonight. There is no alcohol. We are here to have fun and relax, but if we receive the call, we leave." She glanced down at her dress. "Honestly, I'm begging the Cruento to give us this night. We deserve it. And this dress will only be ripped off by one person."

Amerie squealed. "You dirty—"

"You look beautiful," Kaida said, cutting her off. "Every one of you. We don't get to see each other like this, and maybe we should. Because you are more than Ferox. More than dragon riders. You are women. Brave, strong, terrifying women. There is a beauty soul-deep in every one of you that is now reflected outward." She smiled. "It's time we show off that part of us, too. Ready?"

They nodded. Kaida rolled her shoulders back and winked at Maura in unspoken command. Maura swallowed and opened the door.

Aedan was dressed in elegant, classic regal splendor. His black suit fit his lean frame perfectly. A simple circle of gold sat atop his head, gleaming against his sandy blonde hair in the candlelight. He greeted Maura, apparently already forgotten that she had shut the door in his face, and stepped in.

His eyes nearly bulged from his head at the sight of Kaida. They traveled over her face, her body, up and down four times before he took a single breath. Kaida cocked her head before turning just slightly, giving him a feral grin over her shoulder. His mouth parted at the sight of her bare back.

"You look nice," she cooed, lifting to her toes and planting a soft kiss on his cheek.

He blinked quickly. "You look," he rasped, "I–you–"

"Words are hard," Amerie whispered. "Just treat the dress gently when you take it off. Maura's work deserves that."

Maura's face was positively on fire. Aedan took the seamstress's hands in his. "Thank you." He kissed her on the cheek, sending another wave of red flooding her face. She nodded wordlessly and scurried from the room.

Aedan inspected the rest of the riders, his eyes wide. "Deadly," he whispered. "All of you."

"Don't you forget it," Cielle winked. "Now what?"

He inhaled deeply in an attempt to get his wits back. "Now we walk in. Koen and Oryn are already inside. It took them three minutes to get ready. Everyone else has arrived and the revelry has started."

A jolt of nerves ran down Aisling's spine as they walked down the two sets of stairs and toward the ballroom. A violin's sweet song sailed through the open doorway. The chandeliers in the hall twinkled with orange flame against the stone walls. Gentle chatter and laughs echoed inside. Anwir stood guard, hands clasped behind his back as he stared inside. He started at the sight of Aedan.

"One at a time," Aedan told them, his arm wrapped tightly around Kaida's waist. "Each of you deserves every eye on you for a moment."

Anwir nodded at the silent command, his dark eyes averted to the floor as if he was unworthy to see the women of the Ferox like this. A simple charcoal gray suit clung to his lean body. He stood in the doorway, spindly hands clutching the ornate doorknob.

"I'm going first," Amerie declared.

Cielle laughed. "That's shocking."

Amerie stuck her tongue out before lengthening her spine and rolling her shoulders. Anwir lifted his weak voice. "Please welcome the women of the Ferox."

The gentle chatter stopped. The violin continued.

"Calen's rider, Amerie."

A brutally predacious smile lifted her lips as she walked inside.

Aisling stepped forward but Elaila stopped her. "We want to see Koen's reaction," she whispered before walking in. Cielle went next. Both seemed to glow with the attention.

Aisling wanted to throw up. She stared at the open door. "Go," Kaida whispered, nudging her forward. "You deserve every second of this, Aisling. Go enjoy it."

Before Aisling could stop herself, she rolled her shoulders back and lifted her chin. She had faced far worse than a silly dance. She nodded once to Anwir.

"Morana's rider, Aisling."

She stepped into the doorway.

The ballroom had been transformed. A string quartet played in the back left corner. Food and drink rested on long elegant tables on the right. Flowers in every shade of white littered the tables and walls. The glass chandeliers gleamed in the soft torchlights, refracting light as they danced to the soft beat of the music. Hundreds of people stood inside, all dressed impeccably. Hundreds of eyes trained on her. Her throat bobbed with the weight of them.

Troy stood at the front of the crowd in a simple black suit. His long hair had been pulled back in a low knot. His eyes glittered as he took her in, a magnificent smile on his face. Oryn stood beside him in a suit Maura deserved awards for. Pale golden threads twisted in a brocade pattern on his jacket, shimmering in the light like Nyssa's wings.

She stopped seeing everyone as she met Koen's burning stare. There was no more music, no more talking.

His suit clung to him, accenting his lean waist and broad shoulders. His jacket was made of viridian green velvet in the exact shade of Neera's scales. A simple black shirt sat under it—the top few buttons undone to show a sliver of his strong chest. His dark hair was brushed back from his face. Black pants hugged his thick thighs.

Aisling's heart thundered when Koen stepped forward from the crowd, his eyes never leaving hers, and stopped just inches away. He lifted her hand and kissed it softly before interlacing their fingers and guiding her to the rest of the Ferox.

The girls beamed. Troy whispered from the corner of his mouth, "You could rule an entire planet looking like this, Ash."

She smiled. "You look very handsome."

"I know." He straightened his lapels. "Get a good look because you'll probably never see me like this again."

She glanced around him. "You look wonderful, Oryn."

"Words would not do you justice, my dear," he said softly. Aisling blushed.

Koen's hand squeezed hers. She looked up, unable to keep the awe from her eyes as she marveled at his beauty. Her mouth opened, but Anwir spoke.

FORTY-TWO

KOEN

"Ladies and gentlemen of Kairossen," Anwir called, his annoying voice painfully weak against the quiet strings of the violin, "it is my honor and pleasure to present His Majesty, King Aedan, and his Queen, leader of the Ferox, Kaida."

The air sucked out of the room. Koen's jaw fell open. Aisling's hand went slack in his.

No one spoke. No one moved.

Aedan and Kaida appeared in the doorway in matching circular crowns of unembellished gold. They were a picture of power in brutal black. A pairing worthy of Soren. Worthy of ruling.

The crowd knelt. The Ferox stood dumbfounded.

"Married?" Amerie screeched and rushed the couple. The rest of the Ferox followed, their faces as shocked as his own. The crowd stood and clapped before returning to the party.

"Last night." Kaida beamed at her husband and extended her left hand. A simple golden band rested on her third finger. Koen turned to Oryn for confirmation. His green eyes nearly glowed as he smiled at his twin.

"She makes a stunning Queen, does she not?" Aedan cooed, kissing the side of Kaida's head.

"Why didn't you tell us?" Elaila asked.

"This is about all of us," Kaida said. "We did not want to take the attention from you."

"Well that's shot to hell," Amerie muttered. "Do we have to start calling you Queen?"

"Yes," Aedan insisted at the same time Kaida said "No."

Cielle laughed. "So far this is off to a seamless start."

"We are so happy for you," Aisling started, her hands clasped at her heart.

Amerie threw her arms around Kaida and Aedan and kissed them on the cheeks. "I'm mad at you for keeping it a secret but I'm too ecstatic to deal with it right now." Cielle, Elaila, and Aisling each brought them into a hug and murmured happy words to the couple.

Koen shook Aedan's hand. "You know if you fuck up, she'll kill you?"

"Her or Soren," Aedan sighed. "Worth it."

He pulled Kaida in for a hug and kissed to the top of her head. "You're happy?" he whispered, pulling back enough to meet her eyes.

"No," she shook her head. "I'm euphoric, Koen."

He shook his head. "I never thought you would marry. Let alone the King."

"I live to shock." Her eyes drifted behind him for a second. "Are you happy?"

"Euphoric," he whispered.

Kaida smiled and kissed his cheek. "Go to her. Leave me with my husband."

He turned to find the girls standing in a tight circle, mouths moving far too quickly at the same time for anyone to understand what was being said. "I saw Declan in the back," Koen mused and glanced sidelong at Amerie.

She balked. "How do you know about that?"

"I was in the common room."

"I'll beat your ass if you even look at him, Koen."

"I won't say anything, I swear." He looked between the girls. "You all look wonderful. Much nicer than normal."

Amerie huffed and disappeared. Cielle looked him over. "We could say the same about you. Green is your color. Maybe that's why Neera bonded with you."

Elaila brushed the velvet on the sleeve of his jacket. "Maura is a magician, I think."

"Have you seen Oryn's suit?" he asked. She shook her head. "You should. If you think this is nice, his is better." Cielle and Elaila walked off, eyes peeled for Oryn.

Aisling looked up at him. He hadn't been able to speak when he saw her in the doorway. Hadn't been able to think or breathe at the sight of her.

Her eyes trailed over him again, slow enough to build heat in his blood. "You look..." she shook her head and smiled. "You're so hot."

He barked a laugh, loosening the knot of tension in his chest.

"You look amazing," she breathed, running her hands over his jacket. "I mean, normally you do, but this? I fear you've ruined any other man for me."

Koen's hand found her waist. He traced her sides, memorizing every inch of the dress. "Oryn was right. There are no words that will do you justice." His arms clasped around her back. He stilled at the feel of her bare skin against his fingers. He swallowed thickly as she turned and smirked over her shoulder, exposing her delicate spine and creamy skin.

"Maura offered me a necklace," she turned and whispered, her fingers tracing the scar at her neck, "to cover this. But I thought I didn't need it."

He bent down and brushed his lips against hers, unable to hold back for a second longer. "You were right. You look perfect."

She smiled against his mouth. "Do you remember any of the dances?"

Dancing was the furthest thing on his mind. "No."

"Me either. Should we only dance with each other? Save us the embarrassment?"

He bit down against the thought of someone else touching her bare back, of being close to her when he wanted to be the only one. "Who else wants to dance with you?"

"The light and the shadow!" Leonard called, pushing through the crowd to their side. A navy-blue suit clung to his burly body. "My dear, you look absolutely radiant." He bent down and kissed her cheek. "I do not like to beg, but for you, I will. Dance with me?" Aisling laughed and glanced at Koen. Leonard glared over his glasses at him. "I let you use my kitchen to make her soup, boy. Give me this."

Aisling lifted her brow in surprise. Koen cringed. Leonard took his silence for an answer and guided her to the dance floor.

"Should we get this over with?" Cielle nudged his shoulder as the tempo of the music changed into something fast and lilting.

"Do we have to?"

"I think so." She glanced over her shoulder. "Aedan's watching. He wants to see if the lessons worked." They sighed and walked onto the floor defeatedly, molding into the sea of bodies with more ease than he expected. "Not half bad," Cielle said after their first few steps. "I figured you would need practice before you danced with her."

Koen cleared his throat. "I never thanked you."

"For what?"

"For everything. You took all the patrols when Aisling was gone. You talked me off the ledge when I was being stupid."

"Koen –"

He tightened his grip on her hand and forced himself to meet her eyes. "No. I need to thank you. You never stopped looking for her. You were there for me when I didn't deserve it. Even before she came, you were there. I took you for granted for years. I don't want... I want to make sure the people I love know that I love them. That I appreciate them. You're important to me, Cielle."

She tilted her head to the ceiling and pursed her lips against the growing glassiness in her eyes. Their steps faltered. She laughed as they struggled to regain their composure. "You're important to me too, Koen. But you never had to tell me you loved me. I've known, because I love you, too. We all do."

The song ended and she lifted to her toes to kiss his cheek. Elaila slid into her place, immediately leading him in the next song. He opened his mouth, but she shook her head and glared at him. "I love you too, Koen. Do not make me cry when I look like this."

He let out a broken laugh as she twirled them around the floor. "How do you do this so well?"

She shrugged, her smile as effortless as her steps. "I have no idea. It just feels good."

"You should take lessons."

She scoffed. "Please. We have enough going on."

"Never too much to make yourself happy."

She glanced up at him. "You're different." He stiffened but she smiled. "I didn't say worse. You're better because of her." She squeezed his shoulder when the song ended. "I'm proud of you."

The words sank into him like a punch. Elaila seamlessly glided into Oryn's arms. The ethereal pair disappeared into the crowd of choreographed bodies. Time passed with a never-ending supply of songs. Cielle smiled broadly as her father twirled her on the floor, his normal uniform of linen and leather replaced by a dashing black suit. Koen relaxed when he found Aisling in Troy's arms, brilliant smiles on both of their faces as they stumbled together. Her laughter climbed above the music, tickling his skin with an angelic caress.

"The boy is in love," Leonard sighed from beside him. Koen nodded. "I always wondered who was going to bring you happiness. The second I met her I knew there was something about her that was different. And I was right." He looked down his nose at Koen. "She did not know about the soup."

"No," Koen sighed. "I never told her."

"Why not?"

He shrugged. "What would it have done? She was healing. I just wanted to make her feel better. Soup seemed like the right decision."

The chef was quiet for a moment. "Everyone thinks soup is easy. That it takes no skill or practice. But soup can be the one thing to keep a soul alive. Its warmth seeps into the bones, into the blood, and sits there." Leonard looked at Aisling. "The soup healed her because of the person who made it. Never forget the power of a little warmth." He disappeared in the next breath, leaving Koen to stand alone in the mass of people.

Oryn guided Aisling in the next song. Amerie yanked on Koen's sleeve. "Come on."

The dance was a mess. They fought the entire time, each pulling against the other until they gave up and trudged off the floor. "Wonderful as always, Amerie."

"We're too alike. That's why we wouldn't work out."

"But I love you."

She gagged. "Not interested."

"And Declan?"

"He's nice," she said, her voice softening. "And he doesn't seem scared of me."

Koen looked around the room and found Declan's eyes locked on Amerie with pointed interest. Koen smiled. "Just be nice to him. He's a good guy."

"I am nice," she hissed. He cringed and walked away as the song ended, looking over the bustling crowd for Aisling. The music softened.

"The King and Queen will take their first dance," Anwir's strained voice called above the whispering strings.

The crowd stepped back to form a large open circle in the middle of the room. Aedan led Kaida inside, his eyes locked on his wife. The band started a song of joy, of triumph. They twirled together in their all-black ensemble, their matching crowns glimmering in the flickering lights. Kaida had never looked so happy. Never looked so at peace in the entire time Koen had known her.

"They're beautiful," Aisling whispered from beside him. Her eyes gleamed while she watched them dance, their bodies whirling while the music built to a crescendo.

The song ended with a slow, romantic twinkle. Aedan dipped Kaida impossibly low before pulling her up and kissing her with feverish intensity. Oryn's groan punctuated the air after a few seconds. The crowd clapped, and Aedan released Kaida with a jerk as if remembering they weren't alone. He rolled his shoulders back, his hand around his wife's, and addressed the crowd.

"This is a night not for me, but for the Ferox. Year after year we have relied on them for our safety and protection, and year after year they've delivered." Aedan glanced around the room, his voice strong and commanding. "They have given up their own lives for this. For us. They dropped everything to follow the bond of their dragons. A bond that could lead to their death. And still, they fight.

"I am embarrassed, I must admit, that it took so long for me to thank them. They live noble lives, ready at a moment's notice for mayhem and battle. I have never known a group of people so brave, so willing to fight for what's right. Dedication and tenacity are just the qualities you see on the surface. I know this group well. Very well, obviously," he glanced at Kaida, "and I can tell you with every fiber in my being that the Ferox at its core is good. They are kind and funny. Selfless and determined. They lay themselves bare before the Cruento, before evil and oppression, for you. For me. For Kairossen. And not once have they asked for thanks or appreciation. Not once have I heard them complain about their circumstances."

Kaida stared up at him with tears in her eyes. Koen blinked against the pressure behind his.

"There is one member in particular I would like to recognize," Aedan said, his eyes narrowing directly where they stood. Aisling tensed at Koen's side, her hand clasping his in panic. Aedan strolled through the crowd that parted for him and stopped before her. Koen stepped to the side, but she refused to let go of his hand.

"Aisling was captured by the Cruento during the attack at Impellor. She was held captive and tortured for three long weeks. She could have given up. She could have succumbed to their hatred. But she fought," Aedan told the crowd, a fire in his eyes as he stared at her, his voice lined with nothing but absolute veneration. "Aisling did not break. She did not falter. Not only did she manage to escape, but she escaped with Favilla. She managed to save two lives that day. Two beautiful, courageous lives."

The ballroom stood in hushed silence, hanging on every syllable that came from their King's mouth and staring at Aisling.

"Because of Aisling, we were able to stop the Cruento's ability to breed their beasts. We learned about their structure and their nest." The King's voice broke. "Because of Aisling, we have hope again in a world we believed lost to eternal turmoil."

Aisling wasn't breathing. Her body trembled with the attention.

The crowd gasped as Aedan knelt before her.

Kaida followed.

Anwir knelt.

The crowd knelt.

The girls smiled as they knelt on the ground in their gowns. Oryn bowed his head. Tears raced down Troy's face as his knee hit the ground.

Koen bent his knee, softly landing on the ground before the woman his soul loved. The woman he would follow into any battle, into any life.

Tears clung to Aisling's milky cheeks as they spilled from her eyes. She glanced at Koen, her body trembling and hand still clasped tightly around his.

Aedan stood and took her face in her hands, his eyes glistening. "We owe you everything, sweet girl. I owe you *everything*." His voice shook. "I will not apologize for this." He kissed her forehead before lowering his hands and turning to the crowd. "Now," he called out, signaling them to stand, "we dance. We celebrate. We live for the hope of a better world. We hope because we can."

The music started again, a lively bouncy number that promptly instilled energy into the room. Aisling remained rooted to the floor, her eyes blank and wide. Koen brushed a tear from her cheek and kissed the top of her head. "Dance with me?"

She swallowed and nodded once. His arm wrapped around her waist, the other lifting her hand in his. Her body was tense and cold as if part of her had died from the attention. He brought her in close, willing his warmth into her, and guided her through the song as best he could remember.

Aisling inhaled once. Twice. Deeply. And slowly, her body returned to her. She melted into his touch. "I was wondering when you would ask me," she murmured against his chest.

Koen twirled her on cue, unable to take his eyes off the perfection in his arms. "You've been very popular tonight."

"It's the dress." she sighed, running her fingers over the velvet of his jacket and ignoring the steps of the dance. "I love the feeling of this."

He splayed his fingers across her bare back, addicted to the feel of her skin against his. "I'll wear it every day then."

She smiled up at him, her eyes soft and open. "I love you."

He would never tire of hearing it. "I love you. And," he lifted his hand from her back and shamelessly slid it over her curves in the middle of the ballroom, "I love this dress."

Her eyes widened and lit from within with a fire he desperately needed to stoke. She pressed against him until there was no room for air or doubt. Her hand curled around his neck and pulled his face to hers with a searing kiss.

They were a roadblock on the dance floor. Couples jostled against them in a whir of colors and patterns. The music grew to a cacophony of strings, the song heavy in his bones. She pulled away as the song crashed, leaving him breathless. His name was a whisper on her lips.

Koen looked down at her in question.

Aisling answered with a smile that could melt worlds. Wordlessly, she took his hand and led him through the crowd. He didn't register any of the voices he left behind or smiles directed at him, as she guided him from the ballroom.

She walked steadily through the Keep and out the doors into the cold night air. Her grip tightened as the crisp breeze dove into their lungs with a welcoming and gentle nudge forward. The night was quiet and heavy with anticipation. He felt it against his skin – felt the blood pounding in his ears and the desire coursing through his veins with feverish intensity.

His bond fluttered as two shapes moved in the sky.

Just above the light of the torches on the Pit's outer walls, Soren and Neera flew, their tails and wings tangling as they reached higher in the sky. They disappeared into the clouds and darkness. The bond went silent.

Aisling led Koen through the doors of the Pit in silence. She walked down the stairs without glancing back at him, an intoxicating confidence radiating from her bare shoulders. Her heels clicked along the stone floor. The bottom of her dress slid along the ground and caught the light of the torches. He held his breath when she stopped in front of their room and stared at the doorknob.

A smile lifted her cheeks. She turned it.

FORTY-THREE

AISLING AND KOEN

Aisling walked inside. Tendrils of the roaring fire licked the stone, sending orange and red dancing against the bright white moonlight peering inside. She stopped in front of the bed and turned to face Koen.

Everything about him was too beautiful. His suit and the solid body beneath. The way his hair was brushed back. The cut line of his jaw. The feel of his hands against her back and the possessiveness of his fingers digging into her skin.

The way his soul seemed to know hers.

His chest rose and fell quickly. He stared down at her, a raw hunger in his eyes that she wanted—no, needed—to sate. "Are you sure?" he rasped.

She nodded. "Only for you."

Aisling would only give herself to him. For the rest of her life, no one would be able to stake a claim on her. She got to choose who and what she wanted, and she chose him.

No one would ever threaten or punish her without dealing with Koen, too. They were a unit. A promise and a threat in union.

She was his. He was hers.

He shuddered at her words. She swallowed the nerves crawling up her throat and kissed him.

Koen kissed her slowly, forcing himself to memorize every second.

Only for you.

Did she know how much those words meant? How utterly devastated he was because of her? He would have waited a decade for her like this. Two decades. If she never wanted to, he wouldn't have pressured her.

He lifted his trembling hands to cup her cheeks. She sighed at the touch and leaned into him until their chests brushed.

Out of two worlds, two planes, she chose *him.*

His fingers tangled in her mess of curls. Aisling's hands slipped under his jacket and around his waist to pull him closer with her ever-evolving strength. He deepened the kiss as her mouth parted, savoring the taste of her on his tongue.

He unbuttoned his jacket and threw it on the ground in a heap. Aisling ran her hands along his arms, his back, his neck. A low, primal rumble came from his throat at her touch. She breathed a laugh into his mouth. His hands left her hair and roamed her body. "This dress," he whispered hoarsely. "I fucking love this dress."

"Then don't break it," she murmured against his lips. Aisling pulled back and undid a button on his shirt.

He clasped his hand over hers. "Don't." A flash of hurt flew across her face. "Let me." He was not going to let her lift a finger tonight. Maybe ever. The buttons fell away quickly under his fingers. Aisling's breath hitched as he threw the shirt to the floor on top of his jacket.

She traced the muscles of his chest and stomach with her fingertips and smiled at his stilted breaths. Everything in him turned molten with her touch. He held his breath as her hand slid lower with an aching slowness. A hiss left his lips as she palmed him over his pants, and every thought eddied from his head as she pressed a kiss to the hollow of his throat and whispered, "I want you, Koen."

He removed her dress with an air of worship that could never be recreated in any church.

She stood bare before him, her breaths shallow and rapid.

Her body had been doused in flames, and she had no desire to control them.

Every muscle in Koen's body flexed taut as he stared at her. She wasn't sure he was breathing.

Aisling didn't see him move before he took her in his arms and lifted her from the ground. She wrapped her legs around his waist and curled her fingers in his hair as he lowered her to the bed.

Koen took his time exploring every inch of her, noting what she responded to and what made her squirm.

She reached for him twice, but he pulled back. This was not about him. It wouldn't be for years if he had his say. Just seeing her like this—unraveled and wild, her eyes heavy-lidded and full of lust—was enough to send him to the edge.

He could live on this, live strictly on her pleasure.

A whimper escaped her lips. "Please," she begged against his mouth.

He hesitated, needing to hear the word.

"Yes," Aisling whispered.

He obliged.

Koen took her with a reverence that sealed the cracks in her soul. The damaged bits Aisling feared would never heal disintegrated as they moved together and forged an entirely new soul of light and shadow, of fire and darkness.

She kissed him until she couldn't breathe. Until tears fell from her eyes and his.

He whispered promises in her ear, promises she knew he would keep. He pledged his devotion, his loyalty with every heavy breath. She had never been so wonderfully overwhelmed or enveloped in a love so violent and pure.

And as Aisling shattered around him, as her blood fizzled and her heart strained against her ribs, his name was the only word she knew. The only word that mattered.

Koen went breathless and rested his forehead against hers as his body shuddered. He doused her in kisses, uttering her name like a long-awaited answer to a prayer she would never know.

They lay together afterward, panting and smiling as the fire popped and cracked.

She turned to him after a minute of silence, immediately transfixed by the warm hue of the fire across his relaxed face. "When can we do that again?"

He laughed, loud and bright, and tightened his grip around her. "I don't want to hurt you."

"You didn't. I'll say something if it hurts." She kissed his jaw. "Is it always like that?"

"No. Never." He shook his head. "But I might need another demonstration to make sure."

She smirked. "We didn't even get a full dance together."

"We made it half a song. That's something."

"I danced with other people more than I did with you."

He kissed the tip of her nose. "Just say the word, Aisling. I'll dance with you whenever you want."

"Even if I wake you up in the middle of the night tomorrow? Or in the middle of sparring?"

"Even then."

"I don't think we would have made it through a full song, anyway," she admitted with a sigh.

His brows pinched. "Why not?"

"This was inevitable." She ran her fingers down his stomach, over the dips and valleys of his abs, and shrugged. "I wanted you too badly. Being close to you for too long was like a ticking time bomb. I can hardly think half the time you're near me. Even if you aren't." She paused her fingers just low enough to make his breath hitch. "And you looked so good in your suit. Making it half a song was an accomplishment if you ask me."

With a single yank of his arms, she was on top of him. She gasped at his readiness under her, the fire in her blood raging. "You can't say shit like that, Aisling," he growled, "or we will never leave this room again."

She rested her hands on his chest and brushed her lips against his. "What if I don't want to?"

It took two more times before they managed to leave the bed. They sank into the bath together, barely avoiding a third, before dressing in their robes. Aisling crawled into bed, her body and mind fully content, and curled into his side.

"You swear you're okay?" he whispered against her hair.

"I've never been better."

Koen wrapped his arm around her. "I don't know how we're going to get anything done now. I won't be able to function around you."

"Just picture me naked. Or in that dress."

"That's not helping."

"Never said it would."

His finger coaxed her chin up. She sighed into his kiss. He rested his forehead against hers. "Get some sleep, Aisling. I have plans for us tomorrow."

Her eyes fluttered shut at the purr in his voice. She rested against him, her body and mind too fully satisfied for her to do anything but fall asleep in his arms.

FORTY-FOUR

KOEN

The warm rays of morning sunlight gilded Aisling's face. Koen couldn't peel his eyes off her. He brushed her hair from her cheek and smiled as she stirred, her nose pinching before relaxing again in slumber.

Last night had broken him. With just her touch, she had put him back together until he was finally whole. She filled in all the holes, all the rancid, ugly bits of him with her own bright soul, and unknowingly made him the person he was always supposed to be.

Her dress hung on the back of the couch. Every bead glistened in the sun, reflecting and shimmering against the dark stone. He needed to pay Maura for it. For her work of genius.

He hadn't known what to expect. His suit, still crumbled on the floor, was art. Oryn's was a masterpiece. But when Amerie walked through the doorway in her deep crimson dress, a perfect representation of both her and Calen, he felt his heart stutter.

How would Maura get Aisling right? How could she accurately portray the beauty and strength of both Morana and Aisling in a single outfit? He was terrified that the dress wouldn't be enough for her. But Cielle walked in. Then Elaila. They were both stunning in their gowns. Their personalities had been put into fabric perfectly.

And when Aisling walked in, he felt the world go quiet.

It was a dress Morana would be proud of. A dress that perfectly showcased the light and hope Aisling was against Morana's shadows. She was flawless in every way.

He had wanted to kneel before her in front of everyone and devote himself publicly. But he froze, paralyzed by his own will, his overwhelming love for her, and could only reach for her. Could only stake his claim in the most pathetic way imaginable.

Aisling inhaled sharply and squinted as she opened her eyes. She blinked twice against the light and smiled as her eyes focused on him. "Morning."

Her low voice still heavy with sleep sent a flurry of heat down his spine. "Sleep okay?"

"Great," she stretched her arms above her head. "What about you?"

"How do you feel?"

Her brows pinched. "Fine. Sore. But nothing hurts." She smirked. "A good sore." He recoiled at hurting her at all. Aisling noted it and rolled her eyes. "You've punched me before, Koen. You have thrown me on my ass hundreds of times and left me covered in bruises. Don't you dare refuse to touch me now. I won't allow it."

He cringed. "I don't want to hurt—"

She climbed on top of him and sank her delicious weight against his. "Kiss me, Koen."

He wondered how he had ever lived without her as he met her lips. This woman from another world, another life, sent to him by some divine fracture of time and space, the perfect final piece of his heart.

FORTY-FIVE

AISLING

"You made me that soup," Aisling said as she dressed in her leathers. Koen came out of the bathroom with droplets of water sprinkled on his chest. His towel hung low around his waist, exposing the perfect lines of his abs. It took everything in her to keep from ripping it off.

He nodded. "Leonard let me use the kitchen."

"Why?"

"He—"

"No," she rolled her eyes. "Why did you make it for me?"

"Because you needed to eat."

"Why not ask Leonard to make it?"

"Because I know how to cook."

She angled her head in surprise. "Do you really?"

"I do," he smiled and dressed. "Leonard taught me when I first got here and for a few years after. Kaida was sick of me begging her for food in the middle of the night."

"Is that why you had Zain come to work with Leonard?"

He paused. "You know about her?"

"I remember her from my first battle. Then I saw her that night you found Leonard and I baking. He told me the story."

Koen shrugged. "I remember what it was like to feel lonely when I first got here, even with Kaida and Oryn. Leonard was a good person to be around. And cooking is a great skill to have."

"Do you bake?"

"No. That's all you." He took their towels into the bathroom. "I didn't want to tell you about the soup because there was so much going on. I knew you would make a big deal out of it, and you were already going through a big deal." He stopped in front of her. "And I think if I told you I made it, I would have told you everything else within seconds."

"It would have saved us some time."

He brushed his thumb across her jaw. "You needed that time, Aisling. I wasn't going to take it from you."

Aisling's heart was exhausted. Every time she felt it couldn't swell any larger, Koen spoke and filled it to a painful, pleasurable level she thought impossible. She leaned up and kissed the hollow of his neck, earning a deep inhale from him.

"This is going to be a problem," he murmured and wrapped his arms around her, resting his chin on top of her head. "I have to check on Neera. She's been going through it, and I've been too selfish to—"

Aisling pulled back. "What's wrong with her?"

"Soren wants her as his mate. And for some reason, she hesitated, so he's been grumpy. Kaida's not pleased about it. But I saw them flying last night when we left and the bond went silent, so I want to make sure she's okay."

"What if they're..."

He made a face. "I don't think they'd do that in the Lair."

"Morana would be pissed."

He laughed. "They all would be. I'd never hear the end of it."

She twisted her hair into a loose braid. "I'll grab muffins and meet you in the Lair. Maybe we can go for a morning ride with the girls?"

He arched a brow. "The girls or the dragons?"

"The dragons."

He relaxed. "Okay."

They walked out their door and up the stairs before parting ways. She made him kiss her cheek, knowing if he touched her lips they would be hurtling back into their room for the rest of the day. Maybe the rest of the week.

The common room was empty. A single tray of stale muffins sat on the counter. The kitchen staff had to be exhausted. She had no idea how long the ball lasted, but judging by the lack of food and heavy silence of the Pit, it had to have gone well into the night.

Aisling chugged a quick cup of orange juice and glanced outside. The morning sun peeked between gray clouds with a weak brightness. Flowers and long grasses danced wildly in the wind. It would be too cold for them to fly without their jackets. She brought the muffins down the stairs but stopped at the sound of a quiet shuffle against stone. She peered forward.

Troy, still in his suit from last night, tiptoed from Oryn's room, opened his door, and slunk inside in silence.

Aisling's jaw hit the floor.

Oryn and Troy. She had called that a long, long time ago before Troy had even known she made the switch. Her letter to him had been prophetic, then.

She didn't stop the smile from creeping over her face as she grabbed their jackets. Koen was not going to know how to handle this information. They weren't the only two who had enjoyed the night, it seemed.

She ascended the stairs two at a time and walked toward the Pit, a lightness in her steps despite the delicious ache between her legs. Koen had sated her more thoroughly than she thought possible. There was no chance of stopping now that they had started. The cycle tea was going to be the most important thing she drank.

"Hello, Aisling."

Everything in her froze.

She knew that voice. Knew it like her own.

The stone around her was suddenly too dark, too constricting.

Fear like she never felt before, not even in the cave, speared down her spine.

She turned.

FORTY-SIX

AISLING

"What an amazing night you had," Anwir said, his head cocked. "An entire room kneeling for you. The praise of a King. And you looked breathtaking."

Aisling's chest hollowed. She was no longer in the Pit. She was drowning in dark stone. She was cold and full of raw, undiluted terror. Her body was broken, her mind close to it.

"It's remarkable what you've done since you've been back. It's been a pleasure to watch, truthfully. I thought we were so close to breaking you, but we hadn't even brushed the surface. Your strength knows no bounds."

Light leather armor decorated his thin body. Two swords gleamed at his back. His hands rested casually in his belt loops. She had never noticed the tethered hatred in his narrow stare or how his thin lips seemed to lift in a sneer when he spoke.

But why would she have noticed any of it? He never spoke unless he had to. He was unremarkable. A wraith of a man who enjoyed lurking in the shadows. And that's how he wanted it.

His voice was exactly how she remembered it—dark and venomous, the total opposite of the weak lilting voice she had come to know in the light.

"You and Koen will have to end, of course. I will have no one else's seed taking what's mine." His dark eyes danced with delight. "You should have seen the pain the boy was in when you were with me. It was riveting, borderline addicting, to know that I had something a powerful man of the Ferox wanted so desperately. And he had no idea." A breath of a laugh left his lips. "Maybe it's a good thing you escaped. You gave him a brief glimpse of happiness."

Aisling couldn't feel her hands, couldn't feel anything but her heart thudding against her chest. All this time she swore she would know the man's voice anywhere, but he had been right in front of her for months and she suspected nothing.

He had been present the whole time. He was the King's advisor. He knew everything. There was nothing they did that he didn't know about.

But he hadn't been told about the Latebros raid. Aedan kept him in the dark and he lost an invaluable number of men and eggs because of it.

Aisling clenched her jaw. Her voice took on a quiet air of confidence as she spoke to him for the first time. "Did you see what I left for you in the mountain?"

He shrugged. "They were grunts. And the women? Pathetic. None of them as good as you."

Revulsion curdled in her gut. Her lip curled. "You will never touch me, Anwir."

"I already have, remember?" He pointed at her neck. "Seeing a piece of myself on you every day has been intoxicating. It's something not even Koen can fix, my sweet."

"I am not your anything," she hissed.

He smirked, the movement so oily, so disgusting, she physically roiled against it. "You are mine, Aisling. Make no mistake about it."

The ground trembled beneath her feet. Anwir tensed.

Pure rage coursed down the bond.

Cool shadows billowed at her feet.

Aisling smiled as Morana's giant head snaked through the large Pit doorway, her amethyst eyes burning just over Aisling's shoulder. She locked them onto an ashen Anwir, shadows curling between her teeth and twirling in the air.

Anwir sneered, his dark eyes widening in barely contained fear, and alternated his attention between Aisling and Morana. "You couldn't keep your mouth shut, could you? Aedan almost believed he had won."

"I will not rest until you're dead, Anwir." Shadow danced over her body, wrapping themselves around her shoulders and caressing her neck with a lover's touch. Aisling twirled her fingers through them absentmindedly.

She would not be scared anymore. Not here. Not with Morana at her back and her family a floor below. "Tell me again how I belong to you? Tell me again how you're going to take me."

A rogue grin lifted his thin lips. "We'll have all the time in the world after today, my sweet. Worry not." Anwir took a step back. "I think Favilla should meet the last of her children, don't you?"

Aisling's lungs hollowed.

Anwir took another step back. "Let's have some fun before our reunion. It's time for the last stand of the Ferox."

He disappeared around the corner before she could get her legs to work.

Aisling worked to keep the bile in her throat from rising any further. "Koen," she whispered. "I have to tell Koen." Morana blinked once in answer. "Tell the dragons, tell Soren," Aisling ordered as she ran through a narrow gap between the doorway and Morana's head into the Pit. "Tell him to wake Kaida, wake everyone."

Koen walked into the sand from the Lair and smiled broadly at her sprinting toward him. "Neera and Soren are out. Gareth hasn't seen them all night." The smile dropped at the panic on her face and Morana's shadows at her back. "What? What happened?"

Aisling stopped before him and vomited, unable to keep it inside any longer. He lifted her braid from her shoulder. "Aisling, what happened?"

"Anwir," she hissed, hating the way his name tasted on her tongue. She wiped her mouth with the back of her sleeve. "Anwir. He's the Man from the cave."

Koen's face paled. "Anwir? Aedan's—"

"Yes, him. He's the one—" Her body trembled, her fingers involuntarily tracing the scar on her neck. "The voice he uses here isn't his real voice." She retched at the memory of his smile just feet from her. "It's him. And he's not done yet."

Koen didn't hesitate. He looked at Morana. "Get Soren and Neera. I don't care if you have to fly directly into them, get them back here *now*. And tell the other dragons to get ready. We need someone flying over the Keep immediately."

Morana was in the sky a heartbeat later flying at breakneck speed into the clouds. The other dragons stirred from inside the Lair, their rumbles deep enough to shake the sand beneath her feet.

"Come on," Koen pulled Aisling's hand. "We have to tell Kaida."

He stopped at the weapons store at the edge of the Pit and handed her two swords and a few daggers, grabbing a few extra for himself. She strapped them behind her with unfeeling precision. He stopped and tilted her chin toward him. "What did he say to you?"

"The usual," she whispered. His eyes flared with a rage so potent she was sure Neera would answer immediately.

His hand cradled the back of her head. He kissed her forehead. "You're here. You're safe. But he will die today."

He led her in a sprint down the stairs. They burst through Kaida's door, earning a scream from the King and a slew of curses from the Queen. "It's Anwir," Koen said, his voice laced with barely controlled wrath.

"Anwir is head of the Cruento," Aisling supplied, ignoring the blatant nudity of the two in front of them. Aedan's eyes widened, but Kaida's were quiet and contemplative.

"You're sure?"

"Yes," Aisling answered. "It's him. I'd know that voice anywhere."

"Where is he?" Kaida left the bed, unbothered by her nakedness. Koen averted his eyes.

Aisling swallowed against her dry throat. "He ran out but said he was going to have some fun first."

Aedan jumped into a set of leathers Kaida threw on the bed. "What does that mean, have some fun?"

"I don't know," Aisling admitted, "But he was dressed to fight and said Favilla was going to meet the rest of her children."

Kaida was fully dressed in her armor in under a minute with her hair twisted on her head and swords strapped to her back. "Wake them all. Leathers and armor. Meet in here."

Aisling and Koen ran door to door waking every rider, but all were already awake and dressing from the urgency flaring down the bonds. Aisling burst into her old room. Troy sat on the couch with a medical textbook in his lap. "Get out of here," she nearly shouted. "They're coming. Go to the Keep. It's safer."

Troy's eyebrows knitted together. "What are you talking about?"

"They're coming!" she cried, panic shrill in her throat as she pulled him to stand. "The Cruento. They're here. You need to get to safety."

He grabbed her shoulders, his eyes darting between hers. "What about you?"

"I am Ferox." Her throat tightened. "I will fight. You need to get out of here. Don't stop for anyone until you're inside the Keep. Get medical ready. The Cruento won't stop until we're all dead." She paused at the door, her heart threatening to shatter. "I love you."

She ran back to Kaida's room where the rest of the riders had congregated. Their sleepy eyes were replaced by a hard-edged ferocity she had missed. Large swords glinted in the light of the fireplace. A tangible energy thrummed between them. Koen, somehow already fully dressed in his armor, helped her into hers. She donned the vial of light and hid it beneath her armor just in case Morana wanted to have some fun. Oryn walked in last, his golden armor tight around his wounded abdomen.

"Find Anwir," Kaida commanded, her jaw tensing at the sight of her injured twin. "Find him and kill him on sight."

Aedan's face was hard. "Anyone he's with, annihilate. We kill without questioning this time. It's death by association."

"Dragons?" Cielle asked.

Aisling gasped as the floor shook under her feet.

As the walls around them spit dust and cracked.

As the Pit exploded.

FORTY-SEVEN

AISLING

Elaila screamed.

Her hands clutched at her chest, blue eyes glossy and unseeing as tremors racked her thin body. Aedan threw her over his shoulder and ran out of the door. They sprinted up the stairs as best they could against the rumbling stone and into the Pit.

"Osiris," Elaila gasped, throwing herself off Aedan's back and into the sand. Her body shook as she crawled toward the Lair where dust and sand and stone hung suspended in an unmoving cloud. "OSIRIS!"

Cielle grabbed and tugged Elaila's shirt. Tears glimmered in her eyes as she pulled her friend away from the crumbling Lair. "Elaila!"

But Elaila was past hearing anything. Past rhyme and reason.

Her sapphire eyes bulged from her head as she wrestled Cielle to the ground with a strength and agility no one had ever seen before and sprinted into the Lair. Her guttural scream echoed against the fallen walls, splintering Aisling's heart in half.

The Pit crumbled stone by stone. Gareth appeared through the dust, coughing into his shirt. Cielle whimpered at the sight of her father.

"What happened?" Kaida shouted.

"Bombs," Gareth wheezed. "I don't know how they got inside."

Aisling clenched her jaw. That's why Anwir was in the hall. The snake had been in the nest the whole time, waiting for the opportune time to strike.

Gareth wiped the dust from his face. "The rest of the dragons were already out before the explosion, but Osiris..."

"Get Elaila now, Gareth," Kaida commanded. "I don't care what you have to do to get her out. Then suit up. We need you." The Dragon Master nodded, his normally soft eyes hardening at the command of his Queen.

Another deep rumble rocked the ground, but the Pit didn't fall. Screams from far away echoed through the air. Aedan blanched. "The Keep."

"Go," Kaida told him. "Go now. Get them ready."

He stared at his wife for a long moment with heartbreaking tenderness. "Since we were children, Kaida, you have been my Queen." He kissed her forehead. "Come back to me."

Aedan grabbed several swords from the store and ran through the main doors a heartbeat later. Kaida's throat bobbed once, twice, as her husband disappeared from sight.

A giant shadow passed over them. Aisling looked up. Soren bellowed from above. A weak roar replied from the Lair. Cielle and Amerie both let out a sob of relief at the sound of Osiris.

"At least three hundred men," Kaida said, staring into Soren's red eyes. "He says they're minutes from the Keep."

"Bombs? Beasts?"

She shook her head. "I have no idea. He can't tell. We need to get out now."

Gareth reappeared from the Lair. His burly body was covered in silver armor and blades. His warm eyes glittered with the same brutality Cielle displayed in the hive just days ago.

Elaila walked at his side. The fury in her eyes was a brilliant, dazzling, terrifying blue. Dirt and dust covered her face. Her long hair was twisted in a thick braid over her shoulder. Two swords gleamed at her back. Two more hung in her arms. Kaida smiled. "Good girl."

"Is he okay?" Cielle asked.

Elaila trembled, a dissociated gleam still in her eyes. "He will be."

They ran out the doors just as another blast shook the Pit. The entire western wall crumbled. The windows of the common room that Aisling loved so much shattered and crashed against the stone in shards. Their bedrooms, their sanctuaries, gone. Elaila's jaw clenched, but she didn't look back.

"He got out," Oryn said beside Aisling, his green eyes fuming as they sprinted ahead. "Troy ran to the Keep the second you left the room."

She could have cried with relief. "Are you going to be okay?"

He winked at her, the movement unfeeling. "Freshly cleaned and wrapped."

"We fight like always," Kaida called as they sprinted toward the Keep. "The dragons will assist from the sky. This will be a test of the trust in our bonds. They know what they're doing. You know what you're doing. Make them proud to have chosen you." She unsheathed two daggers. "Anwir is the target. Find him, kill him, and we kill the Cruento. Do not offer him a single shred of mercy."

The Keep was a stone cage of chaos.

Soldiers bustled in controlled order along its outer walls and lined the turrets above. Women and children scattered into its depths for safety, guided by Troy and the rest of the medical team now dressed in pure white linens. He glanced at Aisling and Oryn as they ran past and nodded his head with a grim tightness on his face.

Aisling allowed a torrent of rage to enter her bloodstream. There were refugees inside. Victims of the Cruento's hatred who barely escaped their clutches were about to endure another vicious attack. Dozens of orphaned children like Zain. Maura. Leonard. Innocent, loving people she cared about.

Morana licked the bond with a puff of shadow—not to douse Aisling's rage, but to stoke it.

Gareth hugged his daughter and caressed her cheek with his knuckles before disappearing into the sea of soldiers. Cielle didn't wipe the lone tear from falling down her cheek. Amerie did it for her.

Kaida led them to the far side of the Keep where Aedan screamed a slew of orders for the hundred or so soldiers in front of him. They stood in straight lines, faces blank and swords in hand. Aisling grimaced at their youth. Had they ever seen battle before? Did they know how brutally the Cruento fought? Did they know men turned into animals when fueled by fury and hatred? How dangerous fighting became when too many unstable men wore the same armor?

"We will be the last line of defense," Kaida instructed, passing through the lines of soldiers to the doors of the Keep. "They will never enter our home."

Soldiers called out in shock as Aylim and Calen perched on the stone walls next to the archers. Amerie glanced back at her dragon. Her jaw clenched. Cielle stretched her neck from side to side and nudged her. "Focus, Amerie. They're going to be fine."

Amerie rolled her shoulders back with a scoff. "This would happen when I finally found someone."

"Where is he?" Kaida asked.

"In the Keep. He went to steal some of Leonard's cake for me."

"For breakfast?"

"Don't judge me, Kaida."

A grin lifted Kaida's lips despite the battle preparation around them. Soren and Neera landed on either side of the soldier lines. Morana, Nyssa, and Favilla sailed above. "At least four hundred now," Kaida murmured.

"More soldiers are coming," Aedan said as he walked to her side. "The falcons went out immediately."

"I don't think the falcons made it," Koen murmured. Aisling followed his gaze. Her stomach dropped. Soldiers gasped.

What was left of the Cruento beasts flew at them. A solid wall of black wings darkened the sky. Dozens of Favilla's unwanted children made without consent or respect, come to murder their mother and her family.

The ground shook with the footsteps of four hundred men cresting the southern hill to the Keep. Aisling lifted her lip in disgust as they came into view. They came dressed in ragtag armor and sprinted toward the Keep, her home, in a tidal wave of hatred.

And leading them, his face twisted in a grotesque smile, was Anwir.

Fury bubbled in her blood until it was the only thing she could feel. It seared the bond, turning the golden thread at her soul molten.

Morana called out from the sky, shadows leaking from her open mouth as she felt Aisling's rage. Soren answered, shooting his blue flames high into the air as he took to the sky with Neera at his side. Nyssa's golden scales dimmed before she disappeared inside a dark cloud, Favilla at her tail. Calen and Aylim remained perched on the wall, their jaws snapping in anticipation as the wall of beasts moved closer.

"Spread out," Kaida instructed. Aedan walked toward the front doors of the Keep with her. "We will be covered in blood that is not our own. No one bows. No one dies."

Cielle, Elaila, and Amerie walked to the left of their King and Queen. Oryn, Koen, and Aisling walked to their right.

No one looked each other in the eyes. No one offered goodbyes.

Oryn stood beside his twin. Aisling ran halfway down the length of the wall and unsheathed her blades. Every muscle in her body vibrated with the need to release her fury upon the world.

Koen lifted her chin with his finger. "I'm holding the match. It's time for you to light it." He pressed a kiss to her forehead. "Show them the monster they created." He moved to her right, his beautiful face carved from stone as he unsheathed his weapons and morphed into the weapon he was.

"I love you," she said, her voice low and calm.

It wasn't a goodbye. It was an anchoring.

The wall of black beasts crashed into the dragons in the sky above.

Shrieks filled the air. The dragons bellowed. Fire danced in the clouds.

The Cruento men slammed into the soldiers of Kairossen.

FORTY-EIGHT

AISLING

It wasn't like inside the mountain.

These men were prepared. Ready.

They crashed through the lines of soldiers like hundreds of battering rams.

They were snakes in a field. Sharks scenting blood. They barreled through the lines as if they felt no pain, felt nothing but their undying hatred.

The soldiers held but were overrun almost immediately.

The Ferox stood steady, the last line of defense, as Cruento forces plowed into them.

Aisling sliced through the rebels one by one. She made no sound as her blades met flesh. She did not yield a single step. Did not lower her blade unless it was through flesh.

Oryn was a beam of light on her left. Koen was a show of brute strength on her right.

Blood rained from the sky. Fire singed flesh. Metal scraped against metal.

She lost herself in the chaos of battle. The monster she hid came back with a vengeance, but this time she welcomed it with open arms and allowed it take up as much space inside of her as it could.

The bond raged. She sent wave after wave of her own fury down it. Morana answered with a bellowing roar and took two beasts in her claws, ripping them in half and dropping them with a sickening thud onto the Cruento ranks.

The ground shuddered as bomb after bomb detonated behind them. Screams pierced the air. The Keep shook with each blast, but its walls held firm.

Calen and Aylim raged at the walls as they watched the rest of the Ferox dragons demolish the beasts. Smoke filtered from their mouths while their unused flames grew inside.

"Archers!" Cielle screamed over her shoulder to Aylim, her blades deep in flesh. "Use the archers!" The dragons understood immediately. Flames oozed from their mouths in small plumes. The archers didn't hesitate, their fear of the beasts diminished as adrenaline coursed through them. They lit their arrows with dragon fire and plunged them into the mass of Cruento.

Bodies crumbled, but not fast enough.

It never ended. Man after disgusting man came at her. Aisling had never been so grateful for her long runs with Koen and the endurance the unending hours of training had built.

Koen's roar hit her ears. Aisling's heart stopped.

A fresh gash bled on the side of his head. Crimson oozed down his face in a heinous curtain.

She stopped feeling human.

Rage was all she knew. Rage was all she felt.

Neera echoed it, then Morana. The sky plunged into clouds of shadow and flame.

She forced bodies to fall unceremoniously at her feet until she was at his side.

"I'm fine!" Koen shouted, barely dodging an axe.

Aisling plunged her blade straight into the man's chest and twisted, reveling as his familiar face turned from disgust to devastation. His yellowed eyes softened, his hands covering his wound as his mortality leaked from between his fingers. His axe fell from his hands. Aisling did not waver. She grabbed it before it could hit the ground and plunged it into his neck.

His head rolled in front of Koen's feet. Koen stared at it in shock.

Amerie screamed down the line. Aisling and Koen whirled. Calen bellowed.

Her daggers twirled in her hands like windmills. Cielle's long blade slashed toward her through the melee.

Not toward Amerie, but toward Elaila between them.

Elaila, butchering the men who used her for years. Elaila, with her lavender-blue armor covered in bright red blood, her sword still swinging despite the gushing slash on her neck.

Elaila, her beautiful face a mask of rage and retribution despite the paling tint of her skin.

Tears raced down Cielle's face as she came to her friend's side. Amerie covered them while Cielle dragged a faltering Elaila toward the Keep.

A flash of lavender-blue scales flew crookedly over the turrets and landed in the mass of Cruento men. Bright white eyes glowed as gigantic plumes of orange decimated all in his way. Osiris didn't seem to notice, didn't seem to care that half his tail was missing. His brutal roar shook the ground beneath them as his bond went limp in Cielle's arms.

Leonard forced the doors of the Keep open and grabbed Elaila from Cielle. He disappeared inside with her lifeless body a heartbeat later. Cielle stood numbly at the closed doors, her shoulders drooped forward, her chest rising and falling rapidly. Amerie screamed at her. Cielle steeled her shoulders and turned, a new brutal rage lining her face. She sprinted to the fight and leapt to Amerie's side, blade swinging with untethered wrath.

The dragons demolished the beasts above. Morana's shadows pocketed the sky. Soren's flames tinted the gray clouds blue. Neera's nets herded the monsters in the sky. Bodies of Cruento beasts slammed into the ground in various states of disintegration. Smoke billowed into the air from where they fell.

The soldiers worked with vicious efficiency. Gone were the clean lines of preparation, but their intensity, their bravery, never wavered. They gleamed in silver armor as they took down the raggedy rats of the Cruento with shouts of glee. The number of rebels diminished with every swipe of Kairossen blades.

A flash of movement far to Koen's right caught Aisling's eye.

Anwir raced alone toward the edge of the Keep where only two guards stood at a small hidden door.

Aisling didn't pause to think. Didn't allow herself a single second of hesitation.

Koen screamed at her as she rushed past him and the lines of battle. Anwir turned over his shoulder and smirked as he met her eyes. He threw his blades into the guards at the door with terrifying precision and wrangled the door open before disappearing inside.

"Aisling!" Koen's hand wrapped around her bicep. He wrestled her to face him. Dried blood covered half his face. "What the fuck do you think you're doing?"

"He's inside!" she screamed. "Anwir just got inside!"

"The soldiers know what to do if they see him." His eyes were hard as he tightened his grip on her arms. "You cannot chase him. Not alone."

"He can't live," she spat, the monster inside of her seething. "There are innocent people inside! I have to get him before—"

Morana landed at their side, her bright amethyst eyes glittering with delight at the carnage she inflicted. Blood covered her beautiful scales, but she had no open wounds. Neera and Soren landed on either flank of the battlefield. Calen and Aylim joined Nyssa on the periphery and shot their flames with beautiful precision at the enemy. The dwindling number of Cruento men hesitated at the realization they were surrounded. The Kairossen soldiers monopolized on their pause.

"I'll go with you," Koen said.

Aisling's jaw clenched. "No. They need you out here." She couldn't let him get hurt. If Anwir even touched him she would explode. Koen looked over her shoulder where the dragons had started having their fun, eating and burning their fill of filth while swords gleamed in the late morning light.

"I think they'll be okay."

Morana blinked once in encouragement. "Fine," Aisling gritted. She glanced at Morana. "But you cannot get hurt. That is a command." Morana rolled her eyes and lumbered to the battlefield.

Koen took her hand. "In through the side door. We'll be quick and quiet. He's either gone for the –"

"He's waiting for me in the throne room," she answered. "He knows I'll follow him."

"The throne room?"

"That's where he wants to be. That's his whole objective."

Koen's jaw feathered. "Okay. Then we'll go. But we're going together. You won't be anywhere near him alone again."

They sprinted to the side doors where two armored bodies lay covered in blood. She unsheathed the small dagger from the cave in her left hand and kept a sword in her right. Koen's eyes hardened, his jaw clenched tight as they stepped over the bodies just inches from the open doorway where an eerie stillness waited inside.

The screaming on the battlefield behind them stopped.

There was no more metal on metal. No more shouts or commands.

Even the dragons were silent.

The bond inside her chest slithered with cold fear, icy and painful against her bones. Aisling looked at Koen, his face contorted with the same confusion and discomfort she felt.

Morana yanked on the bond with a force that sent Aisling's legs moving without her consent. She stepped over the bodies again. Stepped over the stone ledge and onto the craggy rocks littering the ground back onto the battlefield.

They paused at the sight of every soldier unmoving. At the Cruento smiling.

The hairs on the back of her neck stood straight up at the sight of Aedan and Kaida standing together, bodies painted with blood, staring into the mass of men before them. At Cielle and Amerie frozen in place, eyes wide. At Oryn's barely leashed anger. At the main doors to the Keep splayed wide open.

The dragons stared from the sidelines into the center of the field, their teeth bared, their wings splayed in a show of dominance. A promise of pain. But they didn't move. Didn't breathe a single flame.

Aisling pulled on the bond at her chest in question as she walked toward the stillness. Morana didn't move, her eyes furious as she stared into the center of the field.

Koen audibly swallowed as he glanced over the crowd. His face paled. He looked down at her with a flurry of emotions she couldn't decipher.

Fear latched onto her heart.

Koen walked at her back as she came to Aedan's side and stared down the walkway that had formed down the center of the bloodied field.

Aisling's stomach pitched forward. Bile raced to her mouth.

"I think we should have a chat, my sweet," Anwir called from the center of the field, his blade against Troy's throat.

FORTY-NINE

AISLING

Tears lined Troy's hazel eyes. His shirt and hands were covered in blood. Anwir's blade pressed into his dark skin and illuminated the wild pulse bounding in his neck.

"I fear this is the only way for you to take me seriously," Anwir pouted.

Aedan stepped forward, sheathing his blades and lifting his palms in placation. "Leave Troy alone, Anwir. Drop the blade. We will listen."

"I have no desire to talk to you," Anwir spat, his black eyes narrowed on the King with such vitriol it tainted the air. "You are a sham of a King. A worthless, spineless idiot." The Cruento men laughed. "You have ruined our beautiful land. We are trying to fix it. Why would I ever waste another breath on you?"

"How long?" Aedan demanded, unable to keep the hurt from his voice. "How long have you been against me?"

Anwir smiled, his thin face so serpentine that Aisling involuntarily shivered. "Since day one."

"Why?"

"Why?" Anwir yelled, shaking Troy. "Why? You will never be a great leader like your father was. You are a scourge on our land. A blight against these hardworking, deserving men. I despise everything you stand for."

"Then why waste your time working with me? Why not kill me and get it over with?"

"My blade in your back almost did the trick."

Aisling's eyes fluttered. Impellor. Aedan nearly dying. Anwir disappearing during the battle, found too conveniently hours later with an injury difficult to confirm.

The revelation rolled through every member of the Ferox. Koen's hand squeezed the hilt of his blade tighter. The silver in Kaida's eyes roiled.

"You think I never debated killing you before that?" Anwir laughed. Aisling flinched at the sound. "I have pictured your death a thousand different ways, Aedan. Each one more brutal and embarrassing than the last." He tightened his grip on his dagger. "But I would have been found out immediately. You keep such a small circle. Everyone knows it would have been me, not the whore you've decided to make our Queen," he spat.

Soren's eyes turned molten. Blue flame danced between his teeth. All the dragons echoed it, their splayed wings tensing around the Cruento and Kairossen forces.

Aedan didn't flinch. Didn't move. Pride rushed down Aisling's spine that he didn't take the bait. The King simply lifted a brow. "Leave Troy out of this, Anwir. He is innocent."

"He's not from our world!" Anwir yelled. "You're letting people who aren't from here make themselves at home. He doesn't belong here. He should have been killed on the spot like I suggested."

"You only suggested that because he requested Aisling's presence," Aedan retorted, his voice turning sour. "You couldn't let go of your obsession with her, though she is not from our world, either. She is a plane stepper."

Anwir blinked quickly. "You never—"

"Tell me why I would tell you when I knew this was how you would react? Some information is not worthy of you, especially recently. You haven't had a clear thought since Aisling came back. Do you think I didn't see it? Do you think I didn't recognize your boldness? Your pathetic excuses for reports and the information conveniently missing?" Aedan took a step forward. "It's exactly why I didn't let you know of the Latebros raid. Exactly why I didn't let you know of my marriage until just before the ball. I knew something had changed, but I didn't realize the extent to which you let your putrid soul fester."

Kaida stepped to Aedan's side. "Let Troy go, Anwir."

"I don't answer to whores," he sneered. Koen tensed at Aisling's back.

Aisling refused to allow him to speak to her Queen, her friend, like that. She stepped forward too quickly for Koen's hand as he reached for her. She stood in front of Aedan and Kaida, her fear for Troy molding into impatient rage. "What do you want, Anwir?"

He smiled and pressed the tip of his dagger flat against Troy's neck. "I want you, Aisling."

"I am not from your world. Does that not disgust you?"

He shrugged. "A female is a female, no? Power is power. You were mine. I will have what is mine."

"You're starting to sound a bit like a stalker," she sighed dismissively and took another step forward down the aisle of men. Morana's fear pulsed down the bond. Aisling drowned it with her adrenaline. "You had hundreds of women in your cells."

"None of them as sweet as you."

She smirked. "Resorting to flattery now? I remember a man much different than this." She ran a finger along the scar on her neck. "I remember a man much stronger than this."

Troy's eyes widened. Anwir's upper lip curled. His voice lowered to a growl. "I have yet to show you how strong I can be, Aisling."

"Hmm," she murmured, squinting up at the sky in thought. "Frankly, I don't want to be with a man who begs like this. It's all so public. So embarrassing." She looked to his men, her boldness intoxicating. "You put your faith in a leader who begs a woman to sleep with him? A woman who escaped him once before? I thought that was against your whole system?"

They shifted on their feet, their eyes darting between her and Anwir. She braved another step. "You know your men called dibs on me in the cave? Since day one. They didn't respect you enough to listen. One got so far as to almost take what you think belongs to you. What kind of leader inspires such little obedience from his followers?" She cocked her head. "Boys make threats and hide, Anwir. I thought you were a man?"

Anwir's blade pushed into Troy's throat. Her friend gasped as blood trickled down his warm skin and soaked into his white shirt. Aisling bared her teeth.

Troy was her soulmate. Her one piece of life from both worlds. She would die before she let something happen to him, before she let one more drop of his blood spill after he followed her through planes just to know she was okay.

The dragons rumbled low in their throats as her anger melted through the bonds. Anwir's men glanced at them nervously as if suddenly remembering they were surrounded by flame and teeth and claws.

She swallowed her fear and let the adrenaline of her hatred keep her from exploding as she stared into Anwir's venomous eyes. "Let Troy go. Let Troy go free and unharmed, and I will go with you."

Koen inhaled sharply behind her. The Ferox's surprise and disbelief tainted the air. Morana snarled.

Shock flashed across Anwir's face. He tightened his grip on Troy's arm. "I am in no mood for games, my sweet."

"Neither am I." She kept her bond neutral as she stopped just feet from him. "Let him go and I will comply with whatever you want. I'll be yours in whatever way you desire."

"No, Ash," Troy whimpered before her. Tears rushed down his ashen cheeks.

Everything inside of her twisted at the pleading in his voice. The same sound she had only heard once before when he begged her to be present in her old life.

She couldn't be there for him then, but she could now.

"I love you," she told him, her voice cracking as she stared into his bright eyes.

There was no time for goodbyes. She threw everything she had down the bond as she took another step toward Troy.

Aisling refused to look into the faces of the King and Queen who had been nothing but supportive and caring as she navigated her new world. Refused to look at Cielle and Amerie, her first friends in her new life. Refused to think about Elaila injured inside.

She refused to look at Koen. Refused to see his devastated face. The face of the man she loved. The man she would die for.

Anwir smiled.

Aisling returned it, bright and beaming.

And Favilla lowered from the clouds, maw open.

FIFTY

KOEN

He was rooted to the ground.

The love of his life, the woman he lived for, was a foot away from the man who had nearly destroyed her, and he couldn't move.

Neera's bond ran raging hot in his chest.

She is going to fight.

His stomach pitched forward at the deep feminine voice in his head. *Neera?*

Yes, obviously. She paused. *Morana will act. So will we.*

Koen clenched his jaw. *What's the plan?*

Patience, Koen.

Aisling took another step toward Anwir.

Favilla dropped silently from the sky, her giant black body a shadow above the ground. Flame ropes sprouted soundlessly from her open mouth and wrapped around Anwir's arms, yanking him backward. The blade at Troy's neck fell to the ground.

Anwir's face twisted in shock and pain as the flames singed his skin.

Aisling leapt headfirst and grabbed Troy's shirt. She flung him backward toward the rest of the Ferox. Oryn raced forward and caught him a heartbeat later. He pushed Troy behind him, a raging fire in his eyes at the frank red blood on Troy's neck.

Favilla's flames disappeared. She landed behind the Ferox and in front of the Keep doors with her brilliant black wings fully extended. She did not make a sound. Her eyes narrowed on the now terrified Cruento with unwavering intensity.

Anwir screamed. Red and black lines marred his skin. The Cruento men took several wide-eyed steps back from their injured leader only to bump into Kairossen soldiers.

Koen watched in awe and horror as Aisling confidently stalked toward Anwir. As she smiled at Anwir's screams.

She's magnificent, Neera whispered.

Morana bathed Aisling and Anwir in shadow.

FIFTY-ONE

AISLING

Morana had listened. She had trusted the bond, trusted the rush of feelings Aisling had thrown down in a desperate attempt at explaining.

Aisling welcomed the shadows as they caressed her face. It had been far too long since she'd played in the darkness. Not as prey, but as the predator.

She was Aisling, Harbinger of Shadow and Death. The Pearl of the Ferox. She had traveled worlds and conquered her dreams. She had fought against oppression and pain. She had escaped.

She would never be prey again.

She was the darkness, and the darkness was her.

She threw herself into Anwir, loving the way his body collapsed against hers. He gasped as the air leeched from his lungs and his burnt flesh scraped against the rocky ground.

She could only hear Anwir's gasps. Only hear her even breaths and steady heartbeat.

He struggled to stand. She let him get his bearings before thrusting her heel into his knee, smiling at the crunch that echoed in the shadows.

Morana purred down the bond.

"I am going to break you," Anwir seethed from the ground.

Aisling laughed. "You cannot break the darkness, Anwir. It breaks you."

He struggled to stand. His blade whistled as it sliced aimlessly through empty shadows. She ducked down before shoving her shoulder upward, slamming into his diaphragm and knocking him to the ground.

The darkness didn't laugh at her. Not anymore.

"I came from another world to destroy you, Anwir." She moved to his other side, laughing while he scrambled the wrong way. "Everything you stand for is a sham. You will die knowing that what you fought for was in vain. And I can't wait to see the fear on your face when the light leaves your fucking eyes."

She lifted her foot and slammed it against his chest.

His spindly fingers wrapped around her ankle and pulled her to the ground.

FIFTY-TWO

KOEN

The dragons moved in unison.

Morana stood still and stared down at her shadows without blinking, never taking her eyes off the darkness.

Soren shook the ground as he landed in front of the retreating Cruento men. His wings splayed to their full length to reveal a magnificent leathery wall of pure black. Aylim and Calen stood on either side of their leader, their mouths covered in smoke as they chirped in excitement and spread their wings. Soren herded the men closer toward Osiris, his white eyes still unnervingly bright with pain and distress. The Kairossen soldiers silently moved to the periphery of the field to allow the dragons to take their place.

Kaida and Aedan moved forward. Oryn walked at his twin's side. Nyssa hovered above. Her golden wings glittered in the dappled sunlight while she sailed over the Cruento ensuring none escaped. Favilla remained where she was and nudged Troy into her wing with a soft purr in her throat.

She will keep him safe, Neera explained. *Come.*

Koen glanced at the ball of shadow. There were no sounds from inside. Nothing to show what was happening to Aisling. *Does she need—*

Nothing. She needs nothing, Koen. She is shadow. She is light.

He gritted his teeth, fighting the overwhelming urge to come to Aisling's side.

You taught her well, Neera murmured as she stalked toward the now tightly packed group of Cruento. *Let her have her fun.*

Cielle and Amerie came to his side, their eyes wide as they watched the scene unfold before them. Together they walked toward Kaida and Aedan.

FIFTY-THREE

AISLING

Anwir forced himself on top of her.

He fumbled with his blade. Aisling shot the heel of her hand upward and laughed as his nose crunched. His answering scream ripped through her ears, but he still fought.

He slammed his forehead into hers. Something in her face splintered.

She wrapped her hand around his burnt wrists and squeezed, digging her fingers into raw flesh. His blade clattered to the ground. He lifted with a snarl and shoved his knee into her thigh.

Koen's training danced through her mind from all that time ago.

Anwir lifted his knee to slam into her again, but she slid her leg to the outside. His knee came down on the ground with a shattering crack. He gasped in pain, shuffling just enough for her to slide her other leg from under him.

"Is this what you wanted?" she whispered. Her legs wrapped around his narrow waist. Anwir paused, his heavy breathing pulsing against her face. Nausea curled in her gut at his closeness, at his touch.

Use that awful core of yours, Koen had said.

Aisling clenched her core and flipped Anwir onto his back with more ease than she had ever found with Koen, and slammed Anwir's burnt wrists on the ground above him. He groaned as the air slipped from his lungs. She straddled him horizontally with her full weight, one knee on his throat and the other on top of his groin.

Aisling pulled out her necklace and let her light shine through the darkness while twirling Anwir's dropped dagger between her fingers.

The shadows lifted.

Anwir's broken, bloody face came into view. Crimson poured from his now crooked nose over his cheeks and onto the dirt below. Gashes covered his forehead and mouth. His face pinched against the brightness of her necklace. She cocked her head. "Hello, sunshine."

Morana huffed a laugh above her. She smiled up at her dragon. Morana leaned down and nuzzled Aisling's head with her snout. Pride and utter devotion filtered through the bond and settled in her chest with an intoxicating brightness.

Anwir's eyes finally opened. His muscles tensed to move, but he hesitated at the sight of Morana just above him. Aisling pressed his dagger over his groin and sliced the fabric of his pants.

"This seems familiar." She pursed her lips. "Oh! Yes. I sliced your man's hands to ribbons for touching me. I wonder what I should do to you?" His sneer dampened. She winked. "Don't worry. I won't kill you just yet. There's something you need to see first."

Aisling lifted her gaze to find Koen just feet from her. He stared down at her with a tantalizing mix of reverence and desire. She threw her love for him down the bond knowing Morana would share it. A heartbeat later he inhaled sharply, his pupils dilating. "But I need the man I love, the only man I will ever give myself to," she paused and smirked at Anwir, "to handle you. I won't allow myself to touch such filth."

Koen's russet eyes blazed as he came to her side. His hand wrapped around Anwir's throat, fingers overlapping. Aisling stood. With one arm, Koen lifted Anwir's narrow body to standing and tightened his grip until Anwir's eyes bulged from his sockets. He scraped at Koen's arms, finding nothing but unyielding muscle in his way.

"Not yet, Koen," Aisling cooed, smiling up at him. "Let's have some fun first. Let him see the last stand of his Cruento."

With his fingers still wrapped around Anwir's throat, Koen bent down, cradled the back of her head with his free hand, and pressed a punishing kiss to her lips. She parted her mouth, needing to taste him, needing to know he was okay.

Morana plucked the bond. Aisling broke the kiss with a scowl.

"Remember when you said you wouldn't be gross?" Amerie called out in the distance.

Koen smiled against Aisling's forehead. She pressed a kiss to his jawline, utterly overwhelmed in the best way, and nudged him to move. Koen dragged Anwir by his neck toward the rest of the Ferox. His toes scraped against the ground and left a line in the dirt. Morana followed behind, her tail swishing happily.

Koen stopped before Kaida and Aedan. He threw Anwir to the ground with far more force than necessary. Anwir's broken body landed with a pained grunt. Cielle's blade hovered at the back of his neck. Amerie spit on his head.

Aedan took a step toward Anwir, his normally warm eyes blank and unfeeling. "Where did you transport the beasts before our raid?"

A wet laugh bubbled in Anwir's throat. But he didn't answer.

The silence echoed painfully in Aisling's ears. Aedan's jaw feathered. He turned to the herd of Cruento men hidden behind the wings of the dragons. "Where did you transport the beasts before our raid?"

A moment of silence. Then, "We took them to Impellor."

Aedan's eyes widened before his brow furrowed. "Impellor?"

Calen lowered his wing. A young man covered in crimson and brown limped forward. Calen lifted his lip, stopping him after a single step. "There is a network of tunnels far beneath the surface," the man responded. His weakened, wobbly voice traveled across the battlefield. "They start in the Latebros. We moved a majority of the older beasts just the day before to make room for the eggs about to hatch."

Kaida cocked her head. "Where are these tunnels?"

"Everywhere," the man breathed. Anwir's eyes sparkled with rage at the weakness of his men. "Every major city, even some minor ones, have tunnels beneath them. They aren't big, just big enough for us to wheel the cages through."

"And you would release them—"

"They were stupid. We had to release them close to the city we wanted, or they would go anywhere."

"We found no tunnels besides the one we destroyed."

Another man from the Cruento crowd took a bold step forward. "We have tunnels deep in every peak, not just that one."

Multiple hives, Aisling realized with horror. All hiding in the deepest pits of the mountains. How many more women would they find? How many eggs?

Kaida echoed Aisling's train of thought. "How many should we expect?"

The men glanced at each other before shrugging. "Dozens of women in each peak. We only have twenty eggs left."

"And who is watching them?"

"A few grunts."

"Where is the rest of the Funestum?" Aedan's hand clenched at his side.

Anwir rolled his eyes. "If we had any, do you think we would have wasted our time fighting you?"

Aedan didn't move for a long minute. Silence echoed as he stared down at his closest friend, his faithful advisor. "I trusted you, Anwir. Trusted and loved you like a brother." His voice caught. "This brings me no pleasure."

He turned toward the wall of dragons. The two men stood still where they had planted their feet, a gleam of hope in their dark eyes. Kaida came to her husband's side and clasped his hand. "You gentlemen were very helpful."

A heaving breath of relief rolled down their spines.

Kaida's smile was anything but reassuring. "And yet..."

Their hopeful smiles faded as Calen ripped a snarl just feet behind them. Amerie cackled with delight. They lunged away, only to be herded by the red dragon's wing back to the mass of men now cowering in fear.

"I will not waste my breath on any of you," Aedan addressed the Cruento, his voice strong and commanding despite the pain in his eyes. "You deserve no final words. No respect. You each deserve a painful death. You do not deserve the honor of being known before you die for a cause so pathetic as yours."

Kaida angled her head, the movement both serpentine and sultry. "Know that the dragons answer to me. Know that your death was demanded by the will of a woman."

She smirked at Soren. Her dragon bellowed a roar into the sky. It reverberated through the rock at their feet. The heavens shook.

The Cruento cried out in fear.

Soren chirped, an aching softness in the sound. Neera came to his side and nuzzled against his neck before turning her burning yellow eyes to the group of men below.

Osiris, Calen, and Aylim took a step back as Neera cast a dome of flame around the men. They screamed as the heat enveloped them from every angle. As the edges of the dome flickered and tasted their skin.

Slowly, painfully slowly, Neera shrank her power until there was no space for the men to move. They writhed against each other in panic, their shouts and pleas for forgiveness muted against the crackling flames.

Oryn nodded at Koen, and together they lifted Anwir by the shoulders. Koen grabbed a handful of Anwir's dark hair and yanked his head up, forcing him to see the end of his cause.

Anwir made no sound or plea for his men. Neera's flames reflected in his dark, blank eyes.

Soren leaned over the net of flame. Nyssa hovered at his side, her wings outstretched like a gilded shield. Osiris, Calen, and Aylim purred as they extended their necks.

Together, in a ball of glittering orange and red and blue, the dragons of the Ferox burned the last stand of the Cruento.

Time passed. Neera's dome dissipated. The flames stopped. Smoke billowed from piles of ash on the scorched and empty ground.

Aedan swallowed thickly and turned his attention toward Anwir. A flicker of pain crossed his gaze, but disappeared in the next blink, replaced by hardened resolve. "I will not bring your punishment," he said softly. "The honor does not belong to me."

His eyes lifted and latched onto Aisling's.

She pinched her brows in confusion and glanced at Kaida. Her Queen simply nodded once in answer.

But Aisling knew it was not her death to claim. It never had been. There was someone else who deserved it far more.

So she turned from Anwir, from the Ferox. She gently pulled her hand from Koen's and walked toward the Keep.

The black beast stared at her, sapphire eyes blazing. She lowered her head until they were eye to eye. Aisling placed her hands on either side of the dragon's face.

"He's yours, Favilla. Whatever you want to do, whatever you've dreamed of, now is your chance." She rested her forehead against Favilla's snout. "He deserves nothing but the worst from you, sweet girl. Make him regret ever letting your name leave his mouth."

Favilla puffed hot air against Aisling's chest and lifted her head. She glanced down at a still ashen Troy tucked in her wing. Aisling stepped forward and took his hand in hers. "I've got him."

Troy collapsed and trembled in her arms. Favilla covered the two of them with her wing. His silent tears flooded her shoulders. "You almost died," he croaked.

"Not the first time." She pressed a kiss to his wet cheek and led him to the rest of the Ferox. Favilla walked behind them, her steps slow and deliberate.

Aisling looked at her King and Queen. "I appreciate the opportunity, but it isn't my death to claim." A rush of pride flickered across their faces. They dipped their chins in answer. "You can drop him now," she told Oryn and Koen.

They dropped Anwir on the rocky ground. Oryn took Troy's hand and brought him to his side as they took a step back. The rest of the

Ferox followed, leaving Aisling staring down at a sneering, bloody Anwir.

She kept her voice even and bored, the monster created by him in her heart quelled and content with the promise of his death. "You will never be remembered, Anwir. After today, no one will ever speak of you again. Your name will never be known to history. The last of your men are dead, and your cause will disappear with them. The hatred you insisted on will end. Kairossen will blossom with your death."

Memories of the cave flooded her, but they did her no harm. "You wanted to break me. You wanted nothing more than for me to crawl for you. But you forgot that I am a rider of the Ferox. I bow to no one. Dragons bow to me." She smiled. "And now you are on the ground before me, Anwir. Let the last thing you see be me standing over you with love in my heart and hope in my soul."

The bond in her chest nearly exploded with a torrent of emotions. Anwir's black eyes narrowed on her, switching between hatred and fear as Favilla stalked behind her. Aisling patted Favilla's snout on her way to Koen's side.

The dragon stared at Anwir with a ferocity unmatched by anything Aisling had ever seen. Gone was the injured, weak Favilla. Gone was unassuming, unconscious Favilla. That version of her died as soon as she opened her wings over the sea and burst from the mountain with swords at her back and freedom before her.

Favilla was retribution. She was proof of hope, proof of trust and love. She was righteousness and innocence and resilience in one monstrous package.

As she opened her mouth, Anwir shrank against the ground. He trembled in the way Aisling had in the darkness. He tasted his own fear, acidic and burning on his tongue. He shriveled in the same way he made women feel for decades.

Favilla's ropes of flame scented his terror and slid toward him along the ground. His eyes widened and he cried out as the strands found his ankles. The crispy sound of burning fabric echoed in the silence around them. The fire wrapped its way up his legs with a painful, deliberate slowness.

Favilla did not move as she urged the flames forward. They crept over his hips, curling and twisting purposefully between his legs before shooting more tendrils up his abdomen, his chest, like a jumpsuit of fire.

Aisling pictured every woman in the cells. She remembered the decimated cities, the bodies of innocent men, women, and children scattered about that had died at Anwir's command. The refugees living in the Keep behind her. The orphans like Zain who didn't deserve the horrors they'd seen. She thought back to the terrified mother and her infant at her first battle. To Elaila. To herself.

As the flames wrapped around Anwir's neck, she smiled.

As they curled around his head, his dark eyes wide and bulging, she laughed.

And as Favilla's flames shot down his throat, burning him from the inside where his black heart beat for the last time, Aisling knew it was over. Knew the pain and terror of her people would end.

Anwir's lifeless body slumped as Favilla rescinded her flames. Smoke billowed from his crisp skin. His dark eyes stared into the clouds above, blank and unseeing.

Koen's hand found hers. Silent tears raced down his battle-covered cheeks and left trails of clean skin in their wake. Relief shone in his eyes. Relief and love. Aisling echoed it and smiled up at him despite the blood covering her and the smell of burnt flesh in the air.

The dragons stepped forward. At once, they each threw a sliver of their power onto Anwir's corpse. He burned in a dazzling rainbow of flame.

Morana leaned over the ashes and wrapped her shadows around him.

The wind blew in a raging gust and dissipated the shadow after a breath.

There was no burn mark, no blood. There was nothing to remember the man full of hatred and unrequited lust—the man whose voice Aisling would never hear again.

FIFTY-FOUR

"I feel... great," Elaila mumbled from the bed, her barely opened eyes hazy and unfocused.

Cielle huffed a relieved laugh. Amerie stroked what was left of Elaila's hair. "I want whatever they're giving you."

"She's getting the best of the best," the physician smiled and walked inside. Troy and two other medical apprentices trailed her. The physician looked at Kaida and Aedan, her smile dimming. "The surgery was successful, if only just." She shook her head. "Her thick hair slowed the impact. The braid acted similar to armor, but exponentially weaker. If the blade hit half an inch higher, she would not be here."

The Ferox let out a collective shudder. Cielle clasped her hand tighter around a now sleeping Elaila's. Her dainty neck was covered in a slew of bandages. More clean ones sat in a basket at her makeshift bedside along with various other tools and poultices.

"We had to get rid of her hair, obviously," the physician grimaced. Elaila's hair was now barely longer than Cielle's.

Amerie pursed her lips but nodded. "It will grow back."

"How can we help her?" Kaida whispered.

The physician shrugged. "There isn't anything you can do from my standpoint. She's going to be okay. We only gave her a mild sedative to calm her down. She was almost impossible to wrangle once she woke back up." She glanced at Elaila. "She'll be with us for another day or two to ensure proper rest and stitch recovery. I presume she will want company to keep her from boredom."

"I can stay with her," Cielle murmured, looking up at the rest of the Ferox. "I don't mind."

"You'll clean up and take a minute first," Kaida instructed without hesitation.

"One of my apprentices will be with her at all times for her own safety," the physician offered. "The Queen is right. You need to clean up before you stay with her. The chance of infection is too high." She glanced at their blood-covered bodies with an arched brow. "Clean and rest. Go eat something. Then you're more than welcome to come back whenever you want for however long you want. We will keep her comfortable the entire time she's with us." With a gentle bow of her chin to Kaida and Aedan, the physician walked out. Troy remained in the room with the other apprentices.

"Where do we clean? The Pit..." Amerie trailed off. She didn't need to say more. Smoke still hovered above the crumbled walls of the Pit. Their sanctuary was gone.

"We planned for this situation when we built the Pit," Oryn said softly. "The riders have a block of rooms on the top floor of the Keep. They've never been used."

"I can take you there," Troy offered. The blood from Anwir's knife at his neck was gone. Only a small scab remained.

"That would be wonderful, Troy," Aedan said. He glanced down at Kaida. "We have much to do."

"Oryn, will you handle messages?" Kaida delegated. "Word needs to spread immediately." He nodded, his glance flashing to Troy for only a blink before turning back to his twin.

"Kaida and I will be sending units to recover the women still locked inside the Latebros." Aedan kissed Elaila's head before making his way out of the room.

"Cielle, take your time cleaning up, then come back for Elaila. Amerie, figure out what happened with Osiris's tail. Find Declan and Gareth and see if they can offer any suggestions." Kaida turned to Aisling and Koen. "You two. Use your skills in the kitchen. Go clean up—Leonard won't allow you inside looking like that— and then help him feed our people."

They moved in unison.

"Stop." They paused and turned on their heels. A tear ran down Kaida's cheek. She shook her head. Her voice came out just above a whisper. "I don't know what our future holds. The Cruento is gone, but I cannot imagine my life without each of you in it." She lifted her chin. "I am so proud to have been a part of this fight with you."

Amerie stepped forward, tears brimming in her bright eyes, and took Kaida's hands in hers. "You have become a gigantic softie since you got married."

Kaida tilted her head back and laughed. "I know, I know. It's awful."

"We could never have done it without you," Amerie said softly, the playfulness in her eyes dimmed. She pulled Kaida into a bone-crushing hug. "We aren't going anywhere. You can't get rid of us that easily."

A knock sounded. Declan stood in the doorway, his tall body covered in dirt and debris, his bright gaze immediately landing on Amerie. Cielle bit her cheek to keep from smiling. Koen cleared his throat and glanced at the ceiling with feigned interest.

"I'll take you guys upstairs," Troy said with a lift of his brows. Aisling smiled at Declan as she passed, but he didn't take his eyes off

Amerie, who was flustered for maybe the first time in her life. Troy led them up winding staircases and down a narrow stone hallway. He pointed to a block of ten rooms at the end. "Kaida, and Aedan, I guess, have the last room on the left. Oryn has the one across the hall. The rest are up for grabs."

"Why ten rooms?" Cielle murmured, her brows pinched.

"No idea, but I'm stealing one."

Cielle smirked and squeezed his bicep before taking the room beside Kaida's. "You can take the room next to mine. I have no desire to listen to Amerie and Declan all night."

"Which one do you want?" Koen whispered. Aisling pointed to the one beside Oryn's. He silently agreed and glanced at Troy. "You okay?"

Troy arched a brow in answer. Koen nodded with a knowing grin as he went into their room and closed the door.

Aisling crossed her arms and glared at Troy. "That was rude, don't you –"

"You almost died for me."

She stilled. Every muscle in Troy's narrow body pulled taut as he glared down at her. She rolled her eyes. "I also saved you, if you don't remember that part."

"Do you think this is funny?" he whispered. "Do you think I want to laugh right now?"

"I think we could all use a laugh right now." He glared at her. "Fine. Just say what you want to say, Troy."

"I only came into this life to make sure that you were taken care of. I don't need to live here, Ash. I was okay knowing you were alive and leaving. Dying. Whatever. But you do. And what you did today –"

A sharp acid ran through her blood with his words. "You deserve to live as much as I do."

"You were reckless and impulsive and so fucking stupid out there."

"Don't hold back. Tell me how you really feel."

His jaw feathered. "If you died for me, if you went with him, there was no reason for me to leave the other world. This whole thing would have been a waste."

"Oh, really?" she countered. "Coming here would have been a waste? Learning and growing and becoming exactly who you're supposed to be would have been a waste? You would have rather made coffee forever and been miserable?"

"Yes!" he shouted, the sound echoing against the stone. "None of it would have mattered if I couldn't share the growth with you, Aisling. Don't you see that? I'm only here for you. I followed you through worlds because we are meant to be together. And you almost threw it all away."

"I was never going to go with him," she countered, ignoring the pang of shock at his anger. Troy scoffed. "I'm serious. I wasn't. I just needed to get his focus off of you."

"You could have –"

"Morana knew I had a plan."

"You can't talk to her."

"I know," Aisling snapped. "But I can throw emotions down the bond. She interpreted them correctly and told the other dragons. I was going to kill him one way or another. Blasting him with Morana's shadow put him at a major disadvantage. And it was fun."

He stared down at her, unable to come up with a retort as he digested her words. After a long minute, he sighed. "Fine. Whatever. You're kind of insane now."

"How long are you going to be mad at me?"

"At least a week."

She smirked and walked to her room. "Great. Then in a week, you can tell me every single detail of your little sleepover with Oryn last night."

Troy's jaw fell open as she shut the door in his face. Aisling leaned against the door and closed her eyes. A heavy sigh released from her chest before she examined their new room.

It was almost as large as the one in the Pit. A small fireplace crackled on the left wall across from the large bed. A pale cream couch twice the size of what she had before looked out of large windows on the far wall. The coastline glittered below in brilliant shades of blue against white sand. Every dragon of the Ferox danced joyfully in the wind above the sea. Their power, their beauty, was almost too much for her to handle.

"Aisling?" Koen called from the bathroom door beyond the fire. She followed his voice inside. A large tub sat against the far back wall with wafts of steam dancing on the surface of the water. A tiny door to the right of the tub opened to a water closet. Numerous candles along the walls cast the stone in a hazy orange glow. Koen stood shirtless at one of the two sinks with a blood-soaked washcloth in his hand. "Everything okay?"

"It will be," she replied, shrugging off her armor and coming to his side. She dampened a clean washcloth and lifted it to the gash on the side of his temple. Bits of crusted blood came off at her touch. He watched her for a long minute. She smiled softly. "Does it hurt?"

"You killed him," he said, his deep voice almost strained.

She barely remembered the head rolling before her or the weight of the axe in her hand. "He hurt you. Of course I did."

His fingers wrapped around her wrist to stop her from cleaning. She paused, her brows pinched.

"I almost didn't recognize him," Koen whispered. "There was so much going on. So many bodies. So much blood. I don't think he recognized me, either. Not until you showed up."

Her arm fell limp at her side with understanding. Her blood pulsed in her ears.

"Tell me I'm wrong, Koen," she whispered. "Tell me you aren't saying what I think you are."

His throat bobbed. "It was the eyes. They're still yellow. Still angry and bloodshot."

Silent tears danced down Aisling's cheeks. The washcloth in her hand fell to the floor with a wet slop.

Koen cupped her face, and she nearly sobbed at the depth of emotion swimming in his dark eyes. "I wouldn't have been able to do it," he rasped. "I thought I could. For years, I would picture every different way I would kill him, but when it came down to it, I couldn't do it."

"I'm so sorry," she whispered.

"I'm not upset, Aisling," he said against her forehead, clutching her closer to him. "I'm grateful."

Aisling pulled back in shock. "You're grateful I killed your father?"

"Yes. If you hadn't been there he would have killed me. I wasn't strong enough to do it myself." He brushed a whisper of a kiss to the top of her head. "All of the scenarios I had dreamed about? None of them came close to what you did."

Part of her knew she should feel remorseful or horrible or disgusting for killing his father, but she felt nothing. There was no guilt, no sadness for the monster who had hurt Koen enough that he had aimed to jump from the cliffs to escape. She would not waste a single shred of emotion on the man who could have denied her this love. "Are you okay?"

"Perfect." Not a single trace of a lie laced the word. He cringed. "How mad is Troy?"

She rolled her eyes and pulled from Koen's touch to undress. "Could you hear him?"

"Just once."

"And you never came to check on me?" She stepped into the bath and dunked her head under the water, scrubbing the dirt and blood from her hair. She resurfaced to find Koen leaning against the sink, his thick arms crossed over his bare chest.

"I think your assessment of him was correct in the dungeons." She cocked her head in question. Koen shrugged. "I believed you when you said he couldn't lift a full bag of trash. You would hand him his ass before he knew which way was up."

She laughed. "He's mad, but most likely over it already despite how he's acting." She scrubbed the marks of battle from her skin. "He won't be able to keep his mouth shut, anyway. I'm guessing by tomorrow I'll know every detail of what happened last night in Oryn's room."

Koen's jaw dropped. A playful twinkle lit his eyes. "You're not serious?"

She rinsed and stepped out. He handed her a clean towel and she dried off. "Very serious. I saw Troy sneaking out this morning when I went back for our jackets." Her eyes widened in disbelief. Had it only happened this morning? "He thought no one saw him. You should have seen the look on his face when I brought it up."

"Hard to say what the biggest news of the day is," Koen sighed and pulled her to him. He pressed a kiss to her temple. "Are you okay?"

Aisling hadn't had a chance to think since the morning.

Anwir was dead, the Cruento with him. His voice would never travel in the wind. He would forever stay a memory, never to bring a single ounce of pain to anyone again.

Her dragon was healthy. The Ferox was alive. Troy was with her again.

She was violently in love with the man in front of her.

He was violently in love with her.

She was safe. She had a future ahead of her. Her life was full of nothing but love and hope and possibility. She was finally happy – living, not surviving.

Aisling lifted to her toes and kissed Koen, letting her love for him, her excitement for their future, convey everything her voice couldn't.

FIFTY-FIVE

SIX MONTHS LATER

Smoke puffed from the chimney, curling and disappearing with the strong cliffside breeze. Koen smiled as he opened the door and the scent of warm bread and Aisling struck him.

She glanced over her shoulder and broke into an easy grin. "Hey." Flour coated their wooden counter. Aisling gently lifted her latest creation into a tin and placed it in front of their large kitchen window to rest. "Trying something new today." She pointed to the twisted loaf. "Orange and chocolate."

He pulled the bouquet of flowers he had taken from the meadow from behind his back. Aisling's grin grew. She jerked her chin to the empty vase in front of the window and he placed them inside.

Koen wrapped his arms around her waist and rested his chin on her shoulder. "I'm sure it will be delicious. You haven't had a bad one yet."

She leaned back into him. "It looks nice out today. Want to go on a run while it rests?"

He splayed his palms over her stomach. "I can think of other ways to pass the time."

Aisling laughed and turned in his arms, resting her hands on his shoulders. "I'm sure you can." She lifted to her toes and pressed a whisper of a kiss to his lips. "But we can't hide in here all day again. They'll know."

"They already know," he countered, snaking his hand up the nape of her neck and into her hair. He tangled his fingertips inside and pulled gently, angling her face to him. "And I don't care."

Her hands cupped his face as they kissed, easy and languid with a steady burn. Koen pulled her closer, his feral need for her still as strong as it was all those months ago.

"I'm giving you ten seconds to be decent before I walk in!" Amerie shouted from outside. The low flame in Koen's gut billowed into one of annoyance. He broke away from Aisling with a snarl. She breathed a laugh and kissed the hollow of his throat before waltzing to their door. Amerie slid in, sent an unimpressed glare his way, and kissed Aisling's cheek. "Smells amazing, babe. What's on the menu?"

"Why are you here?" he groaned.

Amerie pouted. "Always so rude. Can you believe you've made him more tolerable?"

Aisling smirked. "I can, actually." She pulled out a small tray of simple rolls and handed one to Amerie. "How's Declan?"

"Perfect. Nice. Friendly. Kind. Phenomenal kisser." Amerie lifted her brow at Koen. "He finished Osiris's fake tail thing, so we'll try that today."

"And you two living together..." Aisling trailed off with an arched brow.

Amerie smirked. "Well, if you must ask."

Koen sighed and took his cue. He walked out of the small kitchen past a cackling Amerie, through their living space where a large fire crackled, and into their bedroom. A floor-to-ceiling bookshelf held a growing collection of Aisling's books, none of which he had read yet. The bed was made, thanks to Aisling, and one of the large windows was cracked, allowing the briny scent of the sea to swirl inside. He stared at the newly rebuilt Pit from the window on the far side of the room.

The last words of the Cruento had been correct. The entrances to the Latebros hives were found quickly. Aedan's forces annihilated what was left of the Cruento, freed the women, and destroyed the remaining eggs.

A week later, access to the Cruento tunnels was finally discovered deep beneath the demolished Impellor castle. Aedan's soldiers took three weeks to explore and create a map of every tunnel that had been delicately carved underground beneath the noses of every citizen of Kairossen. Each entrance was filled with stone and dirt and whatever else was on hand, ensuring no one else would ever have access to the web of hatred and pain beneath their feet.

The reconstruction of the Pit had ended just a few weeks prior. Kaida and Aedan decided almost immediately after the final battle that the Pit would be their main estate. Inside was a wing for the King and Queen, a new sand Pit, and rooms for guests and events. An entire wing twice the size of the one before was dedicated to the dragons. Soren and Neera received half of another wing for privacy, but Neera could often be found gossiping with Morana at all hours.

Each rider received their own house surrounding the Pit. Aisling chose the furthest point closest to the cliffs, giving them an unimpeded view of their running route and the sea she desperately loved. Their house was the only one with a working kitchen and was frequently used as another common room. Koen didn't mind it, not usually, but there were times like this morning when he wanted to lock the doors and keep Aisling to himself.

"Hey," she whispered, popping her head in the doorway. "Breakfast?"

"Inside?"

She smiled. "Yes. The bread still needs at least an hour and I don't feel like cleaning up after your cooking."

"Is she still here?" he whispered.

"Right here, babe," Amerie drawled from their couch. He gritted his teeth, took Aisling's outstretched hand, and followed her to the Pit.

Aisling piled her plate with an array of eggs and fruit and sat across from Koen. Troy slumped into the seat beside her, sleep pulling at his eyelids. She lifted a brow. "Morning, sunshine."

He mumbled a reply and stuffed a forkful of food in his mouth. Oryn leaned forward and grimaced. "Surgery training. He's been up for hours."

A jolt of pride ran through her. Troy was excelling with the medical team. The head physician was thrilled with his progress, insisting that Troy train directly under her. He had started the surgical portion just a week ago, and the workload was proving heavy. "Do you need a latte?"

Troy choked on his food. "Is it weird that I never want to drink coffee again after coming here?"

"Yes," Amerie snapped.

He rolled his eyes. "I just need a few more hours in the day is all." Oryn rested his hand on Troy's and squeezed. Troy's eyes flashed. His mouth failed to tuck in a grin. "But I'll be okay."

Cielle and Elaila walked in and threw their books onto one of the scattered couches in front of the giant new windows on the far wall. "Morning, everyone," Elaila sang. Her hair had grown into a shag that hit just below her chin, exposing the thin scar from battle. She glanced at Aisling. "No morning run?"

Aisling opened her mouth to answer, but Koen glared at Amerie. "Nope."

"However will you live?" Cielle sighed dramatically and sat beside him. "You didn't come to any meals yesterday. You must be starving."

Aisling blushed despite herself. They spent the entire day locked inside, unbothered by the world as they devoured each other. Koen's eyes glittered with the memories from across the table. "We have a kitchen, you know. Unlike you incapable idiots."

"Weird," Cielle murmured as she bit into her toast. "Elaila, did you see any smoke coming from their place yesterday?"

"None," Elaila shrugged. "Not a single puff."

A devilish grin lifted Koen's lips. He turned to Cielle, his mouth opening, but stopped.

His eyes widened, jaw slack.

The table went silent. Aisling held her breath. She knew that look. Knew Neera was talking to him.

He gasped and leapt from his chair. The rest of the Ferox hesitated for only a heartbeat before following him at a sprint from the common room into Neera and Soren's wing. Aedan stood inside, his face a mask of shock mirroring Koen's.

Koen skidded to a halt beside Kaida in front Neera and Soren's room, the two of them silent as they stared inside.

The ground shook below them as the dragons of the Ferox walked in. The bond was numb with disbelief. Morana stopped behind Aisling and chirped softly.

Neera answered, her trill lilting and lyrical. Morana extended her neck into the doorway and followed Koen and Kaida's stare. The bond fluttered with excitement and love, nearly exploding with joy.

Tears lined Koen's eyes as he extended his hand to Aisling. She took it and came to his side.

Soren's bright crimson eyes were the first thing she saw. He curled around Neera, his massive snout nuzzling at her neck. And resting just beside Neera's stomach, two enormous eggs.

Every thought eddied from Aisling's head. Tears came without warning. She squeezed Koen's hand, the only thing she could communicate. The rest of the Ferox gasped collectively as they made their way inside, followed by a smattering of sniffles and tears.

"Three new souls to join our family," Aedan whispered to Kaida. She smiled through her tears and rested her hands on her ever-growing stomach.

Koen said nothing as he stared at his bond. His eyes flickered with pure, complete adoration for his dragon. Neera returned it, a soft glow in her gaze.

Oryn stepped forward and pressed a kiss of congratulations to his twin's forehead before ushering the riders and dragons from the wing to leave the bonds to bask in their happiness.

Aisling kissed Koen's cheek. "Congratulations," she whispered.

The bond fluttered with excitement. Aisling sprinted from the rest of her family into the new Pit and climbed onto Morana's bare back. They leapt into the sky a heartbeat later.

Morana spouted shadow in happiness, dousing the sky with her power.

And Aisling smiled on the back of her dragon, eternally grateful she had chosen to live her dream.

TYSM

Am I crying again? Irrelevant. I'm also eating ice cream (coffee with hot fudge and toffee—trust me), and must yap before I get into my unending gratitude list.

When I was little, I wanted to be an author. But I became a nurse. And I loved it, truly. But in caring for others, I lost sight of myself.

A nagging tug pulled in the deepest pits of my soul, one I could not rid myself of no matter what I tried.

Then I started writing. And writing. And plotting and scheming and smiling. And word by word, page by page, I found myself again. I found that little girl with notebooks full of nonsensical stories and daydreams and nurtured her as much as I could.

That's what all of this has been, really. A reverie.

The idea for this series came to me in a dream. It hounded me for three weeks straight until I finally gave in and put a little note in my phone. "Dragons? Asleep but also alive? Two worlds?" I drafted and wrote Reverie in 4 weeks. Rebirth in 6. And now here we are.

As cliche as it sounds, I have followed my dreams. I am doing what I've always wanted to do. And I cannot start off this train of gratitude without pleading with you to do the same. Find what makes you happy, and dedicate time to it. You do not have to be good. Or viral. Or famous or rich or any of the stupid things we often find ourselves aiming for.

In the end, we need to be happy. Fulfilled. Content with what we have done with ourselves in this short time we are given. And I hope, I pray, that you find what brings your soul light and happiness and run with it.

Now, onto more important business.

My baby daddy- Hozier was right. Heaven is not fit to house a love like you and I.

My baby- Sleep Token was right. You are my favorite color.

Brody- you're snoring again. I love you pup, but stop stealing my food.

My parents- there is something remarkable about unconditional support, and you two are full of it. There are not enough words to express how much you mean to me, and I will not embarrass myself by trying. Instead, I'll just say thank you, and I love you.

My siblings- writing sibling-like relationships is easy when I had to deal with you two. "Just tie the towels together and climb out the window." (she did not do that, we got yelled at, and the door unlocked, don't worry.)

C, G, and K- I think friendships are hard to maintain after a certain age, and when you become a mother, all bets are off. But never with you three. Thank you for being my (sometimes) sane sounding boards when I feel the world closing in on me and for being so low maintenance. I wouldn't survive without you.

Thallia and Cait- again, it was a dream working with you. You're gonna be so sick of me but I don't care, you're mine now.

Sleep Token- you're never going to read this and that's fine. Thank you for putting into words the things my soul cannot articulate. You have allowed me an output for my happiness, rage, sadness, and confusion in a healthy way, and I have no way to repay you for that.

Just know you have a fan until death, and probably in the afterlife, too.

Magistra Ramsey- your enthusiasm and rich knowledge of the Latin language still lives with me today. I think back fondly on my years spent learning from you, especially when I brought in Monty Python for extra credit and instead of teaching you let us watch it for the rest of class. You will always be my favorite teacher.

My readers- There are a lot of days when I wonder what the whole point of this is or if I'm wasting my time fighting the universe to become something I'm not supposed to be. Then I see your kind words and excitement, and it sparks the light inside of me again. You took a chance on an unknown debut indie author, and I don't think you'll ever know how much that means to me. My gratitude for you knows no bounds. Let's keep going on adventures together. xo

Bridgette is a simple woman. She loves Diet Coke, watching TV with subtitles, and the Philadelphia Eagles (go birds).

When she isn't writing, you can find her yelling at Peloton instructors with tears/sweat in her eyes, baking, eating, or watching a concerning amount of carpet cleaning videos.

Find her socials and fun extras at www.bridgettehooper.com

Also by Bridgette Hooper:

REVERIE

www.ingramcontent.com/pod-product-compliance
Lightning Source LLC
Chambersburg PA
CBHW020540120726
47903CB00001B/56